The Faceless W
Sargent's First

CW00702629

J. Ewins and L. Telfer

WORD**HIVE**
CREATE EMPOWER COMMUNITY

WordHive Ltd: London

Published by WordHive Ltd, 2017

First published in Great Britain in 2017 by WordHive Ltd, 77 Victoria Street, London, SW1H 0HW.
www.wordhive.co
WordHive Limited Reg. No. 105153310.

WordHive Ltd: London

New Recruit Jack Sargent had a premonition that things were too easy. Two months into his role as Police Constable, Camberwell, he received a transfer instruction to Leman Street Police Station, which was a different kettle of fish to his beat out of New Road, Camberwell.

How was the faceless woman linked to the death of the American diplomat? Who is the poisoner and is the same person responsible for the two murders?

As Inspector Tom Hunt and his trusted team go into plain clothes again Jack's transfer comes at a convenient time.

This is the first story of the young Constable, Jack Sargent, experiencing crime in London in 1872, and learning from the men and women who mentor him. He invites you into a world full of ruthless murder, treachery and pretence, and love.

Acknowledgements

The staff at: London Borough of Southwark
Archives and local History;
London Borough of Tower Hamlets Local History
and Archives;
The staff and volunteers at the Metropolitan Police
Museum and those working on the family history.

Dedication

For Olive, granddaughter of Jack and Harriet

One

Jack Sargent did not take in the Inspector's news at first. A transfer at this point made no sense to him. In truth, Jack had only had half an ear on what the Inspector was saying and frankly, had been distracted by the columns of water streaming down the pane of glass.

It was wet again. London in December continued much as 1872 had started, with incessant rain. Everyone had grown sick of it. The growing time from May to harvest had been the wettest the young policeman could remember. The weather had played a part, he would admit, in the decision to leave Sussex and join the Met. The ambition to shake off the generations behind him of farm labouring had surfaced with the rain from January onwards. The poor yield on the farm was like a hiatus to his decision. Jack saw his chance for a better income and accommodation and had taken it as it may not come again.

And the rain had continued. Almost since he had boarded the train at Battle back in October he had spent the end of each patrol ringing out his water sodden woollen coat. The Inspector's news of a transfer was the last thing he had anticipated.

Jack turned his face again into the wind and sniffed. South westerly, just like the last four weeks, and there was no hint of sea in the air here. He was two miles from the Thames, landlocked in Camberwell Green. There was no taste of salt on this wind either. Even with a change in wind direction it was just too far from the cold winds of the river to carry the salty wind on the tide. And he found that he missed the change in the air that a tide brought with it so much. Standing under a street lamp he looked at the children sitting half clothed by the muddy troughs in the road. No frost as yet or they would be done for. If the wind changed direction though how long would they survive?

Jack squared his stocky shoulders, like generations of farm labourers before him. Built to dig in his heels and put pressure into shifting a barn door from a young age, Jack shifted his weight from foot to foot, used to more movement than just the endless walking of his eight hour beat. The strength in his arms gave him away as a farm labourer. He could lift his own weight up and down on a door frame and Sergeant Brooke had seen him do it for a bet on the first day and had decided to ignore the quarter of an inch short of regulation height as a recruit. Brooke had seen that the twenty-year old was strong, keen and literate to boot. As an orphan, there were no family ties to take him back to Sussex so the Sergeant decided the young man was a good bet. Not being from London meant there would be no local connections to twist his arm and get him to turn a blind eye. He wasn't arrogant either like some of the recruits from London. Yes, he was a good bet as a recruit and would probably survive longer than most.

Captain Harris, when he had sworn him in on the fourteenth of October, had also taken in the new man's build as he cast an eye over the line-up before him. Jack's power to weight ratio out of the three recruits before him highlighted which one the Captain would want with him in an arrest. The clerk from the City, Sam Curzon, would not be top of his list in a stand-off, that was for sure. The other one, the quiet one, Charlie Banks, was willing enough, but getting a word out of him was a problem and he suspected he would not do well in testifying in court.

'Name?' the Captain had barked at Jack.

'Sargent, John, or Jack.'

'How are you in a fight?' the Captain asked, choosing to ignore the hesitation about the name.

'I can hold my own.'

'Can you.' Captain Harris said sarcastically. It was a statement rather than a question. He had sworn in so many this year following the national recruitment drive. Lads from all over. Accents, and dialects, he had never come across before.

This one was no exception. Funny way he had of pronouncing his words in a broad way, almost drawling. He had heard it when Jack had said good morning to him. It had come out as good "marning".

The signature had surprised him. It looked more educated than most from the country schools. There was an interesting flourish on the S. Captain Harris had looked at Jack's hands and noted the callouses from the farm labouring. Most of the recruits from the country had hands the size of plates. This one was no exception. Labouring from the age of nine in the fields, thought Harris, as he looked the recruits over. Jack was ruddy faced from the outdoor work, hair and skin dried by the elements and with an unusually shaped nose that his mother had kindly told him as a child was Roman. The blue eyes had a direct gaze and the teeth were still good for his twenty years. Curzon now, should have no trouble with the record keeping. Banks, on the other hand, had answered in monosyllables when spoken to, the word "sir" frequently being the sole response.

'You'll need to,' the Captain said to Jack. 'You look like you could stand your ground. Alright, Sargent, it's Camberwell for you. Curzon and Banks, you're going with him.'

Now it was mid-December, two months on from that first day in October, and his hands were recovering. Jack had taken to wearing gloves with relish when out on patrol. It was a new experience having warm hands in winter but London still felt an alien place to him. Waking each morning Jack had not yet lost the expectation of birdsong instead of the noise of congested streets.

The first indication he had of changes to come was that morning when he arrived at the station in New Road. Sergeant Morris had told him to forget going out with his mentor, PC Ted Phillips, and to go and see Inspector Hunt.

Ted had said that he had a lot of time for the Inspector. Tom Hunt had survived his time since he had joined the Met and the press had not broken him when he had strayed into enquiries about middle class suspects living in the Grove. Inspector Hunt displayed the occasional ambiguous ways though, at least according to Ted Phillips.

A hangover, Phillips had said it was, from the Bow Street days when a lot of the work now being done by the detectives was done by uniform on "special duties." Tom Hunt had quietly changed his uniform for plain clothes on many occasions and had equally as quietly resumed his uniformed duties when he had tracked down his quarry. Jack's opinion of the Inspector was high. He knew Tom Hunt stepped outside the rules at times, but he got the job done. Detection was the name of the game, Ted said. The Inspector could almost smell when something was wrong in a situation, because this sense was to him like an aroma of rotting meat from a kitchen. He had been nicknamed "Le Nez" for his tendency to search for clues. Edgar Allen Poe's novel "The Murders in the Rue Morgue," had excited interest in detection in Jack. Ted said that there were few like him left now and that Jack should learn all he could from Hunt. Jack considered himself fortunate to have the inspector as an example. Going undercover was his ambition, and had been since he had read the "Moonstone," by Wilkie Collins, when the Squire benevolently allowed his intelligent young servant to borrow it. Preventing crime by simply showing up was not the way forward as far as his own career was concerned. Jack was also picking up an attitude from the tradesmen and school teachers on his beat that prevention was not all they wanted. Solving crimes that had actually happened was clearly on the minds of the regular residents of Camberwell, from New Road to the Grove.

Then the rain had distracted Jack and he had almost missed it, the mention of the word "transfer."

'Transfer, sir?'

'That's what I said, Sargent,' said Hunt.

Jack stared straight ahead, fixing his eyes on the picture of the Queen, hanging slightly above the inspector's head so that his range of sight was not fixed on the Inspector's eyes. It was a tip Phillips had given him for when he stood to attention. The portrait was a little dated now, having been put up before her widowhood.

'Before I go into that you did well on the break-in to the offices off New Road. PC Williams would have been dead without you,' Inspector Hunt started.

'Thank you, sir.'

'Sit down, won't you. You did well. It was the first road on your beat, I think?'

'Yes, sir.'

'Good. I've been through your note book and Williams gave an account to the Sergeant before the Police Surgeon signed him off. He'll be off some time, poor man, he's in a bit of a bad way,' the Inspector held out Jack's notebook for him to take. 'You've outlined the basics but we need to go over the detail of the assault on Williams for the court. Run through what happened by telling me.'

'I was at the front of the building, Williams had gone around to the back. I could hear scuffling noises inside and tried a door which was locked,' Jack started to relax a little as he got into his account. 'I heard Williams start shouting and I ran to the side of the offices and went up and over a wall. A man ran out of the building and Williams was after him. The man turned and swung

at Williams. I saw blood and Williams went down and the man we now know as Shaw, was on top of him, punching him in the face. I saw Williams was cut. I jumped on Shaw's back and then realized he was in a fight to the death. We wrestled. I was surprised he meant to kill us and wrongly assumed he would give up. He was getting the upper hand with me frankly, sir. I won't make that mistake again.'

'No, you won't. Remember arrests will be vicious, Sargent. The man was caught. He wasn't about to give up. He's going to be treated as a pariah, even after punishment. That's our system. I don't believe it takes away the bad. In my experience over the last twenty-five years it continues the bad behaviour. He's going to be punished for the rest of his life and, if he emerges from prison and completes his term, the public will carry it on.'

Jack waited to see if the inspector was going to continue. He wondered if this was a rehearsal for court or a delaying tactic about the transfer.

'What happened next?' Hunt asked. Jack referred to his notebook.

'I managed to hold him and Williams was on him then as well. The two of us pinned him down eventually, although Williams was bleeding a lot and not focusing. He's the more experienced one of us, as you know, sir. I managed to do a bit of a search and found silver items on him in large pockets stitched inside his coat. He had papers from the office as well, and twenty sovereigns.'

'Go on,' Hunt said.

'I shouted at him, who are you working with? Who are you? He didn't answer, he was making grunting noises and was angry. He was writhing around a lot too. Williams said to me to get him to the station, which we did. Williams was bleeding a lot. The Sergeant sent for the surgeon from number 94 New Rd for Williams, that's Mr Seagrave. He said to me, the Sergeant, that is, mind you salute him when he gets here. He had a complaint in about a young constable who didn't.' Jack paused, unsure whether to go on.

'And did you? Salute the surgeon, I mean?' Inspector Hunt waited. He sat back and looked at Jack and the eyes narrowed a little. Jack smiled slightly, relaxing a little more than he should have done. As a result, he went into dialect, which meant nothing to Inspector Hunt.

'Of course. He was dupping along so I knew he was late. I don't think he noticed. He looked dog-tired.' Jack leant forward, putting one elbow on the desk.

'Dupping?' asked Hunt.

'Sorry, sir,' Jack grinned at his lapse. 'I mean he was walking fast. It's what we say at home.'

Inspector Hunt looked stern. 'Don't do that, Sargent, when you're giving evidence you will get Counsel ask you irrelevant questions to make you relax, put themselves forward as the policeman's friend. They're not.'

Jack sat upright in the chair. If he could have stood to attention he would have done. Hunt relaxed his features and began again.

'It's good we're doing this. You'll give evidence, you see. Williams may not be able to for some time. We don't want the case held up until Williams has recovered. So, you saluted the doctor?'

'Yes, sir.'

'Excellent. I've seen very good policemen go because they've forgotten the social status of the squire, surgeon, or parson. This one in particular. A complaint would go in, I can tell you, whether you think he's noticed or not and a good man disciplined and dismissed for such inaction. Waste of training and potential. If a man has to go let it be for dishonesty. Remember to do it regardless, or you'll be back to farm labouring and no one will take you on in a better job.'

Jack appreciated Inspector Hunt was putting him through preparation for court and trying to give him insight, as if he needed it, into the tight social divisions he would encounter so much in London. Expectations of his from his elders and betters was engraved into the ex-farm labourer and he knew what he had to do from the time he had stood with his father in the fields. Jack understood the expectation was that he would take orders from ranks of individuals in society. Now he had joined an institution where that would continue. Only he saw his chance to eventually rise in a way that he would never do if he had remained on the farm. The hierarchy would still be there but his authority would count as he climbed.

'Did the surgeon take a look at you?' Hunt had relaxed his tone again. Jack was not going to make the same mistake twice. He stared at the wall to the side of the inspector's head and remained on his mettle.

'No, sir. PC Phillips got me some hot, sweet tea, really sweet, until the shaking stopped. It was the way Shaw fought us, sir. The shock was because the man didn't stop once the uniform was in front of him. He'd have killed Williams, you know. I thought he'd stop once a second constable was there.'

'First one, isn't it?' Inspector Hunt asked.

'Not the first fight,' Jack pulled a face.

'Not what I meant. The first time you've realized they don't respect the uniform. They'll kill to get away. It's more dangerous than being a soldier. You're going to encounter hard men and women. You'll need to prepare your mind for that. You're already physically tough. Keep it up. It's your mind you need to prepare. You're going to go into situations where you will have to make up your mind to inflict damage or you'll be dead. Policemen I started with died making arrests. Others decided it wasn't for them. The locals will soon get to hear you're a fighter. The word will already be out. That's good. You're always going to get the one criminal that will think they can beat you. Expect it daily and you'll survive. Especially once you're in the slums. Which brings me to the transfer.'

Jack swallowed and hoped his superior had not seen it.

'It's unusual to transfer a recruit so soon. As you know, Sargent, on the sixteenth of November there was a mutiny in the Met. You trainees, I know were not involved. PC Goodchild from Camberwell Division was reported for insubordination. When he was dismissed for refusing to obey the Superintendents and move to a different part of his division, various stations, like Bow Street, supported him when they paraded for duty at ten o'clock at night.

Fortunately, the Assistant Commissioner, Labalmondiere, was able to explain why he was dismissed and went to the stations. But the police authority has suspended one hundred and eighty men. Scotland Yard has been on stand-by but frankly, some are not coming back. You're to be transferred. Its early I know but there's an upgrade with it, unusual after two months I must admit, but I hope you will see it how it's meant,' Hunt said.

Jack waited. Inspector Hunt stared at the paper on his desk, then picked the order up and handed it to Jack.

'I can't emphasize enough how unusual it is for a recruit to be transferred and upgraded within the first year,' the Inspector looked at the rain on the glass.

Jack said nothing. He moved his position though, back straight, hands on his knees, poised as if for flight while he looked down at the order.

'I was asked to provide two men. I think you will do well although it's early. I made the decision as the Sergeant is to change and the replacement is someone you know, Morris,' Hunt paused again. Jack was hovering between treating this as bad news and hanging on to the fact that Hunt had mentioned an upgrade.

'On that basis, I agreed with the Superintendent that it should be you to take the upgrade from constable third class now. That was because of the way you equipped yourself on the Shaw case, as we've just been discussing. But there's also been other times you've shown that the Sergeant can rely on you. So, you will be upgraded to Constable second class. It's very early,' Hunt said yet again, as if justifying something to himself, paused, as there was still no response except in the eyes of the young man. 'I'm assuming we're not going to have a re-run of Goodchild's behaviour with you?' Inspector Hunt sat back, and his mouth twitched at the corners as he tried to suppress a smile at his own joke.

'But, sir....' Jack started, frowning slightly. He stopped as he watched Hunt's eyes narrow and harden.

'I mean, it's not that I'm refusing, it's just I'm so inexperienced and had hoped to be here with PC Phillips…' He stopped as the Inspector held up a hand.

'And that is who is going as well. Not that we can do without him, but between him, and Sergeant Morris on your training, we've got you to a standard that the other two who started with you haven't reached yet. We'll keep in touch, you and I. We'll work together again. Sergeant Morris is standing in for a short time at Leman Street.'

'Where, sir?' Jack wondered if the Inspector could hear his heart pounding as well as he could.

'Closer to the Thames. It's to Leman Street, that you're going,' Hunt paused and allowed a small smile. 'You'll be back for the Shaw trial, and there may be an occasional use of you at times south of the river. I may need a man to cover my back on a case shortly. Phillips says you're keen. You go with two of the best so take encouragement from that. At least for a while you'll have Phillips and Morris to keep an eye on you.'

'Are you going plain clothes again, sir?' Jack knew he was taking a liberty.

'I'll be in touch. That's all I can say now,' said Hunt, standing up and pushing his chair back. Jack followed him and stood.

'Going back to the upgrade, sir, do the others know. I mean Curzon and Banks?'

Inspector Hunt breathed in sharply. 'Curzon will be going as well. He'll know. Banks doesn't need to. Curzon hasn't got your brawn but he's sharp and quick, and they'll make good use of him in Leman Street. Banks stays here. He's reliable, but slower than you and Curzon. However, he's showing he's got potential and you may work with him again some time. Well, you've got your order details now so off you go and find Sergeant Morris.'

Arriving at Sergeant Morris's desk, Jack realized he was alternating between feeling the adrenalin pumping and sickness overtaking him. Morris looked at him as Jack approached the desk and knew that the inspector had told him.

'Leman Street for you, lad. Constable second class as well. Keep that last bit under your hat here. It's not normal. After Goodchild's antics and the amount of discontent there's been in the service we don't want anything else surfacing. That's why you young recruits were taken on nationally by the way. The London blokes were getting a bit arrogant. Too much of a turnover of constables as well,' Sergeant Morris paused as Jack's mouth had opened and closed a couple of times as he had questions.

'Where's Leman Street?' Jack finally asked.

'Down from Whitechapel to Shadwell and the river and over just before Poplar. H division to you. Make your mother proud. Tell her you're helping to guard the Crown Jewels, the Royal Mint and the traitors in the Tower.'

'Mum died,' Jack said in his matter of fact manner. Seeing it register on Morris's face he moved on. 'There aren't any traitors in the Tower now Sergeant.'

'Always room for more, lad. It remains an option. Look, you've been allowed off patrol this morning so you could go over the details of Shaw's case with the Inspector. He wanted to give you the news himself about the transfer and the upgrade from third to second class and it will be a while before Phillips comes back. What say you about getting yourself down to the Baker's at number 285, and get us both a hot sandwich. This afternoon you're coming with me to the office on the Shaw case to interview the clerk,' Morris took some coins out of his pocket and put them down on the desk. 'Here's some money. Have a celebration. See what they've got in the stock pot today but get us a sandwich as well.'

'Where will I live, Sergeant? Isn't it slums up there?'

'Look, lad, we can sort that out. Curzon and you can find something together if there's no room at the station. Get yourself off now.'

It was not going to go away though, the question of where he would live. It held a real issue for him and there was something innately instinctive about needing a home after his parents had died and he had been taken on at the farm. The stories he heard of the living conditions the other side of the river were not appealing. Jack had almost adapted to Camberwell but the numbers of people crowding into London made him feel ill.

The Baker's had a basic cooking pot of a stock soup on the go all day and it was a common practice for the Sergeant to send out for a jug of it and leave it on the stove at the station. That and chunks of bread meant   a man always had something when he came off a patrol. The hot meat had gone by the time Jack got to the Baker's.

'Today, you're too late, Constable, but I can give you dripping with the bread.' Janet's green apron was covered with flour and her hair strayed out from under her cap. Her face was sweaty.

'No chalk in it is there?' Jack grinned at her, knowing the answer.

'That uniform you've got on saves you,' Janet said, offended.

Jack headed back to the station, sheltering the jug and the rest of the purchases under his greatcoat from the rain. His uniform was wet by the time he returned and he put the jug on the blackened stove and the chunks of bread, smeared with dripping, piled up onto a plate. In a back room, he would get away with taking off his coat and tunic and hanging it above the stove. The drips made a scalding noise as they fell onto the stove that was too hot to touch. Sergeant Morris liked a good hot stove. Jack leant an arm against the chimney and felt the heat off the stove warming his face. He stood in front it and opened a small fire door to let the room fill with yellow light and even more heat. Slowly the warmth seeped into his bones and he could smell the damp from his clothes while he started to think about where, and what, he was likely to live in around Leman Street.

He had been shocked at the shabbiness and facilities in the police dormitory generally. Sleeping was a problem as they were over the cells and could hear the row each night as prisoners were brought in. It was much worse than the farm had been. At least they had kept it clean, white washed the walls between the five of them who had grown up together. He had told Sergeant Morris to put him down as much as possible for night duty. At least he slept during the day as most of the arrests seemed to be made at night. Some of the men had gone as lodgers with married couples in the area, two men sharing a room even, but the conditions he had heard of were more like a home to return to and the diet was better. Jack made a mental note to speak to Curzon about them both looking into sharing if necessary if it avoided the dormitory again.

*

Jack looked at the station clock and wondered what Harriet would be doing now. He had met her on his patrol and like him she had come from a farm but there the similarity ended. She was one of a large number of children, with a mother still alive, and one older sister in London working as a dressmaker in Lewisham. The difference to his own situation struck him as extraordinary. Seven surviving children and a mother alive. What chance was that in one family, he thought. It had been the fact that they were both from country places and had a farm background in common that had helped the conversation develop daily as he passed the house that she worked in as a scullery maid. After the first exchange when he had seen her beating a rug at the bottom of the steps outside the kitchen door, the cook, Mrs Ardle, had called to her to find out who she was talking to and hearing that it was a "nice" young policeman new to the area, had invited him in for a plate of some left-overs from the servant's lunch. Harriet was from Honiton, Jack from a farm near Battle but he had been born in Bexhill. She was seventeen and he twenty. He enjoyed talking to her about her background in Honiton and knew she understood the sense of loss that surfaced about his own boyhood in Bexhill before his father died. Harriet was also pretty and enticing. She had appeared regularly at the time he was due to walk down the road and seemed to be waiting for him with some spurious duty given to her by Mrs Ardle. From that first day Jack had seen her regularly when on his day patrol, the cook allowing him in to warm himself and chat to her scullery maid. The older woman had taken a shine to him and knew the local ruffians would be aware of a policeman being a friend and a frequent visitor to the kitchen.

Service in London was a career option for Harriet. It avoided the poverty of remaining in an overlarge family in rural Devon, with few ways of advancing herself. Jack had been struck by how ambitious she was. Like him in fact. Harriet already had a post office savings account, regularly buying savings stamps. The two had talked in the kitchen while she got on with her duties, under the watchful eye of the cook who plied him with a plate and a hot drink, allowing the young policeman to warm himself by the fire.

 With one eye on the clock on that first day, Jack had worked out how long he could stay in the warm kitchen in Harriet's company before landing himself in trouble with PC Phillips, who was sure to check up on him. By December, Jack had developed a regular routine of seeing Harriet under respectable conditions, being well-fed and watered in the middle of his patrol, regardless whether it was the day or night patrol. It had become a daily occurrence. Jack was aware that his diet was improving and of the cost to the cook as she could have sold the scraps and left overs that she was feeding him. The relationship had developed from just a friendship over the last two months. Each time Phillips would appear in the street looking for him. Phillips had realized, of course, what was developing. He gave him twenty minutes before Jack would hear the knock on the kitchen door and see his superior's moustached face peering in as the door was opened. There was always a plate ready for Phillips as a sweetener so that he did not come down hard on his young recruit. Then it was a question of Jack picking up his helmet and getting off up the steps to the street to accompany Phillips on the patrol.

 Harriet had told him she would one day own a house, take lodgers to pay for it and be independent. There was no mention of marriage as an aim, which puzzled Jack, as she had let him kiss her when he delivered her back to the kitchen door from the few walks together when he got a Sunday afternoon free.

 He could just make it if he went now. He knew if he was late for Sergeant Morris there would be hell to pay. Probably he would be dismissed. He could make it back by two o'clock when they were due to go and interview the clerk in the Shaw case. And he was sure that the cook would have his usual plate ready and Harriet would be dealing with sorting the knives from the washing up ready for the Butler's inspection after lunch. She would be expecting him as his patrol should have started at ten o'clock that morning. Sergeant Morris would think he was on other duties and would find the change Jack had left on the table with the bread and dripping. If he ran he would make it. Running would look like a constable after a criminal but that would not matter. Jack grabbed his tunic and put the steaming article back on.

*

Sergeant Morris held that the population in Camberwell were pretty respectable. Morris should know as he had been in different parts of London. As Jack ran through the streets the route was pleasant, and most of the houses had three or four servants.

'Harriet,' Jack panted almost falling down the steps to the back door. She was in the half-open doorway.

'I thought you weren't coming today. Where's your coat. You're sodden.'

'The Inspector had some news for me this morning. I stayed at the station.'

'Come in, Cook's got a plate ready for you and there's hot soup left over from lunch. You need to take that jacket off really but I'll get you a blanket and the wet will go into that. Where's your coat?' Harriet was already half through the door back into the kitchen to get out of the rain.

'I couldn't run in it. It's drying at the station. Look I have to get back but I wanted to give you the news.'

'Come in for a few moments, Jack. Look here's the blanket. Two minutes and tell me while you have something hot.'

He was in and the blanket was round him, with Harriet fussing about it being held tight. He looked at her happily and did not speak. Harriet was leading him to the fire and Mrs Ardle pushing food at him. He drank some soup from a bowl, more to keep them both happy than out of need, and scalded his mouth.

'I have to go. I'll be back as usual tomorrow,' said Jack. Harriet was holding the tunic in front of the range.

———

'The news? What's the news?' she said as Jack dropped the blanket on a chair. Much of the damp had gone into the wool blanket. He told Harriet and Mrs Ardle about the transfer and the upgrade to police constable second class. Harriet remained quiet, but Mrs Ardle had a smug expression and nudged Harriet.

'See, I told you this one wouldn't stay in the ranks long. Sergeant before you know it, girl,' then she wrapped up the pieces of thick bread and butter that Jack had been meant to eat with the soup. Jack put her food parcel into a pocket and turned to go.

'I'll see you tomorrow, right?' he said. Harriet nodded and her face clouded.

'Where will you live?' she asked.

'I don't know yet,' said Jack. 'Maybe share with one of the others who's coming across the river too. I don't fancy the sound of some of the areas and I've had enough of being in a section house.'

'I'll talk to my sister, Georgina, she's walking out with a policeman. He's been somewhere in the Holborn area. He may know what your new area's like. If you don't mind me doing that?'

'That's kind. So, am I a good bet then? Getting promotion?' Jack picked up her hand. Harriet looked at the cook, who turned to her scones.

'Maybe.' Harriet said. "Depends if I ever see you again once you move.' Harriet pushed him towards the kitchen door. 'Provided you don't get dismissed for disappearing.'

*

Jack made it back by five minutes to two. He burst into the station entrance with two other constables frog marching men in to charge them and so managed to avoid Sergeant Morris's eagle eye. He was sodden though as the rain had come on even heavier.

At two o'clock Sergeant Morris found him gulping down Harriet's bread and butter with his tunic off hanging up over the stove again.

'Assuming you got to see your girl, how did you manage to do it so fast?' Morris asked him, eyeing him up and down and seeing the state that the young constable's boots were in.

Jack's shoulders slumped expecting the worst. His mouth full of bread and butter, he put the remaining crust down on its paper, and waited for the discipline to come. It did not.

The door opened and Inspector Tom Hunt came into the room holding a newspaper.

'You're back then, Sargent. As you've been transferred you're lucky. We have too much to do to be sorting out amorous recruits who are the responsibility of other divisions from tomorrow. Don't you agree Sergeant Morris?'

'I do, sir. Far too much to do. I clocked his run, sir, he's done it in ten minutes there and ten minutes back I reckon. If he stayed five minutes in the kitchen that would explain why he's been twenty-five minutes in total. Very restrained, I would call that, sir.' Morris put his pocket watch back in his tunic pocket. Jack looked from one to the other.

'However, you and Morris are now late for the interview with the Clerk on the Shaw case,' said Hunt. His lips were pursed but there was a hint of humour in the eyes.

'Yes sir, sorry sir,' Jack waited. He was not disappointed but he was surprised at what came next.

'Therefore, I shall be putting you on special duties, PC Sargent. The inter-divisions Sport is in May next year. You'll be representing New Road as we discovered your ability to run. Sergeant Morris will brief you. Play cricket at all?'

'Village cricket sir,' Jack said, frowning slightly.

'That will do. Put him down, Morris.' Hunt dropped the newspaper on the table but Jack was still looking from the Sergeant to the Inspector.

'Excuse me, sir, may I ask a question?' Jack said.

'No, you may not,' Hunt said. 'There's a winter entertainment at St. Luke's Church in Hackney, temporary church, I should say. All divisions have been asked to put forward an officer to go and support it. As you are now a constable second class you can represent the division. It's the third entertainment the Reverend has put on and there will apparently be 'comic recitals.' The evening is to raise money for the new building. Both Morris and I have put in our time at the other two events. So, I would suggest that you obtain the acceptance of that young lady you were so keen to see with the news of your up-grade and transfer, to accompany you. I'm sure she'll agree as I know her employer who will take a dim view of her and the cook sending young constables off with food parcels he has paid for. Any objection?'

'No, sir. I'm not dismissed?' Jack asked.

'You're not my responsibility after tomorrow but you'll represent us before Leman Street discovers your running speed. Now take a look at the paper. The headline in the top right corner.' Hunt pushed the paper over towards him.

Jack looked at the Independent's lead article. "Mysterious Tragedy of the Faceless Woman."

*

Two

'Sergeant, who made the decision to send me to Leman Street? Was it the Inspector?' asked Jack, as he and Sergeant Morris trudged down New Road towards the appointment with the Clerk.

'He would have been asked his opinion but it wouldn't have started with him. Some exalted being in the Commissioner's office. Your main advantage, lad, to be frank with you, is that you're new, not from London, and you're clean,' said Morris.

'I hear you've worked with Inspector Hunt for a long time.'

'What is it you hear?' said Morris.

'Oh, that he was Fairbrass trained.'

'That's right, he was. And you've heard of Fairbrass, I see. Hunt was one of the thousand taken on for the Great Exhibition in '51. Fairbrass drilled him alright, along with the other recruits. Ask him about it sometime.'

'What happened to him?' asked Jack.

'Fairbrass? He retired years ago, moved up to Yorkshire. He's still alive.'

And that was all that Jack got out of him as they arrived at the offices over on the north side of New Road for the interview with the Chief Clerk, Mr Milton, about the Shaw case. Easterbrook, the plumber, acknowledged Sergeant Morris as the two policemen walked past his premises, before they turned in through the front door of the Dispatch Office which was the scene of the arrest. Nothing was said about the headline in the Tower Hamlets Independent by Morris after Jack had read the article. They had been out of the door of the Station House onto New Road as soon as Jack had put the news-paper down on the table. He had barely had time to button up his tunic and get his great coat on before they were out into the rain. Morris walked at a pace. They were already twenty minutes later than arranged with the Chief Clerk and he was working to stop a potential complaint going into the Superintendent.

'This is one of the constables who arrested Shaw, sir,' Morris said, nodding towards Jack, once they were inside the company's building.

'Ah, well done. Looks young,' commented Mr Milton.

'Young recruit, but keen and strong, sir,' said Morris. 'Perhaps we can establish what is missing as far as you've been able to tell. We found silver on the man but that's not necessarily from here.'

'Come through,' Milton said. He led the way into the office to the left of the one that had been ransacked. Two assistants were attempting to sort papers into the correct files. Jack had not expected the company to start sorting out the mess created by the burglary and was surprised they were doing this before the police had carried out a check. Morris gave him a look and Jack remembered to keep a dead-pan expression from then on. Morris did not appear to be at all surprised. At least he was not showing it if he was.

'Good that none of your employees were thrown into contact with the criminals,' Morris said. 'I wouldn't have given much for their chances, as he was a nasty piece of work. Gave one of our experienced constables quite a crack about the head.'

'Of course, how remiss of me not to ask. I heard from Mr Easterbrook that a police constable was bleeding as they marched the burglar away. How is the man?' Milton asked, concerned.

'He's recovering, thank you for asking, sir. I'll mention to the Inspector your concern.' Morris was taking out his notebook. 'Sargent, interview the two clerks here to see if they've come across anything in the mess that they're sorting through, and get their names and addresses. With your permission, Mr Milton.'

'Of course. We can go back into the order of my office, Sergeant if your constable is to remain in here.' Mr Milton was already leading the way.

Sergeant Morris paused as he drew level with Jack and said quietly, 'Get them chatting, and keep your eyes open for anything that looks out of place in this sort of environment.'

'So, what's he like then, the criminal?' asked the younger of the two clerks.

'I didn't catch your name,' Jack said.

'That's because I didn't give it to you.'

Jack looked confused for a moment at the unnecessary stand-off that was potentially brewing. He decided to answer the young clerk's question.

'Tough, fearless fighter, and now, silent,' said Jack.

'Gave you a run for your money, then,' the young clerk retorted. His colleague, an older man, coughed and Jack switched his attention to him. Probably a long track record with the company, Jack thought and one who would not want to rock the boat this close to retirement.

'Your name sir?' asked Jack.

'Owen. Terence Owen, Supervisor and with the company fifteen years. This....clerk, is Bill Harris, started with the company six months ago.'

Jack made a note. He did it more to buy himself time as he could feel his cheeks colouring with the exchange between himself and the young clerk, Harris. A habit he knew gave his inexperience away.

'Addresses, sir?' he asked keeping his gaze on the notebook.

'Why, you coming to tea?' Harris smirked.

'Bill!' the supervisor snapped out the name. 'You won't be helping yourself to take such an attitude with the constable. I live over towards Crystal Palace.'

'You have a bit of a journey, Mr Owen,' said Jack.

'Oh, well, the line comes into New Road, here, and I'm not far from the station.'

'And you get the advantage of nice clean air, no doubt,' said Jack giving the older man a smile. 'And you, Mr Harris? You're accent sounds like you may be a local man.'

'I take the tram out from New Cross,' Harris said.

'I noticed a new section of tram started earlier this year. You go where the work is Mr Harris.'

'Like yourself, Constable,' said Harris. 'That accent of yours is not local.'

'That's right. I'm part of a new intake in the last two months.' Jack and Harris looked at each other, neither blinking. 'I must try the route to Westminster,' continued Jack. Harris nodded.

Jack made an entry in his notebook to get in touch with police stations serving Crystal Palace and New Cross. He noted down the approximate age of the two men before him. Morris may know who to contact, he thought. Jack moved some papers around with a foot and made a play of doing a full stop in his notebook. He sensed Mr Owen flinch.

'Well, I'll have a look around while you gentlemen carry on tidying up,' smiled Jack. Owen and Harris picked up money bags and put them into the desks. Jack watched and then walked over to look at the damaged drawers. These had been broken open and a jemmy and a crow bar were on the floor. Jack picked them up.

*

Walking back to the station Sergeant Morris waited until they were both out of earshot of the Office. 'Let's see what Shaw has to say about his tools you've got there.'

'That young clerk seems to have a problem with policemen,' said Jack.

'Mr Harris has been in a Fenian meeting in Hyde Park in November. We will not be his favourite people,' explained Morris.

'Was he picked up, Sergeant?'

'No. We had a problem with the magistrate. The Superintendent needed summonses against the speakers but the magistrate decided the speakers were acting lawfully. It was a mess. The police had allowed a fair in the park that day so anything that was sold by the Fenians was no different. It doesn't look good. But Harris is on the books to keep an eye on.'

'That explains his attitude to me then. It was as if he was putting a marker in the sand. Picking an argument over nothing to provoke me.'

'Walk around him, Jack, at the moment. We can question Shaw on why he was stealing in case there's a connection with funds for a cause but somehow, I don't think there's a political motivation behind this burglary. Harris feels persecuted at police attempts to prosecute speakers at what he believes is a legal meeting.'

'Is he right?' asked Jack.

'Who knows. Let's leave the Parks Bill to the lawyers.'

They passed the road-spreaders working to get the hard core down. Jack suddenly thought about the mobility of these men around all the areas of London.

'Does anyone keep a check on where they move to?' he asked Morris.

'Difficult to. They've all been coming and going for years. What's on your mind?'

'Moving stolen goods?' suggested Jack.

'Interesting idea. You'll be in Stepney tomorrow so you can keep an eye open for them. Got the newspaper, have you?' asked Morris.

'Yes, Sergeant. I'll have a look at it later. I thought I'd go over to Stepney tonight and have a look at the area,' said Jack.

'Watch your time though. It's either through the tunnel or catching the ferry. You need to be back for the formal transfer in the morning. No doubt you'll be seeing your young lady before you go across the river tomorrow. You and Phillips have a meeting with Inspector Hunt and I after the Parade in the morning.'

*

Jack left his notebook for Inspector Hunt to go through. PC Williams had sent word that he would be taking ten day's sickness. There would be a court day and Shaw was charged with assault and aggravated burglary. He was being held until the date he would go before the magistrate. So far, Jack was told, he had not said anything other than not guilty. Jack left the Camberwell Green station as dusk was falling.

Stepney was pretty close to what he had been expecting, with its omnibuses running to areas all over London. It was dark when he arrived and Jack had ended his shift at four o'clock. He would be hungry soon and looking for somewhere to get dinner.

He was supposed to be packing up his belongings at the dormitory but, as he had very little apart from the labouring clothes, his Sunday best suit, one novel, and a bible, he had decided that he would not wait until tomorrow to go and see where his next posting was but would make his way to Rotherhithe and go through the tunnel as one of the routes that Morris had suggested. He had asked a priest he passed the way to the railway to connect with the East London line. The light from the gas lamps would burn all night in the tunnel and he thought of those who at one time had chosen to walk Brunel's way under the Thames. With the directions that he received from the priest he found the station. Travelling under the Thames himself with the thought of all the water above, made him close his eyes. Growing up, as he had in Bexhill on Sea, he was used to being on the water not under it. Then the train came out of the tunnel's mouth like an angry dragon and he stopped his reverie as they arrived at the station on the north side of the Thames.

Huge warehouses surrounded him with tobacco, wine, and tonnes of coal that would be shipped on the coal boats at Limehouse. Three men leaning over a barrier watched him walk past, one of them holding a lantern, while low level wagons rolled by full of coal on a narrow set of rails. Ships with their sails tucked up like tents that had been packed away for the night were so plentiful that he could not count them all. He was used to the fishing boats along the Sussex coast but had not seen so many craft in one place. At Limehouse all of the activity with the coal business struck him as men moved containers of coal on trolleys. Instinctively he wondered what the level of pilfering was like. He walked on as the stench was hitting his senses. Jack's aim had been to find the station house in Leman Street and to get a tram to the west side of Commercial Road as Sergeant Morris had told him he would find green space off Arbour Square. There he would, Morris had said, be able to breath as he left behind him the smoke and grime of the docks and the Limehouse Pool. Morris had described being able to see the Surrey and Kent hills at one time from Bow Common. It was not likely now with the density of smoke from all the chimneys. Jack would not try anyway as it was dark but intended to get over to Bow at some point in the future. Even the large cemetery in Tower Hamlets was full of the fragrance of Cypress and Cedar according to Morris.

Even though Jack had dressed in his old labourer's clothes but he was aware he was standing out in comparison to the dock workers. He was too clean for one thing and his hands had largely recovered from two months of wearing gloves and writing reports instead of wielding a hoe.

He passed a couple of caravans with the children peeping out over the half door at the back of the first one. The horses were tied up at the side munching into what little greenery there was. Two men with wide brimmed hats sat on the road at the foot of the steps. A woman, perhaps the children's mother, sat on the steps next to a third man who held a clay pipe. They looked grubby, but Jack was struck by the fact that they were a family. If he had been in uniform he would have moved the nomads on. Instead he nodded and received a wary acknowledgment from the man on the steps in return.

Jack walked through an alleyway and found himself on the Commercial Road. A cabman was about to take a fare from a man muffled against the cold. Jack noted the cab's licence number for the future, "75 75."

He walked past a row of brick cottages that looked respectable, and was struck by the Mason's Arms on the corner, as a cooking smell of gravy, pastry and onions enveloped him. He walked around the recruiting sergeants standing outside the public house, their hats perched jauntily on the sides of their heads. The hubbub of noise from the group mixed with the sounds of dogs barking and wheels on the road. It would not do to get picked up by the sergeants. Other men were keeping their distance too, standing watching the group in uniform, tankards in hand, joking and keeping up a lively banter.

A gentleman in a top hat, looking very clean, stopped to let the two public disinfectors pass him pulling their wagon. Street hawkers plying their wares of fancy pottery talked to a woman with a baby in her arms. Jack stared at the grime on her apron. Two little girls on either side of her, as grubby as the woman's apron, picked up some pieces of pottery from the makeshift table the men had erected. The woman backed away and called the children after her. No money to spend on trifles there, thought Jack.

On the other side of the street a man representing himself as a doctor was setting up his concoctions and talking to two women who had come out through the front door of a shop. The street doctor had a sign showing his range of prices. Jack moved on but noted the face.

The aroma of the food pulled him into the Mason's Arms. It could mean pies in Jack's experience and maybe cheese to go with it. His stomach had started to believe that his throat had been cut, he was so hungry. He went in and sat down on a bench seat at a corner table. He would pass for a labouring man but was aware today his hands and face looked too clean. He looked at a group of ship's officers that had walked in. So that they did not have to mix with their crews or the ordinary labouring classes a snug was available off the main room and Jack watched as the uniforms walked past him into the warm little room. All he saw, before the door closed, was the fire, a table and chairs, in the snug.

'What will you have?' the barmaid asked him.

'Any pie that's ready,' Jack said. He put his money on the table and realised he was attracting attention from two men at the bar. The accent maybe, or the fact an agricultural labourer had put money down on the table very readily. Jack leant back into the shadows and hoped they would lose interest. He was annoyed at himself for coming in. He should have picked something up from one of the vendors and started back.

Jack thought of the fresh creamy texture of the cheese from the Weald. Finishing all he wanted he sat back and pulled the folded newspaper from his jacket pocket. Keeping back in the shadows he read the headline again.

"The Mysterious Tragedy of the Faceless Woman." He read on, partially scanning the article in the poor light.

A woman's body had been found, smartly dressed at number five, Golden Square. The woman was found dead with a blanket over her head. A Doctor Brown had been called to the scene and much of the face had been destroyed. The landlady, a Mrs Pope, had let the room a few days before and the lady had given her name as Mrs Timkins. There had been one visitor, a man, and the landlady, reported as a respectable woman who had let rooms for years, had allowed Mrs Timkins to receive him in the front parlour, as she did not hold with gentlemen in lady's rooms. That was all about the male visitor. The lady had paid her in full at the start of the week and told her she would need the room for no more than a week. There was a comment from Mrs Pope that the man who called was not the same class as her lodger, Mrs Timkins. The clothes and his accent had shown her that.

Jack imagined the woman, "the poor woman," as the article described her, but of a better class than her visitor. He saw her in his mind, alone, taking her life. There was a niggle in the back of his mind. Did she take her own life?

Doctor Brown had said the body appeared to be dead for some time. The paper went on to say that a small glass flask had been found next to the body. On the table was a note apologising for causing Mrs Pope so much trouble and a small sum of money, £3.00 was left. The note went on to say that she wanted to have a small quiet burial.

The last paragraph of the article mentioned that no papers were found and it was impossible to know if the name given by the deceased was her real name. The hearth had evidence of papers having been burnt. The body had been taken to the mortuary for the post mortem. A comment at the end by the journalist pointed to the use of strychnine. It was common enough, thought Jack. He knew they had used it on the farm to get rid of the rats. No personal effects were found. No jewellery was mentioned, which would have been unusual in a woman of class. Jack made a mental note to try and talk to the doctor about ring marks.

How did they know that about the strychnine? Jack wondered.

Finally, the journalist for the Tower Hamlets Independent commented on the standard of dress as being refined, hands that had clearly not done a day's manual work, and the age estimated by the doctor of a middle-aged woman.

Jack's thoughts were interrupted by one of the two men from the bar pulling up a stool at his table. Slightly taller than himself, Jack assessed, making sure he remembered the moustache, and the cut of the suit. The waistcoat was beer stained.

'Did you enjoy your dinner?' asked the man.

Jack looked up from the newspaper, surprised that the man had sat down.

'Frankly, not as good as home.' Jack played it right.

'I thought you weren't from round here. Just arrived, have you?' the man visibly relaxed and sat back, tucking his thumbs into his waistcoat pocket. Jack had the newspaper away into his jacket pocket
before the man had any chance of seeing the article.

'How did you know that?' asked Jack, deciding to play the country boy.

'Easy. And people in my line of work notice things. Your clothes are wrong for around here, and the accent says you're a country boy. But you're too clean and your boots are too good for a labourer. You're changing jobs and this is all you have to wear I think. Someone's given you good boots though. Bit worn now so not new. What are you and where have you blown in from?' The man took his bowler hat off, resting it on his knee. The action was not a good sign to Jack as it meant he was not moving any time soon.

Jack smiled, all conciliation and innocence. This man was not going away soon and the last thing he wanted to admit to being was on off-duty police constable on someone else's patch.

'Sussex. New job,' Jack said, leaning back and continuing to smile, working hard at not providing a name.

'There's too many of you country boys coming in now, for my liking.'

'I'm back across the Thames tonight, just came over to see Limehouse. Exciting to see the ships for a lad like me. So many, and all shapes and sizes. Don't get nothing like that on the coast where I'm from.'

The barmaid was back to collect Jack's money and take his half- finished plate. Sitting back against the wall he looked at her and treated her to one of the smiles that only Harriet to date had experienced. It worked like magic, and she nudged the inquisitive customer.

'Don't' you ever stop working? He's paid for his dinner. He's done nothing wrong so leave him. I would have thought you'd had enough today with that lot you took in,' the barmaid said.

'What's your name?' Jack asked her, working his smile.

'Mary,' she smiled back and the distraction worked as the man looked at the barmaid.

'That's more than you've told me in two years.' The man picked up his hat and stood up.

'As if I'd give my name to a 'tec!' Mary said, turning back to the bar. Jack kicked himself for coming in but the "tec" had lost interest and was walking back to his companion at the bar. Jack picked up the coins Mary had put down as his change, belched as the inedible meal repeated, and stood up. Staying as much in the shadows as he could he got to the pub door and went out onto the street.

'Let's hope that detective is not based in Leman Street,' he said to himself. A cab was coming up and he stepped back before it hit him. Jack registered the number on the cab and saw the face of the driver as the man peered over his shoulder to look at Jack. The cab rocked from side to side but steadied and rolled off down the Commercial Road. Across the other side two men were arguing and one punched the other and Jack watched the Blood flow from a nose. The ensuing fight and noise from the onlookers brought the detective and his companion out from the Mason's Arms. The expletives were ripe. One man was down and the other was hauled off by his mate. Normally quick to step up, Jack saw the sense in not being on the scene this time. He turned and walked the other way.

*

The night passed and the day he was to go north of the river dawned. Jack was called into Inspector Hunt's office to have the official transfer completed. Hunt showed him the entry of Public Orders that had come through from the office. Jack and Williams received commendations for apprehension, and the recovery of property. Below the entry was a section headed up "Plain Clothes." Under Division P Jack read his name, "John Sargent, division P, the allowance is granted from fifteenth December." His was not the only name and he saw Sergeant Morris and PC Phillips were also mentioned. Curzon was not mentioned. However, looking further down the Police Order was a section for Transfers. Curzon, Jack, Morris and Phillips were all listed as transferred from P to H division. There it was officially, against his name brackets the words second class. So, they were all going to H division together.

'Plain clothes, sir?' asked Jack.

'When needed. Sit down, Phillips and Morris are coming in shortly. Did you read the article in the paper?'

'I did, sir. Is this tied up with plain clothes work?'

'Before I answer that I want Morris and Phillips in here. Have a look at this,' said Hunt, as he handed Jack a report. It was dated two weeks ago. It concerned a body found just after Jack's recruitment into the police. A body was under a bridge a little way from a crashed carriage. However, the accident had not destroyed the label on the shirt on the dead body which had been traced to a shirt maker in Jermyn Street. Handmade, and silk, it indicated the wealth of the victim. There was sufficient information that had led the police to establish that the body was the missing American diplomat, Arthur Berringer. A journalist had put forward the idea that the wife was implicated. No proof had been found. That was as far as the report went. Nearly two weeks had gone by and the Americans were sending over their own investigator.

There was a knock on the door and Sergeant Morris and PC Phillips entered. Hunt casually pointed to chairs and the two men sat down. Phillips reached across and shook Jack's hand.

'Well done,' he said quietly.

'Thanks, to you both,' Jack looked from one to the other of the two men he was sitting with. Morris and Phillips, clearly, knew much more than he did for this briefing and his mentor, Phillips and the Sergeant, Morris, had been on plain clothes duties with Inspector Hunt before. Hunt's reputation was one of uncompromising duty. One day, it was rumoured in the dormitory, if the wrong men got to the top, Hunt would go because he would not bend with the wind. Niceties and banter from Morris and Ted Phillips about "new boys" muscling their way into special duties over, Hunt started to explain.

'I've shown Sargent the report on Berringer. The wife was suspected, but it all evaporated. We think she has a guardian angel.'

'Right,' said Morris and Phillips nodded. Jack glanced between the three men and felt stupid, wondering why the religious was being introduced. Hunt looked at Jack.

'A protector, as there are relationships between leads and things drying up in the investigation. Clues disappearing. It implies there is a policeman involved. A high-ranking policeman.' Hunt paused.

'How high, sir?' Jack asked.

'Higher than you could imagine, Sargent,' Hunt said.

'Why have you brought me in?' Jack asked, again mystified at his good luck.

'Because we've trained you, watched you, and know all we need. Remember whatever passes in this room isn't to go outside the four of us. Curzon is going to H division as well but it's his eye for detail and ability to understand the implications we want from him. He won't be briefed at this point because he will be in the station and he doesn't quite have your ability to obfuscate in a situation. I'm not sure that he's the risk taker that you are as well,' said Hunt.

'Do you mean that you think it's someone in Stepney, sir?' Jack asked.

'Berringer's body was found there. I want my people in there before the Americans arrive as after that they'll be all over the division like a virus. Thankfully the police strike and suspension of staff has created the opportunity to move the four of you in.'

'Who are you reporting to? I just want to make sure who's got our backs,' Morris asked.

'The Home Secretary,' said Hunt. 'It's become embarrassing, diplomatically.'

'Do you think the policeman is involved in the actual murder or the cover up?' Phillips asked.

'The cover up...maybe the murder itself, maybe both murders, I'm not sure,' said Hunt.

'Just one thing, Inspector,' Sergeant Morris cut in, 'the murderer... both murderers, what would the motive be? Why would a serving policeman, probably high ranking get involved in this cover up?' Morris looked at the Inspector opposite him.

'That news article in the Tower Hamlets independent, sir?' Jack cut in before Hunt could answer Morris.

Hunt's mouth twitched at the sides. 'Yes, go on.'

'You gave me that article yesterday, but call us all in today on what seems an unrelated case. We're moved to Whitechapel but the body of that lady, the Faceless Woman as the press are calling her, isn't anything to do with that area. The body of the diplomat is found in Whitechapel. I'm wondering what the connection is, why you gave me that article to read?' Jack asked.

There was no answer. Hunt carried on looking at Jack. Jack glanced quickly from one to the other of his colleagues, men more experienced, men now treating him as an equal, not as a raw recruit. Men who he could rely on and who had that same view of him, or he would not be in the room.

'The American diplomat's wife went missing on Sunday, lad.' Morris turned to Jack. 'She left their children with the governess and hasn't been heard of since. The woman in the article just might be her. You read the description the landlady gave of her lodger, Mrs Timkins. Refined, well-educated woman, takes a room and gets a visit from a man who's clearly not of the same class. This woman takes strychnine, apparently of her own free will. Doctor Brown is pretty convinced it was strychnine because of the spasms the head and neck muscles had gone through. She loses half her face so that we can't identify her, which is very convenient for anyone wishing to hide the identity, destroys her papers apparently and writes a neat little note, in a fairly uneducated hand, asking for a quiet burial. Not likely she wrote it.'

'The accent though,' said Jack. 'Everyone spots mine, surely the landlady, Mrs Pope, would have known the woman was an American.'

'Mrs Berringer was an Eastern New England woman. Some accents are similar to East Anglia. Maybe she toned it down deliberately. I don't know. But we are trying to tie back anything we can find about the dead woman to the missing wife of the diplomat,' said Hunt.

'And the Americans that are coming?' Phillips asked.

'The Home Office is under pressure to hand it over,' explained Hunt. We have two weeks before their policeman gets here from New York. We're to cooperate. We look as though we've handed it over but we won't have done. When we need to we go under cover, hence the permission for plain clothes that's open ended as far as a date is concerned. But you'll see a difference in the way the New Yorker will operate if he takes the case off us. The other problem we have is that officially we're not on this case. We cooperate by providing the officer with escort. The reality is we're working with him, unless we solve it first. If we do we'll get some insight into who is at the back of these deaths and that's also our aim. He'll know that.'

'Going back then, sir,' Jack said to Hunt. 'What do you think actually happened?'

'Really? I think the woman was after the money. Berringer was a very wealthy man by American standards, super rich by British. One scenario is that she found someone to help her get rid of him. Perhaps even to do the killing without her soiling her hands. Perhaps she offered riches, perhaps there was an emotional entanglement. Maybe, if the Faceless Woman is Mrs Berringer, the diplomat's wife, she became a risk and had to be disposed of herself. Maybe the woman found someone else. Or the person who was involved with her found someone else. Perhaps, the murderer blackmailed her and she wouldn't pay up. There could be numerous reasons.' The Inspector stopped.

'Find the motive, eh, sir? Phillips said. Hunt nodded.

'Well finding the murderer is one thing, but we have two murders now. We also have someone in the Metropolitan Police who is tampering with evidence. I believe, or rather my nose tells me, that we are going very high with this one. I'll get a cable to you Morris, at home when we need to go into plain clothes. Sargent, you and Curzon will be in lodgings round the Arbour Square area, in the home of Inspector Matthew Doyle and his wife, Emily, as it's too risky for you to be in the station house accommodation. I can contact you without arousing suspicion that way. Matthew and I go back to our training days together. I'll need you to be the one to go out in the area as you're not known yet. What is it?' Hunt stopped as Jack had looked down at the floor.

'I need to tell you something about last night. I went over to Limehouse and walked as far as the Commercial Road. I ate in a public house called the Mason's Arms and met a detective who showed rather a lot of interest in who I was and why I was there. I didn't get a name and I played the country idiot as he was doing his best to work me out. I was in my labourer's clothes but had kept my boots on as I don't have any others now. It was the boots that he noticed. I think I managed to put him off. I've no idea where he was based. There's just the chance I could run into him and he'll recognise me.'

'If that happens we'll face it at the time. If it was Commercial Road it could be one of the detectives from Shadwell rather than Leman Street. Keep Morris and Phillips informed if you see him and we'll improvise. I can always get you back here on special duties as the plain clothes permission is open ended.'

Morris and Phillips were up and walking to the door. Hunt stopped Jack.

'Oh, one more thing, Sargent. Not a word to that girl of yours. And no visiting after today. For her own safety.'

*

The evening came although Jack thought that it never would. Phillips and Morris lived south of the river with their families and it was Sam Curzon that accompanied Jack across the river to the lodgings in Arbour Square. They would have separate rooms, they had been told and Jack was grateful for the first time in his life to have his own space. His leaving of Harriet had not gone too well as there was little he could tell her and the attempts to protect her by not disclosing too much made him reticent. They had argued as he would not tell her anything about his address, following Inspector Hunt's directions to protect her. The Leman Street station as his posting was the address he gave Harriet. She had taken his reticence as disinterest in her and that he was moving on. It had not ended happily for either of them.

The house in Arbour Square was owned, and occupied, by a Police Inspector and his wife, Matthew and Emily Doyle, who occupied the first floor entirely for themselves and their family of one child. The ground floor was divided up into a breakfast room and lounge for the use of the guests, with two rooms at the back taken by a married couple. Hunt had arranged it with Doyle based on his knowledge of the man as trustworthy. Jack met Matthew Doyle with his eyes shining that evening having heard some of his exploits from Sergeant Morris.

Breakfast and one other meal was provided and Jack felt like he was living like a king. Emily Doyle chatted to Sam and Jack about how they had made an exception for Tom Hunt's team as she walked them up the three flights of stairs to the top floor. A young clerk introduced himself as they passed the second floor as Michael Culled, and he and Sam found they had much in common.

A maid of all work called Hannah was introduced to the new guests as she was finishing lighting the fires in their new bedrooms. Emily explained that Hannah would bring them hot water each morning but would leave it on the hall stands outside their rooms, with fresh shirts and linen.

Jack wondered what linen was. She would light a fire in their rooms daily as well. Meeting her made Jack wonder how Harriet was and if she would ever forgive him for his silence.

The married couple were George and Ann Black, both involved in some way in the medical profession. The clerk was about the same age as Jack and Sam, told Sam he was working in a business in Whitechapel High Street. Jack liked the situation immediately, as the house faced onto a green. Although it was dark by the time Sam and he arrived at their new accommodation Emily Doyle explained that there was also a public park less than a five-minute walk from the house, that had been saved from developers due to a public campaign that year.

Every time he thought about the access to the green space his heart surged. It was like living in a dream being in this house, with his own room, on an investigation with a man like Hunt, and now meeting another senior trained by a model policeman like Fairbrass. He decided that he would wake early and go for a walk at dawn to see the park.

Sam, like himself, was amazed at the space he would enjoy in having his own room. He confided to Jack that the dormitory in Camberwell Green was the first time he had had a bed to himself without one of his brothers sharing it.

Jack spent the time after the evening meal in his bedroom, enjoying the new sensation of being completely alone, unpacking his best Sunday suit, his labourer's clothes that he thought would become his "plain clothes" outfit when called upon to don them, and the two books that he owned. His mother's bible and the new book by Thomas Hardy, "Under the Greenwood Tree," were both place proudly on the little shelf above his bed. In time, Jack intended to have built his own veritable library upon it.

*

Three

The following morning, as the light filtered briefly through the clouds, Jack made his way from the terrace on the south side of Arbour Square. It was the best experience that he had had since coming to London. He touched his forehead to a gentleman coming out of another townhouse into the square. The man turned the opposite way to Jack and walked towards Commercial Road. The square was only about a mile from the City and still had the air of a garden enclosure. Jack's objective was to find the park. He walked along East Arbour Street which had smaller two storey terraced properties and came to Wellesley Street and then to Stepney Green. The smell of the foliage hit him over and above the coal fire smoke from the houses. He stood and breathed.

Breakfast was laid when he let himself back into the house and coddled eggs in beautifully decorated pots, their tight lids well-screwed down, were on the table. There were slices of bread and butter stacked on a plate in the centre, and a hot tea pot with cups arranged in front of it.

Sam Curzon was finishing his egg as Jack came in. Inspector Doyle had gone out earlier, as had Michael Culley who was already on his way to Whitechapel High Street to open up the business before the manager arrived. There was no sign of the couple and Jack assumed that they had already left as well. Mrs Doyle was trying to get a teaspoon of coddled egg into her two-year old's mouth. It was a good game and the child, Sarah, turned her head away with a squeal of delight each time the spoon was about to pop into her mouth.

'Morning Mrs Doyle, Sam, and Sarah, of course.' Jack grinned at the little girl and she gave another high-pitched squeal at the attention.

'Please call me Emily. I can see that breakfast is becoming far too exciting for this little madam here. You'll be left in no piece and Sarah will think that you both are only here for her. I'll take her out now and see if I get a better chance of getting her to eat with just me as her slave rather than three of us here giving her all this attention. How did you sleep, Jack?'

'Perfect. The first time I can remember without having someone snoring in my ear,' Jack said as he pulled out a chair and sat down opposite Curzon. 'How about you Sam?'

'Same. I've never had a room to myself before. Two older brothers who sounded like trains every night, to say nothing of the dormitory we were in at Camberwell Green, eh, Jack?'

'This home feels like I've died and gone to heaven,' said Jack, helping himself to a coddled egg and a slice of bread.

'That's alright then, and how it should be. I'll leave you two in peace as no doubt you will need to get off shortly. Did I hear you go out this morning?' Emily asked Jack.

'Yes, up to the park. I still can't understand how areas can change so quickly in London from terrible streets of misery to refined squares with gardens like this one.'

'Oh, before I forget, a parcel has arrived for you. I'll get Hannah to take it up to your room. You'll both have a fire each evening and when you're on nights it will be stoked before Hannah goes to bed. Hot water will be brought up when you're both back later. I'll see you both this evening for dinner,' said Emily as she picked up Sarah, who started to protest as she was removed from her adoring public.

Left on their own, Sam stirred sugar into his tea and eyed Jack up as his colleague spread the coddled egg onto two pieces of bread to make a sandwich.

'What's going on, Jack?'

'Breakfast,' Jack said, as he looked up surprised at the question.

'No, what are we doing here, I mean,' said Sam.

'Filling in after all the suspensions,' Jack smiled at him before returning his attention to his egg sandwich.

'Living in this house, which neither of us could afford on our pay. In a neighbourhood like this. A maid bringing up hot water to our rooms. Fires being lit and "stoked" for us when we're on nights like we're toffs. No, come on, what's going on?' Sam put a second sugar in his tea.

Jack shrugged, bit into his egg sandwich, and chewing, said, 'Perhaps the dormitory was full up. Anyway, it's not likely to last is it. We'll be back across the river once they reinstate all those men. Do you think if we make inspector we can take a house like this? Harriet talked of taking in lodgers, a nice house by a park, I wish she could see this one.'

'I think Inspector Doyle might have married a bit of money, either that or he's on the take,' Curzon said. He looked at his plate and Jack, who had been carefully concentrating on pouring tea, glanced up at his colleague at the suggestion. Jack put the tea pot down and looked back at his plate.

'Moving Sergeant Morris, Phillips, and you, says to me something's on. You're the muscle I reckon. Why me, though?' Curzon asked and squinted across the table. Jack had seen him make this expression when he was working things out.

'Don't know, don't care. I'm going to enjoy it while it lasts, which it won't of course. We'll be back in with the snorers before we know it. The closer into the city we get as regards a division the better for our careers, I think. Stepney is bound to be better than Camberwell for that reason alone. But this place, and nice women like Emily Doyle, the little girl as family.

I've never had it, Sam. You've got a family, I haven't. Its why I joined the police to be part of something big and try and get on, you know, break the pattern in my background of being someone's servant.'

Sam smiled sadly at Jack. 'You're still someone's servant, Jack. The Queen.'

'Not what I mean. This is what I want, Sam. And working with men like Morris and Phillips, and you with your eye for detail, it's like family to me.'

Sam carried on looking at Jack, who concentrated on the sugar bowl. The suggestion of something being out of order with the Doyles, had disturbed him. Running out of any inventiveness to divert attention from the real reason why they were both here Jack wiped his mouth on the serviette and threw it on the table. Hunt had put Sam in without briefing him because he had that eye for detail and he would work things out as he came across information. It was protection in case of pressure applied on him. Jack did not think Sam Curzon would be able to cope with physical pain in the same way that he could, and had, in his labouring days.

47

Sam was sharp, and a spell of desk duty was placing him in exactly the right position to pick things up, as far as Inspector Hunt was concerned.

'There, that's me done. It's eight o'clock, we'd better get off. It's a bit of a walk from here,' Jack pushed his chair back and stood up.

'There's a station at Stepney and we can probably pick up transport on an omnibus. Mrs Doyle will know. I don't know whether you're as daft as you're making out or there's some reason why you're not telling me what you know,' said Sam Curzon.

'If they've sent us for a reason, and they've not told us why, there's good grounds for the silence. Let's enjoy it while we can, Sam. You'll not be in uniform for long with your sharp brain. I reckon you'll end up at Scotland Yard and I'll be a lowly Sergeant when you're a Chief Super!' Jack grinned.

'Sergeant Sargent, there's a mouthful for you. And the future Mrs Sargent? How did Harriet take to you coming over here?' asked Sam.

'Not too well. I'm not sure when or how I'll see her again. That point didn't go down
easily with her, but we're only less than two weeks from Christmas and she'll be very busy. We could be back in Camberwell by then. Who knows.' Jack said and stared at the fire.

'Somehow, I think you do,' said Sam as he picked up another piece of bread and wrapped it in his napkin and put it in his pocket.

'If you want to get off, I'll just get that parcel that's come.'

'From Harriet, perhaps?' grinned Sam.

'Maybe. I'll take it upstairs and have a look. I'll be down in a minute, if you can wait.'

Jack tore off the wrapping at the top of the first parcel. There were three bound together but each one contained something different. Inside was a suit, the kind of material that he had seen shop workers wear on a Sunday. There was a shirt in the second parcel, carefully wrapped in paper. The third parcel was heavy and revealed a pair of polished boots. He thought there must be a mistake but the parcels had been hand delivered and his name was on the front. Then it dawned on him that these were his "plain clothes."

He thought with a grin that inspector Hunt was making sure that he did not attract attention by looking out of place in his labourer's clothes.

Jack quickly pushed the parcels into a drawer and put the new boots under the bed. Then he left his room. Running down the stairs he passed Emily, emerging from the Doyles' rooms after the battle with Sarah's breakfast.

'Did you find your parcel?' she asked.

Sam was waiting and watching.

'Yes, it's clothes from home. My Sunday best for church. I didn't think to bring them and just arrived in what I was wearing in October. I thought the Housekeeper would probably give them away but someone at the house must have found them and sent them onto the station in Camberwell Green. Sergeant Morris probably sent them over. Frankly, you wouldn't want to know me in my farm clothes and they certainly look out of place around here, so I'm glad of them.'

*

Jack and Curzon arrived ready for the parade at the police station in Leman Street. The Sergeant on duty that morning was William Thick, recently promoted after transferring back from Chelsea in September.

'So, you thought you'd try your hand at policing?' Thick said to Jack and Curzon after parade ended. He looked at Jack and said, 'I hear you're from a farm in Bexhill.'

'Yes, Sergeant, my dad was a market gardener and before he died I grew up helping him from the age of nine. I was on a farm near Battle before I joined the Met.'

'And you're a man with a good eye for detail I hear.' Thick turned his attention to Curzon.

'I'm used to paperwork, Sergeant.' Curzon said.

'Well you'll see a lot of it here, Curzon. How are you finding being in London after the farm?' Thick asked Jack while he positioned himself behind the counter.

'It takes some getting used to, Sergeant,' said Jack.

'I'm from Bowerchalke myself, not too far from Salisbury, worked as a carter on a farm so I have some understanding of how different Stepney will feel. The harvests were bad, that's why I came to London. Been here four years now. I suspect the terrible rain this year and the poor harvest had some effect on your decision to join the police in London?' Thick asked Jack.

'I see it as a way of getting on,' said Jack.

'Same here. I wanted to get out of an office as well,' said Curzon, 'I've been stuck in a back room since I was fourteen, copying out papers. I want to get out there and solve crime.'

'You'll see a different world from the farm Sargent, and the City, Curzon, here. Even Camberwell hasn't got the low life existence some of the people around here have. Curzon, you're on the desk with me this morning according to the orders I've received so I'm afraid that your skills will continue on the paperwork, at least for today. Sargent, you're out with PC Phillips when he gets in. There's been an omnibus accident that's still being cleared and he's involved at the scene.'

'Is your family still in Bowerchalke, Sergeant?' Jack asked.

'Yes, they're all there at the moment.' Thick picked up a paper which he passed to Jack, reverting to the job in hand of getting these two young constables lined up for the tasks. Curzon on paperwork and Sargent ready to go out on his beat. Phillips should have been with him but the patrol had to go out regardless of the man being new.

'Here's a map for you. Don't lose it as we've got a limited supply.' Thick spread the copy on the desk and Jack leant over to look at it.

'You'll head from here to the respectable parts today. Lucky lad on your first day. No stopping off in kitchens now with pretty maids around there,' said Thick, jabbing a finger at the map. 'You see your reputation has gone before you! This is the route and then you'll head back here this way. Now the characters you need to keep an eye on are working at a beer shop, one called Hope, which is a laugh in itself, and another called Lamb, and he's anything but. Both have done time, pinching lead off a building. The other issue we've had complaints about this morning is washing being stolen off the lines.'

'Sorry, Sergeant, washing?' repeated Jack, who was all fired up ready to crack the case of the faceless woman and thought he had misheard.

'That's right washing. An epidemic of it.' Thick grinned at him. 'You're to call at all houses on the beat that have wet linen in their garden and caution them of the risk they run in having it stolen. Good way to get to know the neighbourhood. Sergeant Morris will be on duty when you get back.' Thick stroked his moustache as Jack picked up his helmet.

'Right, Curzon, here's your pile of charge sheets to work through.' Thick banged a pile in front of Curzon.

'Do you a swap with the washing?' Sam Curzon called to Jack as he walked to the station door.

Jack wondered how long it would be before Curzon started to unravel the real reason they were in Stepney. He rather dreaded the time for the man when the revelation would come that they were after a bent policeman, probably a senior one, capable of murder.

When he arrived at the beer shop an elderly man, who was sitting on a pile of sacking on the pavement, offered Jack a pipe. Jack waved it away.

'Thanks, but I don't smoke.'

The man did not speak but filled his own clay pipe from a tin that he produced from his pocket. He poked the tobacco down with his thumb and then struck a match. Sucking in to get the pipe going while he held the burning match on the tobacco in the pipe's bowl he looked at Jack through one eye that was open, his other being closed as a result of the pipe smoke. Jack wondered at why a human being who was breathing in so much smoke already would voluntarily add more to his lungs. Satisfied with the progress of the pipe, the man asked, 'Where have you come from, Constable?'

'South of the river,' Jack answered.

'Not heard an accent like yours since my days around Hastings.'

'Really? That would be about right, what were you doing in Sussex?'

'Working the fishing. Bit of smuggling, I don't mind telling you, it being so long ago, thirty years or so. The laws having changed now, that I doubt you'll arrest me. Uncle Ben they called me on the boats.' The man paused and turned his head away to spit.

'What brought you to London?' asked Jack.

'A woman, what else.'

Chatting, Jack was aware the man was not the only person listening to him. The word would go around soon enough that there were new policemen in the area. Everyone would know him soon. He could play it as he wanted. The old man would pass on any information Jack would give him.

'I've not seen any of the new 'uns with your build. Scrawny office workers most of them. Some of them don't last long when they try and clear the shop.' He nodded backwards over his shoulder, towards the beer shop. 'I reckon you'd last longer than some of them.'

'Reckon I would,' Jack nodded, and clenched and un-clenched his fists. The old man watched him and then spat to the side again.

Everyone would tell the story that a fighter was on the beat. Ah well, it may make a few wary, Jack thought. He drew a breath and asked, 'Have you seen Hope and Lamb this morning?'

'That's why you're sniffing around is it? What have they done this time?' asked the old man with a leer.

'You tell me,' said Jack, grinning at him.

'That, Constable, is what I can't do, because I don't know.'

It would be enough that the police were asking. Word would get back and just possibly, the two men might move on for a while. They would be someone else's problem and not his.

The weather was dry for a change. He wished he could get a message to Harriet and arrange a meeting but he could not risk gossip if he went into the cable house and there was a limit to what he could tell her about where he was staying and working. Deciding to wait until Phillips was with him so that he could check out the wisdom of some word getting back to her, Jack put the situation to the back of his mind as he pulled put the map from his pocket and studied it to check that he was in the right street and not straying into another constable's beat.

As he walked on his route to the better streets there were four or five that ran up to a park, terraced town houses but four stories in height and all with back gardens full of washing. A perfect location to start his duty of advising the inhabitants of the likelihood of losing their laundry.

A couple of the houses had clearly had a bumper wash day. Line upon line of sheets, petticoats, and pillow cases amongst other things, waved in the cold wind. He decided to call at these rather than all of them hoping that he was right in the assumption that the servants would talk to each other about the policeman's visit.

As he entered a front garden the front door opened and a tidy maid, her apron well starched, handed a hat to a smart gentleman leaving the house. The man looked morose and busy. Jack met him on the path up to the front door, which had been firmly closed.

'Yes, Constable, is there a problem?'

'I hope not sir, I'm calling to see the housekeeper.'

'You will be better going to the kitchen door down the steps at the side. Doctor Brown is my name and I am just leaving.'

'Is it Doctor Brown who acts as Police Surgeon?' Jack asked the man as he walked past him. He hoped he had recalled the name correctly and that it was a Doctor Brown that was mentioned in the article about the faceless woman. He couldn't quite remember.

The doctor looked impressed and half smiled. 'Yes, that's right. You've heard of me at the station, I see. No doubt we'll meet there. Please excuse me, my patients aren't as used to your clientele at waiting for a visit.'

'It was a case I think you were called into. The one in the newspaper about the Faceless Woman without an identity,' said Jack.

'Oh, yes, well she wasn't exactly faceless. Someone had worked the face over so she couldn't be identified. You know what journalists are like by now in your line of work. You have the advantage over me, we haven't met before, have we?'

'No, sir, I started today, here, came over yesterday from Camberwell to fill in for the staff shortages for a while. My name's Sargent.'

'Good to meet you. No doubt I'll see you down at the station. It must be Leman Street, if you're round here?'

'Yes, sir. Good to know the surgeon, always.' Jack saluted, thinking Inspector Hunt would have prompted him to do so, and pleased that he would have news for Morris and Phillips about meeting the doctor involved in the post mortem. A chance meeting but one that made him have a spring in his step as he ran down the basement steps and gave an energetic knock on the kitchen door. He would deal with the washing thefts now and caution the housekeepers about the risk of stolen laundry. The real gain of the morning was that he had made contact with Doctor Brown and the man would know him at the station.

Jack turned on his most charming smile for the scullery maid as she opened the kitchen door.

*

The notification from the court came across the river with Sergeant Morris. When Jack finished his patrol at four o'clock, Morris handed the instruction to him at the desk. It was addressed to Jack and headed up "Assault on Constable Williams and Burglary."

Jack was to appear at the Magistrates Court in two days. He felt quite worried by the whole situation of a first appearance in court and unusually for him, it made him irritable.

'Sergeant Morris.'

'Yes, lad.'

'Is it necessary that I go to this?' asked Jack, waving the order.

'Good grief, yes, how could you not be there. You're the star witness and the division is looking for a conviction on the case. Williams is still off sick but he'll attend the court and give his statement. You're the second witness that will ensure the man goes down.' Morris frowned at Jack's question.

'I've not been in court before and this will be the first time I'll have been on the stand.' Jack put his hands in his pocket and balanced on his heels in a way that reminded Morris of his teenage son.

'Look, Inspector Hunt has gone over it with you, hasn't he?' Morris asked.

'Yes.'

'Alright then, what's the problem?'

Jack thought about it for a few moments. 'I haven't seen a court.'

'Well, you're about to. You're a key witness and a police officer and you will be in and out of courts for the rest of your career. This one's easy as you know you got the right man. Both Williams and you know it's him. All you've got to do is tell the truth. Come in the back for a moment.'

Morris led him into the back room and closed the door. 'Look, there will be cases where it will be suggested to you that you imagine things. This isn't one of them so you have nothing to worry about. Tell the truth and the counsel for the defence won't be able to do anything to influence the jury. It's when you're making things up you have to worry, not that I'm suggesting that you should do that but I know of men where their statements are not as reliable as yours is.' Morris started to open the door and to return to the desk. Jack seized the opportunity to tell him about meeting Doctor Brown.

'Sergeant, I met the Police Surgeon this morning, the Doctor Brown mentioned in the article about the woman. I wondered about doing a bit of follow up and going over to his surgery.'

'Not in uniform, you shouldn't. Remember this is someone else's case. You starting to sniff around could get mentioned. Have those clothes come yet?'

'Was that you,' asked Jack.

'The Inspector. After you mentioned about the 'Tec' noticing your clothes the other night. You'll stand out in your farm clothes, even amongst the labourers here. Your measurements were easy enough to get from your file for the uniform. If you go across to the doctor's surgery, go in civvies, with some spurious complaint, shoulder ache or something. Be inventive. See what you can pick up. Got money to pay him? He runs a club you can join, not sure though how much it costs,' said Morris.

'I could call at the hospital?' suggested Jack.

'No, don't go anywhere near the place. It's like a gateway to death.'

'What about here? Does he come to the station to look at officers?'

'Only when we call a surgeon in, and it would have to be serious, so that is not something we can inflict on you. And I don't want you getting yourself into a difficult situation to try and get to the doctor. Look, leave it for now. That house you saw him coming out of?' Morris paused.

'Yes, Sergeant,' said Jack.

'Go back and find out from the kitchen who it is the doctor calls to see. Perhaps its regular and you can be there. I can jiggle around with the patrols. Phillips and you could go together, that way you'll learn from the master how it's done.' Morris pulled the door open and they went into the corridor.

'Sergeant, if I'm going back south of the river for the court, is there any chance I could slip off and see Harriet for a while?'

'Bit risky, frankly. You're likely to tell her too much. Why don't you write her a note and I'll make sure it's dropped off for you? I'm sorry to say this but I'd better have a look at it first so keep to stuff like suggesting a place to meet, if she can get off in the run up for Christmas. That house is always big on entertaining on Christmas Eve. Why don't you get her a present and I'll make sure she gets the gift and the note?'

Jack wrinkled up his face at the thought of a colleague reading something that he would write to Harriet.

Morris was trying to protect the case. Jack was struck at how the job came first. He was putting it first, too, and he wondered what effect being in the service would have on a marriage.

'How do you cope with that?' Jack asked.

'What?' Morris looked askance at the question.

'Putting the job before your wife?'

'I don't, but there are some things for her own safety that she doesn't know and never will. That's all it is. Her and the children being safe is all I care about. Any woman you marry will be expected to help to a certain extent, especially when you're in married quarters. Where you're staying is different because it's owned,' said Morris.

'How does that work? How could he have bought the house?' asked Jack.

'Inspector Doyle bought the house when he and Mrs Doyle married. She brought some money with her, that one. Her father started as a junior clerk in a bank and had an eye for investment. He and his partners started outside London. She was his only child and he settled money on her when she married, Doyle. They make it pay with taking lodgers, usually from the City. Look, you're keeping Emily Doyle and the child safe, Jack, by not disclosing your address to Harriet, hard as that is for you. Hopefully the investigation won't take too long and we'll track the bastard down that's involved in Berringer's murder and the Faceless Woman case. Meanwhile apart from a note and a gift, lad, to let her know that she's on your heart and mind, you keep silent. Harriet knows which station you're at. You're not promised to Harriet, are you?' asked Morris.

Jack shook his head. Morris felt some relief that such a complication was not imminent with his young constable at this point in his career. The lad was dependable and strong and Inspector Hunt had hopes of building a lasting team. Morris could do without pressure on their new lads from women until they had developed the skills. He gripped Jack's upper arm in what was meant to be a fatherly gesture.

'She can send a note via me. Why don't you suggest a meeting? She could take the tram to Westminster from Camberwell Green.'

*

The following evening Jack left Stepney with Ted Phillips. He was to stay at Morris's home for the night before the Shaw case to avoid travel delays on the following day in court. He and Ted left after the patrol ended and Jack and he travelled back to Camberwell Green where Ted had acquired a newly built house. They parted company at the Green and Jack walked south to find Morris's address. He and Phillips had been back to the house where Jack had met the doctor and were starting to ingratiate themselves with the cook, but it was slow going.

Jack had also asked Emily Doyle's advice about a Christmas gift. He wanted to know where to get a gift for a lady and quietly had come down to breakfast earlier than usual when no one was in the dining room except her and little Sarah.

'You could get chocolates. Is this for Christmas? If it is, you'll need them wrapped and with a card.'

Jack exhaled, feeling defeated. 'I haven't done this before, not since a child. The last time I gave a woman a gift it was to my mother and I made that.' Emily looked at him.

'I imagine you were quite small on that occasion,' she said. Jack nodded.

'It was the last time, she died shortly after. It was Mother's Day and a cake. I helped the Cook at the Squire's make it, at least I threw the flower in to mix. Cook called it a Simnel Cake. Then she let me stick the eleven balls on top.'

'Marzipan, balls of marzipan. Its traditional.' Emily smiled.

'Are chocolates enough?' Jack asked.

'Yes, I think they will be a very nice gift. There's a shop towards the City. There isn't too much of a commitment with chocolates or flowers. I can get a small box for you as I have some Christmas shopping to do in the City. I'll go tomorrow, there are some lovely boxes already wrapped at this time of year,' promised Emily.

So, his gift would go with Morris on the twenty-fourth of the month, as the Sergeant finished work for his own family Christmas.

Everyone was being kind but Jack felt that this was terrible that he could not even give her his gift personally, so essential was it that he did not relent and tell Harriet anything about why he had gone north of the river. Phillips had told him that it was damaging to their undercover enquiry if the address Jack and Curzon were living in got out. Ted was taking the same view as Morris.

'If the girl is worth her salt she'll have patience,' he told Jack. His note had suggested that she let him know when she could meet in Westminster as soon as she had a half day free. He would do his best to get the time off and Morris had promised to try and help him with the patrol times.

*

The court gallery was full, so well-known was Shaw. So many people had crowded in that Jack began to wonder if all the one hundred and eleven thousand people recorded as living in Camberwell parish were trying to get into the court.

Jack heard the charges read out.

'Not guilty,' said Shaw.

Williams was in court looking sickly, his head bandaged and an arm in a sling. Jack's mind wandered as he looked around the court, taking in the magistrates, especially the one Phillips had told him to watch out for, a Mr Newbury. The Barrister for the prosecution, a Mr Striker, was calling Jack to the stand, having finished destroying any potential character that Shaw may have had. Jack took the oath, gave his rank and number, and then waited. Striker looked at Jack who met the clear gaze with one of his own. It was a trick, Phillips had told Jack, that Striker always used with the bench. The role of keeping public order and a man who enabled the populace to sleep easy in their beds. Jack did not mind the play. In Shaw's case, he had been well and truly caught on the company premises, pockets loaded with goods and coin, and had tried to kill Williams into the bargain.

'Keep your expression an open one, Jack, meet Striker's eyes and speak up,' said Morris, over breakfast that morning. Striker had finished meeting Jack's responsive gaze and had moved his hands to his back. He clasped them as he turned to the bench to meet the eyes of the magistrates before him. He waved a hand towards Jack.

'Constable Sargent, gentlemen, the saviour of PC Williams, who you see before you in court today, bandaged following a vicious assault. This is a dedicated, young officer, very keen I'm told by his trainer. Exceptionally keen that he has already been promoted to constable second class. Tell us, Constable Sargent, when did you join the Metropolitan Police?'

'The fourteenth of October, sir.'

'And are you from London?' Striker turned, taking his eyes away from the bench and moving them back to Jack. It had the required effect as all eyes left Striker and moved to the young constable on the stand.

'No, sir, I'm from Sussex.'

'You would not have known the accused before?'

'No, sir.'

'As you can hear, in the accent, gentlemen, not a young man from around here. Constable, tell the bench what you found when you went to the assistance of your colleague.' Striker spun around to face the magistrates again, giving his gown a flick as he moved his hands from his back.

'Keep polite and space your words, so that drawl of yours doesn't lose the magistrates.' Morris had coached him. Mr Newbury was peering at Jack over his glasses. He looked disgruntled. Morris had told Jack to try and ignore the man's looks as he appeared to live in a perpetual state of dyspepsia.

Jack explained how he had heard Williams call him and the resulting fight with Shaw. He described the look in the eye, how he had realised this was a fight to the death. All the time Jack never looked at Shaw but stared firmly at the Magistrates. Striker was asking him a question.

'You are a very new recruit, aren't you?'

'Yes, sir,' said Jack.

'Somewhat inexperienced to be able to make that judgement about a man therefore.' Striker suggested, as he turned away from Jack at that point and stared at the magistrates. Mr Newbury's eyes were fixed on Jack. Striker turned back and raised his eyebrows for the response.

'As a policeman, yes, as a man who has been in fights, no. You can see it in the eye,' said Jack, 'and this man was no different.'

'Thank-you, Constable, you can step down now.'

Inexplicably Jack felt in a bad mood. Having to be in court was going to be part of the job but he felt nervous in the place. So much power in a couple of men sitting on the bench, overfed, suffering from gout in the case of the second magistrate and a clear case of too heavy a breakfast as regards Mr Newbury. He realised he felt fear. He kicked himself for reacting and tried to see things differently. It would be important, he told himself, to prepare his mind or he would show how he felt every time he entered such a place. All he had to do was tell it how it was.

He sat outside the court room in a reception area. It was an impressive building, befitting no doubt the dispensing of justice. In Shaw's case Jack had no doubt about the guilt and the sentencing. The din from the people in the waiting area resembled a fairground rather than a court. Jack suddenly felt that he had had enough and needed to get out into the air.

The row of women sitting outside by the wall were hopeful of selling the flowers they had probably picked up from the market that morning. The three women were shrouded in shawls trying to keep warm against the invasive December cold. Their cheap clothing was inadequate, however. The youngest one could not be missed, her skin and eyes still good. Jack put her at about fifteen and wondered what life would hold for her. He could not buy flowers as he was in uniform but called the costermonger over and paid him for three cups of broth.

'Take them over will you,' Jack said. The man nodded and carried the three cups across, and pointed at Jack, when the oldest woman spoke. As it was a Constable there was no argument and the women shyly nodded at the policeman. Jack again wondered, as he had since he had arrived in London in October, whether poverty in the country was actually easier than in the city. At least people knew each other. Of course, there was a disadvantage to that as well but there had been a certain amount of looking out for each other and the Rector's lady had been an angel in visiting the sick and the poor with small parcels of food. Jack moved away in case he could be accused of wanting favours from the women and went back into the reception of the court.

Forty-five minutes went by and he waited in the lobby as per the instruction in case he was called back into the court. What could be keeping the magistrates from making a decision. He felt sympathy for Williams, stuck in the court room still, probably feeling like death.

Then the door opened and Striker came out, rubbing his hands with a self-satisfied look on his face. Williams was behind him looking white. Jack was thinking of walking round Striker and giving Williams a hand. The barrister was not going to be avoided and walked in Jack's direction.

'Well, Constable, Shaw would not say anything. But we have successfully got the magistrates to commit him for trial. Central Criminal Court and you and PC Williams will be needed for the jury trial. The man is heading for penal servitude but still maintaining that inane grin on his face. He must be in the pay of someone big. You'd do well to look into his family, see what you can find out. My money is on someone taking care of them if he remains quiet. A good morning's work! Good day both.' Striker made his way to the door of the building.

'Shall I walk home with you?' Jack asked Williams, who looked decidedly shaky.

'No, I'll go in to the station,' said Williams. 'I could do with pulling round before I go home.'

'You look as though you'd be better at home,' Jack said.

'The station's closer. I'll stay and see how I go on. I can't do the journey at present and I don't want to worry the wife any more. She was against me coming to court today as it was. I said to her what can I do?' Williams lent against a railing along the steps to the street and Jack took hold of his colleague's elbow in case he was going to fall. Slowly they walked the route to New Road Police Station. Once inside the Desk Sergeant urged Williams to go into a back room. Jack went with him to make sure he sat in the room and got some tea, and then he wrote his report on the court appearance and asked the Sergeant if Inspector Hunt was available.

'Why would he be wanting to see you? Get along now, you should be getting back across. Leave your report with me and get off back to Leman Street.'

Jack checked and wondered if he could get a boat across to North Greenwich and pick up the train that ran across the Isle of Dogs up to Millwall Junction Station. He had been told there was a terminus at North Greenwich that had opened in July earlier in the year. It linked with the line that ran west from Blackwall. The station that had opened in Leman Street had been declared unsafe and closed so it would be a walk from the station at Stepney for Jack.

There was a ferry in and he got on at the back. A policeman boarding attracted unwelcome attention and Jack had to make the ticket seller take his money for a ticket so that he was seen to pay. He stood on deck enjoying the cold wind after the court room and the unfriendly station Sergeant. He heard a shout and realised he was being called to a group of people huddled over a body.

A woman had fainted and was on the deck, unconscious. She had dropped her bag which had been picked up by a couple of children and was fast becoming a source of interest. Jack took it off them quickly before the contents were emptied and the bag thrown over-board. As regards women collapsing he had no idea what to do. She needed help though and there was an expectation from the on-lookers that he, a policeman, would have all the answers.

'Stand back,' shouted Jack. The mass moved away. The woman was coming to and he thought she had probably just fainted. Some respectable looking women were asking him if they could help and he was glad to let them go ahead, standing to one side to make sure nothing threatening happened to the woman. Smelling salts were produced from a bag by one of the helpful ladies and slowly, the woman who had fainted was sitting up, leaning into the arm of one of the other women. Seeing that Jack had her bag she held out her hand for her it and Jack gave it to her.

'Where do you live?' asked Jack. 'Have you far to go?'

The woman shook her head and said something quietly to one of the ladies that were helping her.

'Expecting,' mouthed the lady.

'Right,' said Jack, feeling this was completely out of his sphere. 'You alright then, with these ladies?'

The woman nodded and gave a wan smile. Jack held out his hand and with an arm around her back from another lady she was pulled up and helped to sit on a vacated bench seat on deck.

'I'll leave you in the capable hands of these kind ladies. Could you just check nothing's gone from your bag? A couple of children had it and we had better make sure,' said Jack.

She did so and smiled again at him. 'Thank-you,' she said, her eyes going briefly to the numbers on his uniform.

Satisfied he had done all he knew how, Jack went to the back of the boat and breathed deeply, feeling more at home in a scrap with Shaw than assisting ladies who faint.

*

Four

Jack thought about his conversation several days before with Sam Curzon. He had dwelt on the fact that Inspector and Mrs Emily Doyle had acquired the house in Arbour Square. An idea gnawed into his mind like a rat at a storage barrel that he had seen in a barn on the farm. The rodent would not let go until it had made a hole. It was especially bad in the early hours of the morning. At the back of his consciousness an idea had taken root that he could not utter to his colleagues. A suspicion had formed as to where the Inspector and his wife had obtained the money to buy such a house.

Jack got up and felt the chill in the room. It was cold now as the last embers of the fire in the grate had died. He could not work out the time but the cold made him think it was after two in the morning. He struck a match and lit the candle. Getting back into bed he pulled down his copy of "Under the Greenwood Tree," from the shelf, in an effort to occupy his mind. His mother's bible was really heavy and he could not manage to hold it open and get back under the blankets. He read for half an hour until he felt his eyelids droop. The book fell to the floor and he managed to blow out the candle before he fell asleep.

He was up later than intended because he overslept. The pitcher of hot water was still outside his door, as the maid, Hannah, had not yet been able to bring herself to come into either Sam's room, or Jack's, while they were in there. Picking it up he realised that as the water was now lukewarm, it was late. Sam Curzon must have left before breakfast or thought that Jack had already gone in on a shift. He had not banged on Jack's door as he was inclined to do every morning. Jack pulled back the curtain and saw the dawn streaking across the sky. Jack pulled back the curtain and saw the dawn streaking across the sky.

No rain this morning for a change, but he was too late to sit with a leisurely breakfast. The main thing was to get to Leman street in time for the Parade. Sunrise meant it was about eight o'clock. He would pick up breakfast from the kitchen and go to Leman Street.

Pouring the water over his head, he rubbed his hair dry with the shirt from the day before, and dressed. Going quietly down the two flights of stairs he turned for the kitchen and frightened Hannah who was busy immersing the breakfast plates in to the sink. She suddenly froze, as she had believed that he had already left for the station. Jack raised a hand in greeting, smiled at her, and said, 'Morning, I over-slept!'

The only help in the house, Hannah was skinny and long limbed, with a constant expression of shock. Jack had never seen her sit down as there seemed to be endless tasks for this one servant to do. She did not move now, but watched him as Jack picked up a piece of buttered bread from the left overs of breakfast which was now on a plate on the kitchen table, and quickly smeared jam on it. He poured milk into a tin cup from the rack above the sink and drank hungrily. Buttoning up his tunic part way he went out of the kitchen door, devouring the bread and jam while he walked to the omnibus stop on the Commercial Road.

Jack tried to bring a vehicle to a stop, but it was full and continued past him. He walked on along the busy road knowing that he was going in the right direction towards Leman Street. He passed the Mason's Arms, where he had met the detective that they had assumed probably came from the station in Shadwell. An omnibus was coming up behind him and he turned to flag it to a stop. Seeing a police uniform the driver slowed and Jack jumped on to the platform at the back. It was standing room only at that time of the day and all the shop workers were on board. He stayed on the platform hanging onto the pole, while he looked down the bus. The whole of the group of passengers seemed to be talking and he heard some giggling as a couple of shop girls looked him over and took a shine to him. They were in the first two seats, and giggled and whispered to each other.

'Going to arrest us, Constable?' asked the dark-haired girl.

'Perhaps he's going to take us to the station,' said her friend, who was sitting next to her. With a high-pitched squeal of laughter that would deafen the dead, they lost interest in him as the next stop came into view. Their attention was on the queue at the stop as it consisted of young male clerks. Jack swung around on the pole by the stairs to avoid the young men coming down them who needed to get off. The vehicle was then turning for Leman Street before he knew it and he arrived at the Police Station in time to see Morris and Phillips walking along the street. He stopped and waited for them.

'Thought I was going to be late. It's a comfort to see you two are only just here,' said Jack.

'Going off duty, or coming on I expect you to pay attention to your uniform!' hissed Sergeant Morris and Jack realised that his top button was not done up.

Ted Phillips nodded at him as he struggled with the stiff button. 'Can't have you drawing attention to yourself not being properly kitted out,' he said quietly, as he drew level.

'Sorry, Sergeant Morris. I overslept. I only just made it.'

'Too easy a life for you, obviously,' joked Ted.

After Parade Jack got Morris on his own in the kitchen with the offer of tea. Sergeant Thick was still on the desk and Morris realised the young Constable had something that he could not say in front of other officers.

Jack put the kettle back onto the stove to bring the water up to the boil again and while they waited he voiced his concern to Sergeant Morris.

'Sergeant, given we're looking for a policeman that's a high rank I had a few thoughts in the night. In fact, it stopped me sleeping.'

'Hence the poor attention to your standard of dress, I presume,' said Morris.

'I overslept and had a bit of a rush to make Parade,' said Jack.

'You'd have been carpeted if it had been anyone other than me.'

'Yes, I know. Thanks,' said Jack.

'What is it that you've been working out then?' Morris asked.

'It's about how Inspector Doyle managed to buy a house in Arbour Square. It looks fishy.'

Morris managed to control his humour at the suggestion and restrained the laugh that was building into a twitch of his moustache and a twinkle in the eye.

'So, you think our man is a mere Inspector, do you? Well I'm sorry to disappoint you if you think you've found the murderer in Matthew Doyle, to say nothing of an adulterer moving in exalted diplomatic circles.' Morris said.

'It's not a normal situation though is it Sergeant? Someone of Inspector Doyle's poor beginnings having money like that,' said Jack.

'Because it's not normal doesn't mean it won't happen. Look at the American heiresses arriving by the boatload at the moment. Ask a few questions about their backgrounds and you'll find you're two generations from the blacksmith. Anyway, the money isn't his. It's nothing to do with him making it actually. It's come in a trust carefully drawn up by Mrs Doyle's father who was a banker. They married before the Married Woman's Property Act and everything went into the care of her husband. Doyle declared it to the Chief Super on the engagement and it was all looked into.'

'It's all above board then?' Jack asked.

'Look, its good you're thinking about things but you're on the wrong track there. I was the Constable on a burglary case of her father's home five years ago and I saw her father welcome a man of integrity in Matthew Doyle. There were others trying to land the money all right but, you see, the trust her father left is to be placed in assets that accrue value. Doyle insisted the trustees continued to manage it in and that the money pass to the child. Of course, they could undo it now since the Act. He would have none of it for himself. If they have more children the property and money will pass to their children on Emily's death.' Morris poured them both a mug of tea, spooning two sugars into his own. Jack took the mug that was offered to him.

'So, you're of the same view as Sam that Emily Doyle had come to the marriage with wealth? That's a relief,' said Jack.

'Curzon thought it through, as well, did he? Good that you're both mulling over the case. I'm encouraged. Here's what happened. Matthew Doyle and Tom Hunt worked together on the case of an aggravated burglary of the home Emily and her father lived in. The two had been frequent visitors, Tom Hunt as Inspector and Matthew Doyle as his Sergeant at that point. Emily Doyle was the only child of a banker, remember, and a banker with humble beginnings but a bright man. He wasn't a fool and she inherited shares in the Joint Stock Bank on his death which were held in trust. Once Doyle gave in to his feelings, they married quickly. There was a wedding and little Sarah was born two years ago. Several times Matthew Doyle pulled back due to the difference in position but Emily got her way in the end. Her trustees did not object to the purchase of a property in a prestigious area on her marriage. It built the value of the trust you see.'

'So, I may encounter heiresses in the job,' Jack laughed.

'As you said, it's unusual. There were a few ruffled feathers in the local bucks who were after a wife with an income from a trust but she married Matthew Doyle, newly promoted to Inspector, (Tom Hunt made sure of that once he got wind of the attachment). Sam was right. He has a keen sense that one, weighs things up rather than jumping in. You'd do well to take note of that. Action isn't always the right answer, lad,' Morris downed his tea and put it on the drainer ready for washing later. 'Well, back to it. Where is Curzon?' asked Morris.

'I don't know, he had left by the time I woke up,' said Jack.

'There must be an order that's come through. I'll have a word with Thick.'

The orders for that day were clear. Towards the bottom of the Metropolitan Police Order was an entry for a transfer from Stepney out to Windsor Great Park for Samuel Curzon. Morris signalled to Thick that he was going to have a look at the sheet in the back room. Ted Phillips came into the counter area looking for Jack, as they were due to start their patrol. Morris beckoned to him to follow him into the back.

'Odd,' said Ted, 'Its special duties.'

'I told him he'd end up in Scotland Yard!' said Jack. 'How's that happened?'

'I'll make some enquiries,' said Morris. 'You both need to get off on your patrol. There's some bad flooding at Windsor. Odd though as it's effectively royal duties.'

'There's been a lot of flooding this last week. Bad before Christmas. I saw the Illustrated London News about it, maybe that's why he's been sent over,' said Ted, 'because of his background.'

'He's not alone. Matthew Doyle has been transferred for the day as well. I'll find out who's behind this.'

Jack and Ted Phillips left for their laundry patrol, as Morris had started to call it. They walked at a reasonable pace as Phillips was in no hurry to receive the amorous attentions of the cook. Jack had started to play up to the parlour maid in a way intended to get a reason to visit the house each day but the unforeseen had happened. The cook, a Mrs Prescott, had taken quite a shine to Ted and this had been the route into the kitchen. Ted was not a philanderer and therefore the cook had assumed that he was just a retiring type. In reality he was horrified at being expected to flirt in order to extract information about when Doctor Brown was next expected at the house.

'My Margaret will shoot me,' he had said in an aside to Jack.

As they approached the cook's domain Jack broached the subject of why police would be drafted into a flooding situation at Windsor.

'The paper said that the floods have covered miles on both banks of the river this week, Windsor town and Eton are under water by several feet and people are having to use punts to get out at all. Sunday had the congregation from the parish church being ferried back and forth in boats. You would think the Market would have been called off, given the conditions, but folk were coming in from Maidenhead by boats. The town was surrounded by water and its apparently like a peninsula. There's usually looting in that sort of situation. Doyle was sent across there and asked for Sam as he's got some background knowledge.'

'I thought Sam had a job in the City. How do they stop the water then?' asked Jack.

'Yes, he did, but he grew up over there and his father's a Waterman. All I know is what I read in the paper. There was an article on the comments from the Deputy Surveyor of the Royal Park about the weirs and tumbling bays reducing the water level. This is fairly new apparently, and they've managed to keep the level down by two feet compared to what it was in the floods in 1852. Oh and, you'll laugh, The Windsor Castle Sewerage Farm work has gone on without being interrupted! Ha, ha, can you imagine how that would have been if there'd been a leak. There would have been royal…. oh, good morning Mrs Prescott,' Phillips stopped in mid flow after the two men turned into the front garden of the five-storey house. The cook was coming up the steps towards them.

'Good, morning, Constable Phillips, Constable Sargent. I've just got a batch of biscuits out of the oven, all fresh, and some cheese scones. I thought you were due on your beat about now. You'll appreciate a little something while you check our washing is safe. Do come down Constable Phillips, while your young assistant checks the garden.'

'Not a word,' said Ted Phillips, as Jack started to open his mouth to say something to the cook. 'Get on round the back into the garden and don't take too long about it. I don't want to be left alone with this woman. She's got a look in her eye.'

'Yes, Constable. Save me a scone,' Jack smiled at Mrs Prescott as she turned to lead the way below stairs to her domain. A widow and professional cook she had a good position in the house she worked in but was clearly on the hunt for husband number two. Jack could smell today's offerings and they would be excellent if yesterday's scones had been anything to go by.

Jack went through the garden gate into the back of the property and looked briefly at the rows of sheets hanging in the yard outside the kitchen. He locked the back gate so that no theft of laundry could occur and had a quick peer up the garden along the high walls separating the properties. How anyone would get over the nine foot walls studded with broken glass he could not imagine. His duty done, he knocked on the kitchen door ready to rescue his mentor from a dalliance or which Margaret Phillips, on the south side of the river, was ignorant. The call to duty that her husband was having to perform this week was not helping his nerves or the fit of his uniform around his stomach.

In the kitchen, the parlour maid ignored Jack, which suited him fine as he saw no reason why two constables should be flirting. Not that Ted knew how to flirt. Jack had only agreed to ingratiate himself with the parlour maid as Ted had suggested he would be the better one as a single man. Neither he, nor Ted Phillips, had foreseen the cook taking a shine to the older man as a potential husband number two.

Ted was eating a cheese scone with a mug of steaming tea. Jack stood respectfully in the corner until Mrs Prescott acknowledged him.

'Oh, do sit down, Constable. There's plenty more scones, or would you prefer shortbread with your tea?'

'A scone will do famously, thank you Mrs Prescott. Ah the life of we single policemen, eh Phillips! We don't know what we're missing, do we until we enter such a treasure trove of culinary expertise as this,' Jack said, smiling and taking a scone. He watched the cook heap sugar into a cup of tea for him. Obediently he took a sip and said, 'Mwwm,' and then put it to one side.

'What have you been reading? Give over,' Phillips muttered. But Jack was not to be put off.

'A busy time for you, Mrs Prescott, with Christmas in the next couple of days,' said Jack.

'Oh, you have no idea what my life will be like until the second of January. It isn't a couple of days, bless you, it started on December first with advent – stir up Sunday, you know, the pudding. My speciality - everyone has their own recipe. Mine goes back three generations. I make five for upstairs and two for down here and they keep until Easter, well, in fact they will keep a year but no one eats them in warm weather now. You stirred one, didn't you?' the cook asked Jack.

'Not this year, I was in a police dormitory on December the first. We need to be in a home, eh Ted?' said Jack. Phillips gave him a look.

'Ted, is that your name? Edward, for the Prince, a royal name and a strong name.' Mrs Prescott smoothed imaginary creases down her apron.

Jack tried a distraction. 'How many things did you stir into the pudding Mrs Prescott? The cook in Sussex used to put thirteen things into the mix for the disciples and Christ.' Jack said.

'Will you be on duty on Christmas day, Constable Phillips?' asked Mrs Prescott, giving all her attention to pouring more tea for Ted Phillips.

'Not this year, away from here with family,' said Phillips, as he held up a hand to refuse the second cheese scone. Mrs Prescott wrapped it up for him to take away.

'And your young Constable here? We can't do without both of you. How will we be safe? Are you on duty on Christmas day?'

'I am and you can rest assured that I will patrol here,' Jack said firmly.

'Then you must come and join us for the servant's dinner, no, I won't take no for an answer. We must look after our police force. A place will be ready for you when you can get here,' said Mrs Prescott in a queenly manner, to Jack.

'Oh, what was that?' said Jack suddenly. 'I thought I saw a man dash across the courtyard.'

'Right, we must go and look,' Ted Phillips grabbed his helmet.

'Oh, no, saints preserve us.' Mrs Prescott dropped the knife she was holding and the scullery maid in the corner squealed.

Jack was up the steps and Ted Phillips, weighed down by cheese scone was behind him. Jack kicked the dolly tub stored in the corner of the yard and shouted for the imaginary thief of washing to stop. Finding himself now safe from the matrimonial machinations of the cook Ted Phillips was the first through the back gate and onto the street.

'Did you find out when the doctor is due?' asked Jack after they had put a street between them and the cook.

'Yes, every two days. He will actually call on Christmas Day morning, so your invitation needs to come forward a bit to coincide with him. Here, take this,' and Phillips passed the second cheese scone to Jack.

'We're going to have to find someone else to do this beat with me, Ted,' Jack started to laugh. 'I sense a transfer coming on for you.'

*

'Do you remember those Gangers you saw in Camberwell Green?' Morris asked Jack when he was back at the end of the patrol.

'What's a Ganger, Sergeant?'

'A roadman to you, lad. We've had a report from a Surveyor about a potential theft. The man isn't sure but thinks there's something strange about a period when he was away. There was a stand-in and the temporary Clerk became suspicious about material being ordered and never being delivered. He thinks the Ganger, a man called Knowles, paid a man in the office to turn a blind eye to how much was being ordered. Shame Curzon isn't back yet, he'd probably spot anything untoward in the ledgers. There's word out on the street that Knowles has come across the river. Did you get that parcel from Inspector Hunt yet?' asked Morris.

'Yes, Sergeant. But I'm not used to offices, they'll spot me a mile off,' said Jack.

'This is an office, you're used to this. In the right clothes, you'll do fine. You think on your feet and that accent of yours can be controlled if you slow down your words. But we'll wait for Curzon I think. The Surveyor has come in and says that Knowles threatened to cave in the head of the man he had paid to turn a blind eye. The Surveyor followed him at a distance on the train and thinks that the team that were spreading the hard core on New Road, are now over here. That's why he's come into our police station instead of New Road. Come and see him with me and take the notes. His name is Bryant.'

Jack and Morris walked to the side room. Bryant, the Surveyor, a well- dressed man as expected in one who reported to the trustees, was asked if had anything to prove who he was and how long he had worked in the parish of Camberwell. He had a letter of appointment with him and other correspondence addressed to the Surveyor, with his name inserted and his address. Jack sat to the side with his notebook to start taking down details while Sergeant Morris asked questions.

'Mr Bryant, what made you suspicious of theft?' Morris began.

'The person standing in for me while I was away, I'll call him the Locum, was approached by the very man who had turned a blind eye to the theft of material. The man asked my Locum to take the money from him that he had been paid by Knowles as his conscience was pricking. The Locum refused and was told that Knowles was likely to bash heads if they didn't go along with the deception.' Bryant flicked a small piece of fluff off his knee.

'We'll have a look around this side of the river. Where do you believe this man, Knowles, may be now?' asked Morris.

'Somewhere around Poplar I have been told. I saw some of his men around there but not him. These men move around all the time,' said Bryant. 'One of the men says he's been seen working in a factory in the Stepney area.'

'The name of the man who has told you this?' asked Morris
'Evans.'

'We'll need to speak to him. In the mean-time the Constable
here will look around Poplar. He's familiar with Knowles's
appearance, as am I. It would be helpful if one of our other
constables could look at the records. He's used to office work
and ledgers, worked in the City, that sort of thing. If there's
anything odd about the records he'll spot it,' Morris said.

'Very good. When will you come to the office?' asked
Bryant.

'Tomorrow, sir. The Constable here will brief his colleague
later and we will be across in the morning.'

When Bryant left the interview, Jack realised that the only
way he would be able to brief Sam Curzon was if he actually
returned tonight.

'Sergeant, how are we going to get hold of Curzon if he's
been transferred across to Windsor,' asked Jack.

'I'll telegram to get him back here. It's bound to be tied up
with Inspector Doyle somehow. We'll do a telegram now.'

'Why was he sent there? It sounds odd to me,' said Jack.

'I think it is. We may get to the bottom of who sent him and
the Inspector at some but I doubt it at this point. It may have
been a ruse to get him out of the way, but I can't think why.
Probably more likely that there's something, or someone, in
Windsor that Inspector Hunt wanted him to see. Anyway,
tomorrow you're going out in plain clothes to track Knowles.
Use the train along to Poplar and go out when the office
workers are making their way to work. You'll blend in better
in a crowd. I'll remain with the clerk in the morning and,
hopefully, we'll have Curzon with me to see if we can get to
the bottom of what's going on.'

'Is anyone going to talk to me in plain clothes? I mean the
other men. I could start with them on New Road first thing
and get back across here, change out of my uniform and scout
around for Knowles,' suggested Jack.

'I want your eyes and ears, Sargent. Knowles is the key aim
tomorrow, we can interview the other men at any point. Go
plain clothes in the morning.

When Jack arrived back at Arbour Square he went to check if Sam Curzon was in his room. He could hear movement in Sam's room as he came onto the small landing and decided to knock on the door.

As Sam opened the door, Jack could see a steaming bowl of water on the stand behind him and realised he had interrupted Sam in his toilet.

'Sam, you're here. What on earth happened today?' asked Jack.

'Inspector Doyle collared me to help over in the Windsor area,' said Sam.

'Right, because of your father?'

'I suppose so, I don't have much experience but there are things you just seem to know when you grow up in a place. My father's a Thames Waterman and they were short of men to help do some of the rescue operations. There was a bit of looting going on as well so having the police involved was understandable. I'll finish up in here and see you downstairs. I want to soak my feet, they're really cold.'

'Right, I'll leave you to it. I wondered where you'd gone, this morning. Morris showed me the order that had come through. See you downstairs later.'

Jack sat in his room for about half an hour, flicking through "Under the Greenwood Tree," but he was unable to settle to it. He lay down for a short while and must have dozed off as the gong for dinner sounded from the hall below. Hannah was putting her heart and soul into hitting the instrument. A wail went up from little Sarah and Jack thought Emily Doyle would not be pleased that the little one had been disturbed.

The table was decorated with sprigs of holly and in the centre, was a large bowl of steaming liquid. Jack had seen punch before but not a hot one. With the time of year, he realised it was a mulled drink. At the head of the table stood the Doyles, together, Emily holding little Sarah. Matthew Doyle had changed out of his uniform and was in what looked like his Sunday best. He beamed as Jack and Sam walked in, George and Ann

---

Black already at the table, were standing behind their chairs. Only Michael Culley's place was empty but the door opened and he came in, panting. 'I am so sorry. I had to stay at the office until seven o'clock tonight.'

'Well its good you're here now. I'll start the festivities as this will be the last time over Christmas and New Year that we'll all be around the table. An old toast to you. Waes hael! Be well,' shouted the Inspector.

Jack nodded, remembering the squire in the church hall doing the same and he answered, 'Drink hael.'

'Oh, where did that come from?' asked Ann Black.

'I don't know, just a memory from childhood,' Jack said. 'I think it means, drink well.'

'Take a cup and George would you do the honours?' Emily asked, passing George Black the punch spoon. 'We thought, as its nearly Christmas, we would celebrate wassailing so we could pass on good wishes to you all. Jack you're with us Christmas day night so we will have a dinner for you but everyone else will have gone to other parts.

'Who knows the Wassailing Carol?' Matthew Doyle asked, looking expectantly round the group. Jack grinned and Sarah gave a squeal of delight as he started them off.

> 'Here we come a wassailing
> Among the leaves so green,
> Here we come a wassailing,
> So, fair to be seen.
> Love and joy come to you,
> And to you your wassail too,
> And God bless you and send you,
> A happy New Year,
> And God send you,
> A happy New Year.'

With much laughter, they toasted each other and took their seats for the first course of the soup.

'We should be doing the Mummer's play if I was back home,' said Jack.

'I haven't seen that done for an age, Jack,' said Doyle.

'I've never heard of it,' George Black confessed. 'Growing up in the city, I suppose. How does the play go?'

'I know this one,' volunteered Michael Culley. 'I was in Winchester last Christmas and saw it acted in the local hall,' he cleared his throat and started to recite.

'Here come I, Old Father Christmas…

and that is all I can remember!'

'Well I can help you out there,' said Doyle, and he stood up and made three chins.

'Don't frighten Sarah, Matthew,' said Emily.

'No, I won't.' Matthew Doyle held up a finger for silence and walked in front of the fireplace. 'Jack what can you remember, help me out will you? Here goes:

Here come I, Old Father Christmas.

Christmas or not, I hope Old Father Christmas

Will never be forgot…. Jack, what's next?'

'St. George, I think. Let's see what I can remember without scaring Sarah!' Jack joined Matthew Doyle at the fireplace and made two fists with his elbows out to the side and bobbed up and down as if he was on a horse. Sarah squealed with delight and Jack smiled at her.

'I think that's probably enough from the two overgrown boys in the company if we're to get any dinner and keep this little girl calm,' Emily said, but she laughed as they both sat down again.

Jack turned to Sam and asked about the day. Sam raised his eyebrows.

'Oh, I spent most of the day on a punt, getting people out of their bedrooms!'

'I wondered what you'd actually been doing. Sounds good work,' said Jack.

'Short of men, that's all, and I had talked to Inspector Doyle about the help I used to give to my father on the river while I was growing up. It's not the weather for a punt though,' said Sam.

'What does your father do in his job? See anything interesting?' asked Jack.

Sam gave him a look. 'He's a Waterman, and trains the apprentices. You're digging, aren't you to find out what I know? I know we're here for a reason, Jack, aren't we? Yes, as it happens I did see something interesting, but that was why I was there, wasn't it, but save it for later.' Sam turned to Emily Doyle, who was on his right, and was passing soup to him.

*

With the meal over the Black's adjourned to their own sitting room and the Doyles saw to putting Sarah to bed. This was a special treat for the little girl and her father and an infrequent opportunity for Matthew Doyle. Generally, he was not able to get home before his little girl was asleep. Sam suggested a game of cards in his room and Jack took it for a signal that this was the opportunity for Sam to tell him about what he had seen in Windsor.

Sam pulled up a chair at the small table in his room and Jack brought the chair in from beside his bed while Sam took out a pack of cards from the chest of drawers and shuffled them. Jack waited as Sam dealt the cards and then said, 'By the way, you're going with Morris to Camberwell tomorrow. A case came in from a Surveyor called Bryant about theft of material. Sergeant Morris wants your eagle eye on the ledgers.'

'More ledgers! I was in a boathouse on the Windsor side of the river, looking at ledgers. There was a swollen stream between Eton and Windsor and it rushed between the two places. It took us quite some time to get the punts out safely and we had to wait for the rush of the water to slow before we could get on them. While we waited Doyle and I went through the boatman's records. I don't know if you've ever been on a punt?' Sam asked. Jack shook his head.

'Only fishing boats, off the shore at Hastings,' he said.

81

'So, there was quite some time before we went out. Doyle has a background on the river too, before he joined the Met. Anyway, being interested in the records of how they log the movement up and down the river there, my attention wandered onto to some books on a desk. Doyle was interested in them too and actually called me over.'

'Doyle did?' Jack asked.

'Yes. It's your play, by the way.' Sam pointed at Jack's cards.

'Eh?'

'Your hand, put a card down.'

Jack randomly placed a card on the table. Sam looked at it and studied his own and then said, 'You should concentrate on your game, Jack, you're going to lose.' Sam put a card down and Jack grinned at him.

'Real life's what I concentrate on, Sam, not games. Go on, tell me what you found in the ledgers?'

There were lists of names of who had boarded, dates, and destinations. There were some who visited from Windsor Castle too. The clerk had clearly been very taken that he had important guests using the service. Not royalty, but the diplomatic level and the senior officers who accompanied them, out for the day in better weather. You're ahead of me, Jack.'

'I can't be, I don't know what game we're playing,' said Jack.

'It's rummy, but I don't mean the cards. You know I've seen a name, don't you?' Sam said.

'Come on, Sam, you're looking in a ledger, in an area like Windsor and Eton. Of course, you're likely to have seen a name which is well known. I should imagine there are families whose names we'd see in the papers every day with children at the school, or visiting toffs at the castle.'

'No, it won't do, Jack. No more prevaricating with me. Whose name is in your mind?'

'There could be half a dozen or more, frankly, that I could think of likely to visit the castle,' said Jack.

'Well when you're ready to come clean with me, I'll do the same with you. You need to put another card down,' Sam looked at the table.

'Sam, I can't say anything. I don't know who we're looking for. I've been told not to discuss anything with you, for your own safety, but no one has given me any names. So, you're ahead of me if you've seen a name. What has Doyle said to you? Tell me as it may give me permission to disclose what I know. Either that, or we both go and see him now.' Jack said, putting the cards down on the table and standing up.

'Good idea. Let's do that,' Sam stood up. 'It's obvious why we're in his house.'

'Is it?' said Jack. The two men looked at each other. The question had been spontaneous. Jack did not know how to answer that statement from Sam. 'What's obvious?' he asked.

'That there's a rotten apple in the barrel. Doyle was hungrily scanning the list of names using the boats. He asked me what I had spotted. I said there were interesting personalities visiting the area, but probably not surprising given the school and the castle. He said had I noticed anything in particular. But when I showed him he wasn't interested in the famous Lords and Ladies and their progeny, only an American Diplomat, the members of his party and the protection. It always staggers me how people can look at information and not see what's in there. I found the man, Arthur Berringer. There were other diplomats recorded, wives and families. It's like details hide from most people but I can see them as if someone holds a light over them,' Sam paused.

'So why do you think we're here?' asked Jack, waiting for Sam to tell him that they were part of an investigation into a senior police officer. His question was selfish because he did not want to tell Sam, but he was fully prepared to give confirmation if Sam came up with suggestions. The loneliness of the secret weighed heavily and a desire to have a confidante in the house was almost overwhelming.

'Because we're going to catch him. Question is, who is it and how senior?'

'Why do you think it has to be a senior policeman?' Jack dug a little more.

'Because, my old plate, it would have to be a certain level to be dealing with diplomats and the castle, wouldn't it,' said Sam.

'Not an inspector then?' Jack asked, hopefully.

'No, much higher. I saw the list,' Sam was moving to the door. 'Are we going to go down and ruin a beautiful evening for the Doyles?'

Feeling relieved about Matthew Doyle being too low down in the pecking order to be involved in the murder of Arthur Berringer, he felt it all could wait until the morning.

'Let's leave them for tonight and get up early and grab Doyle before he leaves. Shame to spoil a perfect evening for them, eh?' said Jack. Sam nodded and Jack held out his hand to shake Sam's. As Sam held out a hand in turn, Jack said, 'Just two things. What's an old plate got to do with this?'

'Old plate, mate. You're my mate, rhyming slang,' said Sam.

'Right, dialect?' asked Jack.

'Just what we say at home,' Sam shrugged, and Jack grinned and turned to go. 'And the second thing?' asked Sam.

Jack paused in the middle of opening the bedroom door. 'No such thing as one rotten apple on a tree on the farm, in my experience. There's always more than one. Sleep well, mate.'

*

Five

Jack had to go through the whole night before he would find out the name of the protection that had been with Berringer. Waiting bothered him, as did not being brought into the equation with the level of information that Sam already had. He slept badly, eventually falling into a fitful, dream-ridden sleep in the early hours of the morning, so that when Sam Curzon knocked on his door at six o'clock, Jack did not feel that he had slept for more than five minutes. In reality he had slept for five hours.

The weather this Christmas Eve was like the previous months, wet. He looked out of the window in vain to see frost or snow but the morning was mild again. His boots had a perpetual watermark around the toes.

To be quick he slipped on a shirt that had not yet been collected by Hannah for washing, and his uniform trousers, and joined Sam on the landing. On the table outside their rooms was a pile of fresh laundry. Jack noted again that he would have to start naming his to avoid the usual mix up of items between him and Sam. His shirts were larger though around the neck. He wondered if he would ever really adjust to someone waiting on him, providing him with clean clothing, and bringing up hot water to his room. Jack kept his room tidy, learning during the years of being a child labourer it was the best way to avoid a beating. Now he felt uncomfortable amongst mess. Sam stayed in the doorway and was leaning against the door frame.

'Listen, Jack, the Inspector went into breakfast with Mrs Doyle, and the little one, five minutes ago. I don't know what we're going to be able to get to say to him until the family's finished.'

'Well, we can't disclose anything in front of Mrs Doyle. We have to keep the family safe,' said Jack.

'Agreed, but we have to get permission from Doyle about you having the name of Berringer's protection. Once you know the name, you can keep your eyes open tonight on records of divisions and you and I can join forces and work upwards. We need to get his agreement before he leaves. Either that, or I have to get permission to talk to Morris this morning and go in to the station and see him before I go off home. Maybe Morris can brief you later,' said Sam.

'Doubt it, Morris won't be back at Leman Street when I finish the patrol. He'll have been on duty and will be gone to start his Christmas by four o'clock. He'll not be back until the twenty-ninth.'

'But you're going out plain clothes this morning aren't you. So, you'll be back in by midday, won't you?' asked Sam.

'Yes, should be,' said Jack.

They both went downstairs and Sam put his hand on the door handle, but paused as he looked at Jack. 'Ready?' he asked Jack.

Jack nodded and Sam opened the door. The two men went in to the dining room.

The aromas were overwhelming as Hannah had put down plates on the sideboard of bacon, sausage and black pudding. It was intended to be a special breakfast as it was Christmas Eve and Emily Doyle had arranged it as their lodgers had journeys to do. Only Jack, Sam and Matthew Doyle, were working. Jack could not help himself. After the meal, they had had the night before of roast beef, he had not thought he would be hungry but his lack of sleep drove him to devour a hot bowl of porridge and then two rashers of bacon, two sausages, and two pieces of black pudding.

Sam had played a game with Sarah, covering his eyes with his hands, pulling them away and saying 'peep-oh' to her. Sarah had copied with squeals of delight until each person at the table had had to take their turn. She was not pleased to leave the room.

'Why are you both down here, this early?' Matthew Doyle said, leaning across the table once the door was closed behind Emily and Sarah. Once he was sure they could not be overheard from the hall, Sam turned to Doyle.

'I wanted permission to fill Sargent in, sir, on the name that took your interest yesterday,' said Sam.

'He already knows it. It was Berringer,' the Inspector picked up his cup and concentrated on swirling the remaining tea around the inside.

Sam shut down, Jack could see it. Either he had made a mistake and it was the fact of Berringer having visited the castle that had caught Doyle's eye, or the Inspector was flannelling.

'I think, sir, that Curzon is under the impression that there was a name of a police officer with Mr Berringer, and that this name was the one that really caught your eye,' said Jack.

'Pity, I should control my excitement better. That's a lesson to me.'

Doyle smirked and set his cup down. He looked across the table at Sam. 'Alright Sam, yes, too bright by half, aren't you? However, I must get the information to Hunt today before we start sharing it. Preferably this morning if I can,' Doyle looked at the two young constables before him. They were almost bristling with anticipation.

'In the unlikely event that you and Curzon could meet with an accident this morning, would it not be an idea that a third person knows, just in case?' Jack suggested.

'Are you polishing me off, Sargent?' Doyle laughed.

'He has a point, Inspector,' said Sam, staring at Doyle.

The Inspector, shrugged. 'I realise there's a possibility of someone picking us off one by one but I think at this stage it's pretty slim. There's no indication of our investigation at all. No, I've still no intention of passing on the name.' Doyle thought briefly and said, 'Alright, Sam, but only the rank. It was a Sergeant from Great Marlborough Street Police Station. My base.'

'I thought it would be higher than that sir, from what Inspector Hunt said about a senior policeman?' said Jack.

Sam answered for Doyle, who had paused to take a sip of tea. 'It's who the Sergeant reports to and then up to the top of the tree, Jack.'

'What, Superintendent?' Jack stuttered the question out.

'Perhaps,' said Doyle. 'And that is as far as I'm going before Tom Hunt knows.'

'I'm going over to Camberwell Green with Sergeant Morris this morning. If I can give him a message that we have a breakthrough could Inspector Hunt get hold of you somehow today?' Sam waited for the answer. Jack counted ten and still Inspector Doyle said nothing at all for several minutes. Jack and Sam barely moved, barely breathed and Jack watched the clock hands move slowly for a tedious two minutes. Minutes that would never come again.

'It's Christmas Eve, I and Mrs Doyle are invited to a party tonight at Inspector and Mrs Hunt's home. Suggest to Morris if you have problems getting to see Hunt today that Morris lets Hunt know that I have information to make his Christmas special. Only give Morris the same as Jack knows, Sam.'

'Right, sir,' Sam looked deflated.

'We mustn't give any indication that we have a lead. The position of the person under suspicion implies that there will be others down the pecking order involved. A wrong word and we're done for. I won't have Mrs Doyle and Sarah put at risk. Or the other families of men involved in the investigation. Is that clear?' said Matthew Doyle firmly.

Jack nodded as did Sam. 'What's going to happen, Inspector? Jack asked.

'Christmas and New Year. We draw breath and think. Sam, you're with your family tonight. Jack you're on duty, I believe. You volunteered, didn't you? Is there no one you could be with tonight?' Doyle asked.

'No, sir. It means the men with families get time off. That gives me pleasure. Anyway, Sergeant Morris is delivering a gift to my girl for me today so you never know what might come out of that by New Year,' Jack grinned.

*

Doyle left the house and Sam and Jack went back to their rooms to carry on getting ready. Hannah had left the pitchers of hot water outside their rooms as usual and Sam picked his up. He turned to Jack and nodded towards his room. Jack followed him in and Sam put his water down and involved himself in brushing some dirt off his jacket.

'Do you know any names right at the top, Jack?' Sam asked.

'I've seen a few when I joined but I'm not sure I can remember them. It was only brief when I was being sworn in. There was a list on the Captain's wall.'

'As there would be in every division. And the layers in the divisions beneath them. Where are we going to get you a list from?' asked Sam.

'We're assuming Great Marlborough Street, I suppose, is the one to focus on, but it may not be. You've seen the name of the Sergeant so it's just a matter of knowing where he was based, if he was on special duties, who he reports to. Then we work our way up. Morris might know. Look, tell me if I'm jumping to conclusions, but this is going to be someone in plain clothes, isn't it? And someone on special duties if he's with a diplomat who just fancied a boat trip while at Windsor?'

'Exactly. We want a complete list and one which gives us a lead of everyone directly above them. Then there's the layers beneath them.' Sam stared out of his window, and Jack wondered what lists were appearing in his colleague's mind.

'Just police? How about family as well?' said Jack.

'And background. This is too wide we need to narrow it down,' Sam frowned and shook his head.

'What about cases, maybe high priority ones, in case of criminal links? asked Jack.

'Too much detail. Go with a lead as you turn something up,' said Sam.

'It's going to be a long night this Christmas eve, for me. At least until me and the duty Sergeant start dealing with the drunks they haul in tonight, and characters trying to steal people's presents,' said Jack.

'And, assuming that you can get hold of the name to start you off, what comes next?' asked Sam.

'Well, you're back after Boxing Day. That gives me two days. Inspector Doyle is here over Christmas and I'll have dinner with him and Emily tomorrow night. I could slip something to him and watch his reaction,' suggested Jack. Then he remembered. 'Oh, blimey? I forgot, I've got two Christmas dinners to eat tomorrow. And I've got to see the Police Surgeon at a house on my beat in the morning.'

'You've got a busy day! I am going to be so envious of you getting on with this,' said Sam.

'I'll have it cut and dried for when you get back. See, your eagle eye for information! I told you that you were heading for Scotland Yard. Go and enjoy your family, later. I'll see you after I've been to Poplar and then tonight I'll keep busy on this if I can make some progress. We'll see how many names I can turn up from the Commissioners at the top, down to the woman who cleans the steps,' Jack saw the reaction in Sam's eyes as he mentioned the Commissioners. It was just brief, but it was there. Perhaps it was shock that Jack could not even contemplate someone in that position being involved in two murders. Maybe it was another reason. Perhaps they would have to go that high. Jack thought Sam would be no good under pressure, if he reacted so obviously. No wonder Doyle was being cautious.

Smiling, Sam got up and slapped Jack on the back. 'I could ask for it by four.'

'What in the morning? You'll be lucky. In case I don't see you have a happy Christmas, Sam. Go and forget this and enjoy your family and I'll see you in a couple of days. I'm off looking for a Ganger this morning over towards Poplar so I'd better get changed.'

'Remember I expect you to have solved it by four! By the way, are you really not going to try and see Harriet?' came the surprising question from Sam. Jack started and knew how right Hunt and Morris had been that the best way to care for his girl, if she still was his girl, was to stay as far away from her as he could until the Berringer case, and the case of the Faceless Woman, were solved.

'Not now this has come up. I'll need to focus completely on the case.'

*

Jack deliberately took his time getting ready to make sure Doyle and Sam had left the house. He rearranged the position of the bed, moving it away from under the window as the noise from outside became more muffled towards the back wall of the room. He tried the clothes that Hunt had sent across, running his hand down the material of the suit jacket and the waistcoat, which was cut straight in the front. The shirt had a winged collar and necktie. In the bag was a bowler hat. Jack laughed as he put it
on. He had been told a bowler hat could be stamped on without losing its shape but he couldn't summon the guts to try it. Instead he put it on, walking back and forth across the room, past his shaving mirror, trying it at different angles. Hunt had got his measurements from the uniform details alright. Everything fitted pretty well. The small shaving mirror did not really help him see how he looked in total but it gave some feel of how the farm labourer, turned constable, was transformed into a clerk. Each time he walked past the mirror, his smile widened until the confidence built so that he felt he was ready to wear the outfit outside comfortably. The boots were still a hard-wearing leather but with square toes. Jack decided Harriet would be proud to be seen out with him dressed as he was in the plain clothes outfit.

'Certainly, this beats my old labouring clothes,' said Jack to his reflection.

He would leave the house by the back stairs again. There was no way that he would be seen letting himself out of the front door in his plain clothes. Servants in the neighbouring houses were used to seeing uniformed officers and the two lodgers, George Black and Michael Culley, leaving for work. An unrecognized man, as he would appear to be in the suit and hat, leaving after Matthew Doyle had gone on duty may affect Emily Doyle's reputation.

91

Around half past eight he decided to leave. Passing through the hall he could see Emily Doyle and Hannah starting to put paper streamers and jewelled decorations in the front room, and he noticed that the number of candles seemed to have doubled on the dining table. The Doyle's would entertain friends, he realised, and he kicked himself for thinking that when he returned later that night the house would be quiet and with just the family.

He arrived at the station in good time to catch the train going in the direction of Poplar. The siting of Knowles that had been reported by the Surveyor was in a factory around Poplar. The factories connected to the area down to Blackwall had had a shift change at eight o'clock. Men were leaving after the night shift and Jack walked from Poplar against the tide of workers on their way home in order to get a look at those leaving the area. He positioned himself at a place with a room off the street, serving a breakfast and ordered tea without sugar. It was a good position to see men walking for the train that would take them to Millwall junction.

The smell from the docks always took him by surprise. It was a mixture of something decaying, pools of stagnant water and half-baked sea-weed caked against the sides of old wooden props. Men standing around added to the stench as they reeked of the goods they had unloaded. Fish that had fallen from the baskets as they were carried added to the mix within the general stench. It was over-whelming and reminded him of things dying in contrast to the sense of life and freshness from the sea by Bexhill.

He had a basic description of Knowles and opened the pocket book that Doyle had thoughtfully provided for him containing some money. He was gambling on the hunch that

Knowles would still cross from North Greenwich to Camberwell for lodgings he had no doubt taken, or maybe there was a woman waiting for him that drew him back. He put half a crown on the table and waited for the money to attract attention from the girl wiping tables. She came over with his mug of tea, hot and strong, and he suspected the only benefit from it here would be the warming effect it would have rather than the taste. She would remember the way he liked it because of the money he was pushing in a pattern around the table.

'Got an idea about a man I'm looking for?' Jack kept pushing the half a crown around the table but kept his finger on it. The girl looked around but apart from one other man finishing up his breakfast plate everyone was already on their way to work. She looked hungrily at the money, taking in the respectfully dressed man with the stunning smile. An office worker she had taken him for, probably from the offices at West India Dock, unusual in here but now she thought he could be a bailiff and was after someone who owed money. Still dressed too well, she thought, maybe a private affair. Maybe a supervisor after someone from one of the factories.

'Why would I know who you want. Stands to reason I 'ave no idea who it might be, look at all of them walking by, 'undreds of 'em.'

'But it would be a man with a journey to do, I reckon. Probably likely to pick up food coming off a shift, on his way to catch a train down to cross the river. Someone new around here, who lives on the south side of the river.'

The girl was very relaxed suddenly, seeing the coin being hers. Jack saw the change in her expression as she looked at him and waited. She knew who he wanted, Jack could tell from the triumph in the eyes. She lifted her face and deliberately stared over his head. He followed the direction of her stare. But she tensed and he saw the direction of her gaze change to the door. Momentarily she glanced at Jack and he knew a new regular had arrived, one who caught a boat across the water at the end of his shift, buying food for the journey after a long night. Jack took his finger off the half crown and the girl scooped it up in her cloth.

'Usual,' the man said to the girl, who nodded and disappeared into the back room. Jack stood up and decided he would join the man while he waited for his food.

This early on in his career Jack had not thought about proving who he was. He had no evidence on him that he was a policeman. He would have to bluff it out.

'Knowles, you left your shift early,' said Jack and the man whirled round, taking the speaker as a clerk from the factory.

'It's a lie!' he said.

'Is it?' Jack pushed down the pride he felt at getting his assumption right. He had to get the man to talk to him yet.

'Well I'll miss my boat, maybe a few minutes early today.' Knowles looked at Jack, and it slowly dawned on him that something was wrong. Jack saw him brace himself. Taking in Jack's build Knowles was working out that this was no clerk. He moved and Jack instinctively put his hands up, as a fist came up. He pushed Knowles back against the wall, and the plates on the shelf above Knowles's head shook. Jack kept hold of him, relishing in the fact that he had been right.

'Bit of a clumsy attempt, Knowles,' said Jack. 'Sloping off early as well as fraud across the water.'

'I don't know what you're talking about,' Knowles spat out. Jack put an arm across the neck and pinioned the man. With his other hand, he wiped the spittle off his face.

'Let me remind you. Signing off on material not actually delivered. Probably not just you I suspect. You don't strike me as being very bright to work all this out on your own. Threatening people as well. I think we'd better just get on with a caution and anything you say will be used against you. What was that?' Jack heard a moaning noise as Knowles had realised his way out was blocked by a policeman. Jack had no idea if cautioning the man out of uniform would matter. He hoped Knowles would not think of asking for his identification. 'Happy Christmas, by the way. Not the best way to spend Christmas Eve, is it,' said Jack.

'I never had more than threepence off the buyer. He walked home with me the first time and saw where I lived. Then he drank with me. It's the road spreaders you want,' said Knowles.

'Well my Sergeant is over in Camberwell looking at the docket books today. My money is on you taking the cheap stuff. Probably there was so much of it in different locations no one really checked. Perhaps you'd like to give me a few names? Then you and I can have a short trip to the station.'

'Why are you asking me?' said Knowles. 'You seem to be the one with all the answers.'

Jack felt irritation mounting. Getting Knowles to Leman Street could be a problem, especially as he was not in uniform. Grabbing Knowles by his collar Jack had the superior strength. He looked up and down the road and started to realise the potential mess he could be in attempting to get the man back to the station house. Jack marched Knowles out and took a right turn towards the train station in Poplar. It was a dead-end and Knowles started to exert his strength. Jack shouted 'Police!' He heard running and two Constables came around the corner. Lucky, he thought to himself. Jack was the respectably dressed one of the two men that they saw, and true to form, an assumption was made as to who was in the wrong, although it was a correct one in this case. Jack stepped back onto a step while one of the Constables received a hard punch from Knowles. The second Constable forced Knowles back against the wall, and his colleague pinioned an arm so high up his back that Jack expected to hear it break. Jack gave them his number, name and told them he was ordered on special duties today.

The second Constable made a couple of entries in a notebook, and Jack corrected the spelling of his surname, and fished his own notebook out of his pocket and asked the two officer for their names.

'You at the station in Leman Street?' asked the Constable, licking the point of his pencil.

'Yes. This man, Knowles, has been cautioned in connection with theft in Camberwell Green. I need your assistance to get him to Leman Street. Keep him ready for Sergeant Morris who will be coming back from the Green later this morning. I'll be at the station in about an hour.'

They were new, like him. He watched them struggle to hold Knowles and to operate the handcuffs. They took it on face value that he was a higher rank than them and a police detective. All of a few days, boys, Jack thought, with a smirk.

Knowles was finally handcuffed and brought under enough control to move him back into a street. Jack followed as they made their way up an alley and out on to the main street towards the railway station. Jack turned back towards the place where his tea still waited realising he had left his bowler hat. He went in and found the mug cooled and finished the tea, grimacing slightly at the taste of it and looked for the serving girl. He nodded, as she came out from a back room carrying his hat.

'Have a happy Christmas,' said Jack, as he took it from her. 'You alright?'

'I am now,' she said, patting a pocket. 'Happy Christmas to you, sir. Come again, won't you. We get them all in here.'

Ted Phillips had told him to look after his informers. Jack though, did a double take at being called "sir."

*

Leaving Arbour Square, only this time in uniform and by the front door, Jack made his way to Leman Street. Morris and Sam Curzon were back as he checked in at eleven o'clock. They were both in the room behind the duty Sergeant's desk with two ledgers on the table. Jack could see from where he stood by the door that the writing was different in one half to the first book provided by the Surveyor. The book itself was similar in design to the official ledger from the Surveyor's office, and the entries were in the middle of the book. The fraud had been carried out at a time when staff changed and the Ganger, Knowles, had taken advantage of things being disorganised.

'Well done, lad, Knowles is in a cell,' said Morris, slapping Jack on the back.

'We've gone through both ledgers,' said Sam, turning them round for Jack to see. 'The writing's so different.'

'Yes, both of us went through them, but Curzon spotted the difference in the type of detail required. It's not just the writing, the spurious ledger has insufficient detail of weight and quality of the grade of the material used,' said Morris. 'Where did you find him, Knowles, I mean? He's already provided the duty Sergeant with the names of those involved.'

'Down in a café near Poplar, collecting food for the ferry trip back across the river. It was a hunch, that's all, that he may be coming off the night shift and still living on the south side of the river. I got there shortly after eight o'clock. The girl serving knew who I meant.'

'Good work, all round, then. How did the suit fit?' said Morris assuming Jack had not gone in uniform. Sam poured tea from a pot on the range and Jack grinned and moved the kettle off the fire as it was starting to boil.

'Fine, I'll just hot it up, thanks, Sam.'

'Well done, all,' Morris raised a mug of steaming tea to his two young colleagues.

'Ingenurious plan, and a good finish before Christmas,' said Jack.

'What did you say?' asked Sam Curzon.

'Clever, I mean,' said Jack.

'Do you mean ingenious in that funny way of speaking that you have?' asked Morris.

*

'I was wondering if you managed to see Harriet, Sergeant?' asked Jack.

Morris looked at him, surprised. 'Hardly, lad, I've been at the Surveyor's office all morning.'

'Do you think you'll still be able to deliver her gift today?'

'Am I likely to forget, as its Christmas Eve? I'll knock off at four o'clock, today and I don't break my promises,' said Morris.

'I bet she thinks I've forgotten all about her,' said Jack.

'Then she'll have a nice surprise later. I suspect she's not given you a moment's thought today. They'll be busy in that kitchen and there will be the Christmas Eve party, probably later, in the house for the staff. Shouldn't you be calling in on your regular route by now?' Morris glanced at the clock.

'Yes, Sergeant. Ted's off over Christmas so I'll make a move to get started.' Jack finished his tea, and picked up his helmet.

'What time do you finish today?' asked Morris.

'I'm doing extra as we'll be shorthanded tonight. I'll finish around ten o'clock. There's supper back at the Doyle's later and I might do a midnight mass, after that.'

'Curzon's filled me in about Windsor and I've passed the good news to Inspector Hunt before we left New Road. And tomorrow? You'll have Christmas dinner with the Doyle's in the evening, will you?' Morris stopped, not wanting to over-emphasise the fact that Jack did not have a family to be with.

'Yes, I'm back in here for eight o'clock in the morning, and will see Dr Brown hopefully during the Christmas morning after he's made a call at a house on my patrol.' Jack grinned. 'I'll get two dinners tomorrow. I'm on a promise from the cook on the patch for Christmas dinner in the Servant's hall. Good job Ted's off duty or I reckon he'd get a kiss on Christmas day. You'd better re-assign him Sergeant, the cook's after husband number two,' said Jack, the grin widening. 'Bit of a drawback with the job.'

'Watch yourself in the servant's hall, lad. Not too much to drink, it loosens the tongue. Remember you're on duty.' Morris shook Jack's hand. 'Happy Christmas. Get off with you now.' Morris looked pre-occupied, he stopped at the end of his good wishes, as if embarrassed. Impulsively, he said, 'Look, Christmas won't always be like this for you. One day, you'll have your own family, someone else will cover for you, like you're doing for the married men this year. Alright?'

'Yes, I hope you're right,' Jack answered.

'Right. Get along then.' Morris said, back to his gruff expression.

*

It was a gastronomic experience that day, as he was called into each kitchen by every pretty maid on his beat. He realised after the first one that the Mistletoe would be positioned over each kitchen door in every house and that he was fair game in the Christmas festivities. Remembering, as Sergeant Morris had cautioned, that he was on duty, he wanted to be friendly but also treat the ladies with respect and not put a foot wrong in uniform. So, he allowed the peck on the cheek, smiling more bashfully than he really felt and preparing himself then to be kissed by the cooks too, with much laughter and teasing.

That process over, he was treated to a "little something" to keep the cold out from the preparations of dishes ready to go upstairs. Jack wondered how much of the Christmas food that the owners of the properties were expecting on their tables was finding its way into the stomachs of each delivery boy as well. Making a show of how delicious each little morsel was required no acting ability as it truly was all splendid. He thought how it was a good thing that he would spend eight hours walking on his beat. Declining alcohol that was proffered by some butlers below stairs, he took several sips of each cup of tea he was given, regardless of how much sugar was ladled into it, poured for him by Elsie, or Karen, or Susan. Then, having given the house a quick check from the outside, watched by the servants in the kitchens, he would salute and move on down the road, only to experience the same process again, and again.

'We'll sleep easier in our beds, tonight, knowing you're around, Constable,' said one maid who pressed a note into his hand, signed Becky.

'Oh, Constable, what a shame you won't be here at midnight as the party upstairs finishes, to see our guests safely into their carriages,' said another who's name, he felt ashamed of himself in having to admit, he could not remember.

Jack took it all as part of making the staff feel safe. He also had a few parcels pressed upon him as little "thankyou's," handkerchiefs, carefully embroidered with a "J" on them, a scarf knitted by the fire. Apart from an orange and an apple on Christmas Day, he had not had a gift for years.

He remembered his father playing a game with him at Christmas of finding the stockings and his mother singing. He could almost taste the jam that she had made. The memory was strong and he could see the red and green colours of the holly in the small front room kept for Christmas and birthdays, and the visits of stiff looking people who smelt of camphor, after his father died. Then another memory of playing with a ball on the sand at Bexhill-on-Sea came to him from nowhere. There was an overwhelming desire to have it all again and he felt deeply disturbed by the intensity of the memories. Pushing them away deep down inside he walked a little more briskly to the next street. Perhaps the thoughts were surfacing due to all the changes he had gone through this year. He turned up another front garden path ready to knock on the kitchen door and give the greetings of the season to another set of servants below stairs.

'Pull yourself together, Jack,' he said aloud, as footsteps approached the door, 'At least you're not alone, today.'

Later, on the same beat, Jack made a note about the houses he had checked, and who he had spoken to. He noted for each one what he had found. No one at the station was likely to check today but the record was there if they did. At eight o'clock that evening he returned to Leman street. The noise from the back room behind the Sergeant's desk showed the men were going on leave. Some of the wives had sent in gingerbread, shortbread and other sweet stuff and it was all on the table to be sampled. Jack took one of the biscuits and brushing the crumbs from his uniform, took his position on the desk. Knowles had been charged and taken back to New Road in Camberwell. Jack wondered if Knowles's woman, as he was sure that was the reason why the man was returning each day to the south side of the river, would get word tonight of where Knowles was. It would not be a happy Christmas for her.

*

The need for physical toughness at the desk as the arrests came in was no less than normal that Christmas Eve. If he thought he would have a quiet evening Jack was wrong. His colleagues on the streets that night still had to deal with tough men who wanted to get away and were ready to use force to try and do so. A robbery, an attempted forced entry into a shop, and a woman stealing clothing from a street hawker, all came in by ten o'clock, before Jack took his leave with a cheery, 'Happy Christmas' to the Duty Sergeant. His journey home in uniform was no less eventful and he turned back with one seventeen-year-old who was drunk and disorderly. Consequently, he did not leave Leman Street for his supper in Arbour Square until half past eleven, and at that point decided to go straight to church for the midnight mass. Still in uniform Jack was posted on the door by the vicar so that St Thomas's did not experience any trouble. So, there he stood at the back of the church, giving the congregation a sense of security as they entered, holding a carol sheet and singing his heart out.

  The guests were gone as he returned to the Doyle's home, Hannah let him in looking exhausted, as he probably did. There was a look of sympathy between them, as neither had spent a Christmas Eve off-duty. On a corner of the table in the breakfast room, already laid for Christmas Day breakfast, was a slice of chicken pie and sticks of celery, sliced oranges and a piece of fruit cake. A glass of port was waiting in one of the beautiful crystal glasses that Jack had admired in the cabinet. A nice little touch, he thought, and probably a kindness from Emily Doyle. Jack looked at the clock on the mantelpiece and realised he would get six hours sleep if he was lucky before it would be time to be up and off back to Leman Street. Devouring the Chicken Pie and the oranges he left the rest. Thanks to his time on duty in and out of the kitchens he was not short of food on Christmas Eve.

  'Happy Christmas, Hannah,' said Jack as he carried the remains of his supper into the kitchen. She was slumbering in a chair by the fire which was on its last legs. He realised that he had kept her up and she had been waiting for him to finish and go to bed. 'I'm sorry, I've stopped you going to bed, haven't I? Will you see your family this Christmas?' asked Jack, realising that he knew absolutely nothing about the maid.

  'Tomorrow afternoon,' she said. It was a first. She had spoken to him instead of looking like a frightened rabbit caught in a trap. 'Mrs Doyle's given me the night off, so I go once lunch is served.'

'I won't see you until Boxing day then,' as a second thought, Jack cut the piece of the fruit cake in half, deciding to take it up to bed with him. He took a sip of the port as Hannah stood up.

'Happy Christmas, sir,' she said, and he realised it was the second time that day that he had been placed in a class above his expectation.

*

Six

The next day the smell of Christmas pervaded his room and Jack felt that he was living in a story as every scent he could have expected hit his senses. Cinnamon and ginger and sweet fragrances from bowls and baskets carefully placed on every floor of the house rose up to his room. He washed and dressed and went down stairs carrying the four small parcels he had carefully wrapped and labelled. He had bought sweets for the Doyles and Hannah. The house looked like a picture he remembered from his childhood. The other lodgers had gone to their families around the country and he realised that as this was little Sarah's second Christmas Matthew Doyle was home, focusing on making it a wonderful one for his daughter that morning as she was now more aware of everything. She had his full attention. Emily was working hard to keep the level of excitement down for Sarah. The Inspector was sitting by the Christmas tree, leaning against a chair, his legs open to make a v shape while his little girl sat safely in the space with bits of paper and ribbon scattered around her. Jack's small gift was added to the pile around the Christmas tree.

'You're going to be busy, this morning, Inspector. Happy Christmas, to you all,' said Jack, holding his hand out to Doyle. The two men shook hands and Emily held out her hand to Jack as well.

'Matthew, today, Jack, we'll see you for dinner tonight, won't we?' said Doyle.

'Yes, indeed. I've hopes of seeing the Police Surgeon, Doctor Brown this morning at one of the houses,' said Jack

'Yes, I remembered. Well done.'

'You've been busy Emily. Did you get any sleep?' asked Jack.

'We chatted into the night and were asleep quite late but Sarah chose for the first time to sleep longer so there was a little dash then to finish things off. I let Matthew sleep on for a while but I fear that Sarah's squeals when she saw the tree woke him. I hope she didn't disturb you, Jack?' said Emily.

'Not at all. I'll get my breakfast and get along to the station.'

'I'll come and sit with you,' said Matthew.

'Don't disturb yourself, sir.'

'No, no, I want to have a chat about Doctor Brown anyway and you shouldn't eat breakfast on Christmas Day on your own,' said Matthew.

Jack helped himself to tea and porridge, he hesitated about the bacon but decided that two Christmas dinners were going to take some serious eating today and that he would be better leaving some room.

'Ask the doctor to come and see me will you Jack, as soon as he can after Christmas, tell him I'll be discreet with anything that he says, and grateful.' said Doyle.

'Yes, of course, sir.'

'Matthew.'

'Sorry sir, I mean Matthew,' said Jack, grinning. 'Old habits die hard. Is there anything specific that you think I should focus on with the doctor today? I'm not sure I know where to start.'

'It's complicated. I think I'm almost sure that the Faceless Woman is Mrs Berringer. I can't explain that. I don't think its suicide either. I was awake until dawn and then passed out into a heavy sleep until Sarah's excitement woke me.' Doyle picked up the poker and moved a few pieces of coal in the hearth to coax the fire. 'Ask the doctor what he thinks about the cause of death. If he thinks it's not suicide he'll have a reason why and we can launch a murder investigation officially into the lady's death. It's a question of motive and proof. I've got to have a reason to stop the burial. Show him this, will you?'

Doyle handed Jack a photograph of a woman, smartly dressed, in an American fashion.

'Is it Mrs Berringer?' asked Jack.

'Yes, we managed to get a copy from the American Embassy. I picked it up at Great Marlborough Street station as Golden Square's covered by the area.'

Jack put it in an inner pocket. 'Are we supposed to have it at Leman Street?'

'No,' said Matthew.

'I'll try and walk with the doctor from the house he's visiting. Only thing is I may have to hang around the area so I do get to see him. It will mean I neglect the rest of the patrol area. I'll get off now, sir, Matthew, I mean,' said Jack, getting up from the table.

'Tell the doctor I've asked you to do this, Jack. He knows me, we've had dealings on other cases and I respect him. I think he'll respond if you start with a message from me,' said Doyle.

Just before eight o'clock Jack arrived at Leman Street. Sergeant Thick on the desk nodded to Jack and beckoned him to come over.

'There's a Constable in the back room looking for you, bloke come over from Lewisham, says he's going off duty but has a message for you.'

'Lewisham? I don't think I know anyone in the division in Lewisham,' said Jack.

'Well, he seems to know you. Get in there before parade starts,' said Sergeant Thick.

Jack hurried into the room to find a constable sitting by the fire.

'Sergeant Thick said someone was looking for me. I'm Jack Sargent.'

'Arscott Ward, over from Lewisham.'

'You've come quite a way to see me. I don't think I know anyone in Lewisham.' Jack looked the man over. He was met with a similar expression. Two policemen sizing each other up. It struck Jack as funny, partly because he realised he was doing it instinctively now after only such a short time in the police.

The warrant number was five numbers like his. So, Jack thought, he's joined the police within the last ten years. Arscott Ward was in his late thirties, Jack reckoned. There was a hint of a West country accent in the way he pronounced an r. The man opposite him was just slightly taller, dark complexion and Hazel eyes. Jack held out his hand and Ward gripped it and said, 'You're new to the police, I gather, Jack. From Sussex, I'm told, a country man, like me. I'm from Black Torrington on the river Torridge in Devon, been in the police eight years now. So many of us country boys have come to London.'

'Yes, fresh blood! I'm from a farm near Battle, but what brings you across the river to find me?' Jack asked.

'Christmas. And my young lady's sister is known to you. I have a message for you from Harriet. My young lady has pestered me to get across to you before Christmas is over. Georgina, is my young lady. Betrothed we are and to be married soon. She's in a dressmaker's in Lewisham. Her younger sister is Harriet.'

Jack looked astounded. Ward took a breath and started again.

'Look, you know what the ladies are like. Feel a bit neglected, don't understand this thing about police duty absorbing all our time and not being able to communicate much. You're over here for a while and can't get back to Camberwell Green. Its Harriet Fildew that's my lady's sister. Georgina's Harriet's eldest sister and helped get her the position she has. It's a big family, the Fildews and farming's not what it was anymore around Honiton. There's a few of them coming up to London now. You'll meet them eventually I imagine. Anyway, your Sergeant Morris told Harriet you were suggesting a meeting at New Year on Westminster Bridge so that she could get the tram across, if she let you know when she was on a half day. That's why I'm here. There's only the station as an address, you see.'

'That's so good of you, to come over with a message when you've been on nights,' said Jack.

'I'll get along then, shortly. So, it's New Year's Day, Westminster Bridge, I take it. Harriet says she'll get the tram. She has a half day after luncheon is finished. Has to be back by eight o'clock in the evening,' Ward stopped and waited for Jack to respond. Jack was smiling from ear to ear.

'I finish at two,' Jack said.

'Right, let's say four o'clock then on Westminster Bridge, at the tram stop. You need to be specific, Sargent, ladies don't like to be kept hanging around waiting. You've not had much experience, by the sound of it. Take some advice from an older man....it is Jack, isn't it, the record has you down as John? Alright Jack, you be on Westminster Bridge at four o'clock on New Year's Day, pick up a bunch of flowers, and just wait for Harriet. Take her somewhere respectable, like a tea room, you shouldn't just stand around on the bridge, that doesn't look nice. There's a nice hotel not far from Westminster Abbey. I used to do a patrol round there years ago, but Georgina and I were looking round the Abbey on a day off a few weeks ago, and it's still there. Get her back to the tram stop in time for her to get back to the house for eight o'clock. She's a nice girl.'

'Right, thanks. Did you say your name was Ascott? It's very good of you to come and let me know. Look, if I write a note would you get it to her?' Jack tore a sheet from his notebook and started to write.

'The name's Arscott. I'll see her tomorrow at Georgina's so I can pass it on then. Look, she's sent this for you. It's got a bit creased in my pocket. I did my best but I've had it all night.' Ward passed a thin parcel across the table to Jack, tied with a ribbon. Jack could smell Harriet's toilet water as he untied the ribbon and pulled back the tissue paper. It was a white handkerchief with "J" embroidered in blue. It made the fourth he'd had this Christmas but this was from Harriet. He closed his eyes and inhaled the scent and could almost see her.

'I must be going. I'll let Harriet know tomorrow I've seen you and that you're well. You look well. I'll give her your note. Perhaps we'll meet again.' Ward glanced at the clock on the wall and stood up, picking up his helmet.

'I'm really grateful, Arscott,' Jack said and they shook hands.

'Anything I can do for you, just get a message across to me. I'm away for my bed now, and then a party later where Georgina works. Do you have family to be with later? My family are all in Devon, as is Georgina's. Now Harriet is here, it's nice for the two sisters to have each other nearby.'

'I'm on duty but get off at four o'clock. I've a promise of Christmas dinner from one of the houses on my beat.'

'Well, Season's Greetings to you. It's not a time to be alone,' Ward put his helmet on, and Jack heard him wish Sergeant Thick a happy Christmas as he went past the desk.

'Just man the desk for me for half an hour,' Sergeant Thick called to Jack. 'Did you get to the bottom of what that constable was here to see you about?'

'Yes, thanks, Sergeant. He'd brought a message from a young lady for me,' Jack had his hand in his pocket on the handkerchief from Harriet.

'Hands out of pockets,' barked Sergeant Thick.

'Sorry, Sergeant, it's a Christmas gift,' and Jack pulled the white cloth out of his pocket with an inane grin. Thick gave him a knowing look and left the desk.

Jack saw his opportunity as Thick walked away. Trying to recall the details from Sam yesterday morning he believed there was a clue. Solve it by four, Sam had said. At first Jack had taken it that Sam had been jokingly challenging him to solve who the murderer of the Faceless Woman was by four o'clock on Christmas Day.

He went into the Chief Inspector's room, knowing that if anyone was looking for him at the front desk he would have to come up with an excuse of why he had left his position. On the wall was a breakdown of the divisions, where the stations were situated, and who the superintendents were. It was not sufficiently detailed for him to establish why Sam had used the word "four" though. By four, to Jack when he had been a child, meant multiplication. Could it be four divisions in a part of London? Was he supposed to look for a name that had four in it. Were there four people involved? How would he ever narrow it down?

Jack looked at the division where the Faceless Woman had been found. There was one Superintendent in the division, more than twenty inspectors, a Chief Inspector and a reserve. Where to begin? Was it that there were four police stations within a certain radius? Was their bad penny linked to one of them? Most divisions were expanding with the population growth in London and had some had more than four stations. But Sam and Doyle had seen something in the boatman's ledger. A name, an address, a party of four?

Had it not been Christmas Day he would have sent a telegram to Morris or Hunt. No one he should communicate with on the case was on duty. He dismissed the idea anyway as who knew how many people would potentially read it.

Back to the number four. Could it be the location of a division? Four streets from the centre of the division in which Mrs Berringer was found? Which way though should he go. He looked at the map, up, down left, right. North, south, east or west? What else could he associate with a number four? Jack stared at the book shelf looking for inspiration. The Post Office directory for the area seemed to be taking up a large amount of space along the left-hand side of the wall. There were years of directories. He pulled one off the shelf at random and turned to Police. There were all the names of inspectors listed for the year, the superintendent was named and all the locations of the stations, whether they had an inspector and where telegraphic communication could be sent from to the Commissioner's office. Matthew Doyle was listed as an Inspector at the Great Marlborough Street Police Station. The Faceless Woman had not been found in that division. Berringer's body, however, had been found in Stepney and it made sense for him to have a list of senior staff for this division. As carefully as he could he tore the page out, folded it neatly and added the sheet to a different pocket holding Harriet's gift.

Jack poked the fire. Perhaps it wasn't a clue, just Sam trying to be funny. Anyway, Sam would be back on Boxing Day, no doubt very disappointed with Jack's poor efforts. He sat on the desk and stared at the wall chart for Stepney. It would make sense to look at who was in this division as it was where they had been sent. Jack's head slumped forward and he momentarily fell asleep as the warmth from the chief inspector's fire made him drowsy and the short night's sleep caught up with him.

'Sargent!' barked Thick from the doorway. Jack jerked awake and moved off the desk. The post office directory fell onto the floor with a clatter and he was caught. Quickly he picked it up and put it back on the shelf.

'Good job for you it's Christmas Day. Get back out here on the desk.' Jack moved, expecting to be disciplined. Thick looked at him. 'What were you doing in there?'

'I was reminding myself where the stations are, how many inspectors there are in the division, Sergeant,' Jack said, truthfully.

'Why?' Thick looked at him incredulously.

'Couldn't remember,' said Jack.

'You won't. You don't need to. Get out on your beat,' Thick watched Jack as he collected his great coat and his helmet and at the door, Jack turned, and said, 'Thanks, Sergeant.'

'Get going!' Thick stood, upright as always, and never took his eyes off Jack until he was out of the door of the station.

Jack pushed past the two constables bringing in a man that looked the worse for wear and went down the steps. He had doubts about his ability to work out the direction Sam was trying to point him to. It was such a funny thing for Sam Curzon to have said. He could not put his finger on where to start.

Maybe he, Jack, was going in completely the wrong direction in the investigation. He felt like he had as a child when swimming off the beach at Bexhill, when he had been caught in the drag off-shore and his father had swum out to bring him in. People died like that. He did not want to drown in the detail by missing a clue.

He undid his great coat. It was too warm, there should be frost not damp, he thought. It felt more like February than December. Turning into the street where he knew the Doctor would be paying his visit, Jack broke into a run as saw Doctor Brown had finished his visit and was already moving out of the garden gate and walking in the opposite direction to Jack.

'Doctor Brown, a word, sir,' called Jack, as he ran after the doctor. The doctor stopped and half-turned.

'Constable, a good Christmas to you,' said the Doctor.

'And to you, sir,' said Jack, remembering to salute. 'You are about your house visits early today.'

'I am, both of us in fact. When do you finish your patrol today, Constable....?'

'Sargent, sir, Jack Sargent. It will be later this afternoon as I'm to join the staff in their Christmas dinner.'

The Doctor blew his nose, 'I'm hoping that I'm not coming down with a cold in all this damp, humid, weather. Excuse me.'

'Of course, Doctor. I won't detain you, but if I may I'll walk with you for a few streets.?' said Jack.

'Yes, glad of the company. How are you settling in to the job?' asked the Doctor.

'I'm enjoying the challenges. It's different everyday too. Still learning though, but I'm working with a good team.'

'Are you? If you're with Tom Hunt you'll learn fast,' said the doctor.

'Inspector Doyle also asked to be remembered to you and for me to mention that he would appreciate it if you can contact him about the victim known as the Faceless Woman. As it's Christmas and the Inspector won't be back at work for a few days I am more than happy to pass on any developments to him. He especially asked me to mention this to you this morning, if I saw you.'

'Of course, but I'm only one of a group of doctors involved in the forensics. Doyle is good but he doesn't take any prisoners. Is that why he asked you to speak to me today? Is he on the Berringer case on the quiet? Oh, don't worry, I've seen him and Inspector Hunt operate on other cases and there's usually a team in place going into plain clothes. Are you working on the Berringer case?' the Doctor had dropped his voice. Jack looked at him and remained silent. Doctor Brown nodded and then smiled. 'Look I have to go to the Peabody Buildings on Commercial Road. Walk with me as far as you can on your beat.'

'It's a grim place to be going to on Christmas Day, doctor,' said Jack.

'Any day, but despite its faults it's an important start to proper housing in this area of London for the poor.'

The two men strode out, Jack aware he was leaving the area allocated to his beat. However, he was prepared to take the risk of landing a disciplinary in order to find out what the doctor knew.

'So, Constable, you'll want to know what I've discovered. Are you seeing Doyle later?' asked the doctor.

'Yes, doctor.'

'What made you go into policing? You're not from London, are you?' Doctor Brown asked.

'Hunger, literally and socially. It was an opportunity that may not come again. The weather and the harvests weren't good this year, there was talk of laying people off on the farm and I saw the advert for the national recruitment. It felt like time to change things instead of staying in the same situation I've been in since I was a small child. I've no family as I know of so moving to London seemed a way forward,' Jack gave the doctor a resigned grin and the doctor nodded.

'Will it bother you, the violence and the death, do you think, after the countryside?'

'Oh, there's violence and death in the country,' Jack smiled. 'Trying to stop human beings from committing violence against each other and having a world where people can walk down the street safely seem good things to aim for. I can see how it gets to policemen if they're dealing with it all the time. Probably the same for doctors too. But I think, if I can focus on the criminal, I'll stay and cope with the awful things I'll see if there's a chance to change them. And there's different sorts of crime. It was that fire in Boston on November 9th that finally decided me,' said Jack. 'I read it happened because no one enforced the building regulations. No one stopped the faulty construction and there was so much over insurance that there was no incentive to build safe buildings. I think that's as much a crime, sir, as a poor person stealing washing off a line. I decided I'd like to catch the people behind the Boston fire. Sounds ridiculous, I know but I applied to the Metropolitan Police and they took me on.'

'I can see why. You have a clear eye on things, Constable. That's why you're with Hunt,' the doctor smiled.

Jack laughed, 'I'm learning. But tell me, Doctor Brown, what have you found about the poor woman in the lodgings? Can we be sure its Mrs Berringer?'

'Murder is a funny thing, it seems mainly to be committed by people not associated by society with being the criminal class. We are taken by surprise with murder constantly.' Doctor Brown paused, realising that they were a long way from where the young constable should be. 'Tell me what you know of that diplomat's death first.'

'Mr Berringer was an American diplomat, found dead under a bridge a little way from a crashed carriage. We've traced a label on a shirt to Jermyn Street. It was handmade, and silk, it indicated the class of the victim. We found a record at the shirt makers, fortunately, so we know its Berringer,' Jack paused for breath. He had recounted the background at speed and the Doctor thought the young constable clearly had a good recall.

However, there were points in the account that he realised would not stand up in court.

Doctor Brown smiled. 'So, there was sufficient information that led the police to establish that the body was the missing American diplomat, Arthur Berringer. Or someone who borrowed a shirt and made it look like Berringer has died.' The Doctor stopped as Jack was looking shocked at the connotations that he was putting on the evidence the police had about the shirt.

'I'm sorry, constable, I've been in the witness stand in front of barristers too long. Seed of doubt is all they need with a jury. But let's go with your case that the man in the shirt is Berringer. How would you prove it?'

'Height, eye colour, known marks on the body perhaps, possessions, same as you would a cow that's been savaged,' Jack shrugged, and then grinned, 'except for the possessions in the case of the cow,' and Doctor Brown laughed.

'Good, good, in fact excellent. I agree. There are things we probably know about the American or have records about him that back up it being him. Do you understand probability, constable?' Doctor Brown asked.

'No,' said Jack.

'Oh, I think you will do. Where did you grow up?'

'Bexhill-on-Sea, and then I worked on a farm near Battle, Sussex.'

'What do you know of the area to stop you drowning? No don't bother answering me, I can tell by your face that you've understood me. You have knowledge about areas, weather patterns, things you understand, it will be the same with people in the village. Not everything is unknown. But how many times can you throw a certain number on a dice? Well you can't answer me now, but science would carry out a study of how many throws bring up the same numbers. We learn which occur more than others. It's a facile example but I'm trying to say that we can investigate and learn and someday I believe we will be able to understand that the blood on the scene can be found to be a certain person's, perhaps with a predictable percentage, say ninety-seven percent, and with other facts we can tie it to a person as the murderer,' the Doctor stopped and patted the policeman's arm. 'Tell me, Constable what else you know.'

'A journalist had put forward the idea that the wife was implicated. No proof had been found. It might mean that evidence has been removed by someone. Then she disappeared and the next thing we know is a lady under an assumed name is found in lodgings, unrecognisable, papers burnt, note left in an uneducated hand, which doesn't fit the impression that the landlady formed of her, and at the same time Mrs Berringer is missing and the children are alone in the world. It looks like someone has tampered with evidence and it might mean we have to look close to home for the culprit,' said Jack.

'I'm glad to see you're taking on board the clues that there are,' said Doctor Brown. 'We have some knowledge we can prove but science is still in a stage of discovery in trying to find the killers. Trying to catch criminals through science is a long way off yet.'

'I thought you had some findings from your visit to the room?' asked Jack.

'As I said I've collected findings but how do I apply them? Can I get to the point where I can tell you, or your Inspector Doyle, who the criminal is? Not now, no, but perhaps one day we will be able to,' the Doctor looked around at the children who were following them. He automatically moved his pocket book to an inner pocket. 'You are welcome to come and see what I've found, and we now have the body of the woman, of course, just as we have Arthur Berringer's body, and there are things that those two, dead people are trying to tell us I believe. But I can't prove at this point in the development of science, who committed the murders. I can use science to detect poison in the stomach,' said the doctor, 'and we can trace bullets back to moulds used t make them, that sort of thing, look at the size of someone's foot, fit boot prints back to actual boots and so on. I also understand, that a civil servant in the Indian Administration is experimenting with taking fingerprints as a security measure on documents. It will be interesting when these things become more widespread.'

'What's the point with the finger prints?' asked Jack.

'Everyone is unique,' said the Doctor, smiling at him. 'Imagine that once we can use it.'

'You said "murders." So, you do think we have two murders? Can we check the idea of poison, doctor?' asked Jack.

'We've done an autopsy on the woman found in Golden Square and we've clarified the time and cause of death, her general health. The investigating officer requested an autopsy by the way. Berringer's body is another matter, however, because he is identified already as being Berringer, an American citizen. We've got him "on ice" to use a phrase from their consulate, until the detective from New York arrives. It's pretty certain that he will request an autopsy again then.'

'How ridiculous. It's a death on English soil,' said Jack, frustrated.

'Ah, you've obviously never worked with Americans before. Wait until the detective gets here, you'll find the difference in the methods of policing interesting,' said Doctor Brown. 'As for the poison issue with the woman, we can check body tissue and the fluids in the body. Those sorts of tests have moved on I'm glad to say. We're not still in the 1700's thanks to the methods of Orfila and Marsh.'

'I don't know who they are. Can we get at whether the woman was poisoned or took it herself?' asked Jack.

'As I said we can get an idea of her general health before death. Every house is full of arsenic, Constable. Even down to the green wallpaper that's so fashionable at the moment. Poisoning cases have been headline news for years. I'm not saying it's on the increase but it appears we are catching the killers more frequently it seems. Let me ask you a question,' said Doctor Brown.

'Alright,' Jack waited.

'How did you kill rats on the farm?'

'We used strychnine,' said Jack.

'You see arsenic, strychnine, easy access to poison. My belief in the case of the Faceless Woman it wasn't arsenic. That's largely because of the state the neck muscles were in. And of course, if you get to someone who has taken strychnine, which in this case I think is what was used, you can stop the process if you're in time,' Doctor Brown stopped as they had reached the Peabody Building. 'I'm afraid this conversation may be about to get you into trouble, as you are a long way from your beat.'

'Don't worry about that, Doctor, I'm acting under Inspector Doyle's orders this morning. If I have to prove why I left my beat I can,' Jack reached into a pocket and brought out the final paper bag of penny sweets that he had kept back for children he may have passed on his route on Christmas morning. 'Would you pass these to any children in the building from the police force?' he asked the Doctor as he held the bag out.

'I will. That's kind of you, I've enjoyed our walk. I'll look for you in Leman Street and see if we can collaborate again. I will be away after at the end of December until early in the New Year, hence trying to cover as many patients as possible, even those who don't pay,' the Doctor nodded at the Peabody Building.

'Before you go in, Doctor, you said that a death by strychnine poisoning can be stopped?'

'Yes.'

'So, someone killing themselves wouldn't take it?' asked Jack.

'Depends on whether they effectively shut themselves away from help. It could be argued no one had any reason to disturb the lady in her lodgings as she was about to leave, apparently. Sooner or later the landlady would have gone in to clean the rooms for the next lodger, so the dead woman would have been found,' said Doctor Brown.

'From what I've seen it does to the rats if the woman didn't self-administer she would have known something was wrong very quickly,' said Jack staring at the building in front of him.

'Not a good way to die. However, we may be talking of someone implicated in murdering Berringer, if the Faceless Woman turns out to be Mrs Berringer,' said the Doctor.

'Thank you, Doctor, that's all been very helpful. I'll pass on what we've discussed. I'm not sure where it takes us though unless we're now looking for someone with American links who mixes with diplomats.'

'Why not? By the way tell Doyle to have a word with that friend of his wife's, who lodges with them,' said the doctor, as he turned to go into the building.

Jack felt confused, running through in his mind who the friend and lodger could be.

'What's her name?' the doctor scratched his ear lobe while he tried to remember.

'It's a lady?' said Jack. 'The only lady they have lodging is a Mrs Black.'

'That's right, interesting woman, Ann Black. Trying to become a doctor. She'll be worth talking to, so tell Doyle to have a chat with her. Brave these women bucking the trend. I have no problem with it, and it has to come, women as doctors. Her husband's a medical student. She's studied toxicology in Paris. Tell Doyle it will have to be New Year now to see me. Have a good Christmas dinner, Constable,' and with a wave of his hand the doctor walked up the steps of the Peabody Building.

*

The dinner above stairs was well underway by the time Jack doubled back and re-joined the route he was supposed to take. He knocked on the kitchen door and as it opened he could smell the aromas of goose fat, Christmas Pudding, and hot cider and brandy, which the butler was pouring into glass cups in his pantry.

He had dutifully stirred the pudding as directed by the cook on previous visits and was to reap his reward by sampling the cooked product. The steaming pudding, wrapped in muslin cloth, would now have silver threepenny pieces, and also a ring inside it to predict marriage for the person who found it in their portion, a thimble and any other small trinket. The process was all being replicated upstairs, of course, only with champagne.

He was treated to innumerable kisses under the mistletoe. It was tied to the door bell, which tinkled each time the door opened. A bevy of housemaids, caught him, followed finally by the cook, Mrs Prescott. With much good nature, he took it as it came. The pudding was now on its way up stairs with the butler, Mr Ball, ready to fire the brandy around it. Once served the staff below would start their first course of pâté from the larder, and proceed course by course through the goose, or ham, the pudding and the cheese.

'I think it will be turkey next year,' the butler said as all took their places around the table. 'Constable, please do us the honour of sitting next to Mrs Prescott and saying grace for us all.'

'Dear God, thank-you for those who have prepared this food and may it bless us and may you bless this house today and in the year to come,' said Jack, copying the one prayer he could remember vicar saying in September, at the Harvest festival supper.

'Amen,' said those around the table.

'Well prayed,' said Mr Ball, sharpening the carving knife. 'Let's enjoy the goose while we still can. From what I hear upstairs, Mrs Prescott, it may be the last year.'

'We will have goose, I promise you, Mr Ball, below stairs. Nasty bird a turkey, very hard to digest. Sprouts, constable?'

'Saving myself for your Plum Pudding as the star of the day,' said Jack, and Mrs Prescott did not press any more vegetables that he had long hated, upon him.

His first Christmas dinner of the day over, Jack took his leave, as he was still on duty. Declining brandy in the Butler's pantry with Mr Ball and managing to dodge the mistletoe this time, he was off up the kitchen steps and at the garden gate before the housemaids realised. Jack decided the walk back to the station in Leman Street would be just what his digestive system demanded.

*

Seven

Sam Curzon was due back before evening and he and Jack were to go to the south side of Drury Lane to a little place famous for its books and oysters. Sam would have the oysters and he, Jack thought, would have the books. The Blacks would be back in Arbour Square as well later and Michael Culley. Jack fully intended to take the doctor's hint and make an opportunity to talk to Ann Black, provided he could do so without an audience.

Jack walked up the Commercial Road. It was like an artery of trade running through the area from Whitechapel to the West India Docks. He looked towards the east where the big domed gateway loomed up and the masts and spars of south bound ships were just visible. Glancing around as he walked, he registered that the road was lined with private dwellings which were still respectable but a quarter of the properties were occupied by tradesmen. The rest were schools, public buildings and public houses, and hotels. He passed a woman with a young baby, sitting on a step of her front door. It struck him as strange in this weather but he thought it was due to lack of space in the accommodation. It was impossible to determine from her face what age the woman was. Behind her Jack caught a glimpse into a room which had little comfort. Poverty, he thought, came in different forms. It was not dirt in this case, as she and the child looked comparatively clean and not badly dressed, just careworn and the clothes had many areas of patching. Perhaps fallen on harder times than she had once known. Like him, he thought, once he had been orphaned. How his life and the expectations of those around him for his future had changed. Teachers, potential employers, even those in church. The fact of being an orphan was like a stigma. However, he had not accepted the low level of aspiration that was foisted upon him for long. Jack had learned to keep it to himself after a while, drawing strength from his refusal to accept the low role in life that society expected.

His mother had prepared him to go into a business with his father. There had been a growing demand for the market garden produce as London expanded and people poured in for work. So, he had worked at his letters and numbers in order that no-one could swindle them. He would look after the accounts as he got older, his mother told him, and then they could expand the business to rent more land for the growing season. There was a story to tell in the detail of what was sold and for how much. He remembered her, schooling him well in preparation for the role he would have in the business. His father had no head for figures, she had said, but he could make anything grow. She had taught Jack to read from the Bible and he could read the hard passages with peculiar names by the time he was eight and had done well in school, with his level of reading. He was always chosen to read a passage in the Sunday School. Jack smiled at the memory of his mother's pride when he brought home a "good attendance" certificate by the age of nine. It had stayed on the mantle-piece, by the clock, for months. He and his father stacked the fresh produce in baskets, taking care not to bruise the lettuce, ready for the train to take it into the market in London. Every day, he and his father had built a wall of baskets on the back of the cart, driving to transfer them onto the London train so that the produce would arrive fresh. The change, when it came, of both parents suddenly dying in a flu epidemic had been dramatic. He suddenly had an overwhelming desire to ensure his own children, if he ever had any, would never know what he had known as an orphan.

Jack stopped and nodded a greeting at the woman. The fear was clear in the eyes, she was clearly worried he would find something with which she, also was uncomfortable.

'Is your husband here?' asked Jack.

'No, he's at the docks, with our other children.' There was no east end accent. A bit of a burr on the r which could mean Oxford or even the West Country.

Jack peered over her head into the one room that was visible. Someone had cleaned the room and used whitewash on the walls. Inside he could see two chairs, a table and a bed. That was all the furniture. There was a range which indicated it had been a kitchen to the house at one time. Now parts of the property were being sub-let to different families. In the corner was a walk-in cupboard that at one time would have acted as the pantry. He thought that would probably be where the family kept the other sleeping arrangements for any older children, bringing it out at night.

His eyes wandered over the full bucket of coal which was by the side of the range. The range was lit too and there was heat coming through the door from the room. Leaving the door open, a lit range and a bucket full of coal. They were lucky. Or was it luck that there was a means to keep warm? Jack realised the fear she had shown could potentially be because her husband and the other children were taking bits of coal that fell from the coal ships. He looked again. A piece of rope was strung over the range and pieces of washing aired there. There was a pot on the range. Soup probably, Jack thought. There would always be a ready meal no matter what time the rest of the family came home. By rights he should question her.

She was uncomfortable with a policeman looking in. Poor woman, probably used to a better life at some point. If she had met him with a hard stare, defying him to action, he would have followed it up but remembering the story of Ruth in the Bible from hisSunday School days, about the poor picking the crops that were left at the edges of the field, or gleaning, he thought the word had been, he decided to walk on. He had not spent a cold Christmas this year, in his warm bedroom in Arbour Square, with a fresh fire laid every-day, shirts washed and ironed by Hannah, and good food on the table. Besides, when he worked on the farm the Squire had always left some crops in the field, at least for the birds. Coal that has fallen on the ground off the trolleys?

Was it fair game like corn on the edge of a field? Was gleaning theft? He was sure the owners of the coal would think so. But if the family were only using it for themselves he would not act. It would be different if he caught her husband selling it on, but the state of that home did not imply any monetary gain coming in.

Jack touched his helmet to the woman and walked on, aware that her eyes were boring into his back. He would have left money for the child if he could but there was always someone watching and it would not do for word to go around the neighbourhood that the woman had been given money by a policeman on Boxing Day, even if it was charity. It could be taken as payment for information and her life would not be worth living.

At the corner a greengrocer, Roswell, hopeful for trade the day after Christmas, had opened his doors until early afternoon. Jack doubted that custom would be brisk today, but the counter was now being scrubbed down and the tiles washed. It would only be local custom and those passing by as the deliveries for the middle classes and wealthier homes would have been made before Christmas.

Roswell and his son were the only staff in the shop. The delivery boy presumably had been given Boxing Day as a holiday, as he was nowhere to be seen. The father and son worked hard every day, closing only on Sundays, and were there from morning to night usually. Jack always cast an experienced eye over the produce and had not yet asked where Roswell got his supplies from.

'How has the season been for you, Mr Roswell? A good one for business I hope,' Jack reigned in his desire to start with a question about the woman and child on the step.

'It has been, and we have a few items left that we could turn some coins for on Boxing Day, so the lad and I decided we would be open this morning for a few hours. There's not much business about, but a few bags of apples from the store and potatoes will cross the counter this morning,' said Roswell senior.

Roswell junior, referred to as "the boy," was a man of thirty, married with three children.

'Would you know anything about the lady and child sitting on the step across the way?' asked Jack.

Roswell peered through the window, turning his head from left to right as he weighed up the person towards whom Jack had inclined his head.

'She seems a pleasant sort. Fairly new in the street, came in October. Husband lost his job on an estate, is what I've heard. Don't know what the full story is there. I think they're been used to better accommodation. Three children, the baby's a recent addition as you probably guessed, Constable. Always polite. She had some winter cabbage and potatoes before Christmas. Tidy soul, I think. Children are scrubbed and you know what they say, "Cleanliness is next to Godliness." Always comes in at the end of the day to see what I am selling off. You've served her, haven't you, Wilf?'

'I've nothing bad to say about any of them,' said Roswell Junior, or Wilf, and continued with his scrubbing.

'I suppose you wouldn't have heard where in the country they came from?' asked Jack.

'North of London, is all she mentioned,' said Roswell Junior.

'The husband took the older children off with him this morning towards Limehouse. I suspect they'll see what work is about. Now Constable, I have a little honey roasted ham in the back, I'd like your opinion on, you being from a farm. It's come in from Wiltshire. Come through, would you?' Roswell led the way and Jack gladly followed.

*

Still chewing as he emerged from Roswell's Jack's mind moved on to Sam's return. He had many questions for Sam later. What had Sam said? Then, as if his mind had thrown a switch, he realised he had the answer. Four, no, Jack thought, "by" four. It could mean that he was not to try and solve the puzzle of who the senior policeman was but that there were four of them to do so. Jack laughed involuntarily. Sam meant them to work together, Hunt, Morris, Phillips and him. Of course, it was obvious! The others had more experience of cases, Inspector Hunt especially, given his years in the force had more knowledge of personnel. They were all due back on duty by tomorrow and Morris, he knew, had passed on information to Inspector Hunt that Doyle had good news for him. Tom Hunt would have seen Doyle at their gathering for Christmas and would probably already be working on the answer. The realisation made him feel hungry as he started to relax and he increased his walking speed to reach the hot pot of tea he knew would be perpetually brewing on the Wilson range in the station. No sugar but a lot of milk were calling to him.

By ten o'clock his patrol had started and he was on a promise from the cook, Mrs Prescott, of a "box" of leftover food from Christmas day. All he had to do was knock on the kitchen door and he had been told that there would be someone to give it to him. Most of the staff had a holiday today with just a skeleton few on hand to cater for the needs of their employers. Jack hoped that Harriet would have a whole day as a holiday too. Many would go home with their box but Harriet could not get to Honiton and back today. Jack remembered that her sister, Georgina, was in Lewisham, so perhaps she would go there for Boxing Day as it was not that far from Camberwell Green. A dressmaker, Arscott Ward had said, and he wondered if the ambitious streak he saw in Harriet was something that the two sisters had imbibed at their mother's knee. Arscott had said that more of Harriet's family were to come to London. Jack tried to recall how many brothers and sisters she had.

Arriving at Mrs Prescott's kitchen door Jack collected a box of leftovers carefully packed up for him by her kitchen maid. He enquired on the health of Mr Ball, but the butler was having a half day off and had gone to see his niece and her family. There would be no maids to dodge today under the mistletoe. It was, after all, now law that servants would have Boxing Day as they worked Christmas Day. The Queen had included the twenty-sixth of December last year in the Bank Holiday Act. Carrying his box, he turned back towards the station. Jack looked at the bank building as he walked past. All shut and in darkness too, there would be no money making today!

A man was hanging around an alley that led along the side of the bank from Commercial Road. Jack registered that it was an odd thing to do on a day that the bank was closed, unless there was some dishonest motive. There were very few people around. Jack estimated how long he had spent walking since he had left the station at ten o'clock. He had stayed in Mrs Prescott's kitchen for no more than ten minutes. It would be about midday. He walked on registering that the man was watching him.

Two more corners and the woman and baby were still on the step and she went pale as she saw him approach. He smiled and her face relaxed momentarily.

'From a cook at a big house,' said Jack, as he put the box on the step next to her and turned back towards the bank. He didn't look back until he reached the corner. The woman was still watching him and the box was open on her lap.

Fifteen to twenty minutes had gone by as he approached the bank again. The man was still there, smoking a pipe and leaning against the wall. Jack crossed the road and the man straightened up, removing the pipe from his mouth.

'Funny day to be hanging around the bank. Don't you have somewhere else to be?' asked Jack.

'Enjoying my pipe,' said the man.

'I shall be back here in ten minutes. I don't want to see you when I come back. Move along,' said Jack, standing, hands at his side, waiting for some physical response. The man knocked his pipe out against the wall and held the bowl of it in his fist. Jack tensed, waiting for the attempt to push the shaft into his eyes that might come. The man was deliberating, he could feel it. Instead the pipe was put away in the coat pocket and the man turned away and moved up the alley. Jack estimated the time it would take to get to the other side of the block where the alley would come out. He would walk it to see if the man hung around at the other side. Jack continued to stand and watch, waiting to see if the man looked back.

At the three-quarters mark of the alley way, the man glanced over his shoulder, saw Jack was still rooted to the spot and then quickened his step. He turned the corner and Jack waited. He gave it five minutes and estimated the time, counting to sixty as his mother had trained him to do when slowing down his tendency, as a child, to gabble. Then he counted again, watching and waiting. No one appeared at the end of the alley, after he had gone through five lots of sixty second counts. Jack tried the doors of the bank. He rattled a sash window, just in case, he thought, something was not locked.

He stood on the step of the bank and waited, listening. There was absolutely no sound from inside. Jack decided to walk around the block and see if the pipe smoker was still in the area. He was running the description of the man through his mind ready to have a word with Sergeant Thick at the station. He knew Thick would have a list of any regulars in the area. He kept his walk steady, trying the odd door as he went. A few householders bid him good morning, glad to see the regular policeman on his beat on Boxing Day. There was, however, no further sighting of the pipe-smoker. Jack turned back up the alley towards Commercial Road to resume his route.

His mind went back to Mrs Prescott and the perks of the job that he had no doubt she enjoyed. It fascinated Jack. He was quite sure she was on a commission from the tradesmen. Still, it was for her employers to keep an eye on their accounts and the amount ordered. Jack knew there was a whole issue of servants and what they managed to cream off from the employers. He had seen the goings on, while a servant himself. The fact of the description in the '71 census still rankled with him and had more than contributed to his decision to leave the farm and join the police. Well, it would not happen again. He would never be called anyone's servant again, except for the Queen. He thought of the perks he had seen at the Squire's hall. The lady's maids had worn the mistresses' cast-offs on their day off, then there had been the ribbons they had exchanged and the excess bottles of eau de cologne their mistress had given them which they had sold on. All Jack had come across were spare turnips and no one wanted those except the pigs.

No doubt the butler, Mr Ball, had received tips this morning from his employer's guests who had stayed the night. Those that tipped the most would get the best service next time, regardless of his employer's expectation that the butler would provide a certain standard. Human nature? Jack wondered how much more it was survival in old age without a pension.

Not for the first time, Jack thought of Harriet's advice to open a post office account and her determination to one day own a property and take in lodgers. How much could a house be bought for and how long would that process take before enough was saved. How would Harriet possibly save out a low wage? Yet, he believed she was doing. Jack knew that she had no intention of remaining a scullery maid and that she would wait and watch for her opportunity to rise in the pecking order. He set his face to make a new year resolution to follow her advice. He would also try and find out how much a house would cost in the Stepney Green area. If Harriet intended to be an independent woman he intended to be independent with her.

By five o'clock Jack let himself in through the front door of the house in Arbour Square. He had given his notebook to Sergeant Thick to check through and would pick it up in the morning. His account of the pipe-smoker outside the bank that morning had interested Thick who thought the description of the man rang some bells. It was part of an account of the buildings Jack had to give to show that he had checked they were locked. Thick had nodded, knowingly, when Jack gave him a brief summary. There was no mention at this point of the woman and her family who haunted the front step today. Jack had determined he would try and find out the cause of dismissal from the estate first. It could be simple. Perhaps the husband had not sufficiently grovelled to a local landowner.

Jack had a shift change tomorrow from four o'clock to midnight and a half day free hence the night out with Sam Curzon. His notebook would be at the Sergeant's desk for him when he got in tomorrow afternoon. Sergeant Morris would be on duty for his shift and Jack only just managed to control the excitement he felt at the thought of being able to recount to Morris what he had discovered from the doctor. Despite Christmas dinner with the Doyles the Inspector had been firm there was no business discussed at home on Christmas Day, and especially not with the family present. Jack had expected nothing less but had spent the evening on tenterhooks just in case Matthew Doyle had relented and brought up the subject of the discussion Jack had had with the doctor.

Now as he closed the front door he could see into the sitting room to the side of the hall. There were George and Ann Black sitting with Emily Doyle. The light from the fire was flickering on the ceiling.

'Jack, come and join us for some tea,' Emily called. He could see slices of bread for toasting in front of the fire, butter and scones on the table. George was obliging the two ladies by doing the toasting. Ever hungry Jack left his helmet on the side table in the hall, put his damp great coat on a hook and unbuttoned his tunic to open the neck, and went to join the small party.

'We are having cold meats tonight, Jack, as Hannah is away for the night with her family, but I will do breakfast for us in the morning as she won't be back until luncheon…. oh, Sarah, Jack is not here for just you,' Emily laughed as her daughter held out her arms to be picked up.

'It's no punishment to get some love,' said Jack, picking the little girl up.

'Sugar in your tea, Jack?' Ann Black asked, as she got up and poured him a cup.

'No, thank-you. How was your journey and was the family well?' asked Jack.

'It was long, smoky, and I've spent ages scrubbing my face to remove the sooty bits!' laughed Ann.

'Well, you should know by now not to put your head out of the window,' said George. 'My family were fine, but it's all over far too fast and it will be Easter now until we see my parents again.'

'Where do they live?' asked Jack.

'Norwich. It takes ages! But they're an age where they don't want to come into London any more. George is the youngest and so we make the journey,' said Ann.

'I wouldn't even have an idea of how to get there,' said Jack, putting Sarah down as she was starting to wriggle. He walked over to the table and Ann passed him a cup of tea having stirred it for him. She picked up a plate and held it out to him, inclining her head on one side and raising her eyebrows in an unspoken question about if he wanted any of the food. Jack smiled a reply and helped himself to a couple of pieces of bread. He could see Emily had sliced it as Hannah's slices were more like wedges each morning. These were slim and would crisp up nicely as toast. Jack went across to the fire and stood in front of it until the warmth became part of him.

'Are you doing your own toasting?' asked George.

'I can do,' said Jack and George took the last piece of toasted bread off the toasting fork and held it out to Jack. 'I need to move away from the fire,' said George. He took a seat at the back of the room.

Jack fixed his first piece of bread to the toasting fork, but it dropped into the fire. Laughing Ann brought him another and this time he pushed it to the back of the toasting fork making large holes in the middle of the piece. This caused more hilarity from the two ladies, and Sarah joined in as her mother was laughing. Jack shrugged in his good-natured way.

'I was always too hungry to wait for bread to be toasted,' said Jack with a grin. 'Going back to your journey, George, I've never been further north than this!'

'Well you should. There are some lovely places. You can go everywhere from London, Jack. All you need is time, which none of us really have much of,' said George.

'We went out of Bishopsgate to Norwich. at the moment, as the new terminus isn't yet open at Liverpool Street. That one should just about be open when George qualifies in two years! I did shudder when we went through Kelvedon though, after the accident in October,' said Ann.

'When will you qualify?' asked Jack deliberately. Ann looked taken aback.

'I can't, you should know that,' said Ann, and then she gave him a sad smile, 'You would be arresting me.'

'I met Doctor Brown, yesterday, coming out of one of the houses on my patrol. He mentioned he thought it would come one day, women as doctors. He knew I was lodging here, and said it should come. He knew of you Ann, and mentioned how highly he thought of your qualifications, as he knew we were at the same address,' Jack smiled and pulled his first piece of toast off the fork and started placing another one on it.

'That's very gracious of him, and unusual,' said Ann, quietly.

'So,' Jack fixed her with a smile, 'when will you qualify as a doctor? It has to happen, surely? Women are nurses, aren't they?'

'Not everyone is of your opinion that it's inevitable, Jack,' said George, glancing quickly at his wife.

'You are, aren't you?' Jack asked George. George met his direct gaze.

'Of course, but I'm not in the majority,' said George.

'Well, there's two men in this room, and we both think Ann should qualify as a doctor, and Doctor Brown thinks she will be one soon, so the tide must have turned, oh, look, I'm not concentrating on my toast,' Jack's second piece had caught fire, and Ann laughed, which relaxed the atmosphere in the room. Passing him another piece of bread while he knocked the flames out on the charred piece of toast on the side of the fire, Emily teased Jack about the cost in bread to having him to afternoon tea.

'I doubt it will happen very often, Emily,' said Jack. 'The chances of us all being free in an afternoon are going to be very rare.' Looking at Ann and George, Jack asked, 'What's stopping a woman becoming a doctor then? Doctor Brown said you're a qualified toxicologist.'

'It's not so much the medical schools as the other students. They're all men and there was quite a to do with the objections. We need the law to change, Jack. Elizabeth Garrett has been trying for long enough. She wasn't able to get a post in any hospital until there was an outbreak of cholera. People quickly forget their prejudices in such times. But she still had to go to Paris to get a medical degree. Now she has one and was working at the East London Hospital for Children and was on the London School Board. The amount of juggling of roles that she has to do! Now she's working with her private practice, the New Hospital for Women and Children, and being a new mother. I can't see her continuing, it really is very hard.' explained Ann.

'Jack's right, Ann, it will come,' said Emily.

'Wait and see what happens in the new year,' said George, putting his hand gently on his wife's.

'I think we need some help, frankly, but I can't see it coming,' said Ann.

'We should campaign for it,' said George.

'What is Toxicology?' asked Jack, removing his piece of toast before there was a repeat performance with the fire.

'Oh, it has a long history, as does poison. It's the study of dosages and the bad effects they can have on organisms. It could be very useful to the police, that's why Doctor Brown is interested,' said Ann.

'Now I'm going to stop you all there, before Jack takes us into a case I know is hovering. Matthew has a rule for Christmas that this is a holiday and there should be no discussion of cases. Save it for another time, Jack,' Emily said, as she stood up and lifted Sarah high, to the little girl's delight.

Jack gave a rueful look at Ann, and then smiled at Emily. Good naturedly he complied with Emily's request, although he found it intensely frustrating. He walked over to the table and spread butter on his cooling pieces of toast. He had no idea when he would get the opportunity to speak to Ann again as they rarely met in the house during the day. Ann had noted from his expression, however, that there was more to say.

*

Michael Culley let himself into the hall as Jack stood debating the choice of jam for his toast. The rain had drenched Michael, giving his partially fitted coat a sagging look. Jack realised that Michael had achieved a respectable start to a moustache in the three nights he had been away, whereas he, fair skinned, at the age of twenty, still struggled to get a meaningful amount of facial hair. He was unusual amongst his peers in still looking clean shaven.

Emily called Michael in to join the afternoon tea, of course. He slipped his shoes off on the door mat and left a dripping umbrella in the hallstand.

'It's come on very heavily. The weather is completely cheerless. There are so many people crowding in the South Kensington museums I could hardly move. Everyone wants to get inside somewhere. Are you off duty tonight, Jack?' asked Michael.

'Yes, and if Sam gets back in the next couple of hours we plan to go over to the Drury Lane Theatre area,' said Jack. 'But tell me why you were in Kensington?'

'I've been to the museums. I had thought of the British Museum but the South Kensington museum has opened a branch at Bethnal Green. the new Museum fitted with my travel. You're lucky you're not doing your patrol tonight, Jack,' said Michael, standing in front of the fire while Emily poured him a cup of tea. 'How was Christmas for you all?'

There were general exchanges until it was Jack's turn. Michael looked apologetic as Jack had had to work. He laughed,

'Oh, don't feel sorry for me, Michael, I ate two Christmas dinners! What did you see at the museum?'

'The Marquis of Hertford's collection, and Sir Richard Wallace's. It's all free.'

'Really? What's in the collection though?' asked Jack.

'Oh, ancient and modern paintings, water colours, miniatures, lots of different European Artists as well as British ones. I want to go back and see the snuff boxes. Look, you should come,' said Michael.

'I'd like to, I've not been to a museum yet,' said Jack.

'Well, no point living in London unless you do,' said Michael.

There was a key in the front door and Sam Curzon completed the arrivals back to Arbour Square. A repeat of news had to be given while he shook his umbrella in the porch, and then decided to give his coat a shake as well. He looked enquiringly at Jack, who gave a brief nod. Sam's face lit up. More tea was poured and further scones were devoured, particularly by the three young men, and, by six o'clock, George and Ann decided to withdraw to their own sitting room.

'There will be plenty of cold meats later, and cheeses, pies and of course the Christmas cake. Hannah has left jellies too, mainly for Sarah, but Matthew has a sweet tooth and he is matching her in her love for them. There's plenty and it will all be in the dining room, all we have to do is carry it up,' said Emily.

'We'll certainly give you help bringing it up,' said Michael.

'I'd love some pie,' said Jack.

'Don't forget, Jack, we are supposed to be going out for oysters in an hour,' said Sam.

'Of course, but they'll slip down nicely with some bread and butter, a little vinegar, and a glass or two of wine. Pie is the thing, now Sam,' and Jack slapped his colleague on the shoulder.

'Wine?' Sam exclaimed. 'What company did you mix with on the farm in Sussex.

'It wasn't too far for a trip or two across to France,' Jack winked at Sam.

'We'll have none of that talk in Inspector Doyle's house, thank-you,' said Emily as she laughed and led the way to the stairs down to the kitchen. Michael carried Sarah down for her. The child looked less than impressed at the growth of hair on his top lip.

'She's noticed there's something different about you,' said Emily, 'that is amazing that she sees the difference.'

'She's a bright little thing,' said Michael.

*

On the south side of Drury Lane, the little passage Sam had wanted to take Jack to was teeming with people. The oysters did indeed slip down easily but there was no wine to accompany them. Jack refused the beer on offer, and closed his eyes as he swallowed the first oyster, taking care to avoid the juice dribbling down his chin and onto his new clothes. He took it straight, without vinegar, to see how good they were. The sea filled his mouth and he set to for the next one. Sam watched with amusement the rapture on Jack's face.

'You look like you're in love,' said Sam, laughing.

'I can taste and see the sea if I close my eyes. I wonder if I'll ever go back?'

'To Sussex? Why not, it's not that far,' said Sam. 'Look, there's a pantomime on over there in the Theatre Royal. What do you say? Shall we do an evening at the "The-atre?" I haven't been to a pantomime for years.'

'I'd like to see inside, I'm not bothered about seeing a pantomime but I would really like to go inside. I'm game if you are, Sam. Have you finished, or do you want six more?' asked Jack.

'I'm not too keen on the slippery little molluscs. Six is enough for me. You go ahead though,' said Sam.

'No, too much pie earlier to find room for more than six. What a Christmas this has been for food! I shall always remember my first Christmas in London. Look there's an old book shop over there. That I do want to go into, not for long, but I would like to see what there is, and if I've enough money to buy a first edition,' said Jack and he got off his stool and looked so excited at the prospect of going into the book shop that Sam laughed.

'Listen to you. First editions! What company have you been keeping over Christmas? It's good to come out with you, Jack, you are so full of enthusiasm I had quite forgotten the problems of the case,' Sam's face clouded.

'There won't be a problem, Sam, we'll sort it out tomorrow when everyone's back at work. Sergeant Morris will be back tomorrow on duty and I'll see him in the afternoon. What's making you so downcast about it. I worked out what you meant "by four." The team of four solve it together! There you are, no problem once we get our heads together.'

'That's what you thought I meant? By the four in the team? I'm sure the four of Phillips, Hunt, Morris and you will get there but that wasn't what I meant, Jack. I was rhyming to point you to a name. It was all I could think of on the spur of the moment. The name I meant was Moore. It was all I could think of to point you in the right direction if you got chance to look at any lists in the station. I think that was the name which triggered a reaction from Inspector Doyle, it was someone Berringer was with at the river. I didn't have enough time before the Christmas holiday to start checking levels of superiority in the divisions, but now we're all back we can get cracking on it, eh?' Sam still looked worried, which Jack found confusing.

'Of course, Sam. Why does this worry you so much? We're only just getting started and, unfortunately, we've had Christmas in the middle to slow the investigation down,' said Jack.

'Someone's killed twice potentially, and the style of murder, Jack, a poisoner, using really violent methods to disfigure a face to make it unrecognisable, evidence going missing, and there's the fact that it's linked to senior person in the police force.' said Sam. 'That's what I call worrying.'

'You think it's the same person?' asked Jack.

'The same person pulling strings, yes,' Sam looked over his shoulder but there was no one obviously taking an interest in the two men. The great doors of the theatres were being thrown open and people were thronging in.

'Look, there's not much we're going to solve tonight. We need to get you in front of Hunt, I think, so let's talk to Sergeant Morris tomorrow. What shift are you on?' asked Jack.

'Four o'clock in the afternoon, same as you. It was deliberate so we could both catch up with Morris.'

'Come on, Sam, let's enjoy the atmosphere tonight.'

'Did you see that man on the Strand, when we came up?' Sam nodded towards a man at the end of the oyster bar who was wiping his hand across his mouth after his sixth oyster.

'Why? Possibly. I'm not sure,' Jack turned and casually glanced in the direction towards the end of the oyster bar. He turned back to Sam. 'Why would anyone be interested in us? There's more than a dozen people we passed that I've seen a couple of times since the Strand.'

'Seriously? You've got a better eye than I have. It might be that we're getting too close?' asked Sam, his eyes showing a hint of fear.

Jack frowned, 'I don't think we've even started,' he relaxed his face and laughed to try and dismiss the tension. 'No one knows we're on the case even,' but he glanced at the man again, taking in the build, and assessing how he would be in a fight if something developed. The man was stocky, a little taller than him. He was older as well and Jack estimated that he would get out of breath quickly if Jack used his agility to keep moving. The gut would be flabby to punch as there was no muscle there, only a beer belly. Jack relaxed, pretty sure the man would come off worse of the two of them if it came to a fight. Still, he would remember him. Another one to describe to Sergeant Thick when he next saw him. Instinctively Jack thought about the detective in the Mason's Arms on the first night he had crossed the river. He had not seen him again, but then perhaps the man had leave over Christmas. Admittedly Jack had deliberately kept away from the public house when in uniform but perhaps it was time to test the water and go back in his labouring clothes. What would Ted Phillips advise? The team would be back together again tomorrow. They should know about how nervous Sam was.

'Look, Sam, you've been thinking too much. Nothing we can do tonight except enjoy ourselves. Come on, I'll keep an eye open for the cove at the end of the bar and if he tries anything, it's more likely to be going for that smart pocket watch of yours. I'll shoot into the book shop over there and then let's go into the theatre and join in the struggle for some space!' Jack slapped Sam on the shoulder and the two men moved towards the entrance of the theatre closest to them. Sam joined a queue to enter and Jack sprinted across the lane to find out what old books the shop had.

Jack did not care what was playing that night on the stage, he was too caught up in the atmosphere. He joined Sam showing the prize he had found, an early copy of Charles Dickens story, "Master Humphrey's Clock," published in 1841.

'What do you want with an old book?' said Sam.

'It's a Dickens,' said Jack.

'Yes, I see. Are you trying to get a book that's got a value, is that why you picked up an old Dickens?' asked Sam.

'The bookseller said it's signed, look there's his signature,' Jack showed Sam the scrawl.

'I think you've been done, Jack. It's not a first edition, look,' Sam pointed to the page in the front of the book.

'No, I know, but it's a stereotype reprint and worth more than a poor quality first edition. It's all I can afford. But it's a start. The Squire had first editions and he taught me a little about collecting and the value. Just another way of saving, Sam. This is in good condition. The Squire used to say the condition is ninety per cent of the book price,' Jack grinned and put the book back into its brown paper and then tucked it into his inner jacket pocket. He looked around at the crowds queuing for the advantage in the rush for the front seats.

'How are we going to get a seat Sam, with this lot ahead of us?' asked Jack.

'Oh, we're not trying for the front seats in the stalls. There's an advantage in going up to the gallery. Look, we're in, come on Jack,' Sam was in a wave surging forward and Jack pushed through, up a long spiral staircase which wound itself through the building ever upwards, past white walls lit by gas lights. It was like a never-ending snake trailing along different levels, sometimes filtering off, first to the circle as the huge bolts were drawn down and the doors were flung open on each level, allowing a wave of bodies to enter while those behind climbed to the gods.

'Made it,' called Sam, over his shoulder as they filed in to the top-most level.

Sam and Jack sat hunched with their knees almost up to their chests on seats which had a view downwards like a mountain drop. Jack closed his eyes and stopped leaning forward. He did not like heights. People in the gods were starting to sing, but there were no musicians in the pit yet.

There was foot stamping to break the boredom. A bottle of gin was offered to him, which he passed on, declining for himself. Gin was not a drink that he liked. Sam passed him an orange, which Jack thought an odd thing to try and eat in a theatre. Sam was busy peeling his, throwing the skin over the rails onto the people below.

'Sam!' Jack exclaimed.

Sam grinned, 'It's a tradition,' he said.

'You're a serving Police Officer,' hissed Jack, looking around, half expecting to see Sergeant Thick behind them.

'No one we know will be up here, have a piece and give it a throw,' grinned Sam.

Jack shook his head and allowed the ambience of the décor to possess him. He was grateful for the dimming gas lights and the curtain rising to a great cheer from the unfashionable part of the theatre in which he found himself. Within fifteen minutes Jack had forgotten he was a police officer and became transported into the humour of a greasy slide on the stage, the pantomime dame in the bonnet, who was greeted with shouts of laughter as the character swayed the crinoline dress back and forth. The joker waved the red-hot poker up and down with all the lewdness with which it was intended and two young recruits into the Metropolitan Police were boys again.

*

Eight

Morning broke through the thin curtains and somewhere in the distance Jack could hear a workman hammering. Except it was not outside. The furious knocking was at his door, threatening to fall down under Hannah's effort to wake him.

Pulling on his trousers which he had draped over the bottom of the bed, Jack partly opened the door onto the landing. Hannah stood sideways on so that she did not take the risk of seeing anything embarrassing. Her eyes were fixed on the top of the stairs and she delivered her message by rote.

'Inspector Doyle says he's sorry to disturb your sleeping but there's a telegram come and would you come down.'

'For me?' said Jack.

'And Mr Curzon,' Hannah stood to attention, eyes still riveted.

'I'll wake him, Hannah, thank-you for coming up.'

Wishing that he and Sam had not made a night of it, Jack partially opened Sam's door and told him to get up. Sam threw a boot at the door and Jack pulled it too just in time to stop the footwear from hitting him.

Ten minutes later though, both he and Sam were in the dining room and sitting at the table with Inspector Doyle.

'I'm sorry to stop your morning's leave but Inspector Hunt will be at the station in Leman Street by ten o'clock, with Phillips and Morris. He wants you both in this morning to do the interviews in the area where Berringer was found. He'll brief you. Get your breakfasts and get off to the station. Morris will alter the shift from tonight so you'll finish by four this afternoon.'

'Sergeant Morris, we missed you,' said Jack, grinning as he and Sam walked up to the duty desk.

The Sergeant looked from one to the other from under his bushy eyebrows. 'Really?' he said.

'No joke, Sergeant, Thick had me on my toes, he must have threatened to discipline me half a dozen times,' Jack leaned against the desk.

'No doubt he had good cause. Get off the desk, and stand up straight when you're on duty,' Morris hissed at Jack, which had the desired effect. His eyes developed a twinkle as the two young Constables both responded to his order.

'Inspector Hunt is in a room three doors down the hall. He's briefed me but PC Phillips is in with him now. Get along down there. You're both going out on duty this morning and I've changed your shift,' Morris turned the register he had been writing in to face them so they saw the changes he had made.

'I'm going out?' asked Sam, amazed.

'Yes, that's what I said. Is there a problem?' asked Morris.

'No, Sergeant, it's such a shock to actually be let out after weeks behind a desk,' said Sam.

'Very funny, you had a day out in Windsor before Christmas. Not moaning are you, Curzon?' Morris controlled his desire to smile at the banter, noting the increase in confidence in the two men.

'Me, sir, no, never Sergeant,' grinned Sam, as he followed Jack along the corridor.

Tom Hunt and Ted Phillips were standing on either side of the fireplace, a mug of tea each on the table, to the side of the window. They had been exchanging details about Matthew Doyle's findings during the Windsor floods before Christmas. Brief pleasantries over with Jack and Sam about the season, Hunt got down to business.

'I need you both to check out the people's stories who were briefly interviewed in the area where Berringer's body was found. Sift through what we were told at the time and find out more about them. Take one side of the road each and liaise with Phillips and Morris at the crime scene as you finish. Make sure you keep notes, as we need to see if anyone shifts their story so we can start to piece together what's true. We don't have the actual interview notes, just a summary from the Coroner,' said Hunt, pulling a sheaf of papers out of an oblong leather briefcase with the initials T.H. on its flap.

He pushed them across the table towards Jack and Sam. 'Here's the summary, and the names and addresses. You haven't got long to look through them. You two will go door to door and Morris and Phillips will be in the background checking over the scene. I'm on my way to the Home Office and I would like you all across the river later this afternoon. We have seven days before the Americans arrive and I want to get this stitched up before we lose the case,' said Hunt. 'I'll see you at the station at New Road.'

'I could do with a tea,' said Jack, as Hunt left.

'We should move out of here, anyway,' Ted Phillips lent forward and started to gather up papers. 'We should make it look normal and read these in the back room.'

'By the sound of it the detective from New York will be here on the second of January,' said Sam.

There was the usual amount of detail in the reports: the location of the carriage found by a bridge on the Whitechapel Road and where the body appeared to have been thrown as the carriage crashed. Business owners had been interviewed, as had a church warden who had given a lot of detail but nothing of any use about the accident. Notices had been put up around the area, on walls, in shops, inviting people to speak to the police. There was a list of names and addresses in the area of people who had come forward.

'Surprising who claims to hear something, or see something. But very little detail,' said Sam.

'That's the point, though, Sam, we haven't got all the detail. It's gone. We can pick up those people listed here today,' Ted Phillips said jabbing the list. He started to make a move for his great coat. 'Genuine witnesses will be helpful, those who have something they want to hide won't be. We should check everyone who's listed here.'

'Ted, Sergeant Thick's got my notebook, I'll need to pick it up,' said Jack.

'No, don't keep records on this in your usual notebook. Take these fresh ones and then give them back to me at the end of the morning,' Ted handed fresh notebooks to Sam and Jack.

Jack had a strong sense of the oddity of a diplomat travelling in the area. It was the same type of feeling he used to feel as a child out fishing with his father when the current would drag the boat further out. Nothing was predictable at that moment, except death. His father and he would both grab the oars and pull as hard as they could to get back into shore. They always made it but each time it happened his father had become even more wary of it happening again, whereas Jack had grown in a young boy's confidence that they were unbeatable together.

'Do you mind me saying, Ted, that a diplomat being in that area does not make sense,' said Jack.

'Of course, it doesn't. However, he was there. We don't know whether he was alive or if he was already dead when the carriage crashed and someone is trying to throw us off the scent, placing it on the Whitechapel Road,' said Phillips.

'Perhaps he had been visiting someone and was on his way back home?' asked Jack.

'We could go on making suggestions for ever. At the moment, we don't know why he was in the area. Let's get out and do some following up and see what we have by the end of the day. You both have four lots of names and addresses. That could take you anywhere between twenty and thirty minutes per address. I think Sergeant Morris is shortly being relieved so the three of us can make a move and meet him in the area without anyone here being any the wiser of what we're up to today,' said Ted.

The team made their way to the Whitechapel Road as the accident had occurred by a bridge there. Jack and Sam split the road in half in order to visit those whose names were listed as attending the scene. They walked past a poster advertising lectures to be run by the university of Cambridge in Whitechapel in political economy, English history and physiology, and Jack momentarily noted the opportunity.

Jack's first call was to a butcher, called Able. He was a large, middle-aged man, in a state of semi-undress as he opened the door of number five. Seeing a police constable on his front step Mr Able reached for a coat hanging on the peg next to a mirror in the hall.

'Come in, Constable, please do excuse me. I'm unwell today and thought you would be my wife returning.' Putting the coat on, he beckoned to Jack to follow him. They went into a back room and Jack wondered what he was likely to catch from the butcher. The fire was lit but there was a smell of damp in the room and Jack noticed the patches under the window where the moisture was seeping through. Badly built, he thought.

'I'm here about the carriage that crashed and the man that was found near it,' said Jack.

'Yes, of course. I spoke to the police at the time the body was found,' said Mr Able. 'Do you mind if I sit?'

'You could do with some air in here, sir, if you don't mind me saying,' said Jack, moving to the window.

'Oh, no, don't open it! I shall catch my death.'

Able's reaction was sharp. Jack gave up the thought of letting air into the room and launched into his questions.

'I've seen some notes on what you said to the police at the time of the body being found. Could I ask some questions?'

'I would have thought it was obvious given the amount of blood.' said Mr Able sulkily.

'In what way, sir, what was obvious to you?' asked Jack, cursing that the detail they had was so brief.

'The man had been stabbed, hadn't he?' Able looked surprised that Jack did not seemed to know.

'Did you see a knife?' asked Jack.

'Well, no. I came up after there had been another four people around the body. Anything could have been moved, or kicked away by accident. It was the amount of blood that he was covered with. I'm a butcher by trade. That much blood means a knife's been used. The carriage crashing wouldn't have produced that. I would have thought the coroner would have passed that onto you?' Mr Able paused, as Jack was making notes.

'Very helpful to hear you say so though. Always good to get an opinion from someone with a relevant skill. Did you know the other people who were at the scene when you arrived?' asked Jack.

'No.'

Short and not sweet, thought Jack. 'Did they stay?' he asked.

'No, they left at the same time as the policeman,' said Mr Able.

'So, there was a policeman at the scene? When you said that you were the first on the scene....'

Jack was interrupted by the butcher leaping in. 'I never said that. When I got there, it was with the other's from around here. Those first people left as we arrived, including the policeman. It made such a noise, the crash, most people were on their doorsteps having a look. But the four of us from the street that went over to where the body was are probably on your list there. Accidents always pull a crowd and people started stopping and going over. You do have a list, don't you?' Mr Able was peering over the top of Jack's notebook, trying to see as much as he could.

'The people that were there first then were not from around here?' Jack asked.

'I've never seen them before.'

'Does that include the policeman? I'd appreciate you confirming the names to me, if you don't mind, of the people you knew,' Jack smiled at the man.

'There was the music teacher Miss Barraclough, her domestic Mrs Edwards, the young man Mr Moore from the bank. And then myself.'

'Moore? Did you say a Mr Moore?' asked Jack trying to suppress his sense of excitement.

'Yes, the young man who took over as Director when his father died. Well, it wasn't his father, his adopted father, or rather the father had adopted the young Mr Moore as a child. Is that confusing you?'

'No,' said Jack a little too loudly, and Mr Able looked shocked. Jack controlled himself and smiled at the man. 'Which bank was he from?'

'The one across the road there, come and look,' the man took Jack back to the front room of the house, which had a chill like death about it. Jack peered through the front window following the direction Mr Able was pointing to and looked at the County Bank.

'Thank you. And the policeman, did you catch his name, or notice his number?' asked Jack.

'No, I didn't get a name. Policemen at scenes of accidents don't usually give their names. They don't turn and say my name is Smith, they're too busy dealing with the incident in front of them,' Mr Able was clearly irritated by the question.

'Alright, sir, I don't mean to upset you,' said Jack.

'I'm not upset, but you don't seem to have all the information. There was no number, by the way,' said Mr Able.

'No number? Do you mean on the uniform of the police officer?' asked Jack starting to feel like he had just had Christmas and New Year in one go.

'Of course, I mean on the uniform. What else are we talking about?'

'Try and keep calm, sir,' Jack said.

'I am calm, but you should know all this from your Constable at the time,' said Mr Able.

'Yes, I should. But I've not been privy to every piece of information, you see, being a low rank. Which constable was it, sir? That you gave the information to, I mean.'

'Evans of course. It's his patch,' said Mr Able.

'You've been very helpful, sir, and I won't take any more of your time. I hope your health recovers,' Jack saluted and turned to go.

Jack was shown to the front door by Mr Able still remonstrating with him that he should have been briefed if he was going to go around the area asking questions. Restraining himself from having a row, Jack thanked the butcher again and walked across the road to where Morris and Phillips were standing at the point where the carriage had crashed.

'It's a stabbing! And the constable didn't have a number.' shouted Jack.

'Quietly, lad,' said Morris. 'Who've you seen?'

'The butcher, Mr Able, at number five. I reckon he knows when a knife's been used. Why don't we know this?' asked Jack.

'For the same reason that we haven't had all the details on the Faceless Woman case. Evidence is going missing,' said Ted.

'Well done, get back and do the rest on your list and then once Curzon has finished the other side of the street we can compare notes back at the station. He's in the bank now. Keep that excitement that's on your face inside. Come on now, compose yourself before you go to the next one or you'll give information away,' said Morris.

The crowds cheering inside Jack's head encouraged him to punch the air but he restrained the tendency in public. He walked back to the houses and knocked on the door of number three. It was opened by a trim woman.

'Miss Barraclough?' asked Jack. From a room off the hall stomped a staccato set of notes from the literal execution of a scale.

'Yes, but I'm in the middle of a lesson,' the lady said. 'Yes, I'm Miss Barraclough.'

'Just a few minutes, Miss, I'm sure it won't take longer. It's about the accident at the bridge,' said Jack who was still on the doorstep.

'Oh, come in, would you just wait while I give my pupil some further exercises to do,' and Miss Barraclough opened the door of a room in which sat a seven-year old, hitting the keys of the piano. The door closed for a matter of moments until the music teacher came back into the hall. She led Jack into a tidy front room, with two small, but comfortable arm chairs on either side of a fireplace. Jack noted the precision with which the furniture was arranged and the amount of lace in the cloths on small tables, at the windows and on the antimacassars on the back of the chairs. Miss Barraclough sat down and indicated for Jack to take a seat.

'Do you remember what happened on the night the diplomat Berringer was found,' asked Jack.

'At what time?' Jack noted the meticulousness of the music teacher. On the background detail that Jack had read Miss Barraclough gave music lessons in her home from early morning to evening. She also had been engaged for lessons in some very respectable homes and had students at the Conservatoire. She lived alone. Clearly music was her life. She had help coming in six days a week from a woman called Mrs Edwards. No-one had interviewed Edwards as far as Jack knew. He had not seen an outline of an interview with a Mrs Edwards. He wrote the name down.

'When you heard the accident. Did you go straight out to the street?' asked Jack.

'Of course,' said Miss Barraclough.

'Bit gruesome, for a lady, no doubt,' said Jack, sympathetically.

'Not at all. One must not focus on one's self at such times. Edwards was with me and we did what we could, but the man was already dead in my opinion. He had clearly been thrown from the carriage as it crashed.'

'You've some experience of dealing with severe injuries?' asked Jack.

'No, only nursing my father in a long-term illness in his later years,' said Miss Barraclough.

'You gave a very detailed account to the policeman who interviewed you,' said Jack, but he was shooting in the dark as he had only read a summary. From that outline, it was clear she had not been at the scene as early as Mr Able. Neither had she been at the front of the group that had crowded around the body.

'You've seen it? Good, is there anything else you wanted to ask, I should get back to my lesson, as I have other pupils on the hour and half hour through the morning,' the music teacher glanced at her clock.

'Of course, Miss, I won't keep you much longer. Where would I find Edwards in the house?' asked Jack, concluding that his time would be better spent with the domestic, Mrs Edwards.

'Edwards? Of course, no-one spoke to her, did they? She's in the kitchen. Let me show you. If there's nothing else, I'll wish you good-day Constable. You know where I am if you need to speak to me again, but I think I covered everything from my perspective. Edwards is in the kitchen downstairs. You can reach it from the end of the corridor. Edwards will see you out when you're finished. I must get back to my pupil. Goodbye, Constable.'

Mrs Rachel Edwards, was in her late fifties. Jack put her down as probably widowed some years ago as there was no mention of a husband. He got the impression she had been used to better times and now lived with an adult son and his wife in Bow. She showed little emotion at the appearance of a cheerful young policeman in her kitchen, and went back to polishing the brasses after seeing Jack's smiling face peer around the door.

'May I?' asked Jack, pulling out a kitchen chair. Mrs Edwards nodded.

'I wondered when you lot would realise no one had spoken to me,' she said with a smug smile.

She had nothing to complain of in her position with Miss Barraclough but had not thought in her younger days that she would ever be called someone's servant. Jack sympathised.

'It's the fact people think you don't have a brain, or that you're invisible. I bring things to her attention.' Mrs Edwards looked up at the ceiling as she said this. Jack followed the direction of her gaze. From up-stairs the thumping continued on the long-suffering instrument.

'What sort of things?'

'Account things. Bills and so forth, costs, unpaid fees. She'd be in the poor house if it wasn't for me managing things and prompting her. They wouldn't pay her. Not that I blame the people who send their offspring here. Why pay for someone making that noise in your house. But still you don't get noticed, do you. Just the same at the scene of the accident, I was there before her, but no one took down a statement from me,' Mrs Edwards pointed a finger at the ceiling towards where she assumed Miss Barraclough was sitting, this time keeping her eyes on Jack's. He nodded.

'Yes, I know what you mean, Mrs Edwards, I was a farm labourer before joining the police. I was expected to be so inward, except with the Squire, he was different,' said Jack.

'Ah, so you played a role, like me. I'd not be doing this work if my Frank hadn't have died. Still, it means I'm independent of my son, and can help him. What did you want to know?' asked Mrs Edwards.

'Well, tell me what you saw, what you heard,' said Jack.

'There was a crash, I was cleaning out the grate in the front parlour, it's the one on the left of the front door,' Jack nodded as it was the room Miss Barraclough had taken him into. 'I called to Miss Barraclough, as the boy she was teaching was murdering Chopin at the time the carriage turned over. I was at the window, and if you look, Constable, you'll see how clear a view of the area you have from that room. I saw a body on the ground, and a turned over carriage. I drew the curtain back, which Miss Barraclough didn't like as I ruffled the lace, mad on her lace she is, and could see other people coming out of shops and houses. There were a few seconds between leaving the window and coming through the front door. Anyway, I went across. I was there before her,' again the eyes to the ceiling.

'What did you think when you got to the accident?' asked Jack, picking up his pencil and opening his notebook while keeping his eyes on those of Mrs Edwards. She was starting to liven up as she got into her account.

'I just had it in my head that I might be able to help. There was a small crowd round the body, so you had to push your way through. Mr Able was already there, and Mr Moore, from the bank was crossing the road to go to it. A policeman had already got there and was bending over the body, he didn't stay though and was gone fairly quickly after I arrived. I was the second on the scene after Mr Able.'

'Did you get his number by any chance, or recognise him?' Jack wanted her to confirm if she had seen a number on the uniform.

'No, there wasn't a number, which I thought was odd, in fact, I did look, because we know the officers round here, and this one was new, or maybe he'd been in the carriage with the man. He was a diplomat, wasn't he? So, he might have had a policeman with him?' Mrs Edwards leant forward.

'Doubtful, round here. Maybe someone in plain clothes, or the Americans might have provided their own protection,' said Jack, screwing up his face and shaking his head.

'In fact, I don't think I did see a number. I do remember thinking it was odd, but I got involved with checking the man with Mr Able. Then I heard Constable Evans behind us, as I know his voice. We got up from the body and moved away to let Evans get closer and when I looked around the other policeman didn't seem to be there anymore. Miss Barraclough arrived at that point. It was all only a couple of minutes.'

'No one asked for your statement?' asked Jack.

Mrs Edwards smirked, 'No, I'm what did you call it, inward?'

'Yes, silent, I think you'd say, and you don't exist. But you should do for the police. They were remiss not to take a statement, you're an important eye witness,' said Jack.

She smiled. 'Cup of tea, Constable?'

'That's very kind, Mrs Edwards.'

Jack wanted to have time for her memory to develop and as Mrs Edwards made the tea, he watched her face as she thought.

'Funny about that policeman,' said Mrs Edwards, distracted as she made the tea.

'Yes,' said Jack and waited. She stirred the tea in the pot, then swirled it round like a ritual. True to form as she reflected she behaved as though she was making a cup of tea for her son. Jack guessed that he must like his tea sweet as, without asking Jack, she placed two spoons of sugar in the steaming liquid and two Arrowroot biscuits on a plate. Putting the tea and biscuits next to his elbow, Mrs Edwards went back to her seat. Jack waited for another minute and broke her reflection.

'He said there should be a knife. I didn't understand at the time, but when Constable Evans turned the body over there was so much blood. I looked around for a knife, because Mr Able kept saying there should be a knife, but we didn't see one. There were a lot of people milling around by that time, and I said perhaps the policeman that had been there had picked it up… he'd gone you see by then, and Mr Moore was now there with M'lady upstairs. Constable Evans told us all to stand back and then bent over the body and started to put the man on his back. It was then I could see Mr Able was right,' said Mrs Edwards, firmly.

'Why? What was there about the body that made you agree with Mr Able?' asked Jack.

'Well, he knows his business, and we all know how much blood there is once we gut an animal. Depends where you do it, of course. You must have been involved in that on the farm?'

'Yes, I know what you mean. What do you remember Mr Able saying exactly?' said Jack, ignoring going down memory lane from the farm. He knew exactly what she meant, but he did not know exactly where he would stab a person if he wanted to get them to bleed to death quickly. He needed to check this out with Doctor Brown, and made a note.

'He said, he's been stabbed, and then, oh yes, he's already dead. It was the amount of blood, I think. He's probably already told you,' reiterated Mrs Edwards.

'Yes, thank-you. Good to have your account though as it was missed,' said Jack, bracing himself for a repeat visit with the butcher. 'Just one more thing, Mrs Edwards, could you describe the policeman in any way.'

'He was bending over the body, height was about like you, but the helmet was pulled quite a long way down. Bit older than you I would say from the stubble on the chin. Moustaches. Dark, swarthy, a bit unkempt,' Mrs Edwards stopped.

'That is very helpful,' said Jack, finishing his notes. He put his pencil and notebook away, looked up and smiled.

Mrs Edwards showed him out and he climbed the steps to the street level from below stairs. He braced himself for calling back at number five.

'What you here again? I've told you everything and you should have checked the report before you came. Very inefficient,' said Mr Able when he opened the front door to Jack. But he had opened the door wide and Jack took it as a tacit invitation to step in. He followed the butcher down the hall back into the over-warm room, biting his lip to prevent a response to the butcher who was venting his spleen. Jack agreed with the man's perspective anyway, under normal circumstances there would have been a full report, whereas the oral record taken had vanished.

'I've been to see Mrs Edwards and she has mentioned your skill in identifying the amount of blood indicating a stab wound. Where would the wound have been to give a fast amount of blood flow?' asked Jack, readying his notebook and pencil.

'Depends, the groin, or the stomach region, depends on what the killer hits. Anyway, he hadn't been bleeding for long, so the killer knew what they were about. Just my opinion. Hasn't the coroner got all this?' said Mr Able.

'Couldn't say, sir, just checking things out. Too low a grade to know,' said Jack, with a shrug, making it up as he went along.

'Well they shouldn't be sending you out to bother people. I should be taking to a Sergeant at least. And Evans has gone. He should have told you. Have you spoken to Evans?' said Mr Able, clearly annoyed.

'Constable Evans? Do you know where he's gone?' asked Jack.

'How would I know? I saw his wife in the shop Christmas Eve, that's all and she said he'd been transferred, out of the area for a spell, with a long journey. Bad at this time of the year. The family has stayed in their lodgings but he's travelling every day. You should know this!'

'Alright, sir, I agree with you, I should. Don't upset yourself, you've been very helpful. Just one more question, where can I find Mrs Evans?' asked Jack, and then he ducked as a newspaper came flying in his direction.

'You keep asking stupid questions. Check with the station. And tell the Sergeant to send someone who knows what they're doing next time.'

'You're sure he's been transferred?' asked Jack stepping back into the hall.

'Of course, I'm sure. I've not lost my memory with this cold! She said so, his wife, on Christmas Eve, I'm not imagining it.'

Jack was outside quickly and turned to say thank-you but the door closed with a slam behind him.

He joined Morris and Phillips who were both on their knees combing through the dirt and rubbish, finding blood stains, bits of lost belongings, which could have been from anyone. Weeks had gone by since the death and the diplomat's stabbing was unlikely to have been the only one in the area, Jack thought. Ted Phillips stood up and pulled his gloves off and looked at the state they were in with disgust. His face registered distaste at the exercise of looking for clues in such a site. Jack noted the blood stains on the brick and the cobbles.

'Find anything?' he asked.

'The world's lost property,' said Ted.

'Have you seen Curzon, yet?' asked Morris.

'No, he must still be interviewing,' said Jack.

'Right, I'll go and call at the two addresses he had and see if I can flush him out. How did you get on?' asked Morris.

'Wonderfully well, I think the butcher....' Jack was stopped by a hand going in front of his face as though Morris was stopping a tram.

'Not now, at the station. Wonderfully well is enough. Detail can come later.' Morris started to cross towards the bank.

157

The four policemen arrived back at Leman Street within a few minutes of each other. Tom Hunt had travelled back over the river to New Road Police Station. It was now midday. They travelled in two's, Jack and Ted Phillips, Sam and Morris, with the pretext of an early New Year dinner in their old division's area. Tom Hunt was waiting for them in his office, sitting under the portrait of the Queen. Jack and Ted took their seats and Jack noted there were five chairs put out around the desk, not four. Who was the fifth person? he wondered. Morris and Sam had not yet arrived when Jack and Ted entered Hunt's office and he and Hunt caught up on news about their respective New Year events to come, while they waited. Jack's mind wandered as he looked at the widowed Queen, counted the chins again, just as he had since being a boy, and remembered, with a smile, his father giving him a gentle cuff when he had told him how many he could count. Morning, Ma'am, thought Jack, your servant here. She'd had a few attempts to murder her, he thought. Not too long since the last one. That made six now. Arthur Connor, aged seventeen, in February 1872, was the last one. It triggered his thoughts about that clerk he had interviewed on the Shaw case before Christmas, what was his name, that young one who was a Fenian? It escaped him. Arthur Connor, who had a self-confessed link with the Fenians. Jack ran the details through his mind: threatened the Queen with an unloaded pistol. Been of unsound mind apparently, which was probably the case, Jack thought, as the pistol would have been loaded otherwise and he would not now be staring at a portrait of Queen Victoria any more, but of King Edward. The fact of activity on the Fenian cause sent Jack's mind straying to the Shaw case. He had not thought of it for days, and with some irritation realised that there would be a court date for sentencing at some point in January. What was the young chap's name? That clerk in the office who Morris had said was a Fenian? The one with the attitude…. Harris, Bill Harris, it came to him. He decided he must keep an eye open for Bill Harris when he came back to work in Camberwell. Jack grinned at the Queen, tough as old boots she was, he thought. Then Hunt was speaking as Morris and Sam walked in.

'We're missing Doctor Brown, but I daresay he's on his way. Well, gentlemen, how did this morning go?'

Morris started, 'Sargent has statements from the butcher at number five, Whitechapel Road, which indicates a stabbing, sir. He also interviewed Miss Barraclough at number three and her domestic, Mrs Edwards. We seem to have acquired an un-numbered policeman at the scene of the crash before anyone amongst the witnesses arrived. It's clear in the two witness statements, of the butcher, Mr Able and the domestic, Mrs Edwards, which is a turn up for the book. Curzon, seems to have found that the witness, a Mr Moore, a director at the County Bank, turns out to be the adopted brother of Mrs Doyle. Maiden name was Moore, which explains Matthew's Doyle's reaction to the name in the Boatman's list at Windsor. Unexpected complication there, sir, although I suspect it's a coincidence. Hundreds of people with the surname Moore in London. No doubt the person in the party named in the boatman's register was some wealthy person visiting Windsor, or the school at Eton, not likely to be associated with Inspector Doyle's family. But I can let the two constables tell it themselves, sir?'

'Yes, do, but briefly, before Doctor Brown arrives,' said Hunt. 'Curzon, you start, please.

'Mr. Moore is a director of the County Bank. He joined the bank on the decision of his adopted father to "put the boy into banking." He was in the bank on the day that Berringer's coach crashed, which certainly was within a stone's throw of the accident and heard the commotion. He says he went out and was one of the first at the scene, along with the butcher and the music teacher's domestic. Sargent interviewed them. Mr Moore says he had never met the diplomat, Berringer, doesn't move in those sorts of circles. However, the name is too much of a coincidence. I wanted to suggest…….' Hunt interrupted.

'Just keep to what he told you. It's not the time to make suggestions. We need the witnesses' facts, perceptions before we try and piece anything together and make two and two equal five. What did Mr Moore say about what he saw and heard?' asked Hunt.

'He said the man was lying face down, there was a policeman present who left quickly before the local man, Constable Evans arrived. He seems to have been transferred, by the way,' that registered with Hunt who looked at Ted. Quietly Ted Phillips got up and went out.

'Carry on Curzon, sorry to interrupt you,' said Hunt.

Sam started again. 'It doesn't have a good smell about this, sir, it's the name….' Hunt held up a hand. Sam stopped.

'Give me the facts, what did he tell you?'

Sam looked at Hunt, then at Morris. Jack wondered what was the matter with him. Sam looked down at his notebook.

'There's a lot about the amount of blood, the unknown police officer, the effect on business at the bank for a few days,' Sam fizzled out. He was clearly unhappy. Hunt waited, watching him and then asked a question.

'Good or bad?'

'Sorry, sir?' said Sam.

'The effect on business at the bank?' asked Hunt.

'Erm, a lot of people going in, but less deposits than usual. Almost like the bank was a respectable place from which to see the scene of the accident.' Sam paused and looked up. Jack looked at him and then at Hunt. Something was up with Sam. He had shut down, the face said it all.

'Any unusual visitors?' Hunt asked sharply. Jack registered that the Inspector had spotted the change in Sam as well. If he had been a witness, Jack thought, he would have suspected he was withholding information.

'Did Mrs Doyle go and see her brother?' barked Hunt.

Sam looked down at his notebook. 'Not that he mentioned.' Hunt's face set. He held his hand out for the notebook. Sam passed it across the desk. Hunt put it to one side, and turned to Jack.

'Right, Sargent, let's hear what you've got.'

There had been a sea change, as if a squall had started to move in. Jack was not sure what had happened in the last five minutes but knew just as with the sea, he must adapt to it. He flicked open the notebook.

'The butcher, Mr Able, was of the opinion from the amount of blood that there had been a stabbing as cause of death. He said he got close to the body, seemed to be of the opinion that there should have been a knife at the scene, but there wasn't, and that if the cause of death was a knife wound, whoever had done it knew what they were doing, would have done it before the accident and that the coroner would have the details. He seemed very irritated with me that I hadn't read the Coroner's report, or seen his interview notes,' Jack paused and looked up. Hunt nodded.

'Quite right, you would have looked an idiot. How did you play that?'

Jack grinned, 'Apologetically, sir, said I was a low grade.'

'Good,' said Hunt, 'Of course we haven't seen the full Coroner's report, all we've got is a précis.

'If Doctor Brown's on his way, sir, will he be able to say if it was a stabbing?' asked Jack.

'I should think so. We can get an opinion from the interview details you've got there. Carry on, what else did he tell you,' Hunt was definitely tense, Jack decided.

'He went into detail about where to cut, sorry sir, it's a bit horrific, but I noted it down as he seemed to have a feel about blood flow. Then what he said was borne out by the domestic to house number three, Mrs Edwards, who arrived on the scene before her mistress, the music teacher, Miss Barraclough. The music teacher said she'd given a detailed interview at the time but we haven't seen it. But Mrs Edwards, her domestic, hadn't been interviewed,' said Jack. Hunt nodded.

'And so, you honed in on her and no doubt you used your charm with the ladies to get her to chat,' said Sergeant Morris.

'Give over, Sergeant, she's in her fifties, a widow and has a son who's older than me. I think I reminded her of him, frankly, as she automatically put sugar in my tea,' said Jack, tracing down his notes with his finger.

'There you are, Inspector, everywhere he goes, he eats and drinks and woos the ladies,' said Morris, taking the heat out of the situation slightly. Hunt's eyes twinkled.

'Both Mr Able and Mrs Edwards mentioned a policeman being on the scene of the crime before them, who did not have an identifying number on his uniform. She, Mrs Edwards, said that she thought at first when she found out that Mr Berringer was a diplomat, that it might have been a special officer protecting the American, and travelling in the coach with him,' said Jack.

'Not likely in uniform,' said Morris.

'No, that's what I said, Sergeant, and he would have known Berringer was stabbed as it would take some time to bleed out, if what the butcher said is correct. I thought it more likely he was the murderer,' said Jack.

'Facts from the report, not assumptions,' said Hunt, tapping the point of a pencil on a sheet of paper to make the point.

'Sorry, Inspector. I went back to the butcher then, despite his irritation with me. He said Mrs Evans, the usual Police Constable's wife, was in his shop on Christmas Eve and told him her husband had a way to travel to work now and had been re-assigned temporarily,' Jack stopped and closed his notebook. Hunt held out his hand and Jack handed it over.

Ted Phillips came back into the room accompanied by Doctor Brown. Hunt and Morris stood up to shake the Doctor's hand, Jack and Sam followed suit. 'I've made an enquiry about Constable Evans, sir,' said Ted.

Sam started biting a nail, Jack thought he was embarrassed about his behaviour, and leant across to him. 'You alright?' he asked, but Sam just shook his head.

*

Nine

'I'm afraid I don't have anything fresh to report on the Faceless Woman case,' said Doctor Brown, as he sat down.

'I wanted to ask your opinion on more than that one case. There's a possibility that the death of the diplomat, Berringer is connected. I hoped we could look at both the case of the Faceless Woman and Berringer's death as linked. We're looking for a charge of murder in both. It's good of you to come Doctor, so close after Christmas. Did you get any rest from your work?' said Tom Hunt.

'Not really, but I have a few day's holiday starting on New Year's Eve. I'll help you if I can,' said the doctor, looking round the room at Hunt's team. His eyes rested on Jack, and he nodded, giving him a knowing look that he had assessed the young Constable correctly if he was part of Hunt's team.

'Thank you for sparing your time, Doctor. Sam, could you do the honours with a cup of tea for Doctor Brown? Hunt asked quietly.

Sam went out and Hunt looked at the Doctor. 'Forgive me Doctor, but I need to deal with something that is happening internally.' Hunt looked around the table at his three colleagues. 'Young Sam is not being open with us, and the reason is something to do with the link to the name Moore. You saw it, how he clammed up. My nose tells me that he doesn't think he can trust us.'

'Sir,' said Ted, 'about Curzon, perhaps if you take him off the case and assign him to different duties? I'm unsettled in his lack of control in a situation. I fear for him that he won't be able to stop himself from challenging someone if he thinks they are the guilty party. I know he would be doing that in the interests of justice but he may not have the ability to make the judgement about timing. He could put himself, and us, in danger before we're really able to make an arrest. Such action on his part would be honest and genuine, but risky. We also can't have someone in the team who doesn't have perfect trust with his colleagues and starts to withhold information.

There's also the possibility that he could start working on his own and that would also endanger himself, and probably us…' Hunt stopped Phillips from saying any more as the sound of footsteps in the corridor came nearer. Sam came back into the room with a large tin mug of steaming liquid for the doctor.

Jack waited until Sam had sat down and then gave him a grin of encouragement. But there was no response from Sam. Jack just saw anxiety and pain in the eyes. At that moment, he realised that Ted's insight was correct, but Jack could not say anything as the doctor asked a question.

'So, you do think the two cases are linked in some way?' asked Doctor Brown.

'Yes, but I can't prove it yet. I think the Faceless Woman is the missing Mrs Berringer and that her husband, the diplomat, has been killed by someone working with his wife, maybe a lover with whom she thought she would have a new life. Berringer was super rich in British terms and she would have inherited presumably, or perhaps had the use of the money for her lifetime with the wealth then passing to the children. We need a motive.'

'You are basing the idea of Mrs Berringer being the Faceless Woman on what facts?' asked the doctor.

'That's the problem, I don't have any facts,' said Hunt. The doctor took a sip of his tea. 'She's vanished,' continued Hunt. 'The Americans were working on her being afraid when she first disappeared, rather than her involvement in her husband's death. They are more than able to protect a diplomat and his family so her disappearance was odd in the least unless she was involved. I fear she walked into a trap and became a risk for whoever she was involved with. We also have some interesting witness statements from those who were first on the scene from the team's work this morning.'

'Not the very first people, sir,' said Jack. All eyes were on him. 'Mr Able said there were four people round the corpse. The un-numbered policeman, and other men before he got there. He didn't know them, said they weren't from the street, and they didn't stay.'

Hunt's face set, 'I see, that's a complication. Alright, let's look at what we've got. This morning we've interviewed four of the original witnesses who were first at the scene when Berringer's body was found by the crashed carriage. Morris and Phillips have combed the immediate area, found a lot of rubbish, of course, and many blood stains but we have no way of knowing if any of it was blood from Berringer's body.' Hunt stopped and looked at Jack, 'Pick it up, Sargent, will you.'

Jack got his surprise under control and momentarily wondered where to start. In the middle, he decided.

'An interesting development that we're now aware of from this morning's enquiries in Whitechapel is that we also appear to have a rogue policeman, someone we can't identify, who was at the scene of Berringer's so-called accident but was in a uniform without an identifying number. We also know details from the Coroner's office have gone missing, as one of the witnesses, Mr Able must have given quite a full statement to the Coroner's clerk as he kept referring to what he had already said. We certainly don't have the initial full interview notes into Berringer' death,' Jack paused. Tom Hunt leaned forward and Jack realised that he had been mustering thoughts while Jack was speaking.

''One piece of fresh information from Mr Able while Jack was with him this morning sounded potentially like specialist knowledge from a butcher about blood flow and a stabbing being evident by someone who knew what they were doing, as if the body had bled out. That was from the amount of blood Berringer was covered in.'

Hunt was stopped as Doctor Brown interrupted, 'A butcher with an abattoir at the back of his shop. I know him, I attended his first child's birth. Yes, there was evidence of a stabbing when I saw the body. But I only had a brief glance, that wasn't the case I was there for.'

'That's interesting. He's given a clear opinion this morning that Berringer died from a stab wound. Based on his butchery skills, what do you think, Doctor?' asked Hunt, despite his set face, Jack thought he must be rattled as it was the first time he had heard the Inspector use his first name.

'He would understand the use of a knife, yes, if that is what you're hoping I will say. I don't think you would stand much chance of making a case to a jury with Mr Able's opinion though,' said the Doctor. 'However, he would recognise the link between a stab wound and the amount of blood, where to make it in order to speed up death. Was a knife found initially?'

'No,' said Jack, 'the domestic that I spoke to today, Mrs Edwards, also arrived at the scene at about the same time as Mr Able. She told me he kept on repeating that there must be a knife. She said they both looked but they couldn't find it.'

'Interesting that he expected to find it,' said the Doctor. 'I wonder what there was that gave him that idea.'

'Yes, a lot of unknown factors. Getting at original interview notes would have been very helpful. Our adversary, whoever he is, has slowed us down. But he will only cause delay. He won't stop us getting at the truth,' said Hunt.

'He?' said Sam.

Hunt let it go. But the comment had registered in the team's minds. Hunt changed tack slightly to bring in the other case. 'The woman who we have not been able to identify, named in the papers as the Faceless Woman, if it is Mrs Berringer, may have left her home in preparation to disappear, having left her children with the nanny. Or, as I said, she may have become frightened. We know that she had been in the lodgings several days before she died. Perhaps she was starting to become a problem to her accomplice, maybe she was seized with a conscience, or became a threat in some way. We are assuming that she knew who had committed the crime and cooperated in the death even if she did not do the stabbing. We know the woman in the lodgings had a visitor, the landlady commented that he was not the same class as the lady. I'm going with her being poisoned by her lover, or by persons commissioned by her lover. I am at this point ruling out suicide, although that is how it was presented.' Hunt stopped.

'There have got to be other people involved, sir. It can't just be Mrs Berringer and a lover. You have to get hold of poison, a knife, a policeman's uniform that doesn't have a number on it, and that sounds like it could have been straight from the factory to me, and the removal of the original Coroner's report and witness statements…. And why was Berringer in the area of Whitechapel? What's he doing round there? It's not exactly the West End, is it? A rich man, in his own carriage, bleeding to death probably for most of a journey. That doesn't make any sense to me at all, and,' said Jack feeling that he was on a roll, 'who is this person he was with at Windsor, called Moore?'

'Exactly,' said Sam, before he could stop himself. Tom Hunt fixed him with a stare. Sam stared back. Jack noticed the hard assessment in both sets of eyes.

'For some reason, Curzon, you do not seem to trust the team anymore. What is it that you sense?' asked Hunt. There was impatience in his tone.

Sam had such an intense expression. His chin jutted out and he started to go pale. Jack thought he was going to pass out and put a hand on the back of Sam's chair ready to catch him, but Sam had started to speak.

'Frankly, I think it's too much of a coincidence of the surname Moore being involved. I think if there's a connection between the person named Moore and Mrs Doyle's family that there is a possibility that Inspector Doyle is compromised. To me, it's obvious why Berringer was in the Whitechapel area. He was intending paying a visit to the Director of the County Bank, Mr Moore.' Sam paused and he sucked in air. Hunt stared at him.

'Go on,' said Hunt.

'Doyle shouldn't be associated with the enquiry, we shouldn't be living in his house, and, forgive me sir, but I have to say this, with Berringer's death and the Faceless Woman case being under your unofficial supervision, you are too close to Matthew Doyle. I feel I have to raise the issue that there's a possibility that you may not see justice through, that you also may be compromised,' said Sam. He sat back, took a few deep breaths and continued to stare at Hunt.

'Steady on, lad,' said Morris, 'you'll find yourself on a disciplinary for insubordination.'

'Sam, no,' said Jack, 'Why would you think that?'

'Well, we are laying it all on the table before you Doctor Brown! Curzon, you will remain behind at the end with myself and Sergeant Morris. We will continue what you've raised then. I'm aware that Doctor Brown's time is limited and we need to address the reasons he's here.'

Sam's opinions had hit home. Hunt pushed a sheet of paper into the middle of his desk with two circles overlapping. He wrote Berringer, in one, and the Faceless Woman, in the other.

'There are two areas I wanted to try and understand from the scientific point of view and that was why I asked you here, Doctor, this afternoon,' said Hunt, turning his face of flint away from Sam.

Jack tried to concentrate on what Hunt was saying but was too shocked at Sam's bomb shell that Inspector Hunt would compromise to protect a friend. Sam sat with his hands on the arms of his chair, looking like a condemned man, his lips pressed firmly together making his mouth turn down. His colour was still a pasty white. But Hunt was asking the Doctor a question and Jack forced himself to listen.

'Can you get into the police morgue without inviting too much attention?'

'Of course, as a Police Surgeon. However, I haven't seen Berringer's body recently. Neither did I see the Coroner's report. I can speak hypothetically from what I've observed in the course of my career and the initial assessment I made, although it was only a brief look, but that is all.' Doctor Brown looked round the table to ensure this registered. The only person who was not hanging on his every word was Sam, who was still gripping the arms of the chair and staring fixedly at the wall. Jack looked at his friend and colleague, thought of the last evening when they had been lads out on the town together, and then made himself switch his attention back to the Doctor. He was rattled by Sam's thoughts, part of Jack thought there was logic in some of the man's points, but not to behave as he was doing in the team.

'Can we understand how quickly someone who has been stabbed would die?' asked Ted, 'the butcher that was interviewed this morning, believed the amount of blood indicated a stabbing and that someone had known what they were doing to make the body bleed out quickly.'

'If I can get to the body before it's taken back to America, I can give you a much better opinion but it would be in the Coroner's report,' said Doctor Brown.

'Which we know is missing,' said Hunt with a wry smile.

'I'm willing to do an examination if we can get at the body. But, if you don't mind me saying this to you, you've got to deal with the problem of some rotten apples potentially high up in the force. It may have occurred to you, Tom, that it may go even higher. However, if I'm to help you, I need to look at the characteristics of the wound and its location, the body position and so forth. There is only so much blood in the body. If the wound pierced an artery or was made in the abdomen area near the aorta the person would lose blood rapidly. It depends what the knife probed. Whoever did the stabbing, knew how to do it to bring death quickly, by the sound of it. There are areas where there is just soft tissue and there would only be a little blood. If the butcher that you've interviewed is right its likely there would have been great loss of blood and death could have been rapid. It's been done before the body fell from the carriage though, of that I'm certain,' said Doctor Brown.

'So, he's been put in the carriage while wounded, possibly, or he's been on a journey and someone has got in and stabbed him some time before he got to Whitechapel,' said Sam, still ashen faced.

'Right,' said Hunt, with a wry smile at Sam. 'Or the person travelling with him was trusted and proved false. My monies on the character in the unidentified Police uniform. Perhaps the person changed in the carriage after the stabbing?'

'Maybe threw his blood-stained clothes from the window on the route?' said Sam

'Should we look at routes from Berringer's home to Whitechapel, sir? Perhaps there are areas more conducive than others to disposing of blood-stained clothing?' asked Morris.

'Can we get at rotas, duties, who accompanied him when he went out?' asked Sam.

'Good, this is all good, Morris get onto your idea, Sam you and I will look at what can be done at obtaining details of rotas, together, but we have to acknowledge that the person with him was probably not a Metropolitan Policeman, could have been an American, or an English civilian,' said Hunt, his face looking energised.

'Hang on, if you're talking about a lot of blood it's not likely that the person doing the stabbing would escape having blood on the face, hands or clothing. So, that un-numbered policeman wouldn't fit, would he, because Mr Able would have seen the blood. And where's the carriage gone?' asked Jack. The others looked at him.

'We don't know, good point,' said Morris.

'If you'll excuse me, Inspector, I can make some enquiries. Being a diplomat would imply he would have use of a carriage with the house the American Legation and Consulate placed him and the family in. I think, as we have the address, I can pay a visit before four o'clock if I go now,' Ted got up and, after receiving a nod from Hunt, started to leave the room. Doctor Brown called to him as Ted opened the door to leave.

'If you do find the carriage, and if the stab wound hit an artery the blood would spout like a fountain,' said the doctor, 'If you can get to look inside it you'll find evidence you won't be able to avoid. Jack's right, the killer wouldn't escape being splattered.'

'Right, good, this is excellent. We need to get you into the mortuary. Morris, can you check who's managing the body?' said Hunt.

'I understand, Inspector, that a couple of visiting American Professors are over assisting with refrigeration techniques, as a result of the Berringer death. Doctor Brown could express interest and go along to see what they're doing. We could get him in tomorrow that way, it will be too late today,' suggested Morris.

'I'll need enough time to look at the body. Can you find out for me the names of the Professors and I can ensure I see them. The work is interesting, I can get them talking on a professional basis about the techniques that they are using and suggest that I see the corpse. Gruesome, gentlemen, but if the full Coroner's report is not available now we need to establish detail,' said the Doctor.

'I'll leave that with Morris and yourself, Doctor. With the body of the Faceless Woman, the Coroner still hasn't released it. Getting access to it is easier at present, and I understand you've been involved in the post-mortem,' said Hunt.

'Yes, but if I may I'd like to suggest calling in an expert on Toxicology that would be immensely helpful to me,' said Doctor Brown.

'Of course,' said Hunt, 'Who did you have in mind?'

'Ann Black, she has a degree from a Paris medical school. She's reliable and discreet,' said Doctor Brown.

'And lives in Inspector Doyle's house,' said Jack, looking at Sam.

'True, she's a good friend of Emily Doyle's, but can be relied upon to be discreet. I've had some occasions to meet her in the St Mary's Dispensary earlier this year. I think she'll qualify as a Doctor one day, we just need to change the law,' said Doctor Brown, with a brief smile.

'I can ask her if you like, tonight. We had a bit of a chat yesterday about the problems for her becoming a doctor so it would be a good way to lead in. If I can get her and her husband on their own I can ask her to contact you, Doctor?' said Jack.

'Yes, do.'

'Right so we're on the ball now with the Berringer murder but what can we hope for in terms of identifying who the woman is, given her face was obviously worked over by some bastard to make her unrecognisable?' asked Morris.

'We need scientific evidence that's sufficient to shift a jury's position. We need it clear and strong to cancel any opposition's evidence. Or we need a confession! The burden of proof will be on the prosecution, so it's down to us and a clever barrister. At the moment, all we've got is a hypothesis, which, frankly, is based on the fact of Mrs Berringer's disappearance, and a smell to the case,' said Hunt.

'Le Nez,' said Jack, thinking aloud about Tom Hunt's reputation. Hunt smirked at the nick-name. He looked from Jack to Sam. Again, he thought about which one he would want to have his back in a fight.

'And none of that will be enough before a court. This has to be firm evidence,' said Hunt.

'Identifying marks on the body, and so on. Teeth present might help if the Americans have got records. This couple were rich people, they would have ensured they had attention when they needed it, for their health generally. Not much work has been done on teeth helping us to identify a person, only on bite marks and matching them to teeth. It's worth exploring how advanced the American forensics are though. I know we're still lacking skills in using teeth as part of establishing who a dead person may be. No one has been bitten as far as we know, but I would advise when you make an arrest just to check arms, hands, in case Mrs Berringer bit her assailant,' said the Doctor.

'Do you think that her face was knocked about before she died then? That she may have struggled?' asked Jack,

'I'm thinking of that newspaper report that you and I discussed on Christmas day, Jack. The landlady mentions a male visitor. She doesn't mention seeing anyone after his visit,' said Doctor Brown. Jack coloured at being singled out on first name terms by the Doctor. He saw Hunt and Morris exchange looks and brief smiles. He was still unsure of being treated as an equal by a man of science and quality. However, his confidence level rose.

'Sir,' Jack said, looking at Hunt, 'Would it be an idea to interview the landlady ourselves about times and dates of that visit and if her lodger had any other visitors?'

'Yes, but it's out of our division.' Hunt looked at Morris, 'Time to bend a few rules perhaps?'

Morris raised an eyebrow, but the moustache twitched in the barest of smiles. 'I think it's more a question of a bit of training for a keen young constable getting used to plain clothes work, sir. Sargent and I could go together but I think he can weave the magic he has on the ladies and lead on the interviewing.'

Hunt nodded, 'Tomorrow. Do an order will you, so the paperwork ties up with his absence tomorrow. We don't want anything drawing attention to what he's doing if he's absent without the correct authority. Can you cover his beat?'

'Phillips could do it on his own,' said Morris.

'Meet Morris at the address given in the article, Sargent,' said Hunt.

'Yes, Inspector.'

Doctor Brown had been watching the interaction. He said, 'It's worth checking, the date of that visit, the article doesn't make it clear to me when the gentleman caller came. The landlady may not have seen Mrs Berringer again, if that was who the woman was. Bite marks have been accepted as evidence, if they match teeth. If we can get the woman's body brought across to the mortuary near Poplar I can go back to pathology and check the teeth that are left and even get impressions. We need a reason to get it brought over though. I can't think of one. Neither can I get into the mortuary where it's being kept. If I can get at her body the other idea is that we can check what state the teeth are in as they survive whereas other parts don't. We are making fast strides now with Forensic science but there is still a lot we can't prove. I know it doesn't help us in this case but in a few years, I believe we will be able to have evidence beyond any doubt as to identity, if we can tie people back to dental records. But, we must work with what we've got on this case, which at this point isn't much. You two going and establishing the date and time of that call will be invaluable.'

'Amazing the pace of change,' said Jack, 'But it's only the rich that will see a dentist.'

'Then that's another thing we must change, Jack,' said Doctor Brown, he smiled and continued, 'Oh, this isn't actually new. Using teeth and individual characteristics to identify a dead body goes back as far as sixty-six A.D.,' said the Doctor.

Jack looked dubious. Doctor Brown looked around the room and realised he was the only one present with a classical education. He smiled.

'I'm sorry, let me explain. A Roman Emperor called Claudius married a woman called Agrippina. A bit of a nasty piece of work, but they were well matched. She was a little worried about her position so decided to have a potential rival killed. A woman called Lollia Paulina. So, a soldier was duly told to kill the rival. As with those times, Agrippina wanted proof that her rival had been killed. The soldier was to bring back Lollia's head and Agrinppina used the dental alignments and particular characteristics of the head, to satisfy herself that her rival was indeed dead. Obviously, the teeth need to be quite distinctive.'

'Good grief,' said Sam.

'It maybe we can get hold of whoever did dentistry for the Berringer's in America, sir, when that "Tec" arrives in a few days. I was thinking about the Squire at home,' Jack paused, staring at Hunt.

'Go on,' said Hunt.

'He lost some teeth in a riding accident and had some dentures made. He only wore them out in public, and didn't bother when he visited the farm or rode to hounds. If the Faceless Woman had lost any teeth and had dentures made there would be a record wouldn't there. Perhaps when the detective comes from …….' Hunt interrupted Jack.

'Oh, I don't think we need to trouble him with this. I'll get access to Berringer's Secretary tomorrow. I'm sure he'll have details of who their doctor and dentist were in America. A telegram will suffice then to the dentist used. I'm sure we can get at records if they did have a dentist. Good work, Jack,' said Hunt, his face had become animated.

'There was a case in Scotland, actually, of dental evidence being used in court about dentures. It's an old case, early nineteenth century, what was the name of the woman? Mc something, I'll check when I get home,' said Doctor Brown.

'Excellent work, gentlemen, this afternoon. I suggest we call it a day now. Thank-you Doctor, for your time. Sargent, get back across the river now and link up with Sergeant Morris tomorrow morning at ten at Golden Square. You'll need to check how to get there,' Hunt stood and the others followed suit. He shook hands with Doctor Brown, and nodded at Jack, briefly as the young Constable stood up. Morris sat down again after shaking the doctor's hand. Jack followed the doctor out of the room, looking back to see Hunt suck in air through his teeth, as he fixed his eyes on Sam and said, 'Curzon, remain please with Morris and I.'

'Sir,' said Sam and the door closed on the scene.

*

The trip back across the Thames was choppy as a wind had got up with the tide flowing in. The rain became heavier and the surface of the Thames was pockmarked. Night was closing in and from the east darker clouds moved across the sky like a curtain. The Thames bent round the land as if the river was hungry to take it back. Much of the industry was down by the river now but the banker's failure in '66 had left local businesses in an exposed position. Many of the firms had failed as they had borrowed heavily. Jack had been told that only nine thousand were involved in the ship building now whereas before the collapse it had been as many as twenty-seven thousand. The glass works kept going though, and the Blackwall Railway Company had acquired the rights to Potter's ferry. Rumours abounded that prosperity was on the way back for the docks. Personally, he could not see it. All the building was starting in Bow and that was the area to go for a house.

Jack braced himself on deck, and held on to the back of a seat as the cold, salty wind cut under his helmet and stung his ears. He had managed to see Charlie Banks as he had left the station at New Road, coming up the steps with a young boot black that he had arrested for refusing to give change for a sixpence.

'I'll just lose him 'ere with the Sergeant, if you 'ang on,' Charlie had said. He was back onto the steps five minutes later and he and Jack shook hands, and wished each other a Happy New Year.

'That's 'im sorted for the night,' said Charlie.

'Charlie, you've not arrested the lad,' said Jack, looking concerned.

''E's off the street for the night. The Sergeant will give his ear a clip before morning and let 'im out.'

'He could be imprisoned!'

'There'll be no court for 'im, but he won't short change anyone again. Nobody is going to miss 'im tonight.'

'Who's he in with?' asked Jack, looking flabbergasted.

'No one, the Sergeant's put 'im in the back room.'

Jack asked how things were going and Charlie confessed, in his Macclesfield accent that he was bored. Charlie confided he had decided to go home and they parted promising to raise a glass to each other on different sides of the Thames on New Year's Eve. Jack realised that they would probably never meet again. Two policemen from different areas. Jack did not expect to go north, nor was Charlie likely to see Sussex, but both understood what it was like to speak in a dialect, and from that an affinity had grown up in the few weeks they had worked together. Jack started to wonder if he would ever again see the other man he had joined the police with, Sam Curzon. He thought on what Sam's fate would be by the end of the day.

Reflecting did him no good, he decided, and he jerked himself out of the mood. Looking around the deck of the boat as it crossed to the jetty on the Isle of Dogs, he was conscious his duty was always to prevent crime, and that he should wake himself up.

He glanced at the Millwall junction station clock. It was already dusk at four o'clock. The darkest day had gone, it would start to get lighter by the end of January. He wondered if he would see less rain in1873.

Ted Phillips had told him he could pick up some hot stew at the side of the station. Where the place was, he could not see at first, but his nose started to pick up the rich smell of onions and gravy. It was only one room with a common table, and a policeman entering was bad for business. The seamen cleared their plates and left and Jack shrugged at the woman behind the counter.

'Sorry,' he said.

'They're inclined to stay too long, anyway. A plate for you?' she asked, good naturedly, drawing the blind at the window and locking the door to show that she was now closed. 'I've no objection to a Constable coming in at the end of the day, just won't be too keen at the beginning if you clear the room!'

Jack laughed, and sat by the fire, putting his helmet on the table. He breathed in the aromas from the stew, felt the texture of the bread and decided Ted was right. This place was now on his regular route if he came over from New Road. There had been no lunch for him that day, which meant seconds. He knew there would be dinner waiting, and reckoned that he could polish that off as well.

'What do you for breakfast?'

'Anything that takes my fancy,' said the woman.

'Marvellous,' Jack said, as he paid and left.

At Arbour Square Jack knocked on the Black's sitting room door. He heard George call, 'Just a minute,' and the door opened and Jack could see that George was on his own. He felt relieved that it was this way round and he was spared the social gaff of seeing Ann alone.

'I've got a message for Ann from Doctor Brown, the Police Surgeon. He would value her involvement in a case if she could contact him tomorrow,' said Jack.

'That's good,' said George. 'I met him at a lecture, on the tracing of arsenic in the Cotton case. It sounds conclusive, I must say. The woman will hang no doubt. What is it that he wants to see Ann about, did he say?'

'I think it's her knowledge on toxicology. He'd like her opinion on a case. If she can get in touch with him he'll provide the details. I'm just passing on the message.'

'She's good on arsenic, if that's what he's after.'

Jack laughed, 'I hope that's not what it sounds like,' he said. 'See you at dinner, George.'

*

The morning found that Sam had not come home last night, and Jack had knocked on his colleague's bedroom door before he went down the stairs to see if anyone was in there. Turning the handle, he stuck his head around the door, but the bed had not been slept in and he feared the worst.

In plain clothes, ready for the Golden Square interview, Jack went down to Hannah's kitchen, to leave by from below stairs. He knocked, and stuck his head around the door.

'Good,' he said, after seeing her face remain normal. She was no longer reacting to him using her kitchen as an exit at times. 'You don't look at me at like a scared rabbit, any more.'

'Nothing to be scared of, is there. You're out on duty again in your civvies, are you?' asked Hannah.

'That's right. Any chance of some bread and bacon to keep body and soul together?'

'It's all upstairs, I can get you some from the sideboard,' Hannah offered.

'Who's in?' asked Jack.

'Just the Missus.'

'No, it's alright,' said Jack, remembering Sam's fears, 'I'll get something on the way. Hannah, did Constable Curzon come back last night?'

'No, sir,' said Hannah, giving him a meaningful look, 'No message, neither.'

'Odd,' said Jack.

'Very odd,' said Hannah. They looked at each other. 'P'raps he's dead?' she added, with a grim look.

Jack looked back and made himself grin, 'No, just out on a job, that went on longer than expected. I'll see him later. I'll take some of that bread if it's fresh, though.'

'Always fresh in the mornings. Here,' Hannah said as she smeared butter on it and wrapped it in a paper bag. Jack stuffed it his jacket pocket, gave her a grin, which was answered by her with a firm nod, and he left through the kitchen door, climbing the steps up to the side of the house and making sure that no one was looking through the front room windows before he turned onto the street.

*

Ten

Jack left the omnibus, swinging from the pole on the rear platform to jump down. Morris had caught the tram from Camberwell to Westminster and walked to Golden Square, and they met at the statue of King George the second.

'First time round here, I suppose?' asked Morris.

'First time west of the City,' said Jack, looking around. 'It's gone down by the looks of it.'

'Oh, yes. You'd have to go back some time to have seen the area in its grander state. It used to be the centre of the ambassadorial district a hundred years ago. Now most of the properties are let as lodgings to gentlemen or boarders.'

They walked into the square and Jack looked up at the sky. 'I feel like I'll never see the sun again, this month,' said Jack.

'It's a wet one, alright. Wettest one I remember,' said Morris.

'I'm sure I've counted over twenty days of rain this month. Here we are, number five. Sergeant, before we go in, Sam didn't come back to Arbour Square, last night. I checked his room before I left as I couldn't get an answer when I knocked on the door. His bed hadn't been slept in. I thought I'd better mention it given the state he was in yesterday in the meeting,' said Jack.

'No, that's alright. He's staying with me for a while. Nothing for you to worry about but keep his whereabouts to yourself, will you. Inspector Hunt and I thought it was for the best. He's likely to blow our cover we think and put himself in a difficult position. The Doyles will be told he's been transferred.'

Jack stared at him, dumbstruck, but Morris was rapping on the door of number five.

The door was opened by a woman of about fifty years of age wearing a shawl across her shoulders and wiping her hands on her apron. Morris explained their visit and reluctantly the landlady, Mrs Pope, allowed them across her front doorstep.

Mrs Pope explained that she let rooms, and the one occupied by the lady known as Mrs Timkins, or the Faceless Woman as the paper had dubbed her, had been one of her more expensive ones as it overlooked the square.

'She was a nice woman, as far as one could tell. I'd understood she was going on somewhere and would only need the room for a short time. Such a shock I can tell you when I found her,' said Mrs Pope.

Morris had taken a back seat once they were in and was letting Jack 'weave his magic with the landlady.'

'If you got the idea the room was being taken for a short time what exactly had the lady said to you?' asked Jack, gently. Mrs Pope ran her tongue over her bottom lip, staring out of the window while she gave the question some thought.

'I think she said it was while the arrangements were being made. Yes, that's right, the booking was being made, that's what she said. Then when the man called… I mentioned him in my statement, lower order type, not her class of man, in my opinion, she said something to him when she joined him in the parlour. I don't hold with ladies seeing men in their rooms, so I always make the parlour available. I'm trying to recall exactly what it was that she said, but it gave me the impression there was a journey to be done. Oh, what was it?'

'Why did you think the man wasn't her class?' asked Jack.

'Oh, the clothing, the cut of his suit, the way he spoke. Reminded me of one of the newspaper types, reeking of smoke, and beer, or some of the 'tecs you get around here. Not like you two gentlemen you are. A good position in the police I should think, I can tell that by your suits and your manners, but not him. No, the lady had a bearing, regardless of taking lodgings, a way of holding her head, speaking, and, although the clothes were simple, they were quality. You can't hide quality. It comes out in the manners too,' Mrs Pope nodded.

One again, Jack was grateful for Inspector's Hunt's eye with the clothes he had sent to him, vowing to try and emulate the style in future if they communicated good taste.

'Could you describe the man? Height, facial hair, that sort of thing, maybe accent?' asked Jack.

'Bit taller than you, most man have a moustache don't they, it needed trimming I remember. Oh yes, and a crumpled look about the suit, bowler hat but it's the fashion isn't it, well-used boots…sign he was on his feet a lot and covered some miles as they were quite dusty. I noticed, see, and said to him, when I let him in, to wipe his boots well. I would say as regards accent? East end I think.'

'Must have been a terrible shock for you when you found the body,' said Morris, while Jack made some notes.

'Very odd really, as the face was covered. There being a file with a label on it, "strychnine" was like something out of a story. Why would you label it? And the note about not wanting to cause trouble, and a simple burial. Not like her hand either, the writing when she signed was educated. The note wasn't written by her. None of it made sense to me,' said Mrs Pope.

'You didn't think it was suicide then?' asked Morris.

'Well I didn't believe it. It didn't fit. The writing wasn't the same, so there was that. I can show you the receipt she signed. She wrote a note on it for me about laundry. I think, as well, at the back of my mind was that niggle as I'd heard her say about arrangements being made and she clearly thought when the man had come that he was going to give her information. What was it that she said to him when she walked into the parlour? It'll come to me,' said Mrs Pope. She got up and went to an old mahogany bureau with a drop drown lid. In a recess was a series of receipt books stacked on top of each other. The Landlady picked up the top one and opened it to a few pages from the end of the book. 'Here,' she said, walking across to Morris. 'There's the note on her receipt that she wrote about the laundry. The writing is a fine style isn't it. Educated woman, you see, a refined hand.'

'You didn't hand this in, then,' said Morris, passing the receipt book across to Jack.

'Never thought about it. The police took the note she was supposed to have written that was by the body. I said at the time I didn't think it was written by her but no one listened. This would prove it, wouldn't it?'

'Yes, it would. Well done, it's a key piece of evidence. Now, I should take it with us so I will have to remove it from your book. If you remember what the lady said to the visitor get a message to me,' said Morris, tearing a sheet of paper out of his own notebook and scribbling a name and an address on it. He passed it to the landlady.

'What address did you give her, Sergeant?' asked Jack when they were back out into the square.

'A mate at Great Marlborough Street Station, he'll cover for us. If she remembers anything more and sends it on to him it will reach me. Now a little bird tells me you like oysters, so there's somewhere you should see, before we go back to New Road. Scott's Oyster Rooms are not too far,' said Morris.

'How do you know this area,' Jack asked Morris, after a dozen oysters had gone down.

'I worked for a while, up to 1865, at Great Marlborough Street Police Station. You get to know the good places to eat. The areas changing now and I think Scott's will move soon.'

'Why did you move out?' asked Jack.

'Family, promotion. The chance of a Sergeant's pay. And a lot has happened about transport in the last five years, linking things up, but it wouldn't have been easy with the shift pattern to stay around here with a young family. Things are better for the children where we are now in Camberwell Green,' Morris said.

'Sergeant, can I ask what's happening with Sam?' said Jack.

'Special duties,' said Morris.

'Leman Street or New Road?' asked Jack having made a decision to be blunt.

'We're all posted to Leman Street at the moment, lad. You and I are out and about, so is Sam. Sam's doing what he's good at. That's all you need to know, at present, just as he doesn't know what you and I are up to today. Safer that way,' said Morris. 'Finished? Let's get going then.'

'The man Mrs Pope described could be anyone,' said Jack as they walked up the Haymarket. 'What role was he playing, do you think?'

'Who knows. Sound like he was a delivery boy to me, even if it was only a message. She was expecting word to be brought to her from what Mrs Pope overheard. She knew he was bringing her. East end accent, she said. Hardly narrows it down, does it,' said Morris.

'She was clearly expecting him, though, if she mentioned arrangements,' said Jack.

'Good point. More likely to be a messenger from someone than the actual person she was going off with, if what Mrs Pope says about her being quality is true,' said Morris.

They walked in silence, Jack taking in the surroundings.

'I was thinking of going back to the pub I ate in on the first night I came across the river, see if I could find anything out about the detective that spoke to me in the Mason's Arms,' said Jack.

'Just watch yourself if you do, time to get back I think. I'll walk you down Whitehall towards the tram stop for Camberwell, so that you see the area,' said Morris. 'What's on your mind about the detective?'

'Not sure, just the behaviour, as if he owned the patch. I'd like to check him out, with rogue policemen around,' said Jack. He paused and froze as a scene played out that he both could not believe but also which needed evasive action. Morris looked at him and then followed the line of sight. It all took no more than five seconds as Jack gave Morris a shove to the right and dived himself as a cab veered off the road straight for them. It was a gloomy day and possible that the cabby had not seen them clearly, but there were screams, and the horse reared up. Jack rolled away from the hooves as they came down, feeling like the oysters were not going to stay down. The cab was lurching off, rocking, down the road and the horse seemed out of control. People were gathering around Morris to see if he was alright. Jack had torn his jacket sleeve and there was blood on the shirt from a graze on his arm. Bits of the dirt and gravel from the road were stuck into the graze and he felt sick.

'Are you alright,' a man asked him.

'I think so,' said Jack, getting up.

Morris was sitting up, holding his arm. 'Is my friend hurt?' asked Jack, starting walk over.

'Don't know,' the man said. Jack steadied himself against a lamp post, and nodded his thanks to the man who had helped him up. He went over to Morris who was still holding his arm.

'I can't straighten it. It may be broken. I landed on the elbow. I think we'd better get across into Great Marlborough Street Station and see my friend. They can get us the surgeon and we'd better report the cab. Did anyone see the number?' asked Morris. Jack was struck with his presence of mind but noted his face was draining of colour.

'Seventy-five, seventy-five, I'm pretty sure that was the number on the licence plate,' said one of the people who had stopped to help them. A man flagged down a cab for them and Jack and Morris rode to Great Marlborough Street Police Station. Morris's contact turned out to be a Desk Sergeant called Gill. The Police Surgeon was on site and Morris's arm was set in a splint and strapped up. He had not been able to straighten it. Jack's bleeding was stopped and cleaned and his arm bandaged. He regretted the tear in his jacket more than anything that had happened to himself. Sergeant Gill got a cable off straight away to New Road for Inspector Hunt.

'I was going to let you know that the Golden Square killing was being looked into and that you might get a contact from the landlady, Mrs Pope, from number five, if she recalls information on a suspect,' Morris told Gill.

'What you doing looking into that, it's not your manor?' said Gill.

'Just a special duty,' said Morris with a wan smile.

'You and Hunt again? He'll get you killed one of these days,' said Gill.

'Not with the Constable here, around,' grinned Morris, flinching from the jerk as the doctor tore the end of the bandage up the middle to knot the two ends together.

'Sorry, Sergeant,' said Jack. He ran the scene again over in his mind, with the cab coming at them and the horse starting to rear, while the cab rocked wildly on its wheels. The face of the cabbie was familiar, but he could not remember why. Then he had it. The cab had been parked when they arrived at number five Golden Square. The number of the cab plate had registered as it was the same one he had seen as he had come out of the Mason's Arms, on the Commercial Road. It had lurched towards him then and he had just avoided being hit by the vehicle before the driver had peered over his shoulder and stared at Jack. The horse had seemed out of control then too. Was it the same man? He pulled up a stool and sat down next to Morris, speaking very quietly.

'Look, Sergeant, I saw the cab earlier today, before we went into number five. It was parked at the side of the square. It's not the first time I've seen it either. I remember the number on the Commercial Road and I think it may be the same cabbie, but not too sure on that. I avoided being hit after I came out of the Mason's Arms as it lurched past then. There was a fight that broke out with a couple of men across the road and I was distracted by that but the driver might be the same person. He did glance at me then as he went by, that first time, a look over his shoulder but I only saw him sideways on then. This time I got a full view of his face. The number of the cab was the same, four numbers, seventy-five, seventy-five, and I think the horse was the same.'

Morris put his head back and Jack notice how grey he looked. 'Right, lad, well done. Check the licence if you have the number. Let's hope it is actually licensed and not a rogue. There's thousands of them otherwise. You think this wasn't an accident, then. Do you think you were followed that night, as well?'

'I don't know, I can't see why I would have been, unless someone already knew about the team being set up. But Hunt hadn't briefed us by then, so how could anyone have known anything? I didn't even read the article about the Faceless Woman until that evening,' said Jack.

'Where did you read it?' asked Morris

'In the Mason's Arms,' said Jack. 'No one saw it though, the 'tec did sit down as I was reading, but I'm pretty sure I got it away before he would have seen anything. Sorry, if something was seen, Sergeant.'

'You wouldn't know, nor would you be expecting anything at that point. Still, this is something to chalk up to experience. We'd better get back across the river,' said Morris.

Sergeant Gill gripped Morris by his good elbow to help him up. Once he'd got him standing Gill said, 'You're going back in a cab and straight home, mate, surgeon's orders. This young lad can go back to New Road without you.' Gill looked over his shoulder at Jack and said, 'Get him home first, will you and then go on back to the station. You can track the cabby down via the licensing authority and get him in for questioning. Someone's aimed for you both, I've no doubt.'

Once on their way from Great Marlborough Street Morris put his head back, bracing himself at the jolting of the cab. The cab had rubber tyres so the journey was not as bad as it might have been. As the driver started to cross Westminster Bridge, Jack peered up the river towards St. Paul's. 'I could get used to this,' he said as an attempt to lighten the situation but Morris grimaced with the jolting of the vehicle.

'Listen, Jack, careful with what you say in front of Mrs Morris. No need to upset her, just play it down a bit and I'd rather you didn't mention the cab coming at us. She gets a bit nervous when I go out with Hunt.'

'Happened before, has it?' Jack asked. 'Don't worry, I'll help keep the peace,' he grinned at the thought of the big burly Sergeant being more worried about his wife's reaction than at the thought that a cab could have killed him.

'When you get the licence details, get the address of the owner as well as the cabbie. Don't go around on your own, and check in with Hunt before you do anything. You don't know yet what you're going into,' said Morris.

'Perhaps they're just giving us a message, whoever "they" are,' said Jack as they pulled up outside Morris's home. The cab waited while Jack got him into the bedroom with Mrs Morris rushing ahead to turn back the eiderdown. The poor woman had turned white as she opened the door, and Jack explained briefly they'd been involved in a road accident while on duty. She took in his words and Jack thought the woman was no fool and did not believe the carefully crafted story he was spinning.

'Thank-you for bringing him straight home,' said Mrs Morris as she opened the front door to let Jack out

'Surgeon's orders,' Jack smiled.

'Usually he tries to hide at the station when these things happen. Did the doctor say how long this would be?'

'No, Mrs Morris, I can ask the station to send the Police Surgeon to you. All I know is that the elbow has a break,' said Jack as he took his leave and got back into the cab which took him straight to the police station in New Road.

Inspector Hunt was sitting behind his desk as Jack walked in. He assessed the torn sleeve to Jack's jacket and the way he was wearing it slung over the left shoulder so that the arm was free of restriction. The bandage showed under the rolled-up shirt sleeve. The telegram from Sergeant Gill was face up on the desk.

'What the hell happened?' asked Hunt.

'We were followed by a cab and then it came at us down the Haymarket. Sergeant Morris has a broken elbow so he'll be off for a bit. I've just delivered him home in a cab to his wife, who doesn't look too pleased. Strong woman, though, held how she was feeling in. I got the impression she was used to this sort of thing.' Jack grinned and added, 'especially when he works with you Inspector. He's been bandaged up by the

Surgeon at Great Marlborough Street and the arm has been set. Sergeant Gill saw us.' Jack paused as Hunt nodded. 'I told Mrs Morris that I'd ask our Police Surgeon here to visit,' Jack said and Hunt again nodded.

'Did you get the interview done or did this happen before?' Hunt asked.

'We'd left Golden Square and enjoyed lunch at Scott's in the Haymarket. Sam must have told the Sergeant I liked oysters. The cab tracked us as I saw it parked when we got to Golden Square. I'd seen it before on the Commercial Road the night I went across the river and had only just avoided being hit by it then. I'm afraid the Sergeant's broken elbow is down to me pushing him out of the way,' said Jack, sheepishly.

'He maybe dead if you hadn't,' said Hunt. 'So, it's tried before then.'

'We don't know that, sir,' said Jack.

'I think we can assume that it was trying to run you down. It's too much of a coincidence. Did you get the licence number then?' asked Hunt.

Jack nodded. 'Yes, and I think I could describe the driver.'

'Get onto it then with the Duty Sergeant. Did anything come out of the interview at Golden Square?' asked Hunt.

'How would someone have known that night that I need dealing with?' asked Jack persevering to try and understand the level of information that was leaking.

'The order was up for the team here to go to Leman Street. Someone was monitoring. You were probably followed that night as you left here. Didn't you tell me that you met a detective in the public house that you went into?' Hunt turned to a cupboard and fished for a register of the divisions. He flicked through the pages, looking for something specific while he asked the question.

'Yes, a man sat down with me while I was finishing a meal. The barmaid called him a 'tec. Oh, sir, I forgot to get the piece of evidence off Sergeant Morris from the interview at five Golden Square. The landlady, Mrs Pope had kept a receipt with a written instruction from the lodger, the Faceless Woman, which she said proved that the suicide note was written by someone else other than the dead woman.'

'Excellent. So, we have evidence. Sounds like a breakthrough. Alright, Jack, don't worry, I'll have to go and make peace with Francis Morris anyway, for the state her husband is in, and I want to have a look at the Sergeant as well, so I'll pick it up. I'll sort the Police Surgeon out. Looks like your jacket needs some work on it. There's a Taylor on New Road. How's your arm now?' asked Hunt.

'Just grazed, sir.'

'Here's the list of staff at Shadwell police station,' said Hunt, as he pushed the register across the desk towards Jack.

The Taylor on New Road promised to have a repair done for Jack before the end of the day. Jack went back into the station and searched for the list of licences granted to owners of carriages, and the cabmen that year, as the fee was now being paid to the Metropolitan Police.

The owner was traced to an office on the north side of the river near Limehouse and he owned a whole fleet of cabs with drivers paying a rental per week.

Hunt called him in as he walked past the Inspector's office. Jack agreed with Hunt that he would call at the cab office in the morning.

'I think we need to establish who this detective is that you met the other night. Don't go doing checks alone, get Phillips in on the interviews with both the cab owner and the detective. Anyone at that public house you could question?' asked Hunt.

'The Mason's Arms? Yes, there was a barmaid. There are a couple of other places, Ted knows one of them quite well, just the other side of the river. One I've been to in uniform, but the other I was in plain clothes when I went in,' said Jack.

'Keep it consistent, as it's how the people will know you. Alright, Jack, get off across the river. I'll call in and see Morris later, and I'll brief Ted Phillips about tomorrow. You're technically back on your beat in the morning but I can extend the duties today.'

'Sir, where's Sam Curzon gone?' Jack asked, as he turned to go.

Hunt looked at him, surprised, and thought about the response for a few moments. 'He's at Windsor, masquerading as a Waterman. He'll work there and keep his nose to the ground and get feedback to me on anything he finds. Keep that to yourself. As far as Inspector and Mrs Doyle are concerned he's been transferred back here.'

'So, he isn't sacked, then?' Jack said, with a grin.

'Why would you think that?' asked Hunt understandably offended.

'I thought he was in for a disciplinary,' said Jack.

'Sam sees things in black and white, with no middle ground. We're right or wrong as far as he's concerned and he'll go down fighting for the right, that one. It's about staying safe at present as we're close, but not close enough. You and Morris have come across a major piece of evidence in a case that we have seen very little detail on to point us in the right direction. Sam challenging people won't help at this point but he's got a good instinct. I don't discipline a man for his honesty,' said Hunt.

'And the connection with the name Moore?' asked Jack.

'We have yet to see,' said Hunt.

*

Jack collected his jacket and thought about trying to see Harriet while he was on the south side of the river. He was tempted, but ultimately shook off the desire to go across to the house where she worked in case he was being followed.

It was for her safety, and the characters he was tracking, although still unknown to him, must have known sufficient about him from the first night across the river to attempt an accident with a cab. New Year's Day was two days away and he would see her then, but he would have to keep a careful eye open. It affected his train of thought that she may be affected just by him calling at the place at which she worked. 'Stay away,' he said to himself, as he swung his arms into his jacket.

*

Jack had crossed the river and picked up the train running from Millwall junction to Blackwall. He would have to give the place at the side of Millwall station a miss today, despite the Hot Pot that he could smell as he walked past. Ted and he could visit tomorrow when he would be in uniform. Keep things as the informant expects rather than muddying the waters by appearing in plain clothes when they've seen a uniformed police constable. He wasn't sure he could stomach food just at that point anyway after the accident.

He swung himself up onto the train and rode until Blackwall. There he disembarked to walk towards Poplar, against the tide of people finishing a shift, to the place with a room off the street to see if the girl he had already established as an informer was in today. The stench of the docks and rotting fish hit him again as it had before.

The girl saw him coming up to the door, and wiped a table in readiness. Jack nodded a hello and pulled out a chair. The room was not empty as it had been before Christmas but a mug of tea was brought and sufficient sugar to sink a ship. He put a half a crown down on the table and rested his bowler hat over it. It was a sufficient movement for the girl to have seen. Jack would bide his time as the tea was hot and he still felt slightly nauseous following the accident.

Slowly the room emptied and he took out his pocket book and added another half a crown to the coin already under the bowler. Five shillings this time would indicate the seriousness of his enquiry.

'How was your Christmas?' asked Jack.

'Busy, and your day?' the girl responded.

'I was working, like you. There's two people I'm keeping a look out for. One is a cabbie, drives a cab with the numbers seventy-five, seventy-five on the licence plate, dark haired man. Would you know any cabs round here and areas where they would park?' asked Jack.

'They're on the road, at times when the bosses come. Bit earlier than this time of the day and by nine o'clock in the morning. I can have a look. So, two people you're after today? That why there's two coins then?'

'Seems only fair. The other is a detective, possibly operating out of Shadwell. Likes the Mason's Arms on the Commercial Road. I wonder if you ever see any detectives from over there around here?' Jack removed the bowler hat, and she scooped the coins up in a deft wipe of her cloth. He wondered if anyone else had spotted her speed when it came to money.

'I can see. I'd be expectin' you back tomorrow as I'm not in on New Year's Day. Come when we're empty like this. The boss's gone by five. Either this time of the day or early like you were the other day. Any other time it's hard to talk.' The girl walked towards the door and turned the sign to "closed." Jack got up and took a sip of the bitter liquid. He nodded, put his bowler hat on and left.

He was dressed in the wrong clothes and needed to be in his labourer's clothes to visit the Mason's Arms. Half of him wanted to move the enquiry along, take the risk, but sense prevailed for a change of clothes first. He boarded the train and rode back on the Blackwall railway as far as Stepney Railway Station where he left the train to wend its way to Shadwell. Jack walked up the Commercial Road, turning into Arbour Street East first and walking towards Arbour Square. He shocked Hannah by entering, this time, through the kitchen. She froze in pummelling the pastry, her long face becoming longer but met his grin as he passed by the kitchen table with a serious, 'Evenin' sir.'

Jack was up the back stairs and into his room, pulling his labourer's clothes and old boots from the shelf at the top of the wardrobe. Then he was changed, and went down the back stairs into the kitchen. Hannah froze again as he had come back, but remembered to speak as Jack stopped in front of her, holding out his shirt.

'Will you be in for dinner tonight, sir,' she asked, her eyebrows disappearing towards her hairline as she saw the dirt and blood from his graze on the fabric.

'I will. What are we having?' asked Jack.

'Pork and apple pie and I'm making trimmin' for the top like apple shapes. Meats been cooking all day so just got to slow bake the pastry to keep the shape,' said Hannah, ''scuse me but my hands will heat up and ruin the pastry so I have to keep going. Do you mind putting the shirt in the bucket in the corner to soak, overnight? Do you need it for tomorrow?'

'Can you wash and dry it that fast, Hannah?' said Jack, taking a piece of apple from the pile.

'Wait, sir, that's a cooker, take one of these,' and she nodded to a pile or eating apples to her right. 'I can dry it over the range while the pies cook. Out on a job again tomorrow in your plain clothes?' asked Hannah, still working the pastry but she turned her head slightly on one side with a curious look. Jack did a swap with the cooking apple picking up a sweet eating apple instead.

'I am, and I need to look smart. You haven't seen me Hannah, I'll come back in this way.'

'I haven't seen you, sir, I've only eyes for my pastry, but do you mind me askin' sir, do you need help with that arm?' She fixed an unblinking stare on his bandaged arm, her mouth set firmly.

Jack grinned at her, and said, 'No, Hannah, but thank-you.' He left through the kitchen door, pausing only to stick his fingers in a flower bed to dirty his nails.

*

The Mason's Arms on the Commercial Road was teeming with men sitting smoking clay pipes, holding tankards. The barmaid who had told him the first night that her name was Mary, was standing pouring beer behind the bar. She looked up as he came in through the door and smiled a welcome. Jack had wondered if she would remember him but guessed it was the sign of a good barmaid to never forget a customer when they returned. He could understand why it was full of men with that welcome. She had a knack of making a customer feel they were the only one there.

Jack positioned himself by the bar and leant half on it. That way he could look around at who was in and see if the detective was a customer. Six o'clock in the evening and men still spending. The day's wages from the work at the docks would not go far tonight for the family, he thought.

'What can I get you? Hurt your arm?' Mary asked.

'Work accident,' said Jack, smiling to give her the news that he was really keen to see her. 'What time do you get off?' he asked, although had no intention of following up on it if her answer showed interest in him.

'Not 'til late and I'll get the sack if I fraternize with customers, so thanks for asking, but sorry,' answered Mary.

'My loss,' said Jack, 'I'll have the house brew.'

'Bad choice, I'll get you something better,' said Mary, winking. She walked to the end of the bar and pulled a pint. Jack vowed to himself that he would only drink a quarter of it, as he had already attracted attention as someone new from men at the bar. Not allowing his system to be affected by alcohol would be helpful for the work ahead that night if the detective showed up. If not he would sleep better without it. Keeping his hand in his pocket he swigged the liquid, and realised it was cider. He put his money on the bar and Mary scooped it up and served another customer. A few minutes later she was back to chat.

'I didn't think we would be seeing you again, after that 'tec's surly welcome,' Mary said, leaning on the bar. Their faces were quite close, and Jack took a step back.

'He isn't here again, is he?' Playing the nervous type, he glanced around. Mary laughed.

'No, he only comes down when they're on a case. He's up in Shadwell most of the time, just fancies his chances if I'm honest.'

'Him and every man here,' Jack watched the smile play about her lips and thought how easy it would be to drown in them. He hoped she was safe each evening when she walked home. 'Would you know his name so I can avoid him if I hear it,' asked Jack, and he thought she would never fall for that one as it was far too obvious.

'He's Harry Franks, father was from Scotland, the lads in the back have theories about his mother, but I'm not going to repeat those stories,' Mary laughed and Jack joined her.

'You can do better,' said Jack, meaningfully.

'What, with a labourer, with dirt under his nails, like you?' Mary laughed and then moved away to serve another customer. Jack stared into his tankard. A man on his left caught his injured arm and Jack flinched with the pain. The man slapped him on the shoulder and apologized, the worst the wear for drink. Jack braced himself as the pain shot down his arm. He must have jarred it more than he thought when he fell. Mary came back, and looked into his tankard.

'You're not a drinker, are you. I thought you'd have seen sense and gone back to the country. No life around here for a country boy, trying to get work every day, unloading ships. Go and breathe some fresh air. That's what I'm going to do at the end of the year. Off down to Brighton, got a job as a waitress, nice hotel on the front. I'll leave it all behind, the muck, and the stench, and this bunch. Maybe see you there if you go back.' She gave Jack a smile to match his own.

'Who knows, if I don't make my fame and fortune here, I may just see you in Brighton. This stuff's too strong for me,' said Jack and Mary laughed at him. 'That detective, why would he come here if he's in Shadwell? That's up the line, isn't it?'

'He's on a case. He was after old Mary. She'd got twenty-four silver forks on her at lunchtime. Silly old girl had been trying to sell them on to a man in the gas works in James Place. She's got so many aliases and the last time she was locked up it was Franks again who arrested her for trying to sell on a workman's tools. He'd seen her and followed her down here. She gives her age as seventy-four! That's what the 'tec does, he waits for them to come out again after their sentence and then tracks them until he catches them at something new.'

'Well, thanks, for the special brew. I must get home before I spend my rent. Good luck to you in the New Year and take a few deep breathes of sea air for me, and who knows, I may see you in Sussex,' said Jack. He headed for the door, turning once to wave goodbye to Mary.

Out on the pavement, he thought, sensible woman to leave. That was enough for one day, he concluded, unsure if it was the cider or the accident that was starting to give him a headache. He turned right for Arbour Square off the Commercial Road, pleased that he had the name of the detective and that his instinct had been right that the man was operating out of Shadwell. Tomorrow he would go out early back to the Poplar café to see his informant in case she had any news on the cabs. Somehow, he had to work out a better way of changing back into uniform without going home to do so. Too much time was being absorbed. He had to get word to Hunt about the detective and he and Ted would visit the place for lunch tomorrow down at Millwall in case that was a potential source of information. They'd have to visit the cab office too. By morning he and Ted should have the addresses of the owner of the cab business and the driver's whereabouts.

He wondered if Hannah's pie would go be as good as he hoped for dinner.

*

By seven the following morning, he shaved and was surprised how a night's sleep made all the difference to how he looked. By ten o'clock the night before, he had developed dark hollows under the eyes, and his arm and left side had developed stiffness from the fall. He wondered what sort of a night Morris had spent, and if Sam had any findings from Windsor.

Avoiding breakfast at the table would be essential, he decided and opened the bedroom door. On the door knob was a freshly ironed shirt, all grime and blood removed from the previous day. Hannah had been true to her word. There was a brown paper bag which had inside a wrapped sandwich and a slice of apple pie. He picked it up and peeled back a corner of the bag and sniffed and the aroma of the apples made him smile.

Jack went down the back stairs, carrying his uniform in the hope that Hannah would have a solution to his need for a bag. He was in his smart suit, no trace of the tear, thanks to the skill of the Taylor on New Road, and the shirt was as good as new. He pushed open the kitchen door and Hannah's eyes went wide as usual when he came through that way.

'Oh, it's you, sir. Did you find your breakfast?' Hannah asked.

'I did, I have it here. And the shirt as good as new. You are a marvel, Hannah,' said Jack, smiling.

'Excuse me, sir, but what are you carryin'? It looks like a policeman's uniform.'

'Yes, I need a holdall or a case for it. I've got to change into my uniform by the time patrol starts. I can't keep coming back here. Is there an old bag I could borrow, until I can sort something out?' asked Jack.

Hannah's face contorted as she thought about it and Jack could feel the struggle going on inside her about taking a bag that she knew of. Then she shot past him up the back stairs, returning five minutes, or so, later with a carpet bag, slightly out of breath after running up and down five flights of stairs. Jack folded his uniform into it plus his police shirt, and managed his great coat on top. His police boots would not go in so he changed into them and decided that he would just have to go with the way he looked in a pair of police boots and a smart suit.

'Thank-you Hannah, we're a team!'

'That's what the Inspector up-stairs always says,' said Hannah.

'See you later,' said Jack as he opened the kitchen door.

He arrived at Poplar and the wind actually made the area smell fresher that morning. He could see the girl inside and a few customers having a breakfast before their journey started after their night shift. The workers on the new shift had already gone through, so all he had to do was wait patiently for these people to leave for the train.

He heard the girl play around with the door catch and then the kitchen door opened. An older woman appeared from a back room and Jack realised with surprise that the girl was not on her own.

'How would this work?' he asked himself. He had assumed that she would have been on her own, but should have realised that being earlier than he had been the other morning there would need to be someone in to cook food if the girl was serving and clearing tables.

'Morning, sir,' said the older woman.

Jack looked dependable in his office suit. She would take him for a clerk from the dock office near West India Dock station. She went back into the kitchen area and he heard the door close. Jack walked to a free table and sat down.

'Your usual, sir,' said the girl. 'Or would you like to see the list?'

'There's a list?' he said, surprised. In her right hand, she was holding a small sheet of paper.

'Thanks, I'll have a look,' said Jack, pointing to the sheet. The girl handed it to him, and he saw two addresses noted down towards the bottom, underneath a set of choices for breakfast. They were under a heading reading "suppliers." A mug of tea and copious amounts of sugar were placed in front of him. He took out his pocket book and placed another half a crown on the table next to his mug of tea. She thanked him and this time gave him change, which he found confusing.

'You've given more than it costs, sir,' said the girl. 'Hope to see you in the New Year.'

'Thanks,' said Jack, learning that he could be over-generous. He took a slurp and put his bowler hat on top of the list. He hoped he would prove to have as good a slight of hand as the girl when he picked his hat up.

Jack could hear the woman in the kitchen singing, and it was a few seconds later when she stuck her head round the door.

'Any cooked, sir?' she asked.

'Yes, I'll have the sausage,' said Jack. 'Only wrap it for me, will you?'

'Seen anything unusual?' Jack asked the older woman as she brought a brown paper bag containing his order to the table.

'You from the docks office?' asked the woman. The girl froze.

'Yes,' said Jack. 'I wondered whether there's a detective around here at times, goes by the name of Franks. Scruffy looking, beer stained clothing, that sort of type. I could do with having a word on some filching that's going on. I've heard he's got the wrong charge on old Mary who he arrested yesterday. Tell him theft won't hold up, unlawful possession's what he needs to charge her with. A policeman friend told me last night when I mentioned the case to him.' Jack started to stand up, managing to grip the edge of the list with his bowler hat.

'Oh yes, him. He passes up the line regularly, stationed at Shadwell. Shall I give him your name. I should think he'll want to thank you.'

'That's fine, thanks. I'll keep my eyes open for him.' Jack opened the door and turned to wish everyone a Happy New Year.

Now to get to the station and change into his uniform before Sergeant Thick turned up and caught him in civvies on a morning he had to present for parade. He made it to Leman Street with fifteen minutes to spare before Sergeant Thick came on duty.

*

Eleven

'Jack!' said a voice behind him which almost made him jump out of his skin. It was Ted Phillips.

'Blimey, Ted, you gave me a shock.'

'What are you doing dressed like that?' asked Phillips.

'I'm about to change,' said Jack, grinning at him but walking backwards down the corridor.

'You haven't been out on your own, Hunt told you not to go alone after yesterday,' said Ted, with a hint of irritation in his voice.

'I'm alright, I've got some findings. I'll fill you in later. I've just got to change into uniform before Sergeant Thick gets in.' Jack disappeared into the back room with his carpet bag. He opened a couple of drawers in a desk and realised that he would have to take the clothes out of the carpet back in order to store it anywhere until he was to collect it later. He looked around and noticed a small square cupboard in the corner. It would probably do for the carpet bag if it was empty. He stuffed his plain clothes in a drawer as he pulled them off and slipped on his uniform. The carpet bag was pushed into the small cupboard. He was ready.

'I've got an address Ted for the cab office and also the name of the detective I met the first night I came over from Camberwell Green,' said Jack as he picked up his great coat and swung an arm into a sleeve.

'You do? Let's have a look at the map then.' Ted went over to the wall map and Jack joined him. They scanned the roads from the Leman Street Police Station to just north of the Whitechapel Road on the map on the wall.

'The cab office is here in Whitechapel,' said Ted Phillips.

'Good, what's the plan then?'

'After parade, we go along there now, and bring the owner, Brackley, in. Then to the driver, who we now know according to the licence is Cunliffe. Unless he's already done a runner. So, we'll start with the owner. We can get the details about the driver that way and pay the man a visit, but my guess is he'll have a done a vanishing act.'

'Don't we need a warrant?' asked Jack.

'I'm sure there'll be one ready, but I don't have it,' said Ted, evasively. 'We may not need one,' he added, apologetically.

Jack was working the likelihood out of neither the owner, nor the cab driver being around for much longer. 'And if we wait word will get about that we're after the driver and the owner could disappear too?'

'That's right,' said Ted. 'With us asking questions today it will become obvious we're starting to work things out. People will start taking precautions and potentially polish off the evidence in human form, or at least help them disappear.'

'So, we need to act fast and sort out the niceties later. But there will be a warrant?' asked Jack.

'If we actually need one, Jack. The Inspector will make sure of that today. But the magistrate is Mr Newbury and he's a stickler for detail and getting a warrant from him is never quick. If we wait there'll be no one to arrest so you and I are going to the cabbie office now and pray everything will be in place by the time we're back here.' Ted picked up his helmet and they left.

The two men walked past the old Garrick Theatre on Leman Street heading up to the Whitechapel Road and then turned left towards Aldgate. The cab office was tucked behind the Boar's Head Yard. Not the most respectable of areas behind the Whitechapel Road.

'Mr Brackley in?' asked Ted, as he and Jack entered the cab front office. Jack positioned himself just behind the clerk, next to a door he assumed led into another office. Ted stood in front of the clerk's desk.

'I think he's in the back. I'll see if he's free,' said the clerk, looking shocked but starting to get off his stool.

'Don't bother, we'll go through,' said Jack, pushing open the door next to him and letting it swing wide. From the doorway, Jack planted his feet apart and put his hands on his hips so that he filled the entrance into a small office. Inside was crammed a large man behind a desk, ledgers piled to his right, and at a smaller table to his left sat another young clerk. The room was far too small for two people, especially given how much space the large man was taking up. Ted stayed in the front office and spoke to the clerk.

'Mr Brackley? We have some questions for you. Do you have a driver renting a cab from you, name of Cunliffe?' asked Jack.

'Police? What's the problem, Constable? Have we called the police?' Brackley started to stand, but Jack put a hand out to stop him and the man sat back down again. The man looked genuinely shocked.

'It's alright, sir. We're investigating a potential hit and run yesterday in Piccadilly, by one of your drivers. We have the cab number provided by a member of the public and it also fits with a previous reported near miss off the Commercial Road before Christmas. Both incidents involved police personnel and one was injured yesterday.' Jack had taken out his notebook, and turned to a blank page, as if he was reading a report. Brackley looked worried and started to shuffle his papers into neater piles.

'Do you have a warrant to come in, like this? Bursting in as if we're criminals?' Brackley took out a handkerchief from his pocket and started to mop his brow. Jack altered his approach slightly as the mention of the warrant was a potential problem that they did not want to develop. Jack smiled at Mr Brackley.

'It's criminal behaviour we're investigating, sir. We understand you're the owner of many cabs but, unfortunately one of the men licenced to this trade is letting you down. We obviously have to look into it, especially as there have been two reports of the same cab driving out of control.'

'Of course, of course. Very unfortunate. Police personnel you say, oh dear. What's the number?' asked Brackley, reaching for a ledger.

'It's number seventy-five, seventy-five, and we have checked with the license that the driver is a man called Cunliffe.'

Brackley traced his finger down a page. 'Are you sure? The driver retired a month ago. He's not the sort to drive like that anyway. A very experienced man, Cunliffe. His horse wouldn't get out of control with him and the animal's elderly now and been put out to pasture somewhere near his home, I understand. There must be some mistake. The licence is valid for another three months, but the vehicle is out of use as a result. The notes here show we are trying to rent it out at the moment and that it's proving difficult as whoever takes it on will only have a few months left in the current licence period. It wouldn't have been driven, you see, officer, not by Cunliffe, anyway. No one has been assigned the licence.'

Ted had positioned himself behind Jack on the other side of the doorway as a fourth person in Brackley's office would not be possible.

'Where would the cab be at present, sir?' asked Ted.

'Well it should be in the overspill yard at the back here. We would be doing it up, getting ready to rent it to a new driver. Probably it's in there now.' Brackley started to rise from his chair.

'No need to trouble you to show us, Mr Brackley, perhaps one of the clerks could take us. We'll need to speak to Mr Cunliffe as well, sir, if you can provide us with his address,' said Jack.

'Who would know when it last went out?' asked Ted, looking at the clerk sitting at a small desk next to Bradley's desk.

Through the back here, is it sir?' said Jack, who was already opening a side door and peering round into an alleyway. The last thing they wanted was for Mr Brackley to insist on seeing the magistrate's warrant before they got into the yard.

'Yes, the yard opens out at the bottom of the alley. But the carriages not being used are stored in sheds that used to be stables for the Boar's Head. The foreman will have the record in the yard office of when the cab last went out. Only the cabs are in the yard and the others are in the sheds. That way we can work on them in the inclement weather. So much rain this year! We've been forced to rent some cover and it all increases costs you know, plus having vehicles off the road, like the one you're enquiring into, affects the profit. I'm sure there must be some mistake as Cunliffe is an old man, very experienced, and he has an immaculate safety record.' Brackley wiped his brow again.

'Is it possible that someone could have got into the yard and borrowed a carriage?' asked Ted.

'There's only one entrance,' Brackley paused, as he thought. 'I suppose if the carriage was being worked on in one of the sheds it might be possible to take it out for a run, see if the work done is effective. But the horse isn't here, anymore, and there would have to be a horse. I don't understand why this would be done?'

'Anyone we can have a word with in the yard?' asked Jack.

'The foreman would be there now but it's still early. However, the carriage going out from the shed wouldn't need to come through the yard, look Simon can show you better than me trying to explain. You'll see how the side of the shed opens up on to Hebrew Place and a cab could wind its way onto the Aldgate High Street or the Whitechapel Road before we'd know it. Simon, the record shows the cab is in Shed two, take the constables over, will you,' Mr Brackley moved out of the way for his clerk, Simon, to wriggle round the desks and take Jack and Ted out into the alley. Once in the yard they nodded at the foreman, who squinted over the smoke from the clay pipe he was sucking, as Simon led the two constables through to where the old stables for the Boar's Head were, now the repair sheds for the cab business. There was a number one and two painted on the sliding doors of the two sheds. A couple of drivers looked uncomfortable at the sight of the uniforms walking past, and talking momentarily stopped. Jack said, 'Morning,' to a group of three men as he and Ted walked past. He knew their numbers were being memorized in case the drivers saw the officers again.

Simon took them inside shed two. It had six cabs in various stages of repair, some involving new seating. However, the licence plates were on all of them and there was no evidence of number seventy-five, seventy-five.

'Perhaps we can have a look in shed area one,' said Ted Phillips and they followed the young man across and into the other repair shed. Again, there was no sign of the licence plate that they were looking for.

'Right, let's check the yard with the vehicles going out and then, if it's not here, you'd better deliver the bad news to your boss,' said Ted, to Simon.

'That makes more sense, if it's been stolen,' said Jack, as they walked towards the foreman. 'It probably explains why the horse was so skittish as well. Maybe the man is using an animal that's not been put into harness for a cab, perhaps it's easier to get it worked up into a state.'

'Could be, but what should have been straightforward this morning with a potential arrest has added to an already complicated case. We'd better interview Cunliffe though, just in case, although I doubt he's our man from the description that Brackley has given us of a retiree,' said Ted.

'The driver I saw wasn't anywhere near retirement in age. I'll get Cunliffe's address from the office if you want to talk to the foreman?' suggested Jack. Ted nodded and Jack followed Simon back up the alley to the side door of the office to give Mr Brackley the bad news that his carriage was missing.

He offered to entered the missing carriage in as a reported crime when he got back to Leman Street. Brackley was clearly a money man and had not been in the sheds for some time, leaving the checking of the stock to others in the business. He relied on his ledgers and it would be easy to falsify records unless someone was on the ball.

Ted joined Jack a few minutes later. He looked dejected after speaking to the foreman. The carriage was entered as "repair" only in the records the foreman kept but the man insisted that he had not seen it go out after Cunliffe's retirement. As far as the foreman was concerned the cab had been put into the repair shed and was still there. He would have no reason to check it without an instruction to use it. They left with an address in Jack's inside pocket for Cunliffe and once back onto the Whitechapel Road relaxed.

'I think we need a cup of tea,' said Jack, as they turned into Leman Street, 'We should celebrate as we didn't get called on that warrant!'

Ted allowed himself a brief smile and then raised his eyebrows, 'I thought we'd be marching a couple of men back to the station now. It fits the twists and turns of this case though for it not to be straightforward. I asked the foreman where the horses are kept. There's a series of small stables or men keep their own horse. Cunliffe's horse went with him out to pasture as he retired. So, the horse being used for those two incidents wouldn't have been Cunliffe's cab horse. Let's check in with Sergeant Thick and then we can have a look at where Cunliffe lives. We've got to get down to the Millwall Station later as well and see what we can find out about the cab and if it's been seen at all. Where's the other place you mentioned to me?'

'Near Poplar, but they haven't seen me in uniform. I'm not sure the girl who gave me the information yesterday would cope with the revelation that I'm a policeman. They think I work at the West India Dock office and am interested in catching pilferers,' said Jack.

'Well we have a choice,' said Ted.

'What's that?' asked Jack.

'Wait for them to make another move. We're expecting them now and there's strength in that, or go and take control,' Ted shrugged, and they turned into Leman Street Police Station.

Both equipped with a mug of hot sweet tea, they checked on the map for how to get to Cunliffe's address, which was out through Bow.

Jack and Ted traced the route of the Blackwall Railway extension east to Bow Road and the railway station. According to the information from the cab office Cunliffe lived up by Victoria Park Station with a daughter in Wick Lane, slightly south of Hackney Wick, and Jack and Ted hoped they would be able to get a train from Bow Road up there.

'There's the line,' said Ted, tracing it on the map with his finger.

'Looks like we can pick it up at Blackwall?' said Jack, looking at his colleague, uncertainly.

'Well, we can try. I've never been up there. There's nothing there really yet, except water works, by the look of it, said Ted.

'Big park, though,' Jack said, looking at the stretch of Victoria Park.

'After that we can make enquiries at Millwall Junction and sample the stew at the side of the station house,' suggested Ted.

'I wonder where he's put the old horse?' said Jack.

'There may be some grazing around the park up there,' said Ted, pointing at Victoria Park. 'Anyway, you're not expecting it to be the same horse?'

'No, I just hoped the poor animal was also having a retirement,' said Jack.

The address was actually in Bower Road, near the Wesley Chapel, a few minutes from the Victoria Road Railway Station. The daughter, Mrs Eliza Blunt, was about forty years of age, and she showed the two constables into the back room, and sent a child to the cricket ground in the park to collect her father, Mr Cunliffe.

It was a small house with two bedrooms. She told the two constables that her father had the front downstairs room now as a bedroom as he had retired and was spending most days tending the horse which had been put out to pasture. There was a strip of grazing on the edge of the park and it was commonly accepted that the horses would graze. He had been quick to go out that morning in order to make sure that the animal had a waterproof cover erected using some of the trees for shelter and had stayed to chat to some cricketing cronies who met at the pitch even though it was out of season.

'I don't know what we'll do with the horse if the frost starts. I think he'll have to put the animal in the outhouse if it turns cold. What the landlord will say I can't imagine. Anyway, that's not your concern. What was it you wanted to see him about?' asked Mrs Blunt.

'The carriage that he drove has gone missing from the sheds it was being restored in. It seems to be the subject of a couple of hit and run accidents in the last few weeks, after your father retired. We've been to see the owner this morning and we need to interview your father,' Ted explained.

'Well, he shouldn't be much longer. Ah, there they are now, coming in through the back gate.'

Mr Cunliffe followed his grandchild in through the back door and greeted Ted and Jack. He was dripping, and his daughter took the pieces of sacking he had over his shoulders and then his wet coat and hat, and hung them in the wash room. He took a seat by the fire and Mrs Blunt poured stewed tea from the pot on the range. Taking a sip her father put his cup down and lent forward. Jack had taken in the alert little eyes that were like black beads. He would not have missed much about a potential fare at the side of the road.

'Gone missing, you say?' Cunliffe looked shocked. 'I can't see how that would happen, given the size of those cabs. It's not new either, it needed a lot of work on it to keep it up to a good standard. I'd have stayed a little longer if Brackley had spent the money on it. But the newer vehicles are what the punters want these days not those old cabs.'

'Where did you keep it, while you were working?' asked Ted.

'Outside my lodgings at night and when I wasn't working, until the last few months when I moved here ready to retire. I gave up my rooms and moved in with Eliza and her husband. They could do with the money and it's cheaper for me and I get to spend time with the grandchildren. I parked the cab on the road, usually opposite here, and it's an ideal retirement for the horse,' explained Cunliffe.

'We wondered if you'd seen anyone unusual hanging around, before you retired, taking more than a normal interest in the cab, maybe someone who could have put a different horse in the shafts?' asked Jack.

'Funny that, there was a young fellah, well, younger than me. Our Leslie drew him actually because he kept walking up and down the road. Where did that sketch go?' Cunliffe looked at his daughter.

'I'll get it, pa, it's up in the children's bedroom,' said Mrs Blunt, getting up and opening a door, which Jack had thought was a cupboard next to the range. Behind the door was a staircase. They heard her move along the floor above.

'Very compact these houses,' said Cunliffe. Jack nodded.

They heard a click of a latch as Mrs Blunt returned through the door into the kitchen. She put a pencil sketch down in front of Jack and Ted, which was a good one. Jack could see there was a similarity in the face of the driver in the picture to the man who had stared at him on the Commercial Road that first night.

'How old is your child?' asked Ted, 'It's very good. The eyes are good. What do you think, Sargent?'

'It's certainly like the man I saw on both occasions. Can we take this? It's important evidence. It will help us track him down,' said Jack.

'You think he's stolen the cab?' asked Cunliffe.

'Not just that but he had nearly killed a couple of people yesterday. Do you remember what day it was when your grandchild sketched the picture?' Jack said.

'Before Christmas as I stopped work before Christmas Eve. It was the afternoon as the children were sitting in the window waiting for the Christmas Party at the Chapel, up the road. They were bored and I said to them to draw something and the best picture would get a sugar stick. It was about three o'clock as it hadn't started to get dark yet, when Leslie drew the sketch,' said Cunliffe. 'I looked out the next time he came up the road, as Leslie wanted me to see how like him it was. That was the picture that got the prize!'

'Where was the cab?' asked Ted.

'Parked across the road, as usual,' said Cunliffe.

'So was that the only time you saw the man in the sketch,' asked Jack.

'Oh yes, because the cab was handed back, so to speak before Christmas. It would have been in the repair sheds at Brackley's by Christmas Eve.'

'Did you see a horse at all, a sturdy, black horse?' asked Jack.

'No, not round here. Is that what was used to pull the cab?' Cunliffe asked.

'Yes, yesterday it was, and on the other occasion there was a near miss it could have been the same animal as yesterday. Could we come and see your horse Mr Cunliffe? Just so we eliminate every possibility,' asked Jack.

'Yes, of course, she's down in her shelter that I rigged up this morning. With it being mild she's alright on the common at the edge of the park. There are some others grazing as well so she's got company. If the weather turns cold I'll have to think of something else as technically we can't stable her here, although the outhouse would do the job.'

Jack and Ted exchanged glances about the fact that there were other horses on the common.

'How would someone get a horse from here to Whitechapel?' asked Jack.

'Ride, of course,' laughed Cunliffe, 'Or walk it there through the park and there's a bridge across the Regent's Park Canal at the bottom of the park, by the gymnasium. You could stay on the tow path until the

Kingsland Road and then drop south through Shoreditch to Commercial Road and then onto Aldgate High Street and you're there at the yard. When you've finished your tea, I'll take you over to meet my Bessie.'

'That's the horse,' said Mrs Blunt, in case the two officers were in any doubt.

They thanked Cunliffe's daughter for the tea and the warmth, and put their great coats back on. Cunliffe gave his coat and hat an extra shake before putting them back on and then the three men left through the back yard to walk to Victoria Park. There was a bridge over the railway line into Wick Lane from Tennyson Terrace, and the entrance into the park was by the Royal Standard Tavern. 'Old Bessie' was a grey and not as powerfully built as the horse that Jack had had bear down on him twice. However, there were other horses in the trees and calling to Ted, he walked over towards the Park Lodge and banged on the door.

The Park Keeper was in the park on his patrol, according to his wife, who opened the door. The horses were from the nomads camping by the railway line, she thought. The group came and went especially in the summer as they moved down to the south coast. Technically, the edge of the park, where the trees were, was a bit of an area of dispute with local people insisting that it was common land. Her husband turned a blind eye to the grazing of the horses by the nomads providing no other "behaviour" accompanied their appearance. If thefts went up in the area he moved the nomads on with the help of the police. Jack thanked her and walked back through the drizzle to the shelter of the trees. Cunliffe and Ted were waiting for him by a large, black horse, with Cunliffe giving the horse an old carrot that he had had in his pocket as a treat for Bessie.

'It could be the one,' said Jack, 'but there's no way of knowing.'

'Too powerfully built and the wrong temperament for a carriage horse,' said Cunliffe. 'You'd have a problem with him in traffic. He'd have the strength for it, mind, but I wouldn't trust the temperament.'

'What do you bet that the man in the sketch is with the nomads?' said Ted. 'Let's go and see that Park Keeper's wife again. Got the sketch safe?'

'I have,' said Jack patting his breast pocket.

'Do you still need me officers?' asked Cunliffe.

'Not now, sir, but would you come to Leman Street and ask for me tomorrow, and I'll have a statement ready for you to check and sign about the man in the sketch and the horse we've found. Constable Phillips is my name and you can see my number. We'll not hang around in case we start to attract attention from the nomads there. I don't want to spark anything off for you being seen with us, or for them to suddenly leave. Thank-you for your help, you've taken the enquiry on a long way.'

Jack and Ted waited at the Park Keeper's lodge with yet more tea until he finished his patrol and returned. His name was Atkinson and he came in cursing the weather and the bad chest it was giving him. His wife quickly explained that she had two Constables in the front parlour about activity from the nomads. Once his boots were off his feet, and a fresh pair of woollen socks had been provided for him, he joined the visitors with a mug of his own.

'Well, gentlemen, what can I help you with? My wife has mentioned there's been some contact with old Mr Cunliffe,' said Atkinson.

'We think there's a connection with one of the horses that's grazing free under the trees being used with the old cab that Mr Cunliffe used to drive. It's been involved in a couple of potentially nasty accidents starting just before Christmas and there was another one yesterday with a police constable injured. If it's one of the stallions out there, and it belongs to the nomads, we wondered if you would look at a sketch of a man that was hanging about Bower Road before Christmas Eve, and see if you can identify him for us. Maybe you've seen him in the park, or by the railway line, or tending the horses,' Ted held out his hand for the sketch, which Jack had ready.

'Let's have a look,' said Atkinson, taking the sketch from Ted. 'He looks familiar, but it's a child's sketch, isn't it? Now I've seen it I'll pay special attention to who tends the horse. I can do a visit over to the horses when the men come over to them. I suspect when the weather improves they'll move on. This group turns up every year because of the grazing. They've been here nearly two weeks now, which is usually the limit to their stay. How can I contact you? There's no police station here yet.'

'Take the railway down to Blackwall and I can meet you there by five o'clock tomorrow afternoon,' said Ted. 'That should be enough time for you to see if the man in the sketch is part of the group. You can leave the rest to me if he is.'

'Good,' said Atkinson and they shook hands and took their leave of the Park Keeper and his wife.

'Well, we still don't have an arrest,' said Jack as he and Ted walked back to Victoria Park Station, carefully avoiding the area running along the side of the railway track to avoid being seen.

'No, but we've moved the enquiry on.'

They crossed the line at Tennyson's Terrace and up along Bower Road to the station. The train took them back to Blackwall and they changed for the branch line to the final call of the day, and a hot meal by the side of Millwall Junction station. The train was busy with people heading for the ferry. It was three o'clock and Jack's stomach was doing a clog dance for lunch. As the got off the train the smell of a rich gravy reached his nostrils and he felt his mouth start to water.

'How has your day been, gentlemen?' asked the woman behind the counter. They both smiled and nodded the information to her as the place was not empty. Ted removed his helmet and sat down next to two seamen. They wiped their plates with their pieces of crust and got up and left. The rest of the clientele suddenly lost their appetites and the bell over the door rang a chime as it opened and closed and the room emptied.

Resigned to loss of custom, the woman came and sat down on the bench next to Ted and gave him a kiss on the cheek.

'How did it go this morning?' she asked. Jack's jaw dropped.

'We've got some progress. Have you anything left for two hungry men?' asked Ted.

'Of course, I saved todays for you as you let me know you were coming. Hadn't you better tell your young colleague who I am, before his eyes leave his head?' the woman nudged Ted, who turned and laughed.

'This is my sister, Rose. She's my eyes and ears at the docks when we're doing a special. We kill her trade that's the only thing, but keep who she is to yourself, Jack.'

Jack smiled with relief that the potential disaster for Mrs Phillips was non-existent and held out his hand. Rose gave it a very positive shake.

'That's a relief, I thought I was going to have to take you in hand, Ted. Family on the ground, eh, no wonder you get information from this side regularly. Stew for me and double the helping, please, if your dinner is as good as the other evening, said Jack.

'Ah,' said Ted, 'You came, did you?'

'Yes, and I had the same effect of clearing the room, sorry Rose,' said Jack, apologetically.

'That's alright, Ted usually comes at the end of a day and you effectively did the same. I'll just put the closed sign on and draw the blinds for a little while. What are you both after?' Rose asked.

'Food first,' said Jack looking pleadingly at Rose. She grinned at him and gave Ted a nudge.

'You'll have to watch this one with the ladies, Ted, he's already the potential to be a real heartbreaker. When he gets a bit more experienced with extracting information he could be lethal with that smile.'

'His heart is committed, Rose. But I take your point. It's not escaped me that he can pull the parlour maids on the beat if he wants to. Better dish up or we'll get nothing sensible out of either of us until we've had food,' Ted passed a plate down to Jack which had chunks of crusty bread on it. Jack started to pull a piece apart and stuffed it into his mouth to quell the shaking that had started with lack of food. Two plates were before them and conversation died as they shovelled up spoons of the soupy stew.

'Show Rose the sketch, just in case she's seen the man,' suggested Ted as the initial appetite abated.

'How did you get this?' asked Rose, as Jack handed over Leslie's drawing.

'From a visit with a potential suspect this morning. However, the day hasn't gone as we thought it would and the whole situation got more complicated,' said Ted.

'Have you seen the man around the ferry area, Rose,' asked Jack. She looked at him and nudged Ted again.

'Dangerous eyes, pleading look, you'll have to watch him, Ted.'

'Give over,' laughed Ted. 'Well Rose, have you seen him, at all.'

'Yes, I think I have. He's a thief. Rolled around in a big carriage before Christmas. The horse was wrong that he had for it. Too wild, like it wasn't broken in. But let me get you your seconds.' Rose picked up a ladle and meat and vegetables sat in huge mounds on the tin plates. Then she sat back and waited while her brother and his colleague fell to on the food again.

'He must have been paid well,' said Ted, wiping his mouth. 'Someone's picked him up to deal with you, Jack. I wonder how?'

'Perhaps he was caught and doing the job of polishing us off was the way he was let off,' suggested Jack.

'That implies someone quite low down the food chain in the force has been on the look-out for someone with this man's potential,' said Ted.

'So, charges are dropped provided he polishes me off? Why would I have had that effect?' asked Jack.

'Perhaps, as you're unknown, they thought you would be the easy one first?' said Ted.

'Thanks,' said Jack.

'I mean, you're an unknown quantity. It might have been because you were coming across the river, dressed as a labourer, looking like you'd gone plain clothes. Perhaps they thought you were onto something, or someone. I do wonder if information about where you and Sam were lodging had got out as well.'

'That would mean someone in New Road?' suggested Jack.

'Or someone in Doyle's team?' said Ted.

'Where is that, by the way?' asked Jack.

'Great Marlborough street,' said Ted, and he and Jack looked at each other.

'There was that detective I spoke to briefly in the Mason's Arms, that first night I came over the river,' said Jack.

'Or Doyle's home?' said Rose. The two men looked at her, 'I mean someone may have overheard something in his home.'

'We're back to Sam's unease,' said Jack.

'Which is why we had to move him,' said Ted.

'Has anyone done any checks on the people lodging there?' asked Jack. 'We could, couldn't we Ted? Just from a point of concern. A friendly chat with each of them.'

'You'll need to give Hunt notice if you're going to start anything like that. He'll have heart failure otherwise. You and I can do this on the quiet, Jack. Young Charlie's still at New Road, isn't he? No one's going to check on Charlie making enquiries. I'll have a word in the morning and get him going. He's quiet but thorough from what I've seen.'

'And bored, Ted, it just might be what he needs. I saw him the other day after that meeting we'd all had, he said he was thinking of jacking it in and going back home. I got the impression it wouldn't be too long, so you'll need to get hold of him quickly or he could be gone by New Year.'

'Who's there at Doyle's?' asked Ted, taking out his notebook.

'Michael Culley and Ann and George Black. That's it,' said Jack.

'Servants?' asked Ted.

'Just Hannah, a maid of all work. She hasn't got time to kill anyone, she never stops working,' said Jack.

'Ever looked in a kitchen, Jack, at the amount of poison available?' said Ted, ruefully.

'Yeah, but that's usually arsenic, not strychnine. Maybe strychnine for rats, of course. There's Sam's point, about the surname "Moore" being Mrs Doyle's maiden name, the proximity of the bank where young Mr Moore, the director, works, to the Berringer body and why Berringer was in the area in the first place.' Ted moved a potato at the bottom of his dish around absent-mindedly. Rose covered it with more stew, and looked enquiringly at Jack, who nodded. Food in his dish and another plate of crusty bread before him put him in an excellent mood. He glanced at the station clock and realised that it was time they were both back at Leman Street and checking in with Sergeant Thick.

He thought of the way Wilkie Collins had presented the culprit in "the Moonstone." Obvious people were not the ones who had committed the crime. But that was a novel, this was real life. Who could have organized him being followed? Why would someone arrange an attempt on his life? His mind ran the picture of the accident in Piccadilly. Supposing he hadn't pushed Morris out of the way? The carriage would have hit Morris, not himself. Perhaps that was not random. Morris had also worked at Great Marlborough Street Police Station, although some time ago. Again, the link to Doyle. One down, one to go in a team that were getting too close? Were they close? It certainly didn't seem so to Jack.

The thought of being targeted made him feel sick. It was getting nasty and Sam's forebodings could be real. Someone they knew, were perhaps living with, could be a potential killer, or colluding with a killer. The situation may involve someone who was well connected in the Met and able to use officers to put pressure on a suspect to become a killer. Everything he and Ted had found out in the last twenty-four hours had been very encouraging, but they were still scrabbling in the dark.

'We need to go. Thick will have us both on the carpet otherwise. How much do we owe you, Rose?' asked Jack.

'Oh, just one plate each. You've paid me in stimulation. See you both soon. I'll put the blinds up after you leave and re-open. I'll keep my eyes open for that man, just in case. As tomorrow's New Year's Eve are you working Ted?'

'Yes, as I had Christmas off. This young lad has a couple of days off though. I'll be across later in the day tomorrow to see you so any information you manage will be very welcome, Rose.'

*

Twelve

Incessant drizzle again in London on New Year's Eve. It really was the wettest year Jack could remember in his twenty years. Puddles of rainwater on the roads and paths as he walked towards Shadwell reflected a grey dawn. The wind from the west was cold but he would have wished it colder to have a frost settle and end a year of rain with a crispness under foot. Anything to vary the dismal sky.

He had faced breakfast alone. No Sam, and Ann and George had left London for her parent's home in Berkshire. Michael Culley had gone to work and the Doyles had left for new year in Oxford apparently. There was Hannah in the kitchen, and Jack had looked at the empty breakfast room and made a decision to take a plate of food down to the kitchen and join Hannah while she did her chores. He had looked at all the food keeping warm and wondered what would be done with it. Bacon, kidneys, sausage, boiled eggs sitting in a basket, bread rolls and home-made marmalade. He had woken in an excellent mood due to the progress he and Ted had made with their enquiries yesterday, but a solitary breakfast was dampening his enthusiasm.

Dinner had also been taken alone last night and one solitary meal with a glut of food in an otherwise empty dining room, despite being extremely comfortable and warm, was quite enough for Jack. Due to his having slipped out early morning over the few days since Christmas he had not had breakfast with the family and dinner had been eaten late with Hannah having kept a plated meal for him. The fact that everyone had plans for New Year was a shock to a person who had nowhere else to go and stay. He had known little other than work in his short life, with church on a high day or holiday and parties in a church hall, or a feast on the long table on the green in the summer to celebrate a festival, and then back to work. Eating alone was not something that sat comfortably with Jack. He would rather stand on the street and munch a hunk of bread and exchange the odd pleasantry than sit in luxury alone. Despite being orphaned he had not spent his life alone, having acquired roomfuls of compatriots initially in the orphanage for whom he had become the natural leader with his physical strength and good humour until he was quickly placed on the farm. Then there had been five of them growing up, working, fighting, and eating together in the same tied cottage. But New Year's Eve alone in a comfortable room with too much food affected his mood. What would he do with himself for the rest of the day? And tonight? He would raise a glass to Charlie across the river in New Road as they had agreed to do, and to Sam at Windsor, but apart from that what would he do on New Year's Eve alone in London.

Although he had very much appreciated the fact of having a bedroom to himself, he vowed he would not eat another meal alone. Jack had made a decision and piled the dishes on top of each other, blown out the candles underneath the hot plates, and carried everything down the back stairs to the kitchen. He had given Hannah yet another shock and sent her face into a frozen stare at the sight of all the dishes he was carrying.

'Thought I'd save your legs,' Jack had said, and he had put them down on the kitchen table and just managed to stop the top dish from sliding off the pile to crash onto the floor.

'I would have used the dummy butler, sir,' said Hannah, and she had taken the dishes to the side table.

'Oh, I never thought of that. I've brought a plate down, in that lot, if you don't mind me eating in here with you?' Jack had pulled out a chair, and noted that Hannah's face, in its long stare at him, took a greater time to relax than usual. He had decided to ignore the shock he was, yet again, giving to the maid of all work.

'What are you doing tonight Hannah?' he had asked and his question extended the length of time her face remained set.

'Church at midnight, drinks and supper in the back hall, and then back to shut the house down.'

'Which church is that? Any time off over the two days?' Jack had asked wondering if he would wake on New Year's Day to a completely empty house.

'St Thomas's up the road.' Hannah had paused and bitten her lip and then had continued with an invitation. 'Anyone's welcome. I'm off after lunch tomorrow. There's you and Mr Culley staying so you'll not have such a quiet breakfast in the morning as he won't be at work. I'm to do a cold plate for you both for lunch if you're here. Then there's dinner, if you're here, that is. If not I can leave some pies, and cheeses. That's the mistress's instruction,' such a long explanation had seemed to exhaust Hannah, as she had suddenly stopped.

'I'll be out in the afternoon, but not sure about the evening. I'm meeting someone at Westminster in the afternoon. Cold plates are fine for me, but go with what Michael wants and I'll muck in. Have you far to go? Is it to family?' It was not any of his business but he had craved the small talk.

They had chatted on. Hannah had told him about her family party set up for New Year's Day and that she would travel to be back in Arbour Square by nine o'clock in the evening. Jack had looked at food left over and she had followed his gaze.

'I'll put it in a soup, and make egg sandwiches for later,' she had said.

'Could I take some of it to a family on the Commercial Road?' Jack had asked and Hannah's eyes had momentarily softened as she had nodded. And that was where he had headed first, leaving some of the remains of the cooked breakfast for the woman on the door step.

'Happy New Year to you all,' said Jack as he put the parcel down. This time she stared in shock at the man in the smart suit and bowler hat, realising too late that it was the young policeman.

Shadwell. That was the destination.

Jack walked back along the Commercial Road until it morphed into the Blackwall Road. The Police Station was in the corner of David Lane down towards Shadwell Basin. He had to get to the other side of the railway line and intended to cut through Shadwell Railway Station. He went on for too long though and had missed the route he had intended. Instead, he turned back and found Sutton Street East and was able to cut across the line from the station. There was a group of men hanging around from the Sailor's Institute near the Police Station and Jack was cautious as they eyed him up and down. A smell hung in the air and he lost interest in the men. Then he remembered that Shadwell Basin fed into the Thames and nearby was the Tobacco dock. That first night that he had come across the river through the Tunnel he had seen this area from a distance and shuddered. The docks were still fairly new but the people standing around looked needy. Jack had debated with himself about wearing his labourer's clothes but there had been good reason not to. He met the aggressive stares with a gaze that held a message. He would do some damage if approached and the men hanging around did not make a move as he turned into Shadwell Police Station.

His target audience in his style of dress was the Policemen he was about to meet so that he would be taken seriously. Making contact may be stupid but Jack had decided he was going to find the detective from the Mason's Arms. Franks, Mary had said his name was. Harry Franks.

If the man was involved in some way with the crimes of Berringer's death, and the Faceless Woman, Jack intended to provoke a response by turning up. Unlike most people walking through the sort of environment in Shadwell Jack was enjoying bringing an unknown quantity to a head. The detective Franks was that unknown element. Was he an enemy or an ally? What was Franks from Shadwell Police Station? He would soon know.

Jack was over the door step into the Police Station on the pretext of having his watch stolen. He was having fun. It was time to stop whoever was behind these crimes, stop the wandering around in the dark and he was about to try and form an alliance, or start a war. Either would create a movement he believed in the Berringer and Faceless Woman cases. He would flush out the people responsible for the corruption and catch the killers. Hunt would crucify him if he knew what he was about to do. So be it, Jack was resigned to whatever the outcome was and he went into the Police Station anyway. It was time to change up the balance in the team's favour and remove whatever advantage the corrupt policeman, or anyone higher up in the social scale that were involved in the deaths, held. They had been calling the shots so far. He and the team had been played with in the last week and Morris could easily have been killed in Piccadilly. Something now needed to give. Jack set his face into an open smile and approached the Sergeant's desk.

The Desk Sergeant took down his details. 'Name?'

'Williams, George Williams,' said Jack.

'Take a seat Mr Williams, and someone will interview you shortly.'

Jack looked at the two women waiting. One about forty and overly friendly. The other embarrassed at being there, constantly checking her dress was in order. Jack wondered what the second woman was there for. The first was easy to work out. She was not unused to being at the Police Station.

'I wondered if a detective Franks was on duty today, not sure if I've got the right name, but I met him in the Mason's Arms on the Commercial Road,' said Jack, before he sat down.

'That sounds like Detective Sergeant Franks. He's going off duty. I can ask him to step in if you know him,' suggested the Sergeant.

So, there it was, thought Jack, a Detective Sergeant.

'I think he'll be interested to see me,' said Jack, and took a seat on a different bench to the two women.

Jack watched the minute hand on the wall clock, listening to the heavy tick as the pendulum swung. A carved German Eagle, wings spread, was fixed to the top. It was an ugly thing but becoming fashionable. He would not give it house room. The Desk Sergeant went into the room at the back of his desk and Jack could see him bend over and speak to someone. He had left the door open and Jack knew he would be observed by someone in the room. He hoped it was Franks. To oblige he took his bowler hat off.

He heard a chair scrape back and waited. The detective from the Mason's Arms appeared as if by magic at the desk with the Duty Sergeant, who nodded towards Jack.

'Mr Williams,' he said to Detective Franks, with a friendly look back at the person that he thought Jack was. The detective's waistcoat was not stained with the evidence of a beer today, as the one he had worn had been that night Jack had sat opposite him in the Mason's Arms. The general odour of tobacco that travelled with him matched was outranked only by the tobacco dock outside. The moustache bristled, the eyes were sharp as he recalled Jack's face and build and Jack knew that he was remembered.

'Williams?' said Franks, staring at Jack. 'Lost a pocket watch and asks to see a 'tec. Room down the hall, follow me,' and the detective led the way.

Franks opened a door three down from the reception area and stood to one side in the doorway as Jack went in. Franks waited, and Jack pulled the chair on one side of a table out and sat down. Franks entered the room and closed the door, but he remained standing, leaning against the wall. Jack waited, leaving the upper ground, at this point, to the detective, and waited for the conversation to start.

'Williams? And you asked for me. Looking a little different from the other evening. What are you, Mr Williams?' asked Franks.

'Metropolitan police, like you. Leman Street,' said Jack.

'No, I don't think that will do. I know all the 'tecs at Leman Street and, frankly, you ain't it. There certainly isn't anyone called Williams. But you and I met at the Mason's Arms and I thought you had a smell about you, frankly, a keen, new smell, wanting to make your name, but I didn't think you were a Policeman, country boy.'

'Police Constable Jack Sargent, special duties, Inspector Hunt's team, New Road, assigned to Leman Street,' Jack stopped as it had had the desired effect. Franks stopped leaning against the wall and walked forward to the table. He sucked the air through his teeth and pulled out a chair.

'Hunt? And you're coming in here and putting all your cards down on the table. Taking a risk that I'm clean. Interesting. My sixth sense says Hunt hasn't sent you, and he doesn't know you're here. Right?'

'Right. Because there's such a natural stink about you it's too obvious. I think you may not be corrupt, and if you are you'll take action so it's win, win for us. You might be someone I can trust. I may be wrong, but I don't think so. The clothes and the stink of tobacco are something you've adopted,' Jack said.

Franks smirked at the honesty. 'Wouldn't last too long round here looking like you, would I?'

'You wouldn't have given me the time of day if I'd come in dressed like a labourer,' said Jack, with a grin.

'Too right. What are you here for, then?' Franks asked.

'I'm after this man,' Jack put the sketch from Cunliffe's grandchild on the table. Franks picked it up.

'Are you now. You're not the only one. Badley. I tried to bring Badley in for aggravated burglary and rape and he ends up with a cast iron alibi and I'm told to back off. What are you after him for?' Franks passed the sketch back.

'Trying to kill two police officers, including me. My Sergeant is off with a broken elbow after avoiding being hit with a cab that this man was driving. He tried to run me down that night I was in the Mason's Arms. We think someone in the force is protecting him, and he's been given a job to do to get rid of us,' said Jack.

'And why would someone do that? You're working on something and this man's been given a job to do to polish you off in exchange for charges being dropped. Charges I brought, by the way. That means something smells in Shadwell other than my jacket. I don't like that, not on my patch. Come on what are you working on? If it's Hunt it's being managed from someone high up. I've been around a lot longer than you boy, I know Hunt's background. I know why he's still only an Inspector. It keeps him within the daily workings of the force, so he can get involved on the ground. He hand-picks his men and it seems he picked you. That makes you interesting. You said the other night you were new in London, from Sussex you said, was that true?'

'Yes, that was true. It was the first time north of the river. I was being transferred to Leman Street and I wanted to see the area,' Jack leant forward. 'As to your question about what I'm working on, it's the same as you. I don't like the idea of crooked policemen, or some toff calling the shots about what crime is tolerated in order to protect themselves. I don't care how high up we go to catch him either. There's a couple of dead bodies in the last month and the fact that evidence has gone missing means someone is pulling strings. I come across the river one night and the man in the sketch, Badley, did you say his name was?'

Franks nodded.

'Badley tried to run me down with a cab he's stolen. But I saw the licence number. That cab is still missing. Then he tries again in Piccadilly two days ago. My Sergeant gets a broken elbow for New Year but if I hadn't pushed him out of the way he would probably be dead now. I reckon you and I can get what we both want by working together. Who told you to back off this man?' asked Jack, deciding he might as well be blunt.

Franks, sucked in air through his teeth again. He looked at Jack and walked round the table, picking up a chair and placing it to the side of Jack.

'My Inspector. He got an order that the man had a cast iron alibi as I said. Badley's attached himself to a group of nomads who turn up in Shadwell Basin a couple of times a year. His name's Badley on the record but that's not his full name but the English always shorten names, don't they, when it's a foreigner. That's how I ended up with Franks. Great grandfather was French, LeRoy was the real name, but it ended up on the documents as Franks because of the accent when he tried to explain he was a Frenchie. No one understood him, see. It's a common story anyway. Badley has done penal servitude, under a number of names, and he's done hard labour more than once and then completed his time and reappeared. I keep a list when they go down and I wait for the date for them to come out, which they always do, and then I'm on them. This time he'd have been done for a rape as I've got witnesses, even if I can't get the aggravated burglary to stick. Trouble is the witnesses are women of a certain order, servants. It doesn't go down too well with the middle-class magistrate generally. Don't' believe them, you see. They end up being dismissed even though they've not done anything wrong. I'd got him with three witnesses who were in the house at the time of the burglary and his attack on the parlour maid. They've all lost their positions. There was no doubt, it was rape alright if you get my meaning.'

'How do you mean?'

'Level of violence that usually goes with the rape, the state the woman was in, shaking, moaning uncontrollably, face a mess. He and his crew broke in,' said Franks. 'I shall have him. I want him and I shall have him.'

'Like Old Mary?' said Jack, staring at Franks intently.

'Was that you? Possession not theft was the message I got from a woman who passes the odd piece of information to me. She said it was a well-dressed clerk working at the West India Dock Office. You're getting around, young man! Told me that some green new boy must have put the wrong charge on the sheet. You don't know him I suppose?' Franks smiled at his own joke.

'No, I don't know any green new boys, and I'd be grateful if you don't let on to the women that the smart clerk is a Policeman,' said Jack with a grin.

'No, obviously not. Alright, Sargent's your name, is it? If we're to be colleagues what do I call you. It can't be Sargent, I'll get a reaction to using a name that sounds like a rank for such a new boy.'

'Jack.'

'Harry. Harry Franks.' They shook hands and an alliance was formed.

'Your rank, Harry? The Desk Sergeant said you were a Sergeant?' asked Jack.

'Detective Sergeant. You're third class I would guess if you're new?' said Franks.

'I was actually made up to second class after the strike lay-offs,' said Jack. Franks registered the speed and nodded.

'Here's a little suggestion for you, young Jack. We should pay Badley a visit. Scare him, make him think we mean him harm. Which I do, frankly. He's coming in and I want to know who he did the deal with to get the charges dropped. We need to find out where he is, though, as he seems to have disappeared, said Franks.

'We know,' Jack blurted out, the realisation dawning that Franks did not have the information about Victoria Park. Jack had assumed he did and that a superior's influence was the only thing stopping the detective from making an arrest. 'At least we think we know, it will be confirmed by five o'clock tonight if he's up at Victoria Park near the station. The Park Keeper, a man called Atkinson, will come down to Blackwall to meet my colleague, Ted Phillips, with information if he's seen Badley up there. The old cabbie, Cunliffe, who gave us the sketch yesterday told us he'd seen him in his street near the park. We interviewed the Park Keeper afterwards and he agreed he'd check out if he was around the horses that are grazing on the common land. Cunliffe thinks the horse that was used to pull the cab is one of the animals put on the land by the nomads.'

'That fits. He's been seen with a group down at the docks. They get the blame and he gets away. Perfect cover for him as people's expectations are that the crime is committed by them, as they're foreigners. He seems to have the group under some form of control. What's the plan then?' asked Franks.

'I don't know. Technically, I'm on leave today and tomorrow,' said Jack.

'Technically! Factually you mean. See, I knew you had the smell of the keen recruit, after making a reputation for himself. Don't you have a party to go to today somewhere?'

'No, frankly, I don't,' said Jack.

Franks gave him a look and then lowered his eyes. 'How would it go down with your colleagues if I'm in the background, looking to make an arrest myself, small team, with a view to extracting information that would be useful to you and Hunt in your investigations, and to me and my Inspector in pursuing our case?' asked Franks, getting up and walking back and forth, while he thought.

'I've no idea how Ted Phillips would react to the fact you and I are even having this conversation. I may be off the case faster than I can blink. It would have to look like coincidence that you've tracked Badley to the park, if he's up there at all. I happen to show up being the "keen recruit" that I am. Just a thought regarding the Faceless Woman case. If you're saying there's violence as regards a rape would he be a candidate for working over a dead woman's face to make it unrecognisable? Come to think of it would he use a knife? If someone is pulling strings and is prepared to get serious charges dropped against this man has he run up a list as long as your arm of potential charges?' mused Jack.

'He usually uses a blunt instrument. His fists even. I've not come across anything involving knives with him. Yes, I could see him working over a woman's face, alive or dead, if it suited him. He may know, of course, who's involved if it's not him but my bet is we can get him to talk and name names. You and I both want the man behind bars for a long time but there are bigger prizes to be had if we can get him to talk,' said Franks.'

'I can find Ted later at Blackwall station, be the keen young constable that he knows that I am. He'll tell me off but my shoulders are broad. Where will you be after five o'clock so I can get word to you if the Park Keeper confirms Badley is part of the nomad group?' asked Jack.

'Why not the Mason's Arms on the Commercial Road? Let's meet for a drink. I'll have a team in plain clothes at the bar, and you'd better change your clothes or you'll get that nice jacket spoilt. I'll wait until six o'clock. Then if you don't show we'll know we haven't got confirmation. I'll probably go after him up at the Park anyway. What do you say?' suggested Franks.

'Don't we need a warrant?' asked Jack.

'I've still got one. Valid too until midnight on the thirty-first December. Happy New Year! I was supposed to hand it back but, you know, one lives in hope that things will turn around, which it looks like they are about to. We're done until later, aren't we?' Franks gave something that looked like a smile. 'I'll walk you back to the Shadwell Railway Station just in case one of our regulars decides to see if you've got anything they want in your pockets.'

'I can look after myself,' said Jack.

Franks looked him over. 'I'll walk back to the Railway Station with you, make sure you actually get there in one piece,' he insisted. 'Yes, I don't doubt you can look after yourself but I want you at that meeting with the Park Keeper and your mate Ted,' he said.

Jack grinned and had nothing he could argue with. 'Just what will you do if I don't get confirmation Badley is up at the Park?'

233

'As I said, go up there anyway and get stuck in,' Franks shrugged. Jack laughed and nodded as that would be what he would do as well. Franks and Jack walked back to the Duty Sergeant's desk making a big show about the pocket watch.

'I'm just walking Mr Williams up to the railway station,' Franks said to the Sergeant, who glanced up and nodded. Jack noticed the two women were no longer waiting and looked at the German clock to see he and Franks had been in the interview room for nearly thirty minutes.

Out in the road, Franks engaged a few characters eye to eye while he and Jack walked back towards the railway.

'Look, I can make sure I get you out of anything difficult later if we get a confirmation it's Badley up at the park. But I'd have to call you as a witness who just happened to be around on an operation we were running, if we make an arrest. I need to know that you'd be ready to back me up,' said Franks.

'You're talking about quite a long way down the line, aren't you?' asked Jack. 'We'd both be after getting a conviction but we want the information about who's at the back of this deal that's been done with Badley, with a view to more arrests, don't we?'

'Regardless who's involved? Yes, we do,' sad Franks.

'Right, regardless of who's involved. Yes, I'll testify in a prosecution, I need more practice in court anyway, I've only done one appearance so far since I joined. Look, I should have mentioned that there's a New York detective arriving on the second of January for the Berringer murder and Mrs Berringer's disappearance,' Jack had almost forgotten about this complication.

'Is there now!' said Franks, 'that gives us forty-eight hours then. No problem, we'll have him singing like a canary by tomorrow. Any plans for tomorrow as you'll be at your own little outing now tonight?' They were at the railway station and Franks saw a constable questioning a man near the steps.

'Only in the afternoon about four o'clock,' said Jack.

'Good, just in case Badley proves a little stubborn,' Franks held out his hand. 'See you later, young Jack, I'll wait until six, remember.'

'I'll be there,' said Jack and Franks walked over towards the constable to give him some back-up.

*

Jack called in at Leman Street to wish his colleagues a happy new year and good-naturedly ignored the ribbing about looking like he was off to meet a lady.

'Chance would be a fine thing, but I'm living in hope,' said Jack. He went into the staff room at the back of the desk and spent a while drinking tea with men going off duty until the room cleared. Quickly he opened the cupboard and found the carpet bag he had left before changing the day before. He pulled his labourer's clothes out of the drawers in which he had stuffed them,
and packed them into the carpet bag.

Walking to the exit he looked like a man who was about to go away for New Year's Eve. He turned for the Commercial Road and Arbour Square.

*

Jack arrived at Blackwall Railway Station at ten minutes to five o'clock. He could see Ted Phillips, and to his surprise, Ted was not in uniform. He had forgotten that Ted would have gone off duty. Jack walked over to him quickly and Ted's face registered surprise.

'What are you doing here, you are off duty aren't you?' asked Ted.

'As are you after four o'clock,' grinned Jack.

'You should be taking your leave. You've worked all over Christmas and this is your first day off for weeks. Surely you've got other things to do?' Ted frowned.

'Not really,' said Jack, resigned to the fact. 'I wanted to hear what the Park Keeper had to say.' He debated with himself if he should be honest with Ted, but before he had come to a conclusion the train pulled in from Bow Street and Ted craned his neck looking for Atkinson, the Park Keeper. They both saw him at the same time and Ted waved an arm. Atkinson raised a hand and walked over to them. Ted thanked him for keeping the appointment and together they caught the train down to Millwall Junction and walked to Rose Phillip's place by the side of the station building. Rose was ready with tea, and the place was closed up so there was no problem with waiting for the place to empty today. She had sat by the window with the blind half down waiting to let Ted and the man he was meeting in but registered that the man in the labouring clothes was Jack. She got up immediately and opened the door for the three men. They sat while she fixed the bolts in place again and drew down the blind fully.

'My sister, Mr Atkinson,' said Ted.

'Good evening,' said Rose.

'How do you do,' said Atkinson.

'Any sighting, Rose, today? Asked Ted.

'No, nothing. If I'm honest Ted I think they'll show up tonight when people are busy out celebrating in the posh West End. Houses will be empty and crowds will be distracted and careless of their pockets,' said Rose, as she poured tea and put scones in front of the men. Jack was grateful for the sister's kindness as he realised it was hours since he had eaten. It would be potentially hours before he would get a meal too, so he made the most of the food on offer.

'I wish I still had an appetite like that,' said Atkinson, watching Jack tuck in to scones and slabs of butter.

'The appetite of the young,' smiled Ted. 'Probably sleeps well too. Now, Mr Atkinson, do we have a positive result to your inspection of the Common Land today?' There was a pause and Jack glanced across at Ted whose face was devoid of emotion. Was the answer going to be no or was the Park Keeper being over dramatic?

'Yes, I believe we do,' he eventually said. 'I'm sure it's the man in the sketch. Nasty looking piece of work. He's not a nomad, I'm sure of it, and he seemed to be someone that they were taking orders from as regards the horses.'

'That's all we needed. Do you think he's there for another day or two, or was the group starting to make a move?' asked Ted.

'No, there wasn't any movement about getting the horses into the shafts ready to move. I would think it won't be long, but the weather is against them moving those caravans off at present. They need some dry days to stop the wheels sinking in the mud. How long will it be before you move on them?' asked Atkinson.

'Possibly tomorrow, so keep clear of the area,' said Ted. 'I'll see my Inspector this evening and we'll go for a warrant.'

Jack thought how it would all be over by the time the magistrate had his New Year's Eve disturbed by a police inspector. He glanced at the clock. He had thirty minutes to get to the Mason's Arms.

Ted would wait for the ferry and was going to see Rose home. Jack offered to accompany Atkinson back up to Blackwall where the Park Keeper could go on to Victoria Park Station and get home. He and Ted wished each other goodbye and a good new year and agreed that Jack would not turn up for work tomorrow but enjoy a day off. Jack went along with it because, as far as Ted was concerned, he would be working at Shadwell later tonight questioning Badley, with Franks. Jack walked with Atkinson and shook hands as the Park Keeper caught the train to take him up to Victoria Park. Jack had fifteen minutes to get back as fast as he could to the Mason's Arms.

*

Mary saw him come in first and like every good barmaid acknowledged the young labourer. He had a smile only for her. Franks was standing at the bar, watching Mary, and registered the effect as the new young man with looks had obviously arrived. He turned, tankard in hand and rested an elbow on the beer sodden bar. Pushing his hat to the back of his head he waited for Jack to join him. Jack saw Franks speak briefly to a man who stood at his shoulder and realised this was someone who had the detective's back. Four other men got up from a table and joined Franks at the bar and Jack realised, with relief, that there would be seven of them. For some reason, he had thought Franks might only have come with a couple of men, but put his fear down to inexperience.

'A tankard for blue eyes, here,' said Franks and Mary gave him a look.

'That's your last, if you're on duty. I'm not leaving on my last day today with you getting the sack being on my conscience,' she said.

'Bah! Who cares about your conscience when you're running off and leaving me in the lurch. Don't fall for a woman, they up and leave you,' Franks slapped Jack on the shoulder and for an instant Jack wondered how many tankards he had had. Then he saw the wink, or had he imagined it?

'Are we on, or not for tonight?' Franks bellowed.

'Depends what you have in mind?' Jack answered, still unsure.

'The party up in Bow?' shouted Franks.

'Well, I don't know, my aunt and uncle are respectable people. I'm not sure they'll be happy you turning up in this state of inebriation,' said Jack, frowning.

'Blimey, get you, swallowed a dictionary. Well Mary, my darling Mary, wife that will now never be, farewell! If you find Brighton a little cold for your taste you know where to find me,' Franks waved his tankard and most of the contents ended up on the floor. The man behind him gripped him by the shoulder and Franks was led to the door, followed by Jack, who turned and shrugged at Mary.

'Enjoy your new life in Brighton. At least you'll be able to breathe down there. Might see you by the pier!' called Jack

'Hope you have a good New Year and try and stop the 'tec from being arrested for being a drunk,' Mary called back, laughing.

Franks and his team were already on the street. Jack joined them and the seven men crossed to pick up the Blackwall Railway. Franks stopped at the archway before the station and waited behind one of the supporting pillars until the five men clustered around him with Jack.

'You missed your way, guv,' said the big man who had stood behind Franks. 'You should have been on the stage.'

'Yes, yes, a wasted career keeping the streets safe. Now Jack, what do you have for us?' said Franks, brushing off the back handed compliment at being able to play a drunk's part.

'A positive identification by the Park Keeper, Atkinson, and Badley was still up there at the time that Atkinson left this afternoon. He's clearly using the nomads to hide amongst and seem to have some sort of authority over them. But Atkinson didn't think that any of them would be moving soon because the road is too wet for the wheels of the caravans to cope in the mud. A source down at Millwall Junction thought they would move into the West End once the celebrations get going later for any pickings they come across. I'm not sure. But it was a reliable source who's watched Badley's movements and knew that he's a thief.' Jack deliberately kept Rose's name out of it as the source.

'So, we have an evening to remember ahead of us, gentlemen. Let me introduce everyone to you, Jack. A man should always know the men he is to share a split lip or a cracked head with. This uncouth lout with a sense of humour about my acting ability is my fellow Detective Sergeant Stan Green. The rest of the group are men you would not wish to get on the wrong side of if your name was Badley, which I'm glad to say it isn't. Detective Constables Alf Bridges, Henry Allsop, Percy Samuels, and Arthur Wilkes. Gentlemen, our newest affiliate for the evening, Police Constable Jack Sargent, in the force since November and already working with Tom Hunt, and now us. Truly in the presence of greatness, gentlemen. Watch his back will you Alf. Are we ready?' Franks looked at the pieces of equipment being brought out of pockets and smirked. Jack realised all he had were his fists. They had always been enough to date but tonight he suspected would be a fight for life, like with Shaw when he had attacked Williams in the burglary case. He grinned at Alf, noting the scar on the neck.

*

Thirteen

Victoria Park Station at night, and a fire in the distance blistering the heavy, dark sky, over towards Moscow Terrace. It was a narrow strip of housing between the railway line, Wick Lane and the stretch of Common Land at the side of the park. Jack led Franks and the others out of the station, past Cunliffe's home, with its curtains drawn to the rest of Bower Road. The squeals of delight from the children on this New Year's Eve were audible as they passed by the old cabbie's home to the route across the railway in Tennyson Terrace.

If the fire was a sign of the presence of the nomad encampment that was the direction Franks wanted to go in. He and his men needed to avoid going into the trees where they would have a disadvantage as they did not know the area. Jack kept them on the roads and terraces until they reached the two taverns on the edge of the Common Land. The yards at the back of the Royal Standard and the Morpeth Castle taverns ran onto the patch of the common land shrouded by trees.

'Where's the Park Lodge that you mentioned?' asked Franks.

'Further down to the left, but the entrance to it isn't on this lane. Hopefully the Park Keeper and his wife have followed the advice and gone away for the next twenty-four hours,' said Jack.

'What do you think, Stan, a couple of the men to go up Wick Lane towards the buildings at the top, and then into Moscow Terrace?' asked Franks.

'I think so, we need to establish just where the nomads are camped and what exits we, and they, have got. The fire probably indicates the spot but equally it could be people out celebrating. Where were the horses, Jack?' asked Stan.

'Cunliffe's grey was on the other side of these trees towards a path running from Atkinson's lodge to another park lodge at the top end of the park. I don't know if the other horses we saw belonged to the nomads. Cunliffe, the cabbie, wasn't too sure,' said Jack.

'The dark makes things difficult and we don't want to be lighting lanterns. I'll go with Henry towards those buildings where the fire is coming from. Jack, you think that direction is Moscow Terrace? Where exactly did you understand that the encampment was?' asked Stan.

'Close to the railway line, I think there are old, unused, station storage buildings so they could camp for a while, be up around them and be pretty much undisturbed,' said Jack.

'And is there another way across the line?' asked Franks.

'No, only the way we came. They could run across the line or go to the right or left of Wick Lane,' said Jack.

'Or go through the park on horseback?' suggested Stan.

'Too muddy at present to move their carts, that's why they haven't left the area yet,' said Jack.

'We're after one man only, I want him able to walk and talk,' said Franks, tersely. 'I don't want the nomads to be arrested but if they get in the way, which they may do, deal with them as you have to, to get around them. We have to return on the train so Badley needs to be suitably restrained to get back to Shadwell. I don't want the added complication of extra arrests being made so don't get too carried away with the breach of the peace routine. Restraint can be done, gents, as you know, in a variety of ways without an arrest following. Stan and Henry off you go. The rest of us will wait here.'

The men stood with their backs to the park. Franks squinted as the wind was in their faces, looking as far as he could in the darkness for anyone watching them. 'What's over the other side of the line towards the east? Anyone know?' he asked.

'There's a ropery, some dwellings, watercourses over towards the Hackney Cut and the Lea River. I only know because Ted and I looked at a map back at the station, just in case we had to do exactly this type of activity,' Jack said. 'There're a spur of the Great Eastern Railway going east out of the station here as well as our line back towards Blackwall.'

'So, if our man makes it to the station there's several routes he could take. I suspect he won't try that, more likely to grab a horse and head into the park. We don't want him doing that as we won't catch him,' Can anyone ride, by the way?' Franks asked, looking round at Alf, Percy and Arthur.

'I can stay on,' said Alf.

'Bareback?' asked Franks, looking at Alf, surprised.

'Yes, well, used to be able to,' Alf grinned.

'What a wonder you are, Alf.' said Franks. 'You see gentlemen not only do I offer you a night out in the park but bareback horse riding to boot. Alright, here's Stan and Henry coming back. What findings do you have for us?'

'There are about twenty people, men and women and some children, around those buildings that Jack mentioned near the station on this side of the line. Their wagons and carts are up there but no sign of any horses. There's also no sign of Badley amongst the groups. We could, however, hear some talking in the trees at the back of the taverns and movements of horses too. He might be there dealing with his horse, but if he is he's not alone. I reckon there were about two other men from the voices we heard. It could be worth us going for that as an option and having a look for him by the horses,' said Stan.

'Good, but not all of us. And do it from a place where you can retreat to other people quickly, like the yard at the two taverns. No ploughing through dense trees for us. Now Mr Badley and I have met before and his chin knows my fist. I'm out as far as a reconnoitre is concerned. So is Jack as he's tried aiming a cab at Jack twice and I would imagine he'll never forget our boy here from Sussex, having escaped Mr Badley's attentions twice. The lucky members of the team who get to sample the beer and have a little wander toward the trees are you four with Stan. Have one on me lads and, Stan, if you see him send Alf back with the happy news,' said Franks.

'We could walk over a bit closer,' suggested Jack.

'You see I knew you were a keen one. I think you and I are well positioned waiting here. We're close to the crossing over the railway line which means we can block it or make our own escape. I'm comfortable here for the present, Jack. How are you in a fight by the way? I ask in case he rumbles the lads and makes a run for it. Unless that happens you and I stay here although I know that you are desperate to meet our quarry. We'll wait for Alf to come back.' Franks, despite his humour, nonetheless paced up and down.

Alf came out of the Morpeth Castle Tavern, carrying two tankards. 'There you are, keep the cold out, there's a bit of rum in both,' he said loudly, as he handed the tankards to Franks and Jack. Dropping his voice, he continued, 'There's three men in the trees at the back of this tavern with a group of horses. We're pretty sure one of them is Badley. We can take three of them if necessary. There's a would-be shelter been put up for the horses, a bit of tarpaulin roped across some of the trees. That's where they are.'

'That will be Cunliffe's shelter for his grey,' said Jack. 'I've an idea.'

'Steady, boy, not the sort of behaviour we expect from the young Constable, is it Alf.' Alf smirked at Franks. 'What is it?' continued Franks.

'The cab must be somewhere around, probably in a building the nomads are near at the back of the station because there wouldn't be anywhere else to keep it. It's a gamble but it's worth a look. If I can get Cunliffe to come and collect his horse on the pretext of the weather getting worse, we could harness up and ride back to Shadwell with Badley under restraint. That's assuming the cab is up by the storage sheds at the station. Cunliffe told us the route back to Whitechapel but I can probably persuade him to drive and we can get the cab back to the owner eventually. Saves taking a struggling man onto the train,' said Jack, uncertain if Franks would go for his idea.

'He won't be struggling when we've finished with him, let me just assure you of that, my friend. I like the idea of travelling in style, keeps the public safe too, as he's a nasty piece of work. But we will be nastier. Stan is a nightmare to travel with on trains. He's only got to have a man speak to him in a carriage and he thinks he's going to be stabbed in the neck. Hates enclosed places where he can't control the security. The only glitch in the plan, is getting the cab and the horse and driving it here, without half the nomad encampment jumping on you and Cunliffe, said Franks, looking at Jack. 'Alright, try it if the cabbie is willing.'

'I'll go back to Bowden Road and see if Cunliffe is prepared to help,' said Jack. 'If he is he'll come for the horse first on the pretext of putting her into an outhouse at the back of his daughter's house because of the rain. I can go and check if the cab is in those buildings. If it's still got the licence number on it that will identify it. We can hitch the horse and bring the cab into the stable yard at the back of the tavern and get Badley and the rest of us in it and back to Shadwell. I need to be clear which tavern yard to use.'

'Alf, go back and give the ridiculous news to Stan and the others. I say ridiculous as it's potentially a nightmare if the nomads challenge Jack and Cunliffe, assuming the old cab driver has the guts to help us. But the fact this lad walked into Shadwell today was also ridiculous and that worked, otherwise we would not be here. What do you say? Shall we go with the ridiculous?' asked Franks.

'It could work, the nomads don't know Jack and they'll have got used to seeing the old cabbie with his horse and cab over the years. I like the idea of getting Badley into a coach as well. If we can knock him out for a bit he would look like he's had too much to drink. That would be easier than getting him back to Shadwell on the train,' Alf nodded at Franks and Jack.

'Alright, Jack, go to it. I'll go into the bar and wait where I'm out of sight. Alf, you join the others,' said Franks.

*

Jack knocked at the house in Bower road and Mrs Blunt opened the door. From her face, she clearly expected more children to be arriving for the little party they were having. It took some moments for her to identify Jack as the young constable that had visited before but once she understood that he was with a team in plain clothes, on an operation to recover the cab, she quickly ushered him into Cunliffe's front bedroom where the cabbie was reading. Jack told Cunliffe the plan. The old cabbie had a glint in his eye as he thought about it and then was keen to go and get his old horse. Giving his daughter the reason for getting his old Bessie into the outhouse, Cunliffe left with Jack. They walked up to the tavern and Jack went into the bar, while Cunliffe walked straight through into the stable yard. From there he went into the trees to the make-shift shelter he had set up. Jack joined Franks in the bar where he was in a corner, smoking a clay pipe and having a game of dice with three other men. Stan and the other men were nowhere to be seen. Jack stood at the bar long enough for Franks to acknowledge him briefly and then he went out of the entrance to the front. He heard hooves on the cobbled stable yard and waited, holding his breath, opening and closing his fists ready in case he had to use them.

Cunliffe came around the corner of the building leading his old grey. He looked a little flushed but otherwise alright.

'I saw him, Badley I mean, he's there with a big black horse. I've not seen it before but it would fit the description of the animal you mentioned being used to pull the cab. The animals are restless, probably the wind getting up. I said the weather was too bad now for this old lady and I was putting her in the outhouse at the back of my daughter's house. He didn't bat an eyelid, wished me a Happy New Year, the bastard!' said Cunliffe.

'Well done, sir, let's get going then up Moscow Terrace to the storage buildings this side of the railway line. Let's hope I'm right and the cab is in there. If not we'll just play it that we're walking the horse back to your outhouse,' said Jack.

The first building was clearly in use by the railway company and they moved on to the next one. It was not locked and the door creaked open on rusty hinges. In the light from the station there was enough to see the numbers on the licence plate on the back and Cunliffe was ahead of Jack at recognizing his old cab. The grey was in her shaft in a matter of minutes and Cunliffe up on the driver's seat with Jack pushing the doors of the building open. Cunliffe encouraged the horse slowly forward to keep the noise level down and Jack jumped inside the cab and sat on the floor so that he was not visible from the road. A small group of men were leading a pony that was restless to one of the carts. They looked at Cunliffe as the cab and its driver rolled slowly out. Cunliffe raised his whip to them in acknowledgment and they lost interest. It was less than five minutes since they had entered the storage building and Jack was grateful for the old cabbie's knowledge and ability to play things normally. Cunliffe slipped the cab out of Moscow Terrace into Wick Lane at the top end of the park and rolled slowly down to the Morpeth Castle Tavern. He parked in the yard at the back and Jack slipped out to go into the bar. He found Franks sitting in a corner positioned so that he could see the door. Jack nodded and Franks barely responded, but started to stand up briefly speaking to the two men at the table. Outside in the yard he took in the cab and Bessie, Cunliffe's old grey horse.

'Who will charge him, you or I?' Franks asked Jack.

'You're the superior officer,' said Jack.

'That's right, I am. But you're one of the people he's tried to kill. Right, I'll do it. Let's have a word with the cabbie so he's in no doubt what's likely to happen,' and Franks walked over to introduce himself and brief Cunliffe. Then Franks burst into song. Auld Lang Syne echoed around the tavern's courtyard.

'Should old acquaintance be forgot,
and never brought to mind?'

Jack, astonished at the noise produced from Franks, and the potential to attract attention, momentarily raised his hands to try and quieten the detective, while shushing him. Then, he realised it was a signal as he heard a shout and scuffling in the trees and the distress of the horses started to produce a response from Bessie. Stan and the four constables were dealing with the three men in the trees. Franks stopped singing.

Mr Cunliffe was enjoying himself, but the glint in the eyes had hardened at the realisation that Badley was being arrested. He climbed down to calm Bessie, holding her nose and talking quietly to her. Jack made to go in to the trees to help, but Franks restrained him.

'In the dark, you don't know the lay of the land. Stay put as they may need both of us to get him into the cab.'

There was the sound of undergrowth breaking and then Badley was being hauled out of the trees by Henry and Percy into the yard. From the sounds in the park the horses were reacting with the fight around them. There was no sign of Stan and the other two constables but the fight was clearly not over yet. Jack could not take his eyes off the trees, imagining what was happening as the Constables dealt with the two men who had been with Badley.

Neither Franks nor Jack moved at first. He could not make his body respond. He made a mental effort to tell himself that would have to be prepared to do damage if needed to help his colleagues. Badley was struggling and managed to pull an arm free and hit Percy. Jack was surprised at how angry he suddenly felt. He ran forward pulling back his arm and his right hand went into a fist. He wished he had a truncheon but Morris had told him never to use it if he could help it and he deliberately had left it at the station in Leman Street. He heard Franks shout to him but it was too late to stop, 'hold the prisoner,' Jack shouted, and he used his fist to knock Badley out.

'That's quietened him down. Now into the carriage before we have an audience,' called Franks. Henry and Percy dragged the now unconscious Badley to the cab and pushed him onto the floor, climbing in after him. Percy's lip was split. Franks was in the other side and Jack went into the trees to see what was happening to Stan, Arthur and Alf. The two nomads who had gone with Badley to tend the horses and settle them under the tarpaulin for the night were sitting propped against a tree looking the worst for wear. Stan was moving towards the yard, and grinned at Jack as he walked past him. Alf and Arthur followed. Arthur was checking his own jaw. Jack was caught in the face by a branch swinging in the wind and did not manage to avoid it in time.

Cunliffe was coaxing the grey slowly towards the exit of the stable yard, deliberately taking it gently in case anyone came out of the tavern. Stan was close to the cab, and climbed up next to Cunliffe. Jack and the other two constables ran to the back as Henry swung a door open. He and Percy had hauled the unconscious Badley inside the cab and he was sprawled out on the floor. Cunliffe was starting to encourage Bessie to quicken her walk and the men inside helped their colleagues into the cab as the pace quickened. Once inside, as Cunliffe pulled away from the Morpeth Tavern, the realisation that the operation had worked started to hit Jack. Seeing the prisoner unconscious on the floor, the men started to grin at each other. The grins turned to laughter and soon Jack was joining in, but flinched at the pain in his cheek.

'I didn't expect him to be so quiet. Obviously, we reckoned without the farm boy's fist. Quite a punch you pack, young Jack,' said Franks. Jack put his head back and smiled, then realised again that his cheek hurt where the branch of the tree had caught him.

Henry leant across and had a look at the face, 'You'll have quite a bruise tomorrow, but the cheek bone is intact.'

'Great, just when I'm going to meet my girl,' said Jack, ruefully.

'She'll give you some sympathy. They like a few scars on their men,' said Arthur.

'There speaks the voice of experience, but he may not fraternize with the same sort of women that you do,' said Franks. 'Now, the only bone I have to pick with you, young Jack, is that we didn't get to charge him. So, he'll have a nice treat when we get him into the station and he comes round. Better search him now lads, in case he has anything sharp and nasty on him. Did he put up much of a fight?' Franks looked at Henry.

'No, not really, we had him before he realised what was going on,' said Henry.

'The two men with him were more of a problem, as they probably thought we were after the horses. Stan dealt with one and I caught the other from behind. Both carrying knives, by the way,' said Alf, with a grimace.

'Pleasant company, our Mr Badley keeps.' Franks banged on the front of the cab and Stan's grinning face looked through the hatch.

'How's it going in there?' called Stan.

'Sleeping like a babe,' Franks said back to him. 'I take it our cabbie knows where we're bound?'

'Yes, Jack gave him the address. He says the streets are quiet at the moment so we should be at Shadwell in fifteen minutes,' Stan let the flap fall back and the men in the cab settled back for the rest of the journey.

*

'Now this man is the kind of prisoner who will fight us all the way. If he sees the light of day again given what we can charge him with now I shall be very surprised. No doubt we will be hunted down once it becomes known he's been arrested. So, we need to act fast and be on our toes. Plus, that New York detective arrives in two days so we want this man to start singing quickly before it becomes known he's been arrested. We want what he knows. If the focus is on Hunt's team by someone above we have forty-eight hours I reckon as they won't know Shadwell station has him,' said Franks.

250

'If either of those two men in the park that were with him tonight are involved in his activities word will get back, won't it?' asked Alf.

'My guess is that it's mainly petty pilfering and theft from the docks that the nomad group work on with Badley. I think he's been tolerated providing he's produced opportunities for them. I doubt they're ready to run fowl of the police on murder charges.'

'We've got the opportunity to find the man who's orchestrating this character's activities. My intention is to up the charges now to attempted murder of two policemen, but I think we'll go for involvement in the murder of the Faceless Woman case, given the way her face was worked over. We have the rape charge and the aggravated burglary but I quite fancy seeing what effect the thought of dangling at the end of a rope has on Mr Badley's tongue. Give him a smack, will you Perc, he's coming to. There's no point in having a difficult journey,' said Franks, as Percy complied.

'We want a confession and we want names. We want to know if he's got any involvement in the Berringer case. I wonder if it would be worth doing an identity parade for three witnesses who were at the scene shortly after the coach crashed and the diplomat was flung out? Given his activity in driving coaches he may have been involved,' said Jack.

'Well let's slap him with everything, shall we? He can only hang once, remember Jack, but it may loosen his tongue to think he's going to dangle at the end of a rope for either of Mr or Mrs Berringer's deaths,' Franks said. 'We need to get those witnesses along in the morning. Do you have their names?'

'And addresses,' said Jack.

'He may be the man who worked over the face of that woman after she was dead, he's no stranger to violence as the rape case shows,' said Alf.

'Exactly. I intend to charge him with everything in order to make him talk. We'll see what the boy's upstairs will say and who starts to apply pressure on us. Then we'll follow the lead,' Franks paused and turned to Jack. 'We'd better agree on a story for your Inspector Hunt. He'll be upsetting a magistrate about now I should imagine, to get a warrant. I ought to send a cable to New Road. How do you want to play it?'

Jack laughed, 'I'm probably for it no matter what story you concoct. I suppose we could play on my being keen, wandering up here this evening and stumbling onto an arrest in progress, enlisting the help of Mr Cunliffe as he would know me, and lending a hand when Badley got difficult.'

'Sounds brilliant, you should write for the papers! That will do, and no doubt you'll be recommended for commendation, as will be all the men on the team,' grinned Franks.

This statement was met with embarrassed smiles. The cab was slowing and Jack pulled up the blind and looked through the window. Cunliffe was swinging off the Commercial Road on to White Horse Street heading for the Shadwell Police Station.

Henry and Percy carted Badley into a cell and cuffed him so that when he came to he would be easier to get into a charge room. They left him still unconscious and locked the door. The team went into the back room and Jack was glad to see the Desk Sergeant had changed from earlier so he did not have any difficult explanations to make. Franks and his men were in the room at the back of the front desk and a bottle of scotch was opened and a toast was made to 1873 and the collaboration they had with Jack. And Jack welcomed it and then they heard Badley start to create as he came to in the cell.

'Better get the Police Surgeon down to have a look at Badley, before we get accused of stuff that's nothing to do with the arrest. He should take a look at that cheek too, Jack. Perc, you should be looked at as well. Anyone else need the saw bones?' asked Stan.

The men shook their heads.

'Where's Mr Cunliffe?' asked Jack.

'He's making a statement with a meat pie and a pint. Then one of the Constables is going to travel home with him on the train to make sure he gets back alright before the service stops running. We've put the cab and the horse in the stables and we'll let the owner know in the morning that we've recovered his property. The old cabbie is singing your praises. He's had a ball, has Mr Cunliffe,' said Alf.

'His daughter will be getting worried that he's not back yet. Funny there's no police station up in that area yet,' said Jack.

'It will come, London's spreading out that way,' said Stan.

'Right, gentlemen, when you're ready, please make your statements, while Alf gets the Surgeon in. Then we'll invite our guest to an interview room. Jack and Perc, see the Surgeon after he's checked Badley and then join Stan and I. The cable has gone to Hunt and I shouldn't imagine he'll be long before he arrives. I'll let Hunt know that you are in the interview, or he'll not trust me,' said Franks.

An hour later, Jack had finished a sandwich and had it confirmed that the cheek bone was not broken as far as the police surgeon was confirmed. Arnica had been applied to the swelling and the bruise. The eye was going to be a pretty picture to present to Harriet tomorrow, Jack thought, as he looked at himself in a mirror. He checked where he could find Franks with the Duty Sergeant. He and Stan had gone out to eat before interviewing Badley. The rest of the men had gone home having finished statements and being dismissed. Deciding to wait in the room at the back of the Duty Sergeant's desk he turned for the door as Franks called to him from the entrance door.

'Gentlemen, shall we take the party to the criminal?' said Franks. Turning to Jack he said, 'Coming? Or do you have an alternative evening planned?'

'Wouldn't miss it for the world,' said Jack smiling and then flinching at the same time as his cheek hurt.

'The cable has gone to Hunt. Whether he'll make it tonight will depend on where he is I suspect. If he's parked in a Magistrate's study trying to get a warrant for Badley's arrest he may not get the news before the morning. He'll also run out of time to cross the river if it gets much later. So, we will crack on, young Jack,' Franks flamboyantly extended an arm for Jack to go ahead of him down the corridor, and Stan grinned, knowing how pleased Franks was.

The interview with Badley consisted of silence from the man at first. He refused to acknowledge his name or last known address. He had an air of confidence that he would not be detained for long, which was understandable as whoever was protecting him had got the charges dropped last time. Then Franks read out the charges almost in a casual way.

'Murder of the American Diplomat, Berringer, and murder of Mrs Berringer, attempted murder of Police Constable Jack Sargent on two occasions, once on the Commercial Road, and once in the Haymarket. Attempted murder of Sergeant Morris in the Haymarket….'Franks was stopped by an angry shout and Badley raising an arm above his head and brought his fist crashing down on the table in front of him.

'You can't pin this lot on me. I've not murdered anyone. It's imagination that I tried to run anyone over,' Badley spat to the side.

'Charming, with our charwoman in mind, don't do that again. Well we'll let you think which ones on the sheet you don't agree with. But you will have an identification parade in the morning from the coach crash on the Whitechapel Road. This police constable has already identified you as the driver of the coach that attempted to run him down on two occasions and which almost killed his colleague. Stolen property you were driving as well. We'll roll the rape and aggravated burglary in if you like, but frankly, it doesn't make much difference as you will hang this time. Justice for the victims of course, which is very important, but you won't be with us for too much longer,' Franks looked at his watch. 'Goodness, is that the time, beddy-bye's for you in a cell so that you look your freshest for the identification parade in the morning, and party time for us.'

'You can't do this, I've not murdered anyone,' shouted Badley, he made to spit again but thought better of it as he saw Stan clench his fist.

'Can't abide spitting,' said Stan, walking closer.

'I wouldn't upset him,' said Franks to Badley, 'under a bit of strain with the types we've been bringing in recently, and unpredictable in his behaviour. Nothing you'd like to say? Anyone spring to mind who could help you? No? I suppose not many people would want to help a bastard like you. Like to tell me who it was who helped you get the aggravated burglary and rape charges dropped?'

'Go to hell,' said Badley, turning his face away.

'Most likely, but I'll see you there, and I will hound you for all eternity just like I will here in this life until I see you convicted of the crimes you have committed. You've had quite a career, bit short lived as you won't be coming out this time. The hang man is on holiday, I understand, until the fifth of January. As is the undertaker. But he'll be back on the fifth as well and they can both pop in, and take the measurements for the drop and the coffin,' Franks sat down opposite Badley and waited.

'Nothing? Right, time for our New Year celebrations. Hope you get a refreshing night's sleep, Mr Badley. We want you looking all pink and pretty for our visitors in the identification parade. Think on the charges. These aren't going to go away. As you're probably aware, with your record, we don't have to release you for a bit.' Franks opened the door and called to the Duty Sergeant. Badley sat and stared at the table top. Two Constables came in and placed themselves on either side of him ready to take him out of the room towards the cells. As he reached the door Badley spat on the floor.

'Wait,' said Stan and the two constables paused. Stan went across the room and planted his feet apart and stared into Badley's eyes who had just the briefest expression of anticipation. Franks leant forward slightly, waiting. Jack looked at Stan's hands but they were not clenching.

'Tomorrow,' said Stan placing his face near Badley's ear and then the man was led away to the cells.

'This is why you can't take him on a train,' said Franks to Jack, nodding at Stan. 'He gets upset about behaviour, these days. Right, give me the names and addresses of the witnesses, who were at the scene when Berringer' s body was discovered and we'll get Constables round there now.'

'There's a butcher, called Able at number five, he was one of the first on the scene, and a domestic at number three called Mrs Edwards, she doesn't live in though, and I don't know her actual address,' said Jack, pausing while he thought. 'I wouldn't bother with her employer, the music teacher, I don't think she was amongst the first on the scene. But there was a director of the County Bank, who has a connection with Inspector Doyle's wife as he's her adopted brother, also called by the same surname she had as her maiden name, Mr Moore. He was one of the first at the carriage crash. I don't know where he will be, though, tonight. I know Inspector Doyle and Mrs Doyle are in Oxford but I don't what their connection is with that city. I didn't interview him.'

'Who did?' asked Franks.

'Sam Curzon,' said Jack.

'And where is Constable Curzon?' asked Stan.

'Away on duties in Windsor, he'll be working as a Waterman. That's his father's background and Sam grew up on the river. The surname Moore was found in a Boatman's register at Windsor with that of Berringer on a specific day. The Berringer's had a child, or children, at the school there.' said Jack, unhappily because of the link to Inspector Doyle.

'Interesting,' said Franks, sucking air in through his teeth. 'Stan, find Constable Curzon in the morning. Right, young Jack, we will go out together with uniform in attendance, in a carriage at this time of the night, and get you back to the Commercial Road so you can get some shut eye. I and a couple of Constables will go to the Whitechapel Road from there now, and arrange a little outing for the witnesses to be here at ten o'clock in the morning. I would love your company, in uniform, please. I daresay your Inspector may be joining us with anyone else he wishes to involve. That's it. If we're to see the New Year in let's get cracking.'

As they climbed into the carriage in the yard at the back of the station Franks called two Constables over who joined the Detective and Jack. The carriage rumbled slowly along the stinking roads with the two Police Constables visible at the windows.

On the Commercial Road Jack climbed down on the corner of Arbour Street East.

'Happy New Year, see you at ten o'clock in the morning,' shouted Franks to Jack, as the carriage pulled out and picked up speed on its way to upset Mr Able the butcher at number five in Whitechapel, and anyone else that Franks could round up for the identification parade on New Year's Day. Jack waved and called back the same greeting.

*

Eleven o'clock, but the adrenalin had not yet drained from the system and he knew he would not sleep. Yet he was tired. He debated about turning for Arbour Square but instead walked on to St. Thomas's church, remembering there would be supper, a face that he knew, and the type of service he had been going to all his life on high days and holidays. He craved contact with someone, anyone, with whom he could have a different conversation than about work. His mind was so tired that he could not work out how to do the change from uniform to his smart office clothes tomorrow afternoon. He had a logistical problem in ensuring that he actually did meet Harriet at four o'clock and knew he could not arrive in uniform, or be late. Supper at the church hall, the Watchnight service, New Year's greetings, were all things that would feel normal to him on this high day and holiday as one year died and a new one began.

Jack stood in the church grounds, looking like he was there to help the grave digger. A gent tipped him sixpence as he walked past him into church.

'You've kept the grounds well this year, a Happy New Year to you,' he said to Jack.

'I...' Jack started to try and explain that he was not a groundsman but realised that he looked like one after scrabbling around in the park and hiding in Cunliffe's cab. He looked at the coin in his hand and then laughed. The night was damp but just before he went into the church hall the first moon he had seen for weeks actually appeared from behind the clouds. He put the coin in the offertory box in the porch, and joined the people gathering for the supper.

*

Fourteen

Jack woke at seven o'clock. 1872 had exited and he had seen 1873 enter with handshakes in the church. His first waking moments in the New Year came with a bang as Jack opened his eyes. He lay staring at the ceiling as he had woken with a start. This was New Year. The banging stopped and a set of pictures rolled through his mind of the previous evening and Badley's arrest. Then he moved, throwing the blankets off. He was due at Shadwell Police Station at ten o'clock, although Franks and his team would be back at work by now.

Today he was likely to have some explaining to do to Inspector Hunt. And then there was Harriet. His face softened into a smile. Harriet. She would expect him at Westminster Bridge on the dot of four o'clock and there would be hell to play if he was not there.

He had had less than six hours of sleep. Jack had left the church at one 'o'clock in the morning with Hannah and they had walked the short distance back to the house in Arbour Square. Like Jack, Michael Culley had not come back to Arbour Square for dinner and Hannah had donated the pies she had made to the Watch Night supper.

'I may get sacked, but I can't stand good food going to waste,' she had said firmly to Jack as they left church.

'Well, we ate them there didn't we, so where's the harm?' Jack had said, in an attempt to encourage her.

He had been too tired to undress, and had slipped his wet boots off in the porch, and climbed the flights of stairs to collapse on his bed, fully clothed. At some point, he had pulled the blankets across himself as the room cooled. Now the banging on the front door had woken him.

Jack poked his head over the bannister to see Hannah on her way up the stairs. In the hall below was a police uniform. An inspector. His jug of water and bowl was already outside his door on the hall stand where Hannah usually left it. Jack wondered how much sleep Hannah had got before she would have been up to start breakfast and lay fires.

'Sir,' Hannah had stopped on the third flight having glanced up and seen him staring at her progress on the stairs. 'Inspector Hunt in the breakfast room for you. I put him in there, as I thought he looked hungry.'

'Yes, he probably is. He's had an early start,' said Jack and then thought that Hunt had probably had little sleep thanks to the telegram. He turned to go back into his room to get ready and then called down to the fast disappearing Hannah, 'Tell him I'm just dressing and I'll be down.'

Hannah waved a hand in acknowledgement and carried on down the stairs. He thought he could hear her muttering under her breath about the time some people chose to come calling on other's days off.

Jack washed and put on his uniform. Franks had stipulated it but thought he stood the chance of Hunt being irritated when he saw him in uniform as it was his day off. He knew Hunt could order him not to go to Shadwell. He'd face that if it happened. Then he packed his office suit in the carpet bag so that he could take a change of clothes with him ready for the meeting with Harriet.

He went down and left the carpet bag on the hall table. To his surprise, Michael Culley was at the breakfast table, and Tom Hunt was helping himself to bacon.

'Jack, a Happy New Year,' said Michael, standing and extending a hand.

With a quick glance at Tom Hunt's face, Jack responded with a handshake and wished Michael the same. Hunt nodded to jack and fixed him with a hard stare. The Inspector looked grim and tired.

'I'm sorry if you've not slept sir, after hearing about the job last night,' said Jack, and his honesty at getting straight to the point had the desired effect of relaxing the atmosphere. Tom Hunt's mouth almost went into the flicker of a smile and he pulled out a chair and sat down at the table.

'Can I get you a cup of tea?' asked Jack.

'Yes, you can. Get your own breakfast and then perhaps we can use another room to talk about police matters if Mr Culley doesn't mind us being anti-social.' Hunt started to cut up his bacon.

'Not at all,' said Michael.

'What are your plans today, Michael?' asked Jack, pouring two cups of tea.

'More fun than it looks like you both will have, given you're in uniform,' said Michael.

'Well, we shouldn't be. But something came up last night and now there's no choice.' Hunt gave Jack a look, his eyebrows raised. Jack helped himself to a boiled egg and Hannah's thickly cut bread, still warm, and again wondered how much sleep she had got since they arrived home at one o'clock in the morning.

'I should imagine you're hungry, sir, you must have left home quite early to get here,' said Jack.

'Yes,' said Hunt, shortly.

'So, where are you off to today, Michael?' Jack soldiered on trying to keep a normal tone. Then he recalled that Charlie Banks would be set to investigate Michael Culley's background by Ted Phillips this morning. Michael and all the lodgers in the house. He swallowed his conscience with a spoonful of egg, and waited for Michael's answer. However, Michael did not get the chance as the door opened and Hannah stood in the doorway with a shovel full of coal in her hand. She fixed Tom Hunt with a stare, and held out the shovel.

'As its New Year's Day, sir and you being the first across the threshold after midnight, and a guest, would you mind goin' back out of the front door and comin' in again for luck. We may be too late to stop bad comin' in as we should have done this when you arrived. It's traditional to first foot where I come from, you being dark haired and a man, like.' Hannah pushed the coal shovel closer to the Inspector.

'What's that for?' asked Hunt.

'It's a symbol of well-being for the house. It's supposed to foretell the household's future,' said Hannah.

261

Hunt had a look on his face that he had completely lost control of an ordered world in the last twelve hours. He held out his hand for the shovel of coal.

'I bring this in, do I?' Hunt asked Hannah.

'Yes, sir, for luck.'

Jack looked at Hannah and frowned at the portent of doom they were all expecting if Hunt did not comply with her superstition. He watched Hunt comply as the Inspector went back into the hall and Hannah opened the front door. He dutifully stepped into the porch and she closed the door. He rang the bell and she opened the door for him. Hunt gave her back the shovel without a word and re-joined Jack, Culley and his cooling bacon. Jack could not explain it but Hannah's actions and Hunt's compliance seemed to be like desperation.

'Finished?' asked Hunt, as Jack put his teaspoon down.

'Yes sir, shall I lead the way.' Jack stood up.

'I think you'd better, as I don't know where I'm going. Goodbye Mr Culley,' Hunt said.

'Nice to meet you, Inspector. Maybe see you later tonight, Jack?' said Michael.

'I should think so,' said Jack. 'I should be back by seven.'

Jack led the way to the lounge on the other side of the hall. He closed the door and shivered with the contrast of the temperature in the room to the rest of the house. Hannah had not lit a fire for the last few days in this room although it was laid. He went to the fireplace and found a box of matches tucked behind the clock.

'I'll just get the fire going, sir, no point in starting the day cold,' said Jack, striking a match.

'No, good point. What were you thinking of last night? You could have got yourself killed going up to Victoria Park on your own? You were lucky you ran into Franks,' said Hunt, grim faced.

'I didn't exactly go there alone, sir. I found detective Franks at the Mason's Arms last night and it became apparent he was with a team. I'd got the sketch of Badley from the cabbie and I had shown it to him. Ted had a lead from a source down at the docks that there were incidents of stealing involving nomads. There was a chance that it could be the group from the park that we thought that the driver of the coach was connected to. Ted's contact confirmed the man was involved. The Park Keeper, Atkinson, met Ted at Blackwall, and he confirmed to Ted, last night that….'

'You showed the sketch to a detective that you hadn't checked out! You could have blown the investigation. There's no way you could have known that Franks was trustworthy,' Hunt sounded irritated.

'He's too obvious, sir, in his smelly jacket, beer stains, and his battered bowler. He's playing a part. They were really good sir, as a team. I wish you'd been there. It was like a proper operation, well managed, and they went in and got Badley,' said Jack.

'You contributed a lot I hear as well using that contact with Cunliffe. But you didn't follow the rules. And you were supposed to be having two days as leave. The reality is that you've worked your leave. You won't survive if you do that. You certainly won't have a family life eventually. Yes, it's a good outcome but it may not have been. You can't just make up your mind that you're going in because you get an idea. You've been lucky with this one and it's worked out and you've probably moved the investigation on. We have yet to see. But you can't disobey the rules based on your instinct, Jack. You should have informed Ted as the more experienced officer and let him decide if it was to be pursued.' Hunt finished and the two men looked at each other.

Jack quietly said, 'We made an arrest though, sir.'

'Yes, I've acknowledged that,' said Hunt, irritated. 'I know you're making the point. Accept I'm displeased with you acting alone. Anyway, there's an identification parade this morning. If Badley is identified as being at the scene where Berringer's dead body was found he'll be charged with murder. We'll see if that loosens his tongue.'

'There's a good chance he was there,' said Jack.

'Well we'd better go and find out.' Hunt moved to the door, and then paused as he turned the door knob. 'I value your contribution, but this could have gone wrong. You may have been killed. You may be relying on instinct, or perhaps you genuinely are piecing details together faster than I am, but you don't go in alone and by alone I'm including working with Franks. Is that clear?'

'Yes sir.' Jack paused, not moving as Hunt pulled the door open. Franks looked at him impatiently, 'What is it?'

'I'm supposed to be meeting my young lady on Westminster Bridge this afternoon at four o'clock. Is that still going to be alright?' asked Jack.

'Essential. If that's the only way I can get you to take some time off,' said Hunt, caustically.

*

Mrs Edwards and Mr Able were to view the line of men separately. Mr Able, still unwell, was seated on a chair in front of a window overlooking a parade yard. A piece of muslin hung in front of it so the observer could not be seen by the men in the yard. He glared at Jack when he arrived. Franks had wanted Jack present as the Constable who had interviewed the man and the butcher seemed to blame Jack for the fact that he had been disturbed to do come to Shadwell Police Station to do "his duty."

Mrs Edwards had been at home with her son and had been glad to come. The music teacher had been disturbed and had provided the son's address. Mrs Edwards waited in an inspector's office with Hunt and a Constable made her tea. She would be brought in to the room overlooking the yard after Mr Able left so that the two of them had no opportunity to speak to each other.

Mr Able was seated behind the muslin. A knife had cut a small slit just sufficient for an observer to see through. In the yard in front of them was a line of men, including Badley. There were at least three Police Constables in the line, a couple of actors that had been pulled in at the last minute, one of whom had applied makeup so that he had the same bruises around the jaw as Badley. They were a similar height to Badley and Jack thought Franks had done exceptionally well in producing a group of men who were similar in complexion and build.

Mr Able took his time, and eventually asked a police constable if all the men could crouch down with their backs towards him, and look over their left shoulder. This was arranged and he named number five, which was Badley.

'He's the Policeman,' said Mr Able. 'The Policeman who didn't have a number on his uniform. I told you,' Mr Able gave Jack a look. Jack nodded and ran a picture in his mind of the group that Mr Able had described to him at the scene of the coach crash. 'That's how I remember him,' the butcher continued, 'looking at me over his shoulder while he crouched over the body.'

'Did he hold a knife?' asked Franks.

'No, he didn't have any blood on him either, so he hadn't done a stabbing on the journey. Then he got up and walked away under the bridge. I looked for a knife. I told you that,' Mr Able pointed at Jack

'Really dressed as a Policeman?' Franks looked at Jack as he had not mentioned this.

'He didn't have a number though,' said Mr Able.

'Thank you Mr Able, you've been very helpful. We'll get you home,' Stan said.

'It's only one man though, there was a group of them around the body. Where are the others?' Mr Able said, dryly.

'You've given us a positive identification, sir, that's the beginning we need. He'll talk now you've identified him,' said Jack.

'I hope so. Terrible thing, you should have seen it, someone knew what they were doing,' Mr. Able called over his shoulder as a Constable opened the door for him.

'A Policeman without a number. Now where would they have got the uniform from?' mused Franks.

'It's got to be straight out of the factory,' said Jack.

'It's a stock of uniforms before the numbers are sown on. Stan, do we have a stock of uniforms on site ready for new recruits to have the number sown on?' asked Franks.

'Bound to have,' said Stan.

'So, any police station would have. That doesn't help us narrow a connection down. How ironic that Badley dresses in a policeman's uniform and the idiots don't even have the sense to stitch false identity numbers on it.' Franks said in his sardonic way.

'It confirms a link with the police though,' said Jack.

'Perhaps, perhaps not. Any theatre company will have costume in the store, why not a policeman's uniform. It doesn't have to be authentic, young Jack, a clever costume maker can copy anything. Maybe they just didn't get around to sewing a set of numbers on, or perhaps they were relying on shock making any witnesses at the scene unobservant. They reckoned without someone that was used to blood, though, didn't they?' Franks shrugged and looked at his colleagues.

'Mrs Edwards next,' said Stan.

Mrs Edwards was pleased to see Jack again and he pulled out her chair in front of the window for her and made sure she was comfortable. Franks intervened when she started chatting about the case to ensure Jack did not lead her in any way. He suggested Jack went and made her another cup of tea to get him away and once he had left the room, Franks lifted the slit in the muslin cloth and beckoned to the Sergeant in the yard to line the men up again.

Jack came in with a fresh cup of tea and Mrs Edwards gratefully thanked him.

'Have you done the identity parade?' asked Jack, surprised as Franks thanked her.

'Yes. Many thanks again, Mrs Edwards, we are very grateful to you and we do apologise for disturbing your New Year's Day. We'll get you back home now,' said Franks.

Stan lifted the curtain and gave a thumbs-up to the Sergeant in the yard. The man slapped the cuffs on Badley and led him out. Tom Hunt came in.

'Right, let's go and do a little leaning, shall we,' said Franks.

'Outcome?' said Hunt, quizzically.

'Both picked the same man. Badley is implicated in the murder of Berringer. Mr Able, the butcher, identified him as the Policeman without the identity number. No blood on him according to the butcher, who, I think, would notice. He's not been involved in moving Badley into the coach if the man had already been stabbed. Nor has he done the stabbing on the journey. My gut tells me that he may have been up top with the driver. Somebody was feeling theatrical and setting a scene. Given his propensity to steal cabs and drive hell for leather down London streets my money is on him being on top,' said Franks.

'How many people did Able and Mrs Edwards say were around the body when they arrived at the scene of the crash?' Hunt turned to Jack.

Jack screwed up his eyes trying to remember. Then he had it. 'Four, I think,' he said.

'Driver, Badley as the false policeman, maybe a couple of people who had been in the cab with Berringer, or what was left of Berringer by the time they did that journey,' said Stan.

'And one of those men potentially involved, or working for someone that was involved, with Mrs Berringer?' suggested Hunt.

'Did we ever find the coach?' Jack turned to ask Hunt suddenly as he had remembered that Ted had left the meeting they had all had at New Road in order to make enquiries with the American legation.

'We're still waiting on a report,' said Hunt, sardonically.

'And the routes Berringer may have travelled from his home?' asked Jack.

'We don't know. I've not had an address. The American Consulate are not proving too cooperative. They told Phillips their detective will investigate when he arrives on the second of January. Berringer is one of their own, was the line they were taking,' said Hunt.

'Sounds like they're keen to cloak a scandal,' said Franks, looking at Stan, who nodded.

'I'm sure they are, but this is a murder on English territory, of two American citizens no doubt involving British citizens and, if what we suspect is true, corrupt British citizens who are Metropolitan Police officers, and this murder may even go higher up potentially. I'll co-operate but I'll be damned if I'll back off,' Hunt's face was set.

'Right, I agree,' Franks slapped his hand down on the table.

'Mr Cunliffe may know,' said Jack. Hunt looked at him.

'Is that the cab driver from yesterday?'

'Yes, sir. It might be worth me asking him if he knows where the Legation staff lived, if he ever picked any up, perhaps which routes would have been taken from there over to Whitechapel. The cab yard is in Whitechapel so if he went over to the West End he can probably give us a route,' suggested Jack.

'Right, you can check with him, tomorrow. Not today. And, good idea,' Hunt nodded, giving Jack a look.

'Is tomorrow early enough, sir,' said Jack, looking concerned.

'You have other plans today,' said Hunt, firmly.

'Well, Stan, time to go and give Badley the good news that we have positive identification. Two Murder charges I think, irrespective of the butcher's statement that he did not have blood on him. Let's sprinkle a little stardust and make believe and add a host of other charges, thrown in for good measure, and then leave him to worry about it all for a few hours. He should be ripe to start to sing. Then we'll wait to see who pops out of the wood work to get him off. I'm assuming that you would like to remain, Inspector Hunt?' said Franks.

'It would make my year,' said Hunt.

'We're approaching lunch, gentlemen. Will you both join us?' asked Franks.

Jack looked at the clock, working out how long he needed to get to Westminster.

'Young Jack, I sense you're nervous about something?' said Franks.

'Actually, I have to get to Westminster by four o'clock to meet someone. I haven't seen her since I moved to Leman Street and if I don't make it….' Jack was interrupted by Stan.

'You'll have two hours. But you should get off by two o'clock or your winter nights will be even colder than they currently are,' Stan said, laughing.

'Come and get some lunch and then you'd better get off,' said Hunt.

'Are you sure, sir?' asked Jack.

'Ah, despite the lady's charms we see the policeman's dilemma when he sniffs that he is close to the kill! Get out of here, Jack, or you'll end up like me, hanging around overly pretty bar-maids, half your age, who have no intention of ending up with you. Wasn't this your day off?' Franks said.

'His second day off, which he hasn't taken,' said Hunt, giving Jack a meaningful look. 'Get off Sargent, and that's an order.'

Jack grinned at Hunt and then his face fell. He looked at Franks, 'How will I know what happens?'

'What time are you back tonight?' asked Franks.

'About seven to Arbour Square, I should think,' said Jack.

'I'll be in the usual place until nine o'clock, perhaps see you there for a New Year drink.'

'But no antics tonight, Sargent, and that's another order!' Hunt barked.

*

Jack saw the tram coming up the damp, dusk filled, Westminster street. He checked the clock for the umpteenth time. Bang on four o'clock. 'Punctual little lady, my Harriet,' he thought, if indeed he could dare to assume that was what she still was.

Through a window on the tram a lady was making a small circle of clear glass on a steamy window using a handkerchief, and peering out through the space that she had made into the fading light. Jack could see a dainty hat perched on some dark curls sitting low over a forehead and he wondered if that could be Harriet. A thirty-minute journey it would have been for her from Camberwell Green. Jack had already been in Westminster for an hour, having over compensated to avoid being late.

Finding a flower seller had not been easy, and he had checked there was not going to be a last-minute glitch in getting the table that he had already reserved in the hotel tea room. But now he was ready.

The people started to disembark from the tram. There were two exits to keep an eye on for Harriet as she disembarked. Half the city seemed to get off the tram, including some smart young ladies, holding onto the platform pole as they stepped down, very trim, and stylish in their dress, like he had seen in Piccadilly the other day, and Jack realised one was the wearer of the dainty hat he had seen through the tram window. He looked away from the alluring curls underneath it. He must look for Harriet. He scanned the crowd looking for the person registered in the picture in his mind as the scullery maid in a hot kitchen.

'Jack!' called one of the stylish ladies, and he momentarily glanced around to see which man had the same name as himself and was lucky enough to be called by the owner of the curls.

'Jack! It's me, I can't look that different just because Georgina made me a new dress,' and the face of the owner of the hat and the curls was alive as she smiled into his eyes. Then the smile faded as he took off his bowler hat and she saw the bruised cheek and black eye.

'Harriet,' he said, and could not think of anything else to say, 'Harriet,' he repeated, and just stopped himself from slipping an arm around her and drawing her close

'Are those for me?' Harriet Fildew it was, and she was very aware of the effect she had had. Concerned at the state of his face she gently took the bouquet and allowed Jack to kiss her cheek. He was lost and all thoughts of Badley, Berringer, and the Faceless Woman, had gone.

'You look amazing. I've never seen you like this,' said Jack.

'Ah, well it helps to have a sister who's a dress-maker and it suits my new position.' Harriet gave a small bounce and then remembered herself. 'I've got a new job, Jack, parlour maid, so no more hot kitchens for me. I joined an agency and I start at a new address tomorrow on the Grove. There's a smart uniform too and better money and I can save more. But what has happened to you, have you been in a fight? Are you alright, Jack? Goodness, it looks awful. I'd not thought that you'd have to fight, but of course you will,' said Harriet, the concern dismissing her smile.

'It wasn't a fight, that was over when I got there, I was helping on an arrest up in a park last night and a branch smacked me in the face. I didn't know the area and it was so dark,' Jack explained.

Harriet put out her hand, hesitated for a few seconds and pulled off her glove and rested her finger tips gently against his cheek. Jack saw the concern in her eyes and he smiled. 'It's not broken, is it?' she asked.

'No, of course not,' said Jack, lightly. He transferred the hand from his cheek to one of his own.

'And your eye isn't damaged?' asked Harriet.

'No, it's just a black eye. I've had a lot of those, growing up on the farm,' he nodded at the Christmastide bouquet he had given to her, embarrassed at the amount of attention his injuries were getting but also torn as he liked it.

'Do you like the Christmastide? I think that's what they called it when I bought them.' Harriet looked into the bouquet he had held out to her of a Christmas evergreen arrangement made up of holly, laurel, with some mistletoe and dried lavender wound through it, wrapped around with rushes.

'I'll get you something better in the spring,' said Jack. 'I know it sounds daft but I'd forgotten there wouldn't be flowers now.'

'I love it,' said Harriet, enthusiastically. 'Can we go down there?' She pointed down to the area called the Cut. 'I passed it on the tram and the area looks interesting.'

'I don't know, it might be a bit rough, I don't know the area at all. I'd wanted to take you to a little café,' said Jack, holding back as she moved as if to go in the direction of Lower Marsh towards the Cut. It had looked a hive of retail activity with many costermongers still out in the streets, and more than two hundred shops open on New Year's Day, hoping to catch some trade for a fresh year. From where they stood they could see donkey carts approaching Westminster Bridge bringing the trade to those more inclined to enjoy the river views. Harriet looked at the mist from the Thames, seeping and swirling into the neighbouring streets, wrapping itself around trams and carts and carriages as she and Jack stood together.

'Penny for them,' said Jack.

'Oh, I was just thinking of the early mornings on the farm, the way the mist would cling to the hedges as though it would stay all day. Ma's had it hard since Pa died three years ago, but she's done what she set out to do and got the dairy business established.'

'Will you go back?' asked Jack, anticipating loss.

'No. Ma said to me to take every opportunity and not be dependent on anyone. Anyway, you know what the harvests have been like this year with the wet. I've got more chance of making my way in London than staying around Honiton now.'

'No one person to go back to?' Jack grinned as he asked but his eyes gave away the uncertainty as he waited for the answer.

'Would I be here with you now, if there was? Anyway, I've no time for being serious like that. And there's no one there now except the farmhands and I'm not interested in them! I've got things to do and I'm not going to rely on a man. This is a new world and there's so many of the young coming into the capital from the countryside. Georgina's here, one of my brothers will come soon and Caroline will follow in a few years when she's old enough. So, the Fildews will be in London as well as Honiton,'

Harriet stopped and withdrew her hand. The initial meeting was over, and there was one of those natural lulls in the conversation as neither of them wanted to show the other they were too keen. Harriet's independence had come to the fore. Jack was smarting at the reference to the farmhands.

'That's what I was,' Jack said.

'What?'

'A farmhand,' Jack looked at the river not wanting to risk seeing the potential dismissal that might be in Harriet's eyes. There was no such message for him as she turned to look at him and shrugged.

'I know. Well, you're not that now, are you. I'm not doing the milking every morning, and I'm not staying in the scullery, either. It was just what we did while we were growing up. You've moved on, and you'll carry on climbing up the ladder because you're determined. That's what I like about you, Jack, nothing stops you. We're alike in that. Anyway, enough of the past, today's New Year's Day and we're having tea in Westminster!' Harriet stood on her toes to look down at the river below. Jack joined her pointing out Westminster pier below them and Acre Wharf and the flour mills on the south side. They crossed to the other side of the bridge and stared at the wharves further up the river past the Palace of Westminster. Sailors and lads, unloading boats, fought to keep body and soul together in any work they could obtain, even on New Year's Day. They called to each other and the echo of their voices carried on the water. On the south bank of the river sprawled St. Thomas's Hospital with its medical school next door. Jack and Harriet could just make out Lambeth Bridge but it was already starting to disappear in the mist. Dusk was heavy with clouds which were filled with the promise of more rain. The moon would struggle to appear later and there was an occasional glimpse of it between rain clouds which made the evening feel darker than on recent wintery days.

Jack moved slightly to start walking again and Harriet followed him. She turned her face in to the wind. 'The wind's a south westerly, Jack. It's from home! Happy New Year, Ma,' she shouted. 'Their love is on the wind, Jack!'

'What a romantic, you are. Such a mix. One minute you're the independent woman and the next a poet,' Jack laughed.

'What would it be like at home, Jack?'

'In Sussex? Well, not this year, but usually by now there would be frost and snow in parts.'

'What a confusing time it's been, Jack. I don't know where you're staying or anything about what you're working on at the moment. You used to come and chatter about everything you were doing, and you were so full of life about the police. Now you're assessing if it's safe to be in the street,' said Harriet.

'It's just that bad things happen in crowds and it wasn't what I had in mind for us this afternoon. I found a nice tea place, and you're so dressed up, I want to take you somewhere nice, somewhere I can spoil you a bit, not down to a market as its going dark. We ought to get out of the damp anyway, and the mist is closing in. The edge of your skirt is a bit damp from that puddle and this rain never stops.' Jack held out a hand, which Harriet did not take, emphasising her independence. She walked towards him and he smiled softly at her.

'That big smile of yours. It's not deceiving and it's full of cheek. But I don't really know if I can trust you, Jack. Calling in at so many houses on your beat, charming the cooks and the maids with your manners and your strong build. You're a bit of a distraction so I'm being straight with you. How many other girls do you have?' Harriet stood in front of him leaning forward slightly, with her pert chin raised and her eyes fixed on his.

There was nothing for it but to kiss her as he thought her lips demanded it, and she gave a gasp, more because they were in public than disliking his action. Jack's grin was almost inane and all he could think of was the girl in front of him.

'I really don't know what to do about you, whether I should move on or persist,' said Harriet.

'Definitely persist, I have never kissed anyone else since I got to London. Admittedly I've been met at the door of houses I've checked with mistletoe this Christmas, but they kissed me, not the other way around, and I only gave a cheek,' answered Jack, with a solemn expression.

'Which cheek, so I can avoid it,' said Harriet, with her eyes starting to twinkle.

'You see, no other girl has your spunk!' said Jack, his eyes melting. Harriet looked away to avoid the sense of drowning that she was starting to feel.

'Well, where's this tea shop then?' Harriet asked.

'There's mistletoe in that bunch of Christmastide I gave you,' said Jack, ignoring her question.

'I saw it, but you've already had a kiss and stolen another. Anymore I shall be calling for a Constable,' Harriet giggled at her own joke.

'Constable Sargent, second class, at your service, Miss Fildew,' said Jack, picking up her hand and holding it to his lips.

'That makes a third kiss. Police!' Harriet raised her voice slightly.

'Shush,' said Jack with a laugh, 'I'll get the boot if I get arrested. Happy New Year, Harriet,' grinned Jack.

'Happy New Year, Jack,' said Harriet pecking him on the cheek which was not damaged. 'Where's this tea room, then?'

'That makes kiss number four,' said Jack, laughing. 'It's by St. Margaret's. Come on as they'll close by five o'clock. You'll see it in a minute once we get past Westminster Bridge Station. I went in earlier to make sure they were saving the table I'd asked for a few days ago. They'll keep it up to half past four as I thought we might talk, or walk on the bridge,' said Jack.

'It's not the first time you've come here?' asked Harriet.

'No, my second, but the first time was for work and I was hurrying on to make a meeting with Morris. The good thing was I got the lay of the land for today. Have you been before?' asked Jack.

'Yes, today's my fifth visit to the Palace of Westminster. Just jumping on the tram is such a different world to home and I can't believe, since I came in the summer, that I can catch a tram from Camberwell and get to the Palace of Westminster and the Abbey. Ma can't get over that we can catch trams and rub shoulders with MP's. Even though the milk from the farm is coming up to London now she still feels it's a different world,' said Harriet.

The two walked together, Jack shortening his stride to slow to Harriet's pace.

'Is there a lot of produce from the farm coming to London, then?' asked Jack.

'Yes, on regular days now. The boys take the milk churns by cart to the station and it arrives ready for the start of the day, and Ma's got a regular contract for London. It makes a big difference to the farm being a recognised dairy supplier. She's done so well since Pa died. She's kept the farm going and got some tenants so she can concentrate on the dairy side of things,' Harriet smiled at him.

'It's such a long way though,' said Jack. 'I'm surprised anyone buys milk from Devon when they could get it locally.'

'Ho, there speaks a lad from Sussex. I can bet you, Jack Sargent, that your Sussex doesn't produce milk anywhere near as good as Devon. Our cream is the best! Anyway, the buyer told Ma that with London expanding they can barely meet the demand,' Harriet said emphatically.

'Good, I'm glad for you all, I really am,' said Jack, smiling at her.

'It's been a hard three years but Ma's got through the bad time after Pa died. We all thought it was the end. The end of life, the farm, the future. But you see, Jack, we don't have to be dependent on anyone to make our way. Ma's proved that and I'm not about to be so daft as to go back and marry a farmhand. I told you, I'm going to have my own house one day. Where do we go now?' asked Harriet, as they had come to a crossroads. She stopped and glanced towards Great George Street ahead of them. To the right was King Street and Westminster Abbey was off to the left.

'Can you see, next to the Abbey, there's a smaller church?' Jack pointed towards St. Margaret's Church.

'Yes, I see it,' said Harriet. Jack carried on moving his hand so that Harriet could follow the direction he was pointing to across a road from St. Margaret's Church.

'There's the Westminster Palace Hotel and some Chambers for the law courts across the road from the church. The little tea room is part of the hotel building. It's usually full of barristers, and civil servants for the emigration office, but today, the ladies serving assured me that it would be quiet and suitable for me to bring a young lady to tea. Good job they'd seen me in uniform before I got the black eye. Come on, Harriet, we're nearly there,' Jack held out his arm, crooked at the elbow for her to tuck her hand in, and grinned at her. Harriet slipped her hand into the space that he had made for her, almost shyly. They walked to St. Margaret's and stopped.

'Fancy getting married in there!' said Harriet.

'What the Abbey? said Jack, keeping his face straight.

Harriet first tutted and half turned to him with a giggle, 'No, silly man, St Margaret's. It's a pretty church but such a funny place to build one next to an Abbey. I wonder why it's there?'

'Come on, tea calls before we're too late and they close. Just a bit further, Harriet and we can get into the warm. We can always come back another day and go to a service if you like, then you can see it properly,' Jack pulled her by the hand and pointed across Broad Sanctuary towards the hotel building shaped like an iron. The west door and the towers of Westminster Abbey were behind them.

'Is that where we're going?' asked Harriet.

'Yes, that's it,' said Jack continuing to pull her along. Harriet quickened her pace until she was level with him.

'This all looks quite new, Jack.'

'I think it is, about ten years since it was built, from what Arscott told me. The slums were all cleared. You see the memorial, Harriet?' asked Jack.

'Yes, can we have a quick look?' Harriet held her hat on and walked briskly towards the monument. Jack caught her up and they both read the plaque to the old boys of the Westminster School who had died in the Crimean War 1853 and also in the Indian Mutiny of 1857.

'What a waste,' said Harriet, 'I somehow don't see anything glorious in this. If it was my brothers I would feel cross.'

'Wouldn't you be proud, though?' asked Jack.

'No, I'd be cross.'

Jack laughed and picked up her hand in his. 'Come on, we need our tea.'

'I shall have something new to describe to Ma in my letter, this week. She asked after you, by the way.'

'That's nice of her, what did you say?' asked Jack.

'I told her I had no idea where you'd gone to live as it was a mystery, but that you'd sent me a beautiful box of chocolates for Christmas, hand delivered by a Police Sergeant with enormous whiskers and that you were taking me to tea in Westminster on New Year's Day.'

*

Fifteen

Jack and Harriet walked across Broad Sanctuary away from
St. Margaret's church now shrouded by the bare branches of
the trees of Parliament Square. The young couple's shadows
lengthened as they hurried past a street light. It was already
half past four and Jack had quickened the pace to ensure their
table. The Westminster Palace Hotel occupied the corner of
Tothill Street and Victoria Street. Horse drawn cabs passed
them, the wheels making such a repetitive noise on the street
that it formed a rhythm in Jack's mind. As they arrived on the
corner of Victoria Street, two men, both riding Penny farthing
cycles, passed as Harriet skipped onto the pavement.

'I would love to have a go on one of those,' said Jack.

'It's a mystery to me how you would even get onto one,
never mind keep your balance,' laughed Harriet.

'If we go further up here,' explained Jack, pointing up Tothill
Street, 'We can catch the underground railway back to
Westminster Bridge Station. I thought we could do that on the
way home and then I'll walk you to the tram stop.'

'Why would we do that?' asked Harriet.

'It's an experience because it's still so new for you and I, and
it will mean we stay dry,' said Jack.

'I'm not sure I want to go underground on a train,' said
Harriet.

'But you're the intrepid adventurer, Harriet, who's come
half way across the country to start a new life. All I've done is
move a few counties to come into London. Let's do it together
from St James's Park Underground. It will keep us dry at
least,' said Jack, as they stopped. The entrance to the hotel was
next to a small Taylor's shop, which had already closed on its
first day of trading of the New Year.

Within the hotel reception area, they walked to the tea room
and as he opened the door it caught the bell above it and sent
it dancing and tinkling to announce their entrance. A waitress
in pristine black and white seated Harriet while Jack stepped
aside to allow his smart young lady to be settled at a table
which was covered by lace.

'Oh, look, Jack, aren't the lanterns lovely, they've all been decorated with holly,' said Harriet. She looked at the way Jack handled himself in the surroundings and thought how he had already gained confidence given the type of place they were in. Harriet, still the servant, was not too comfortable to be a guest in a first-class hotel.

'What would you recommend?' Jack asked the waitress.

'The Darjeeling tea and cherry buns, sir,' and Jack nodded for himself.

'I would prefer Ceylon tea, I think,' said Harriet.

'Of course, ma'am,' said the waitress.

Jack leant across to Harriet as the waitress disappeared through a door into the kitchen.

'Bit different to the docks café, we get too used to bad tea,' said Jack, quietly with a grin.

'She called you, sir,' said Harriet leaning across to him, eyes wide.

'I know, what a laugh, eh, and what did she call you?' said Jack.

'Oh, I know, it's the dress, the hat and the gloves. But you're quite comfortable, here, aren't you? You've changed and something tells me that you've got used to better surroundings than you were living in at New Road Police Station. Would I be right?' asked Harriet.

'Well, I can't say where I'm staying, Harriet because of the case I'm working on. It's part of keeping you safe. That's why I can't visit you. But yes, you're right, I am in a better place, and I do get called "sir" by a servant, I'm brought fresh laundry every day, and there's a jug of water to wash with outside my bedroom every morning, and breakfast on a laid table.'

'Good grief, Jack.' Harriet sat back, feeling even more unsure of the relationship. 'Your bedroom? Aren't you sharing?'

'No, I have my own room. What's the matter, its only what you've been talking about. Getting on and moving up. Things are changing for both of us, we can rise together,' Jack frowned a little.

'You'll pass me by,' Harriet whispered. 'I've never been served.'

'No,' said Jack, smiling at her. 'But today you are being served! You'll get used to it. We look the part today, no one has questioned what we're doing in here. Is that what's worrying you? You look the part Harriet and that's not just the clothes. We're just out having tea in a comfortable place.' Jack looked around the room. 'The hotel is full of tourists, look, where do you think everyone's from?' he touched the tips of her fingers on the table, and she instinctively withdrew her hand so that the occupants of the other tables would not get the wrong idea. Harriet gave a tentative little smile, looking around the room, grateful for her sister making her dress in the latest fashion, in the best fabric that had been left over from another order. No one would work out from her attire what she did for a living and Jack was smart in his office clothes. Apart from the black eye and deep bruise on his cheek, which might pass for a hunting injury or a sports injury, he looked like he could be a clerk, or a supervisor in an office. He had deliberately faced the window so that the side of his face with the bruising was turned away from the other diners.

'Thank goodness you came in before you had your black eye. They might have taken it wrongly otherwise and refused us entry,' said Harriet.

'No, never, with you looking as you do,' Jack struggled to take his eyes off her since they had sat down. The sense of his gaze made her flush and she looked down at her hands. She had left her gloves on as she knew that was what ladies did, knowing that her hands were too red from the kitchen work to risk removing her gloves in a place like this. Jack was comfortable and his confidence carried them both. She just had to try and manage eating a cherry bun with a knife and fork, as she had seen her employer do. Jack was a quick learner and he was watching the way every table was served. No one helped themselves from the tray of cakes but each person had the food placed on their plate by the waitress.

'It's a different world, Jack,' said Harriet, quietly.

'One we're up to getting used to,' said Jack.

'Do you really think so?' asked Harriet.

'Look at what we've both already done. You're seventeen, and you're already changing positions for a better one, with ambition to own your own house and support yourself by taking in lodgers. Two months ago, I was a farm labourer, now I'm in a special team with the police, taking tea with a beautiful and elegant young lady,' said Jack, forgetting that he was not even supposed to hint at what he was working on. However, all Harriet had heard were his compliments about her. It stimulated her confidence and she sat back in her chair, resting her hands in her lap, just as the lady at the next table was doing. Harriet smiled and shook her head a little as she thought of what he said.

'I'm sorry we haven't been together, Harriet,' continued Jack. 'I've been trying to honour the role I've got. I'm not sure why I've got it but my superiors seem to have confidence in me. For the first time since my parents died I really think I can rise again. I never told you but my father had a market garden business which, rather like your mother's dairy, was growing as London expanded. I was being trained by my mother to understand the contracts and the accounts so that I could run it one day. That's over, as hard as it is to think about it now, because there's so much that's lost. But with the team that I'm in I actually believe now I could make Inspector at some point in my career. But that's only one side of what I wanted to tell you. I also wanted to honour you, that's the point of bringing you here. It was the best you see, and you deserve the best.'

Jack reached out for her hand and she let him take it, her eyes filling with emotion.

'In my head, Jack, I have all these thoughts, about you, about my feelings, and yours. If I can't write to you I don't know how I can keep it up.'

'I don't think it will be for long now. We'll be solving a case within the next few days. I suspect I shall be back on the beat in New Road before we know it. You, however, will be working in the Grove and above the lowly policeman on the beat around your old area,' Jack tried to make it light hearted but the way he felt about Harriet had to be declared. 'No one is as beautiful as you, Harriet, and I want us to keep being able to see each other. I would love to write to you and receive your letters, but I promised I would keep you safe by not doing so,' he said, his eyes full of sincerity.

'I want to keep in regular contact, too, Jack. I wouldn't want you to think otherwise,' said Harriet. 'Perhaps there's a way we could devise without me having the address. Like our own undercover system, maybe Arscott could help with messages,' suggested Harriet.

'That's a great idea and a relief! And now here's our tea,' said Jack, letting her hand rest on the table as the waitress came alongside with a large silver tray. On it was a note giving a brief history of the site of the hotel. Jack picked it up.

'It says that this is the site of the first printing press in 1475, that Chaucer's Canterbury Tales was published here, and we can find Geoffrey Chaucer's tomb in the Abbey.'

'They really are aiming at the tourists, aren't they, I suppose it's a good position to stay and see the Thames, Westminster Palace and the Abbey,' said Harriet.

'Well we could play tourist and go and find it another day, and then come back for tea again,' said Jack.

*

The walk up Tothill Street took them past merchants closing for the night, jangling large rings of keys as they locked their premises. Small children ran towards them and forced Jack to drop Harriet's arm from his, as he dodged to one side to make enough space for them to run between. Ahead was a building site with a notice that the construction of Queen Ann's Mansions would be starting.

St James's Park Underground railway was a very new experience for Harriet. Being jammed into a train underground with so many people around her produced a sense of panic for her.

'Look at me, if that helps, not at all the people around you,' suggested Jack. They were at Westminster Bridge station so quickly and they followed the trail of people into the open air.

'I might get used to underground travel eventually if I do it in small stages. It's frightening, though,' said Harriet, taking Jack's arm again.

'I think it's amazing. I'm going back as far as I can on it after I've taken you to the Tram stop then I'll work out how to get back to the Commercial Road.'

'Is that where you're staying, Jack,' asked Harriet, shyly as she was not supposed to know. Jack smiled, realising that he had already given too much away. He tried to recover the ground.

'No, it's not the Commercial Road. You know the station is Leman Street so it's going to be in the area. I can't tell you, Harriet.'

'But it's a nice area?' she asked.

'Yes, it's a nice area. And that, my lady, is all I'm saying. What was that?' Jack spun around as a hollow yell suddenly filled the air. Jack had half his mind on whatever might be happening and also a desire not to involve Harriet in a situation. He stood in front of Harriet and peered through the mist.

'What was it, Jack? Can you see anything?' asked Harriet.

'I'm not sure, and I'm not too clear where it was coming from. Everything echoes near water. Well there's nothing more,' Jack looked at her and smiled and she took his arm again and they began to walk towards Westminster Bridge to reach the tram stop. Another yell, only this time of pain.

Jack realised that they were walking towards the sound and any potential danger. It was the last thing he wanted with Harriet but he could not ignore it. As they reached the start of the actual bridge Jack could see that a crowd was forming and people were craning their necks to see what was going on. Then he heard the shout, 'Police, Police, get a Policeman.'

'I'll take you back to Westminster Bridge station, and then I'm going to have to get involved in whatever is going on over there,' said Jack, firmly turning them both around.

'Do you have to?' asked Harriet. 'It's your day off.'

'I can't ignore something even so. When is a Policeman ever off duty?' Jack gave Harriet a sad smile, and led her back to the station.

'Stay here in the warm, I'll not be long,' Jack called as he started to break into a run towards the bridge.

He was trapped against the bridge wall, down on one knee raising an arm to protect his face and the man Jack had jumped on was pulling his arm back to hit the Constable again, but Jack had a hold of his arm. It did not feel real, as if she was watching a play in the church hall. Momentarily she looked around the crowd, wondering why no one was going to help Jack. Some people were goading the man on to hit the Constable again, others were encouraging Jack to stop the fight. Jack's bowler hat was on the floor and she thought she should pick it up and instinctively stepped forward to do so. When she looked up again, Jack had pulled both the man's arms behind his back and was holding them in a painful lock.

'Get the cuffs on,' shouted Jack to the Constable, who was struggling to stand. The man he held scraped his heel down Jack's shin. Jack's grip loosened of only one arm but it was enough for the man to turn to hit Jack.

'Not his face again,' Harriet shouted, her own face puckering to cry and she clutched the bowler hat to her chest in an effort to protect something connected to Jack. A woman next to her put a hand on her shoulder. 'Know him, do you?' she heard the woman ask, but she was too involved to reply.

Harriet stood for a few seconds only and then decided to follow Jack back to where the commotion had been. She felt as if she was in a daze of curiosity. She pushed through the rows of people, which parted for her as she said, 'Excuse me.' She saw Jack leap onto the back of a well-built man, throwing his full weight on him with a Policeman who had been cornered laying on the floor. Harriet registered that there was blood on the policeman's face, just trickling down from the corner of his eye. He had been hit repeatedly she knew, from years of watching her brothers fight the village boys.

But the Constable had hold of the man's free arm and the handcuffs were going on. Jack had responded by blocking the punch and followed with one of his own. The man was stunned enough for them to get him under control. Men in the crowd were cheering now, and the ladies were clapping and it struck Harriet realised how odd it was that a crowd could change so quickly.

'Thanks, sir,' the Constable said. 'He almost had the better of me. There's been a robbery two streets away and we're a bit short-handed over here. This man and two others raided the costermonger stalls. He belted one of the men and then started on me as soon as I arrived. I chased him onto the bridge and then he let rip. Good job you came along.'

'Constable Sargent, off duty, but it's part and parcel of the job isn't it, mate!' What happened to the other two? asked Jack.

'Constable Tanner,' said the officer introducing himself as he peered round at Jack. 'The other two made off with the money and a pile of goods. Could you give me a hand to get him across to the St. Stephen's entrance of the Palace of Westminster? There are officers there that can help me get him to King Street police station. Not sure I can hold him on my own,' said Tanner, who was shaking with the effort he had to expend in holding the man.

'Settle down, or it will go badly with you,' shouted Jack at the prisoner, gripping the man's arms which were now both cuffed behind his back.

'There's a lady I'm with, she's in Westminster Bridge station, how far are we going?' asked Jack.

'Help me get him into the Palace Yard and there's likely to be other constables around. I can get help then,' said Tanner.

'Jack, I'm here,' called Harriet.

Jack glanced momentarily over to where Harriet was standing. The crowd had largely disbursed and she was still holding his hat. Her face was white, Jack registered that she was there, had seen the fight, and then he looked at the man he was restraining and at Tanner.

'I can go home on my own,' Harriet said, as she walked towards them, holding out Jack's bowler hat.

'Stay back, Miss,' said Tanner.

'I'm sorry,' said Jack, glancing quickly at Harriet, and then at Turner. 'I'll have to help the Constable.'

'I know. I'll send a note to you, somehow. Here's your hat,' Harriet held the bowler aloft and Jack saw the funny side of it.

'Throw it, Harriet, I can't let go. Hold him a minute, Tanner, will you,' Jack bent down and retrieved his bowler hat, looking at her. Her face was still white, but just a little colour was returning to her cheeks.

'How much did you see?' he asked.

'All of it,' said Harriet. 'You're very strong.'

Jack acknowledged what she had said with a nod. 'Sorry,' he called to her again. 'We have to go.'

'I'll send a note, with Arscott,' Harriet called again as Jack and Tanner started to march the man towards the Palace of Westminster.

Jack turned once to look at the small figure disappearing across the bridge to get the tram.

'This is so wrong,' he said aloud.

'Sorry?' said Tanner.

'Oh, nothing. Not a good way to end the afternoon with a young lady,' Jack grimaced.

'She looked like she understood,' said Tanner. Then Jack was relieved by another constable, wrote his police number and station down for Tanner in the constable's notebook and they shook hands and then Jack started to run out of the yard.

He was too late to catch Harriet on the bridge. She had climbed the steps of the tram and taken her seat and used a handkerchief to wipe the condensation off the window again, just in case she could see across the bridge. She looked for him too, her Sussex lad. Her face started to light up in a smile as he was running to the tram stop. Harriet laughed and then got up and started to push her way past the passengers.

'Excuse me, excuse me, I'm sorry, I have to get to the back of the tram.' It was moving, but she made it to the platform at the back and held onto the pole, and waved. Jack was still running, waving, and Harriet laughed. The tram would stop soon and he would get on.

'You're going the wrong way,' she said, as he breathlessly leaned against the pole.

'No, I'm exactly where I should be. I'll work out how I get back later. I'm so sorry, I had no choice, I can't walk away from a colleague needing help. I never thought this would happen. I've ruined our afternoon,' Jack panted.

Harriet kissed him, and he wound his arm around her. They stood together on the tram platform, the only ones on it.

'We should go and get a seat,' said Harriet resting her head against Jack's chest.

'We will, at the next stop. Don't move yet, I just want to get used to the feeling of holding you. Then it will stop but I'll have the scent from your hair in my memory.'

'A romantic! One minute you're big and tough and the next you're a lover,' Harriet held on though. 'This will be what it will be like every time I meet you, won't it? The potential of you having to help arrest someone.'

'It might be. I can't say it won't.'

'I have to get my mind used to it,' said Harriet.

'Were you frightened?' asked Jack.

'A little. Frightened for you more than me. I thought you would have another black eye, but I knew you were able to win. It was a shock to see the violence though, against the man on the floor, I mean. The man you arrested would have really hurt him,' Harriet, started to disengage as they were coming into the next tram stop and there were people making their way down the tram towards the platform to get off.

'We'll work out how we get word to each other. I'll contact Arscott somehow and ask him to pass it on to you,' said Jack.

'I'll wait to hear. Look there's two seats, shall we go and get them?' Harriet pointed down the tram and started to move inside. Jack followed. She turned and looked back at him, smiling, confident in herself and him in a way that she had not been earlier that afternoon.

*

The south-westerly wind was still whipping up the water as Jack crossed Blackfriars Bridge on the train. A niggling thought had occurred to him as Harriet had prepared to leave the tram in Camberwell that he may just have been followed. He told her he would play it safe so that they were not seen together and he remained on the tram as she left it. He waited two minutes until she was out of sight and then made his way to the New Road Railway Station. He boarded the train crossing the Thames for Ludgate Hill Station, deciding that he would work out how he would get to the Commercial Road during the journey.

There were no overt signs of being followed but Jack decided that he would walk a while, crossing roads at various intervals to see if anyone in particular presented themselves as walking too much of the same route. He doubled back towards the river, to Blackfriars Station on the north side of the Thames and caught the railway to Farringdon Street.

As usual Jack's stomach got the better of him and by half past seven he ate in what appeared to be a dining room for clerks from the local offices, or so it seemed, as so many were dressed in the same type of clothes as Jack was wearing. A joint of beef had been suspended above a fire hours ago. Not much of it remained but there was enough for a couple of slices. It was tough but tasty as the outsides of the pieces had become blackened by the fire. It tasted good though with the salted gravy and the potatoes. He mashed the potatoes with the back of his fork and scooped up the gravy.

Jack came out into the night and strolled at a casual pace as far as Fenchurch Street until he was convinced, finally, that he was not being followed and then he caught the train to Stepney and the Commercial Road.

*

Franks was as good as his word. He stood at the bar in the Mason's Arms and sized Jack up as he came in. It was after eight o'clock when Jack arrived. He relaxed as he was in time, but Franks gave a sideways nod towards a man at the side of him. Jack paused, trying to work out what Franks was trying to tell him. The man had his back to Jack but in a moment turned and Jack saw it was Ted Phillips.

'Ted! I didn't think you were around today,' said Jack.

'Developments,' Ted raised his eyebrows, 'Good afternoon?'

'Yes, we had a very pleasant tea in Westminster. I've been killing time a bit, took a circuitous route back here to make sure no one was overly interested in me.'

'Let's go in the snug, shall we? Drink, Jack, on New Year's Day?' asked Ted.

'I'll have a Truman's, thanks.'

'Stan will join us shortly. He's detached himself from the domestic bliss he enjoys and is on his way. You're married, Ted?' asked Franks, as the three walked across the bar to the snug. Ted said that he was and Jack did not manage to hear the rest of the conversation as a shout went up from a group of men playing cards.

Franks closed the door of the snug and the three men sat around the fire.

'What are the developments?' Jack asked Ted.

'I'll let Detective Sergeant Franks tell you,' said Ted.

'Please, it's Harry. I'll hang on for Stan as it saves repeating it. You're all done up like a dog's dinner tonight Jack. Was it somewhere refined that you took your young lady?' Franks pulled a pipe out of his pocket and a tin of tobacco and started to press the tobacco into the bowl. He offered the tin to Ted, who shook his head.

'It was. The Palace of Westminster Hotel,' said Jack, smiling at the memory.

'Was it now? Too many trips there and the boss will think you're on the take. And your young lady was well? Naming no names, of course,' asked Franks.

'Thank you, she was very well,' said Jack, and the door opened and Stan arrived. Jack introduced him to Ted and then Stan drew up a chair and sat down.

'Well, bearing in mind that the three of you are off duty tonight, I must send my thanks to the ladies for sparing you. The news I have is that we have information from Badley. After we'd read the charges to him he got rather chatty.'

'What did you fix him up with in the end?" asked Stan.

'I started with two murder charges, two attempted murder charges against police officers, rape and an aggravated burglary, theft of a carriage, positive identifications of him at the scene of the crash in Whitechapel and I could go on but at the risk of boring you, I won't. The poor dear man was in a bit of a state by four o'clock this afternoon. He became quite cooperative and I shared with him my realisation that he was being potentially wrongly charged, we had quite a bonding time,' said Franks. He saw the light in Jack's eyes at his humour.

'To cut a long story short he came up with what he knew about the occupants of the carriage. He was up top with a driver,' Franks stopped long enough to have a drink.

'Well done, Harry,' said Stan.

'Well done, all, I think, but my thanks, Stan, for the acknowledgement,' Franks looked around the table. 'To resume the sorry story, the man insists that he thought that Berringer was unconscious when he was put into the carriage, two men brought him out of an address in Kensington, put him in the carriage and travelled in it with the him, both spoke quietly but he believed one of them had an accent with a drawl to it, possibly American. He saw no blood, but Berringer was swathed in a cape and they put a rug around him. He had no idea that he was dead. He thought he was either drunk, drugged, or, being kidnapped. Badley said that he had no idea about the cabbie, or driver as we should properly call him as no self-respecting cabbie would have been part of this. The driver never spoke. Franks was kitted out in the mock police uniform and told to get up top. He said it became apparent that the driver was whipping up the horse once they got to Whitechapel and that the crash into the side of the bridge was intentional.'

'He should know, given his antics in Piccadilly. Any sign of the carriage, anywhere?' asked Jack.

'No, no sign at all,' said Ted. 'I exhausted all avenues and we know now that it wasn't a carriage that had been assigned to the Berringer family while they were in England. My bet is that it was stolen, but none of the witnesses interviewed noticed a licence number so I imagine it had been removed. The carriage has vanished from the scene of the accident once the body had been removed to the mortuary. I suspect it's at the bottom of the Thames.'

'We have some more news. Badley has given a name that he heard one of the two men say before he joined the driver up top. It's a lead. But a rather confusing lead as it's the name of one of the witnesses,' Franks paused and looked around the table for effect again. 'By the way, young Jack, Ted here is your minder for tonight to ensure that you don't run off and solve crime. Inspector Hunt strongly suspects, probably rightly, that you will be so seized with enthusiasm at the developments that you will arrest half of London before the morning. Isn't that right, Ted?'

'Not quite,' said Ted looking at Franks with a half-smile. 'It's true that we need to coordinate response, and knowing that you were coming here to find out about development, Inspector Hunt also wanted you to get some time off tonight. You haven't presumably arrested anyone on your afternoon out with your girl have you,' Ted chuckled.

'Well, actually there was a situation I helped a constable with,' said Jack.

'I don't believe it. You're like a homing pigeon!' exclaimed Ted.

'What was the name?' Jack asked, ignoring the potential side-tracking about his afternoon in Westminster.

'Ah, the name,' Franks smiled at Jack. 'It was Moore. As we already know.'

Ted and Jack did not move a muscle.

'The same name as the director of the bank who went to the scene of the crash. We'll pay him a visit in the morning, and Ted and Jack you are invited to the party. Inspector Hunt is sorting out the required papers.'

'And the name in the boatman's list at Windsor. Ted, we need to get Sam back from Windsor,' said Jack.

'That won't happen tonight, Jack,' said Ted.

'Why? There's a Telegraph office at Stepney and there's bound to one at Windsor,' Jack fixed Ted with a frustrated stare.

'Not by you, you will be going home,' said Ted. 'Good point though, it's time we brought Sam back and heard what he's found out.'

'And Sam is?' asked Stan.

'Another keen young recruit, clever lad, good on piecing the jigsaw together. His father's a Waterman and Sam knows a thing or two about the river, having grown up with the trade. The flooding at Windsor meant we could get him taken on there as a boatman quite easily, and he's been helping to rescue stranded people from their homes. He's managed to forge a couple of friendships with the boatmen he's working with and we thought he should stay and keep his nose to the ground. He's been reporting via his father to Inspector Hunt. We've had a confirmation that the person called Moore was in Berringer's party but nothing else. It may be a coincidence, but I doubt it, given what you've told us. Alright Jack, we'll get over to the Telegraph office at Stepney Railway station and that's it. You're off home then.'

*

Jack's sixth sense that someone was following had been correct. Someone keeping their distance, watching, waiting.

Harriet had jumped down from the tram and started her walk back to her employer's home. She had even hummed an old song from her childhood, she was so happy and sure of Jack.

It was half way that she realised the person behind her was getting closer with every corner that she turned. She tried a trick Georgina had taught her and crossed the road. The person behind crossed it too. Harriet thought that she would try not to give away that she knew. But the skin on the back of her neck tingled and she fought down the sense of sickness that was starting to build.

What had she, if anything, in her bag that was heavy and would make the handbag do some harm if it came in contact with the man's head? Harriet gripped the handle deciding that she would use the bag as a weapon if necessary. She had a book, a purse with change in it, quite a lot of change in fact, and a bottle of cologne.

She crossed back and carried on humming. She turned her head slightly and saw the man in the shadows. Oh, Jack, you would fight him for me if you were here, she thought, but you're not here, neither are my brothers. No one to fight but you, Harriet, only yourself. Scream, Harriet, make a lot of noise.

He was closer, about six paces away. Harriet was near the house, if she screamed they would hear. She did not have any option, she needed to turn so that she could see him and be prepared for what he would do instead of him catching her from behind. She was in the wrong shoes to run, little heels and if she tripped?

Harriet turned and swung her bag, she screwed up her face and screamed. The man barged her, catching her shoulder sharply in a blow that knocked the wind out of her. Her bag caught him on the back of his neck and she felt the impact of the blow up her own arm. He staggered with it. But his eyes, full of threat, had been fixed on hers when she first turned and she would know him again. She staggered and he broke into a run as the front doors started to open. The night was filled with Harriet's scream.

*

Sixteen

It was eight o'clock by the time Jack came into Shadwell Police Station. Standing at the Sergeant's desk was Sam with a grin to which the Sergeant had taken exception. Sam, however, was oblivious to the ticking off he was receiving, so pleased was he to be back from Windsor with the team and to know that progress was being made. He gave a casual glance at the paper the Sergeant pushed towards him and scribbled his signature. He picked up his helmet that had been on the desk and walked towards Jack, with his hand extended ready to shake hands. Jack felt the good humour and broke into a smile.

'What time did you get here?' asked Jack, trying to calculate the route from Windsor.

'Don't ask, leave it that I set off early and was here early. Long enough for the Sergeant's voice to become a lasting memory. It's a bit of a rambling route, frankly. What an area this is, isn't it? I thought I was taking my life in my hands just getting off at the station in uniform,' said Sam.

'Ready for Whitechapel then?' asked Jack.

'Is that where we're off to?' said Sam.

'For one of the witnesses that we interviewed but I won't say which. Wait for the briefing. What did Ted tell you in the telegram?' asked Jack.

'Not much, progress, an arrest, needed back and to report at Shadwell Police Station by eight in the morning. Since they never close I was here by seven and managed to scrounge some breakfast from the Sergeant's daughter in the back room here. I think that's why he's taken against me,' said Sam, then mouthed at Jack, 'so pretty.'

Jack gave the Sergeant a quick glance and then turned away and pulled a face at Sam. The Sergeant had stiffened and given Jack the benefit of the same look he had reserved up to that point for Sam.

'Come on in the back room and let me see if Detective Sergeant Franks is here yet. Ted should be on his way, if he's not here, already. At least I can introduce you.'

Sam's eyes looked at him curiously. 'Franks? Not Morris?'

'Don't you know? Of course, how would you if no one's filled you in. Look, let's see who's in there and I can quickly explain what's happened and you can tell me what you've found out as well,' said Jack, who could not wait any more, opened the door for him and Sam to go into the back room.

They were stopped from talking about anything other than their time at New Year though, as the room was busy and both accepted they would have to wait. Jack did manage to tell Sam about Morris's broken elbow which had effectively removed the Sergeant from the operation for the time being.

'Where's the prisoner?' asked Sam.

'Badley's in a cell, here,' said Jack.

'Can I have a look at him?' asked Sam.

'I suppose so, I'm not too sure where he's being held though.' Jack turned to the Constable who was doing his boots up at the side of him and asked which cell Badley was in now.

Sam took a long look through the opening in the door. 'He fits a description.'

'What sort of description?' asked Jack, surprised.

'From Windsor, of a side kick to a coach driver. Where did you pick him up?' asked Sam, closing the space.

'He's the character that tried to run me down on the Commercial Road and almost finished Morris and I off, in Piccadilly. Franks was after him for an aggravated burglary and a rape. He's been identified by two of the witnesses from the day you and I went door-to-door in Whitechapel as being up top on the coach as the false policeman. He's started to sing an interesting song to Franks yesterday, about Berringer being bundled into the coach in Kensington, probably already dying by the sound of it, and there being two men in the coach with him, one who may have been American, who mentioned the name Moore,' said Jack.

'Let's go in,' said Sam.

'What! No, Sam, you need to be briefed first,' said Jack.

'That's what you've already done isn't it?' said Sam.

'And what is it that you two bright sparks are up to down here?' barked the Duty Sergeant, who had followed them down. 'Get on with you, D.S. Franks is waiting for you.'

Sam slid back the opening before he moved away, he paused for about seven seconds before the Duty Sergeant pushed it shut.

'Move it!' he said in a growl, close to Sam's ear.

'Yes, Sergeant,' said Jack, leading the way.

'He was shaking. Badley, did you say his name was? He was shaking,' said Sam, as they climbed the stairs. 'He's got more to tell.'

Franks had not gone into a room but was on the front step of the Police station with a new clay pipe in his hand. He acknowledged Jack as he saw him come from the direction of the cells.

'Having a look at our new friend, are you? How is he this morning?' he asked, giving Sam an appraising examination. 'And would you be the Waterman? Sam, isn't it?'

'Detective Sergeant Franks,' said Jack to Sam, as a way of introduction.

'Harry, or Franks,' interposed the detective.

'How do you do,' said Sam.

'I hear you're the bright one. I think Jack's bright. That must make you a genius,' said Franks, as he shook hands with Sam. 'Special team two months after you joined the force! I'm glad to know you. How was Windsor?'

'The water's bad. I would be looking at better river management if I was there permanently. I know the rain has been unbelievable but it's showing no sign of a change. The ditches and the rivulets are blocked. The College is almost surrounded with water and the Home Park at the north and east end of the Castle are covered by the flooding. Menzies, the surveyor of the Royal Park, will have a job on to convince Her Majesty that the new weirs and tumbling bays will give any relief. We've still had to use punts to get people out,' said Sam.

'Above my head, I'm afraid. And what did you make of our friend in the cells?' asked Franks.

'He was shaking,' said Sam, 'And he fits a description I was given at Windsor about a man that was a side kick to a coach driver.'

'Does he now? That's interesting. That means our friend has not been honest with me, which I find a little upsetting. Lets' go and make him shake some more, shall we?' Franks put the pipe in his pocket and turned into the station. The three men walked towards the cells.

Jack realised that Ted Phillips had still not arrived but reminded himself not to worry.

*

'January the second, Mr Badley,' said Franks from the doorway, as the Constable unlocked the cell door. 'Time for you to get ready for a long sea voyage. You'll not like America too much. But, unfortunately for you, having held out on me, I won't be able to stop you from going with the detective that arrives in London from New York tonight.'

'I've not held out on you, I've told you all I know,' Badley said, looking from Jack to Sam and then back to Franks.

'No, apparently, you have not. You see, this Constable here has a cast iron description of a man working with a coach driver in Windsor. Probably carrying Berringer when he was visiting one of his children at the school. And the person named Moore may have been there too. I know enough that you're wasting our time and we'll be back to a murder charge. I'll be handing you over to our man from America tonight,' said Franks, starting to leave the room. Jack watched Badley's face contort.

'Why? I didn't kill him. Alright I can give you the driver's name,' replied Badley.

'Well, it's not much use to me, as I won't be involved in the case any longer, having tried to cut a deal with you and been misled,' Franks was in the corridor and walking away.

'Wait,' shouted Badley, looking at Jack. 'Get him back in here, will you.'

'I'll try,' said Jack, 'but he's a busy man.' Jack and Sam left the cell, and the door clanged behind them with an ominous finality. Franks stuck his head around the end of the corner and mimed counting to ten. Then he nodded to the Constable to open the door of the cell again and the three men went back in. Badley was sitting on the hard bench with his head in his hands. The hands were shaking. He looked up as Franks walked in first, followed by Jack and Sam.

'What if the driver in Windsor was the same man as drove the coach in Whitechapel? And I can tell you who was in the coach at Windsor.'

Franks came back into the cell. Jack and Sam were breathing very lightly and had stepped back into the shadows of the cell so as not to distract Badley.

'Go on,' said Franks.

'It was the same driver, name of Grace, Clifford Grace, and the passenger wasn't the dead diplomat Berringer. It was his wife, the one that's gone missing.'

'Mrs Berringer? At Windsor? Visiting the child, no doubt. But we know that her husband was also there. So, you're just spinning me a yarn aren't you, Badley? Address of where we can find Mr Grace?' asked Franks with a soft tone.

'He drives for the cab company in Whitechapel,' said Badley.

'I know it,' said Jack, who could not remain quiet any longer.

Franks held up a hand to stop any further interruption. He had not taken his eyes off Badley.

'You would have recognised Mrs Berringer?' he asked.

'Yes,' Badley answered. 'We'd driven her before, her and her gentleman friend, always to Windsor.'

This was news but Franks absorbed it like a stone.

'But never the Berringer's together?' Franks asked.

'No,' said Badley.

'And when you went to visit her in Golden Square she would have let you in as she would have recognised you as someone who had been involved in transporting her around. You were the contact about the journey she had to make.' Franks made a tutting sound, with his tongue. 'Murder number two back on the books.'

Badley was shaking visibly as Jack and Sam followed Franks out of the cell.

Franks looked from Jack to Sam. 'Well, we have got a turn up for the books. We know that Mrs Berringer has a gentleman friend, and that they are prone to take a day out in Windsor, taking in a nice familial visit to the child the Berringer's have at a school there.'

'Do you think it's "the" school,' asked Jack.

'Doesn't really matter. What we've established is that Mrs Berringer has a gentleman friend, to put it politely, and unfortunately for them, they've picked a day to go to Windsor when her husband is there with a party of his own,' said Franks.

'I wonder what the marriage was like?' said Sam.

'I think we could hazard a guess,' said Jack.

'Yes, I'm sure we're all singing from the same sheet now, on that issue, lads. I wonder if they see each other and the cat is out of the bag,' mused Franks.

'Or one of them sees the other and it's obvious what's going on?' suggested Sam.

'I'd hazard a guess that Mrs Berringer sees her husband because he's the one who died first. That she sees him with another woman,' said Jack.

'Yes, lads, but this marriage has probably been one of convenience for some time. You heard Badley in there, this wasn't the first time that he'd accompanied a driver with Mrs Berringer and her gentleman friend to Windsor.'

'Maybe there was something about what she saw in her husband's behaviour with another woman that showed her he was serious about the relationship?' said Jack.

'Exactly. We are looking at the potential of Mrs Berringer being involved in her husband's murder, or at least knowing about arrangements to get rid of him,' said Franks.

'But why resort to murder?' asked Sam.

'Because of the money. The man Mrs Berringer is with sees his meal ticket about to disappear, perhaps that's the motive. He puts things into motion and she goes along with it. Let's go back in,' Franks beckoned the Constable to let them back into the cell.

'Badley, I want a description from you of the man Mrs Berringer was with,' said Franks.

'I never saw his face, he wore a muffler, just what he was wearing said he was toff. It was a cold day, wet, on both occasions,' said Badley, looking from one to the other.

'You wouldn't be holding out on me again, would you?' said Franks, 'the noose is a real shadow for you.'

'No, look, he was well dressed, smart, but he never got out of the carriage. He came from the railway station with her from a separate carriage and she got in first and told us to wait. Then he joined her. But he was behind an umbrella, and as I said, he was muffled up. We could hear her laugh a lot from the inside, like she was a young woman, but his voice was always low. Just the clothes, that's all I could describe. It was obvious there was something going on between them. We'd drive her to the school and he waited in the carriage and we would drive him around for an hour like he was doing some sightseeing. It was difficult last time because of the flooding and we went further than usual to get a clear road. Then it was back to collect the lady and to the train. Only the last time she was upset about something when she came out of the school,' said Badley.

'How upset?' asked Franks.

'Crying in the carriage. We drove around for longer than usual. She stopped crying and we heard his low voice talking to her for what seemed like an age, then we dropped the man off at the station, drove around for another quarter of an hour and then Mrs Berringer got out at the station and caught the train back to London,' said Franks.

'Right. We'll be back. If you suddenly remember anything else that you feel compelled to share remember that right at this moment the noose is still waiting for you. It's in your interests for us to catch the person who murdered Berringer so search your memory,' Franks banged on the cell door for the Constable to open. He walked towards the stairs with Jack and Sam following.

'Are we're going after the driver now, the man known as Grace?' asked Jack.

'Yes, I feel drawn to the man and wish to share with him the mysteries of life. Seriously, we must try and find Stan, I think we will need him with us, but wait here will you,' said Franks stopping. He walked quietly back to the cells and slid the opening of Badley's cell door quietly a fraction to look at the man. Badley was sitting on the floor of the cell, rocking back and forth. Franks closed the opening quietly and walked back to Jack and Sam.

'I wonder what else we have yet to find out from this character. Forgive me, Sam if I talk to myself, it helps me think. Do feel free to join in at any time. He's told us to enough to get the driver, assuming we can find him, and assuming now that they are both implicated in the murder of Mrs Berringer. Of course, Badley may just have been the delivery boy for tickets or may have been bringing her a message. The question is who was she going with assuming she was going on a journey after Berringer's death. Who sent Badley to her in Golden square?'

'The man is on the edge of two murders, isn't he?' said Sam.

'Oh, yes, and knows others involved who he has yet to tell us about. They aren't helping him yet, that's why he's in such a state, this morning. Once we've got Grace we can play a little game with them both, lead them to believe the one is telling us things about the other. See who cracks first. We'll ask the Duty Sergeant to arrange a telegraph to be sent to Inspector Hunt to come to meet us at Leman Street as quickly as possible. I'm afraid, lads, that I don't have a warrant this time, but we'll get the Inspector upstairs cracking with the magistrate after the event given Hunt's suspicions about police involvement in the crimes,' said Franks.

'It still doesn't tie up the link with the name Moore though,' said Sam.

'Tell me, young Sam, exactly how you found that name in the records down at Windsor,' asked Franks.

'Inspector Doyle found it in a list of passengers, not me. I noticed that he was taken aback by it and stood and stared at the records for some minutes, then he went out and I went over to check what he'd been looking at,' explained Sam.

'And what did you see?' asked Franks.

'A list of people in the diplomat's party, including a surname of Moore,' said Sam.

'That was all, not a Mr, Mrs or Miss?' asked Franks.

'No, just "Moore," and about four other names,' said Sam.

'And how was Inspector Doyle when you next spoke to him?' asked Franks

'A bit distracted, like he was dwelling on something. He soon returned to normal though. But it was unusual for him to behave like that because he's always so focussed,' said Sam.

'But within an hour, he was getting on with the task in hand, as if he'd thought a problem through and come to a conclusion which no longer disturbed him?' asked Franks.

Sam thought about the question and then nodded, 'Yes, I would think that was right.'

'We don't have a solution about the name Moore. But one of the witnesses at the crash of the carriage in Whitechapel was a Mr Moore, wasn't he? We'll pay the cab company a visit first, collect Mr Grace and see what we can do about a visit to Mr Moore. Let's go up and we'll check if Stan is available,' said Franks, climbing the stairs and speaking to the Duty Sergeant about Stan's whereabouts. Franks whipped open the room behind the Duty Sergeant's desk.

'Ah, here's Stan. We are going hunting, Stan, and we'll fill you in on the way,' said Franks. Stan nodded.

'What's the time?' asked Franks.

'Half past nine,' said Jack.

'About nine hours before that detective arrives in London,' said Stan, giving Franks a meaningful look.

'Yes, Stan, that's true, but he's going to want to see the bodies first and he will have to find us before he can stop what we're up to. It may be a long day, gentlemen and we will keep moving. Jack, you said that you know where the cab company premises are?' said Franks.

'Yes, just between Aldgate Street and Whitechapel in a set of old stables at the back of the Boar's Head. If we can't find him there Mr Cunliffe may be able to give us a feel for where he would be.'

'At a push he might, but I don't really want to go back up to Victoria Park because we're running out of time. Right, gentlemen, lets' go.'

There was still no sign of Ted Phillips.

*

Jack went alone into the cab office to see Mr Brackley, while the others waited further along the Whitechapel Road. He was not there, only Simon his clerk. Mr Brackley had gone away for a few days as they had all worked hard since Christmas but he remembered Jack's previous visit. Simon was very obliging, asked after Jack's colleague, and hoped that they had managed to speak to Mr Cunliffe. However, he was practically obsequious when Jack told him that there was likely to be a reward if they could find the cab driver, Grace.

'Try the foreman, by all means, but I don't think Grace will come on until this evening. Look,' said Simon, turning over the pages of the rota for the last week, 'He has been working in the West End. He may not bring the cab back if it's in the early hours of the morning, unless he gets a fare this way.'

'No need then to bother the foreman, just his address would be helpful,' said Jack.

'Does the reward count for information as well,' asked Simon.

'Of course,' said Jack.

Just to make sure he slipped up the narrow passage from the office to the yard and nodded to the Foreman. He showed him the name, Grace, but the Foreman shook his head.

'Not seen him since before Boxing Day. He's got the cab and we should have had it in on the twenty-seventh to check it over. Check the sheds if you don't believe me,' said the Foreman.

'Thanks, I'll have a look as I pass,' said Jack. He turned out of the yard but doubled back to the Whitechapel Road. He did not have a licence number nor identifying make for the cab that Grace would drive. He was also pretty sure that it was probably at the bottom of the Thames.

Grace lived in lodgings in Mile End New Town. The address that Simon had given to Jack was for a house in Preston Street near a Catholic Chapel. There was a back gate into an alley from the back yard of the property and Jack had gone to wait on the other side of it with Franks while Sam knocked on the front door with Stan standing by.

Simon had told Jack that the landlady was an elderly lady who had been widowed recently. She nodded when they showed her the name on a piece of paper and she opened the door wide to let the two uniformed police officers in, pointing to the kitchen. Not a word was spoken by her.

Grace was in the kitchen, and leaped up when Sam and Stan appeared in the doorway. He was into the yard and whipped open the back gate to be met by Jack's fist.

When Sam and Stan reached the alley, Jack was already putting the handcuffs on Grace.

'Useful man with his hands, our Jack. However, we are going to have to work out a way to caution the suspect before you hit them, Jack,' said Franks.

'Sorry,' Jack grinned, 'It was a reflex action.'

'And a useful one, I do admit, as it prevented escape but try and speak first. Right, off to Leman Street with this one. We'll charge him when we get there and wait for the headache to come to the fore. Who's the Police Surgeon at Leman Street?' asked Stan.

'Doctor Brown,' said Sam.

'Do you know him to speak to?' asked Franks.

'He's been involved in the cases advising Inspector Hunt and had some involvement in the post mortems, as well,' said Jack.

'Useful, I hope he's around,' said Franks.

'He was going away, wasn't he Jack?' said Sam.

'Yes, he was. I can't remember when he comes back. There's probably a stand-in though.'

'Get Grace over to Leman Street, charge him, get the Police Surgeon on duty to him and then let him stew for a couple of hours. In the mean-time Sam and I will go and have a chat with Mr Moore,' said Franks.

'Any preference as to what the charge is?' asked Stan.

'The worst thing that you can think of. Let him know who shopped him in the course of conversation.' Franks sighed, 'At some point we should eat, gentlemen.'   •

'And I owe a clerk money,' said Jack.

The Director of the County Bank had returned to work straight from his New Year in Oxford. Phillip Moore had arrived at the bank at ten o'clock that morning and made his way across from Paddington.

Sam and Franks were shown into the Director's office and invited to sit. The chief clerk of the bank then went in search of Mr Moore.

'Open for us, Sam, will you, as you've already met him,' said Franks.

'Do you know the background?' asked Sam,

'No, but that doesn't matter at this point.'

The door opened and a well-groomed man, neatly but expensively dressed, entered. He was polite in his manner and walked towards Franks as the senior man, first. Sam and Franks stood.

'Good morning, Detective Sergeant Franks, is it?' Moore held out his hand to Franks. 'And Constable, forgive me, I know we've met but I can't recall the name.'

'Curzon, sir, 'said Sam.

'Do sit, gentlemen,' said Moore, and he walked to the other side of the desk to sit down.

'I hope you had a good New Year, sir,' started Sam.

Moore showed just a flicker of surprise that the Constable had opened the dialogue and Franks noted the assumption of superiority in Moore's expression at being addressed by someone he considered inferior in status.

'I did, thank-you. I doubt you're here to exchange pleasantries. Have you further questions about the accident?'

'Murder, sir,' Sam corrected him, 'Murder we now know it is. As I interviewed you before Sergeant Franks thought it would be helpful if I asked the questions today.'

'Murder? Are you sure? Forgive me, there was nothing to indicate a murder, surely it was a fatal accident, a coach crash which ended tragically,' said Moore.

Franks interrupted, 'Stabbing, to be precise, before the man was in the coach. We know that the crash of the carriage was a set up. As the new boy in this case I would find it helpful, Mr Moore, to understand where you stood at the scene. Could we trouble you to come to the road and describe when and how you came to be one of the first witnesses on hand. It will help with the court case, you see.'

'Of course, but I wasn't expecting to be called to court, it won't do the name of the bank any good if a Director of the County Bank is quoted in the newspapers,' Moore turned in his chair and looked at Franks.

'Oh, surely there isn't anything to worry about, you're just doing your civic duty in giving evidence. It's not as though you're involved, is it?' said Franks, smiling in response.

'Good grief, the very thought! Why would you say that?' Moore came back with self-confidence.

'Just a statement of fact, that you're not involved, and therefore, there's nothing to worry about in attending court as a witness. Upright citizen, good respectable profession, won't do the bank any harm at all,' Franks stood up, smiling, 'Shall we, Mr Moore?'

'Yes, of course,' Moore looked from Franks to Sam and then got up and led the way through the bank to the street. Franks checked with Moore the exact location of where the body had been found. There was an element of distaste in being asked the questions in Moore's expression.

'It would be helpful if we go across, sir, and you show us where you stood,' said Franks, waiting and noting that Sam was making a sketch in his notebook.

'I stood here. The butcher, Mr Able, and the housekeeper to the music teacher, were here before me, they're the people that you should probably be calling to court,' said Moore, with a slight tremble in the voice.

'And we will indeed. Tell me what you saw,' said Franks, standing slightly to the side of Moore, watching his face.

'It was a man on the ground, a policeman bending over him, Able, the butcher who lives across the street, was saying something to the housekeeper and they were looking for something near the body. The policeman left, and Evans, our usual constable arrived at that moment. There were about four other people standing around and three of them left after the policeman, then the music teacher arrived. That's it.'

'Thank-you Mr Moore, we can go back in now. Curzon, you have made notes, I see, that's very useful,' said Franks as he looked around the area and then asked, 'And it was not apparent to you that there had been a stabbing?'

'Good grief, no!' said Moore, shocked.

'That fits with the information that we have that the diplomat, what was his name, Curzon?' asked Franks, frowning.

'Berringer,' said Sam, looking a little bemused at the poor memory.

'That's right, Berringer,' Franks looked around and Moore followed the direction of his gaze. 'Let's go back into the bank, shall we Mr Moore, we're starting to draw a crowd which presumably won't be good for business. You know how people gossip, Bank Director on the street with the police at the scene of the crime. Do lead the way, Mr Moore.'

'Yes, of course,' said Moore, nervously.

Moore walked back towards the bank, with Franks and Sam following at a respectful distance. Sam hesitated and Franks sensed that he was about to ask a question.

'Not now, lad,' said Franks to him, quietly.

The chief clerk opened the doors for them and, once seated back in Moore's office, Franks took a different tack.

'Was there any reason why Berringer would have been coming over here to see you?'

'See me? He wouldn't, I don't, didn't, know the man,' Moore stammered out.

'And yet one of the men under arrest said something about a name. It was the Policeman you mentioned, actually, or should I say, the false Policeman. You would have noticed had you been closer to the body that he didn't have an identification number on the uniform. He said that he heard the name "Moore" mentioned by the two people who bundled the corpse into the carriage. Bit of a coincidence, that, don't you think? It's your name, after all,' said Franks, and then he waited.

'I've never met the man in my life!'

'Are you sure? Not socially? He was a wealthy man, he may have been at a dinner party that you attended, after all you run a bank. It's perfectly possible that you would have met in London, isn't it?' asked Franks, raising his eyebrows with the enquiry.

'Moore is a common name, it could relate to dozens of people. I never met him. I wouldn't have cause to meet him. The Americans don't use British banks, they have their own arrangements,' said Moore as his hand went out to rearrange a piper knife and then he thought better of it as Franks watched him.

'And yet here he was, all the way from Kensington to Whitechapel. Strange, and the name, Moore, is mentioned. It's a mystery! Well, thank-you Mr Moore for your time. We'll not detain you from the world of banking any longer.' Franks got up to go. Sam stood and put his notebook away.

Franks got as far as the office door and then spun around to look at Moore who was a few steps behind. Sam stepped to the side to get out of the way of the focused stare of the Detective.

'Oh, I nearly forgot, where were you in Oxford over New Year?'

'Witney,' said Moore.

'Nice area, some years since I've been. Alone, or with friends?' asked Franks.

'With family, my sister and her family, actually. My brother-in-law is Inspector Doyle, by the way,' Moore had regained some confidence as he trotted out the last piece of information. The name of a superior officer to throw Franks off his line of questioning.

'Is he now? Married to your sister. A family time over New Year, how very nice. And of course, Windsor, were it not for the flooding, would be a charming place to visit,' said Franks.

'Windsor? I wouldn't know, I haven't been. I think Emily mentioned it was difficult last time she was there, but I have no cause to go to Windsor. Why did you mention Windsor in connection with Oxford?' asked Moore.

'My mind is a muddle, Mr Moore, forgive me. Thank-you again for your time, and a good 1873 to you.' Franks turned and he and Sam went out.

'Back to Leman Street?' asked Sam.

'Absolutely not. We're going to eat first. Brain food, Sam, as we've got a lot to digest from that interview and I need food to do it.'

'Have we? It sounded like you were playing with him a bit. You were right about your mind coming across in a muddle. You were working something out, weren't you? It wasn't just a muddle?' asked Sam.

'Oh, no, young Sam, there was no muddle, we confused the hell out of the man. He told us a lot. We had the wrong Moore potentially, although I admit there could be no connection. You heard what he said? His sister's been to Windsor, maybe using her maiden name. Why would she do that, I wonder? What is it, lad?' Franks asked as Sam's face had started to look ill.

'That's the name that Inspector Doyle saw in the boatman's register as part of Berringer's party. She lives in the area. Here I mean. I lived there as well, before I was sent to Windsor, I, er, I mean that she lives in Arbour Square. Why did they bring Berringer over here? Were they trying to get him to Arbour Square? Were they trying to frame her? Jack and I were sent to stay there when the move came to Leman Street. It was to be kept dark where we were living and Hunt thought we'd be safe. Inspector Doyle lives there too. Is it him that they're trying to frame?' Sam's confused splurge stopped as Franks took hold of his arm.

'Quietly, Sam, wait now, wait until we're back at the station. I know where Inspector Doyle lives, and yes, his wife would have been Emily Moore before they were married. Her brother confirmed she was in Windsor for us and you tell me that Doyle saw the surname Moore in the register. Quietly does it. Food first, young Sam, and then we'll get cracking. We've just hours before the New York detective arrives.'

*

At Leman Street, a telegram was waiting when Jack and Stan came back with Grace. It was from Shadwell and was addressed to the investigating officer in the Berringer case. Inspector Hunt had arrived shortly before Jack and Stan had come back so he took the honour of reading the telegram. It said that the landlady from Golden Square had been brought to Shadwell Station by a Constable and had identified Badley as the man who had called on Mrs Berringer, the day that the woman had used the front parlour.

'The man who had brought her something in an envelope,' the landlady said, when she looked through the slit in the muslin curtain and pointed him out down below her in the yard in the identity parade.

Badley was not denying it but he was still firm that he had not killed Mrs Berringer, or disfigured the face after her death.

'What a popular man Badley is in the line-up,' Stan smirked.

'But the questions are still unanswered about who killed Mrs Berringer and who made her face unrecognisable,' said Jack.

'We've come a long way though, Jack. We can lean on him and Grace, get them competing to be the one to make the deal, as you say Franks suggested,' said Hunt.

'One thing bothers me still. Somebody working over the face seems a stupid thing to have done. If they'd not done that they might have got away with the suicide story, although strychnine wouldn't be my poison of choice, it's too violent,' said Jack.

'That's the issue that's interesting,' said Hunt.

'Why?' asked Jack giving him a confused look.

'The only reason the face is unrecognisable is to protect someone. To me that killing was not planned, which means that the death wasn't part of Mrs Berringer's future in having gone missing. Someone unexpected entered the scene and poisoned her. Why?' said Stan, calmly.

'If she was leaving, if the envelope, that Badley brought, had tickets inside, say for a sea journey, perhaps back to America, anywhere to get away, disappear with another person....' Jack paused and looked at Hunt.

'Go on both of you, you're developing this nicely,' Hunt said.

Jack stared out of the window, not seeing the people on the street below but a scene in a lodging house in Golden Square.

'If that person was a man.... If there was some involvement with Berringer's death, if she had never intended to run but had to because her life was in danger....... Maybe she had always intended to wait things out, inherit the money after Berringer was killed and she would be completely blameless, the grieving widow, and then go back to America with her children and finally marry someone else? I don't know, just rambling thoughts,' said Jack.

'Thoughts that start to develop the case,' said Stan nodding.

'The link with the senior policeman, or someone higher maybe linked with the police or the diplomatic service, would fit with evidence going missing, reports lost. Mrs Berringer's face being so unrecognisable that we can't link the death with her, so we can't work out who she was involved with. This is good, we're getting somewhere,' said Hunt, sitting back in his chair.

'But why did Berringer have to die?' asked Jack.

'Money,' said Stan.

'That would imply, if Mrs Berringer was involved with someone else, that they were not rich,' said Hunt, thoughtfully.

'Or as rich,' said Jack, calmly. 'Like a salaried policeman, fairly high up, with enough nasty contacts to get rid of Berringer, make it look like a kidnapping one morning and a crash. Shame for the murderer that Mr Able the butcher happened to be home that morning and recognised a body that had bled out. Once it was in the mortuary there would have been opportunity to dispose of the evidence if the person orchestrating the killing had a contact in there.'

'We're still left with the two questions of who killed Berringer, and who killed Mrs Berringer, and whether or not she was involved in her husband's death,' said Hunt.

'That's three questions,' said Jack grinning.

'So, it is,' said Hunt with a smile.

'I still think some unexpected person has entered the scene. The events of Berringer's death would have been difficult to link back to his wife. The type of death Mrs Berringer had would have been violent, not the sort of poison surely someone would choose to commit suicide. The type of death someone wanted to give a person to get revenge, to me. Someone has got into the Golden Square lodging to administer the poison to her. Perhaps she had become uncooperative, had second thoughts. That poison has to take effect. We could do with the Police Surgeon here to understand how long that would have taken. So, there's a time that's gone by. That person has left before the poison took effect. We need to find out who else called at the house. Maybe the landlady wasn't in when they called and Mrs Berringer let the person in thinking they were not a threat. Then someone has gone back in, or a different person has gone in to destroy the face. Just thinking aloud here, Inspector, so forgive me if it's coming across as if I'm rambling,' said Stan. Hunt half smiled at him. Then Jack cut in.

'We need to get Doctor Brown's stand-in to have a look at Grace, anyway. We could have a chat about using strychnine at the same time. Thinking this through, Mrs Berringer's death doesn't sound as if it was expected. Maybe, the person who found her was the man who was involved with her. Perhaps he went to collect her as it was time to sail. Then he's arranged for some nasty piece of work to rearrange the dead woman's face. I can't see a reason for destroying the face unless it was to protect someone, like you said, Stan. Suicide using strychnine, nah, that doesn't tie up at all,' said Jack.

'Get the Duty Sergeant to call whoever is the Police Surgeon in, will you, Jack,' said Hunt.

Jack stood up and went out to the desk. He was back moments later as Doctor Brown's replacement was already on site.

'We can try and get at whichever Metropolitan Policemen Mrs Berringer or her husband had assigned to them at any point. What do you think?' asked Stan.

'They would have had their own protection as a Consulate, wouldn't they?' asked Jack, looking at Hunt, who nodded. 'What sort of people would have liaised with the American Consulate, maybe attended functions the Berringer's were at if they were a high rank, or linked with the Home Office?' asked Jack.

'That puts me in the frame, thank-you very much, Jack,' said Hunt.

'Were you at posh parties?' asked Jack, surprised.

'Only standing in the shadows on duty, no fun,' Hunt said, and then smirked, 'But I know a man who was and who can get at the information for us. We don't have long do we before the bodies will disappear across the sea. What time's this Detective supposed to get here tonight?' asked Hunt.

'About six o'clock this evening, we've heard,' said Stan.

'Word came through that he stayed in Liverpool, last night, and is making his way up by train today. He's got family living in Liverpool who emigrated from Ireland at the same time as his parents. They live in the port apparently and he was spending the morning with them,' said Hunt.

'I was meaning to ask, sir,' said Jack, 'What's happened to Ted, this morning?'

'Didn't he come?' asked Hunt.

'No, not before we left to go and find Grace,' said Jack.

'The Duty Sergeant should have had word, we'll ask him now as we go back to the desk,' said Hunt.

'Has Constable Phillips arrived from New Road since we've been in the meeting, Sergeant?' asked Hunt.

'Yes, with another Constable and two ladies in a room down the hall. I told them you were in a meeting and were not to be interrupted. They came by carriage,' said the Sergeant.

'Did they?' said Hunt surprised.

'Yes, sir, one of the ladies has evidence to give and Constable Phillips has asked the Police artist to step in. I gather it's a description of a man, sir,' explained the Sergeant.

'Well, at least we know he's here. I wonder who's with him? This is probably linked to the Berringer murders if he's brought them here. Let him know, Sergeant, that we're just stepping out to get a bite to eat. Would you let the Doctor standing in for Doctor Brown know we need to have a word with him when we get back? Jack this is your area, we're in your hands for a meal,' said Hunt.

Jack pulled a face. 'The only place I know is down at Millwall Junction that's any good, and that's Ted's sister's place. Most of my supplies have been via houses on the beat. I can take you to the café at the Junction, if you like, but it won't be quick.'

'No, too far, nowhere at all closer?' asked Hunt.

'There's a public house on the Commercial Road, Stan knows it, but the food isn't too good,' said Jack.

'I know a place towards the top of Leman Street,' offered Stan.

'That's the place, then, lead on, Stan. We'll need to ensure we eat. It's going to be a long day,' said Hunt.

*

317

Seventeen

Stan's place was a supper room, not due to open at midday, but the manager was a contact of Stan's and happy to admit them. Stan explained they needed whatever was ready. Jack steeled himself for something cold but Stan shook his head when he caught sight of Jack's face and reassured him.

'It will be good, there's always something cooking, cheese, and they make their bread. It will be alright.'

The three men ate because they knew they needed to, in order to get them through the rest of the day. If Franks was right and the New York Detective turned up that evening they would have to prove difficult to find in order to continue the case. None of them had an inkling what was to unfold by the evening, but each one ate in silence. Finally, Hunt was the first to push his plate away.

'Done,' he said. 'How about you, gentlemen?'

'I couldn't eat anything else,' said Jack, sitting back and putting a hand on his stomach.

'Stan, what's the payment arrangements?' asked Hunt, taking out a few coins.

'He's not licensed to feed the public at this time of the day, Inspector. We're friends calling in to share a meal with him. I'll settle it with him when I call in again,' said Stan.

'Right, let's get back and see what Ted and the Police Surgeon have for us. I need to send a telegram as well,' said Hunt.

'The Duty Sergeant will get someone down to Stepney Railway Station for you. There's nowhere nearer as yet,' said Jack.

'Sergeant?' called Hunt, as they turned into the reception area of Leman Street Police Station, 'I want you to get a constable down to the nearest telegraph office you know of, it's a sealed message, so it must be someone you trust.'

'I'm off duty at two o'clock, sir, and I'll take it myself,' said the Duty Sergeant.

Hunt thanked him and continued, 'And would you get the Police Surgeon up here for me, now.'

'That would be his Nurse, sir. Doctor Brown is away still. It's his Nurse today, a Mrs, er,' the Duty Sergeant glanced down at the list under his desk, of people who had come in that morning,

'A woman, is it? Is she accompanied when she sees the prisoners?' asked Hunt, sharply.

'Yes, sir, a Constable is with her at all times. She's from the dispensary and Doctor Brown has a lot of confidence in her. She's been here before with him,' said the Sergeant. 'A final issue for you, sir, if I may mention something else? Constable Phillips has asked if you, and Constable Sargent, could step into the interview with the two ladies he and Constable Banks are with. The police artist has finished the picture and they would like you to have a look at the face. I wondered if the Sergeant from Shadwell would be of use in this as well, sir, sort of widens the area covered if you see what I mean.'

'Yes, good idea, we'll do that now, which room are they in?' asked Hunt.

'Number three, down the corridor, sir,' said the Duty Sergeant.

Hunt knocked briefly on the door of the interview room, more to prepare the ladies inside than to request permission to enter. Charlie Banks opened the door and restrained a grin when he saw the Inspector with Jack in tow.

'Bit of a crowd, sir, I'll wait in the corridor with Jack while you and the Sergeant come in,' said Charlie.

'Thank-you,' said Hunt, while Charlie stood back to allow the Inspector in first. Stan followed Hunt into the room and Charlie stepped into the corridor, pulling the door behind him. He motioned to Jack to stay where he was. Once the door was completely closed behind him, Charlie grinned at Jack and led him down the corridor into another room.

'I wanted to let you know a couple of things before you go in to the room, Jack. First, did you have a good New Year? I raised a glass to you at midnight on New Year's Eve,' said Charlie.

'I did, thanks, although it turned out to be a bit of an eventful one with everything that happened. My drink was a cup of tea in a church hall to you, Charlie, but I thought of you and wished you well. How did you get on with the backgrounds of the lodgers in Arbour Square?' asked Jack.

'Well, nothing there, except for the expertise on poison of Mrs Black, but given she's standing in as the Surgeon's Nurse today here I imagine she's been checked again and again. But an interesting bit of work. I decided to stay on as a result, thanks to you.'

'Ann Black is the Nurse? If she's on site I could get chance to talk to her about Mrs Berringer,' said Jack.

'That sounds a good opportunity, Jack. Now, to this morning's bit of work in that room. Ted and I brought a young lady and a person that she works for, here, in order to get to the Police Artist. She's got a rare description of an attacker last night who followed her. The two of us came together as a bit of protection for each other, not that the two ladies are dangerous,' Charlie laughed, 'but you know what I mean. The description is tied in with the Berringer case, and Ted thinks he recognises the portrait. What I have to tell you, Jack is that the young lady is a bit shook up, but not hurt, and she was really brave. She's had a bad night by the sound of it and not slept much. She managed to hit the man who followed her a rare knock on the back of the head with a heavy bag she had with her by all accounts. Sounds like he was trying to frighten her, and she turned as he was following her, to face him, look at him, and got her bag prepared because, as she said, she had no one with her to fight for her.' Charlie paused and took in a deep breath. Jack did not think that he had ever heard him say as much before.

'Do you think I'll know the attacker from the picture, then, Charlie?' asked Jack.

'No, I don't think you and I have enough local knowledge yet. But you do know the young lady and her employer, and that was why Ted wanted me to have a word with you.'

'Is it the girl from the café near Poplar?' asked Jack.

'No, it isn't but you do know her because it's Miss Harriet Fildew and the cook, Mrs Ardle, that she works with.' Charlie stopped as the information started to register with Jack. He looked at Charlie without blinking for a while. Slowly it began to register in his eyes.

'Harriet! My Harriet? I must go in,' said Jack, starting to push past Charlie, who caught him by the arm.

'And you will, Jack. But you must let Inspector Hunt and the other Sergeant finish with the identification first in case you say too much about the case. She's a witness, you see, and may have to give evidence in court. If you say too much, because you're upset and it's hard to think, when you're upset, it may be made out by the defence that you fed her information and that would wipe any value her evidence has from the case. That would be a shame after what she's experienced, and how plucky she's been. She insisted she didn't want to go to her sister's, or go home to her mother for a bit of time to get over the shock. She wanted to get this identification done and she said she wanted to help us because you'd tried to keep her safe,' Charlie stopped again.

Jack felt an inane desire to laugh because Charlie Banks, the quiet one amongst the recruits, the one who hardly had said anything except for "Yes, sir," in the last two months was suddenly quite verbose. The humour quickly subsided though, as the realisation hit him that his sense that someone may be following him on New Year's Day had been right and that it had put Harriet in danger.

'It's my fault. I shouldn't have run after the tram. I travelled back with her to Camberwell Green. The man must have followed me to the tram, and seen us together. You know how it is, Charlie when you've got a girl in your arms, I didn't take care,' Jack stood with his back leaning against the wall and closed his eyes, breathing heavily as the anger started to emerge.

'I know how it is,' said Charlie, keeping a hand on Jack's arm.

The door opened and Ted Phillips stood in the doorway. He closed the door slowly, taking in the scene and how Jack was.

'Fully briefed?' Ted asked, raising his eyebrows for confirmation from Charlie.

'He is, Ted,' said Charlie, and Jack registered that this was the first time that he had heard Charlie use a first name of one of the older Constables. It was bizarre, like he was in a dream.

'Jack, the face in the picture has been confirmed by myself, Tom Hunt and Stan. An arrest is underway. I should tell you that it's a Policeman, and he is likely to provide a link to whoever is behind the murders of the Berringers,' said Ted.

'I want to go and be part of it,' said Jack, stepping forward and moving his arm to detach it from Charlie's grip. Charlie let go with a nod from Ted. Jack was clenching and unclenching his fists but Ted was still in front of the door.

'Your job now, is in that room with that girl of yours,' said Ted. 'We'll get him, and he'll be questioned, but not by you. Too close to it. Get yourself down into that room, now, and I'll bring you both in a cup of tea in a couple of minutes. Then I'll have to remain to just monitor that you don't go telling her everything about the case. Funny thing, emotion, loosens the tongue. She's done well, your young lady. You should be proud of her.'

'I am,' said Jack, quietly. 'But it's my fault, I gave away where she was going by getting on the tram with her. You told me to stay away and you were so right, Ted, I realise that now. I hope she'll forgive me.'

'There's no issue, there. You met her in a central London place. Alright, feelings get carried away and you were being the young lover chasing the tram, holding your girl and so on. She's explained all that. You did stay away, and you did follow orders. Chances were the man would have followed her anyway back to the tram while you were dealing with that arrest on the bridge. Get down to the room, now, Jack, and let her know how wonderful you think she is,' Ted opened the door, and Jack arrived at the interview room door without any recollection of walking down the corridor. He knocked and went in.

There was just Harriet seated at the table with the cook, Mrs Ardle. Her face lit up when she saw him and the effect of that was to feel the water start in his eyes, and his face colour, then drain. Mrs Ardle stood up and patted his arm as she walked past him to leave the room.

'Harriet, I'm so sorry,' Jack said, going to where she sat and kneeling down to take a hand. He held it to his face, closing his eyes and breathing in the scent she wore. Harriet put a hand to the bruised cheek and the edge of his black eye.

'It's alright, Jack, I'm alright. It's not your fault. I looked at his eyes and they didn't register madness, and I knew he was trying to frighten me. It would have been worse otherwise and I couldn't have stopped him if he'd really wanted to hurt me because he was quite big and heavily built. I knew you'd have fought him if you'd been there, so I told myself I had to do it. I was near the house so I screamed and people came out of several houses to help me. I deliberately walked fast back to the road where I work, once I realised someone was following me. It's helped the case, Inspector Hunt says. He said I'm a champion. I bashed the man, Jack, I think he'll have a bruise,' Harriet put her arms around him and he melted into her and then the humour took over, the other side of the coin of emotion that had started with anger and then fear and the desire to laugh became a sob in case he lost someone else that was precious to him. The thought of this tiny woman bashing her bag into the neck of the Policeman who had barged into her made him want to laugh again. Harriet sat back and loosened her hold of him surprised at the sound he had made.

'Are you crying? I didn't think you would cry,' she said, her face contorting.

'It's just a noise, it's all mixed up. I want to kill him, but I'm relieved you're alright, but none of this seems real,' said Jack.

'That would do no good, Jack Sargent. What good would that do for you to kill him? You'd hang and I'd be more upset. No, you've got to catch him and find out what he knows,'

'We will, that's where Inspector Hunt and the other officer, have gone now I suspect. Were you hurt?' asked Jack.

'He only barged me as he went past, I think I did him more damage because I had a big bottle of cologne, which I had bought, in my bag. Oh, and there was the change purse as well in the bag. I clouted him good and proper! I was upset though and sleeping was not something that came easily last night,' Harriet explained.

'I'll make sure there's some protection there at night,' said Jack.

'It'll be alright when he's caught,' said Harriet, smiling gently.

Jack looked at her and swallowed the response he was going to make about not knowing who the man was connected to, or how high up it all went.

Ted came in with two cups of tea on a tray and set it down on the table. Harriet put two spoons of sugar in both, 'for shock,' she said, and Jack excused himself for a few moments, on the pretext of bringing Mrs Ardle back in. He really intended to find out from her how Harriet really was. Ted sat down on a chair in the corner of the room, as Jack opened the door and poked his head into the corridor. The cook was chatting to Charlie Banks and Jack stepped quietly out and closed the door behind him.

'Mrs Ardle, how is Harriet, really?' he asked.

'She's not slept well. I took her into my room and sat in the chair while she lay on the bed. I watched her for a long time. She had her eyes open for hours, just staring at nothing. I tried to give her a tonic but she wouldn't have it. She was screaming and screaming when they found her outside. Good job she was, as it brought people out to her. The master was just saying goodbye to friends who had called for New Year's Day, so it was lucky people were in the hall.

The master said that when they went out to her she stopped, clammed up, and stared at him, probably shock that it was the master rather than one of us. He said it was as if she didn't know him and didn't believe what she was seeing, and then looked from one to another of his friends as if she was working them out. He told me that he saw a man running away in the distance, so they believed her when she finally was able to say what had happened. We did get the doctor to her, Jack. He said it was rest and that she should go to family. But Harriet would have none of it. She kept saying she had to tell Jack, and that you'd known there was a risk if you'd come to the house and that was why you'd stayed away and that if they sent her home her mother would never let her come back. We had to agree about getting the police in the morning in order to calm her down. The man had frightened her but she didn't believe he had meant to do anything this time except that. It was as if this understanding seemed to help her. I promised we'd get word across to New Road Police Station first thing in the morning, to that colleague of yours, Constable Phillips. We weren't too sure where you were, you see. The master said he'd send a runner to the station first thing and Constable Phillips, and this young man, came shortly after we'd cleared the breakfast away. I got Harriet helping with that as I thought it would be good for her to get her mind and body doing something. It's her last day with me tomorrow, you know. She's been a good girl. I'm sorry this has happened.' Mrs Ardle took a handkerchief out of a pocket and gave a sniff while she wiped her nose. 'We'll have to see how she goes on.'

'Thank-you, Mrs Ardle, I'll make sure there's some protection at the house tonight,' said Jack, and then he caught Charlie's eye who returned his look with curiosity. Opening the door for the cook, Jack said, 'Would you like to come back in?'

'Jack, your tea's going cold,' said Harriet, as they went into the room.

Jack sat down and allowed himself to be fussed over, watching Harriet as she stirred his tea and passed him the cup and saucer, noticing how the colour in her face was better. Ted Phillips looked from Harriet to Jack, seeing the future. Mrs Ardle moved a curl away from Harriet's eyes in a motherly, concerned way.

'See how much better she is, Constable Phillips, now her young man is here,' she said to Ted, who smiled in return.

Then the door opened and Franks and Sam walked in. Franks nodded at the ladies. Sam smiled at the scene with Jack being given a cup of tea by the young lady, having no inkling as to what was going on. Ted stood up and made the introductions. Sam registered then who the young lady was to Jack.

'If you'll just step out I can give you an update on the situation,' suggested Ted, to Franks.

'We could do with one. We too have stories to tell, don't we Sam?' said Franks.

'I can take the ladies back across the river,' said Charlie.

'I'll sleep better tonight, now I've seen you,' whispered Harriet to Jack. Charlie and Jack escorted the ladies to the front hall.

Outside, Jack waited with Mrs Ardle and Harriet while Charlie had disappeared to get the carriage brought around to the front.

'It's like being the Queen,' said Mrs Ardle.

'You deserve it,' said Jack. 'Charlie will take you back to Camberwell Green. I'll be around later to make sure you're safe.'

'Are you sure you can do that now?' asked Harriet.

'Yes, it doesn't matter now if I come over to see you, I'll be around later.' Jack was oblivious to whether him seeing Harriet would make anything worse, he was determined to ensure she was safe and felt the need to be the one who would follow her protection through.

Harriet reached her face up and kissed him on the cheek and then she and Mrs Ardle walked towards the carriage. Jack watched, standing in front of the station as they drove away with Charlie, until the carriage turned the corner and was no longer in sight.

*

Near the area with the cells was a small room in which the Duty Sergeant had told Jack that he would find Ann Black. He knocked and the door was opened by a Constable present to provide the protection to the lady who was standing in for Doctor Brown.

'I wanted to try and see you before you left,' said Jack, giving her a brief smile as he went in.

'Jack, I've just finished. How was your New Year?' asked Ann, untying the apron that she had been wearing.

'Busy. How about you both?'

'Likewise, but ours was a very busy time really doing very little. But you're not here for pleasantries, are you?' said Ann, taking in Jack's earnest expression. She turned to the Policeman who had accompanied her while she had performed as many of Doctor Brown's duties as they could get away with. 'Constable, I will be perfectly safe with one policeman, instead of two, and I'm sure you must be itching to get back to more exciting things now. Constable Sargent will stay with me until I leave, won't you, Jack?'

'That I will,' said Jack, firmly.

Once the door closed behind his colleague, Jack asked, 'Did you ever manage to get to the mortuary with Doctor Brown, Ann?'

'I did, and we were able to see the body of the diplomat. But not of the woman,' she said. 'At that point, she was still in a different area and there was nothing to tie her up to being definitely Mrs Berringer. I gather that you've had other information now, and that her body's been brought across the city to be in the same place as her husband's. All nice and neat and tidy for the American Detective, apparently. They're expecting him to escort the bodies back to New York, in the next few days.'

'What did you make of Berringer's death?' asked Jack.

'Stab wounds, someone knew how to do it and where to do it. He was like a slaughtered pig. Difficult to be certain due to the preserving that was being done by those American professors but both Doctor Brown and I thought that he would have bled quickly and probably was dead or almost there, when he was in the carriage. Did you find it, by the way?' asked Ann.

'No, we think it's probably at the bottom of the Thames,' said Jack.

'Quite so, and that's where it would be if I'd carried a dying, bleeding man in one, too. I wish I could help about the woman, but I suppose it's too late now if the Detective has arrived,' said Ann, biting her top lip, while putting away small bottles of tinctures and other liquids.

Jack watched her for a few moments and then said, 'He's not here yet, could you get us both in?'

Ann laughed, 'I'm not sure, without Doctor Brown, it may not work. You may get us both arrested. The attendant does know me from fatalities at the Women's Dispensary, but the problem would be we'd need a male doctor. It's the law, Constable, that's the problem.'

Jack gave the first grin of the afternoon. 'Hang on, I've got an idea.' Jack stuck his head round the door and whistled. One of the Constables appeared to see what was going on and Jack called him into the room with Ann, while he ran to find Ted.

*

Ann had been unsure about the idea of Ted Phillips masquerading as a Doctor in the Mortuary but Ted was willing to pretend that he was a holiday stand-in. Ann was there to brief him, with Jack accompanying to give the air of police authority, to see the bodies before the New York Detective arrived. Ted changed into plain clothes and the three of them had left the station by cab to lend a greater air of respectability.

The three walked in through the section devoted to the Coroner's Court and the Mortuary was at the rear. The attendant recognised Ann from her visits in relation to the Women's Dispensary. It was only days since she had been with Doctor Brown and he showed surprise at her reappearance with the two men.

'Did you want the Professors about the Berringers?' asked the attendant.

'No, there's no need. This is Doctor Smith who is relieving Doctor Brown while he's away. We thought that he should see the bodies before the American Detective removes them to take them back to New York. A sort of signing the whole situation off from the British perspective,' explained Ann.

'Oh, I see. I wasn't informed you were coming. They're laid out in there, we put them together as they were in life,' said the attendant, jerking a thumb in the direction of a closed door further down the corridor. 'I'll take you in. I need you to sign in though.'

Jack looked vaguely panicked but Ted and Ann signed the sheet in the register. The attendant looked at Jack's number and Jack knew he would remember it.

'Thank-you. Do you mind if I leave you for a few minutes? I have to go to the office,' said the attendant.

'Of course, we won't be long anyway, you take your time,' said Ted, pushing a door open. The attendant disappeared and Jack gagged at the smell of preservation.

'Is this safe?' asked Jack as he stood in a corner.

'Well it's not ideal,' said Ann, as she started to turn down the cover of the first body. 'It would be better if the Mortuary wasn't on the same site as other buildings. This post-mortem room is at the back so it's the furthest we can get from where the public would be. The laboratory is in the room off to the side there. Jack, would you mind keeping an eye open in the corridor for the attendant coming back while I do a quick assessment of the bodies.'

'You mean I can go out?' said Jack.

Ted laughed, 'Yes, let us know if he comes back. You'll get used to the smell, with time.'

'That, I doubt,' muttered Jack as he stepped out of the room into the corridor.

He peered through the small window as Ann pulled the sheet back fully from a man's body. Ted moved within Jack's line of sight and Jack saw him take a notebook out of his pocket and start to write while Ann talked. Jack glanced up the corridor again and then back through the window.

Ann and Ted had covered up the man's body, Jack assumed it was Berringer. They were moving to the next covered mound. He turned away given the description in the paper of what had been done to Mrs Berringer's face. Coming across a situation in the course of a crime being committed was one thing, staring at a defaced corpse in a Mortuary was another and Jack was fighting down a rebellious stomach.

Ted was still making notes. Jack could hear talking and thought that Ann and Ted must be on their way towards the door behind him. Then he realised that the sound was coming from the corridor at the back of the Coroner's Court and that the attendant was on his way back with some company. With the attendant was a man in a loose-fitting jacket wearing the whitest shirt that Jack had ever seen, displaying a diamond. His hands were in his pockets and he was smoking. With him were two men wearing navy-blue uniforms and flat peaked caps, which looked like they were from the surplus stock of the Civil War.

Jack knocked on the door behind him with one hand behind his back and turned to smile at the attendant.

'Are they nearly done?' asked the attendant. The man who was smoking assessed Jack as he drew close. 'The New York Police are now here for the bodies to be removed and we need to complete the formalities and release them.'

Jack saluted but it didn't produce a response from the two uniformed men. They simply stared.

'You're relieved, Constable,' said the man with the diamond. Jack concluded that he was the Detective they had all decided to avoid.

'Thank-you sir, but I can only be relieved by an order from my superior officer until the Doctor and his assistant have completed the sign off from the English investigation,' said Jack, standing to attention. The door he was blocking opened and Ted and Ann appeared.

'Thank-you Constable, that is all we needed to do. Good afternoon, are you here for the Berringer couple?' asked Ted, stepping out into the corridor, 'You'll forgive me if I don't shake your hand, but I imagine you would prefer me not to.'

'And you are?' asked the diamond wearer.

'Doctor Smith and my nurse. I'm standing in for the usual Doctor as he's on holiday due to the season, you know. You've come a long way I hear, New York, isn't it?'

'Yes, it was quite a sail at this time of the year. Are you going to tell your boy here to stand down, now?'

'Yes, of course, thank-you Constable, we'll be on our way. When do you sail back?' asked Ted.

'I haven't been dismissed sir,' said Jack, staring straight ahead.

'I'm dismissing you,' said the Detective standing in front of Jack. 'I out rank you.'

'Begging your pardon, sir, but you don't here, sir. I have to be dismissed by my superior officer. My orders are to guard the door until the Doctor and his assistant are finished, sir, and they are not finished as they have not signed out of the register,' said Jack.

'You English, you're so servile. Let's get this done,' the Detective looked at the attendant and held out his hand. The attendant fled for the register that he had left in the office.

'I'm saying you can stop, now,' said Ted to Jack.

'Begging your pardon, sir but as a Doctor you are not my superior officer,' Jack was immoveable.

'Would you move if I asked you to?' asked Ann, laying a hand on Jack's arm.

'Certainly, ma'am.' Jack saluted, and stepped away. Before the attendant returned Ted and Ann started to walk up the corridor towards their way out through the Coroner's Court. Once out onto the street it was already dark. Ted hailed a cab and the three of them climbed in. Jack started to laugh.

'What did you think you were doing?' Ted asked him, incredulously.

'I didn't like him. Did you see that diamond he was wearing? Can you imagine how long he'd last around here sporting that on the beat?' said Jack.

'That man doesn't do a "beat," Jack. He didn't like you either, which means he'll remember you and your identification number,' said Ted. 'We'd better make sure that you and I are nowhere around to run into him in the next few days.'

'Was it worth the visit? What did you get Ann?' asked Jack, leaning forward and moving in time to the sway of the cab.

'Yes, I hope so,' Ann glanced at Ted.

'Definitely,' said Ted.

'Mr Berringer was killed expertly. An artery would have been cut and he would have bled quickly. Someone knew what they were doing as it was a very sharp implement. Like cutting through butter,' Anne paused and Jack visualised how he had put his knife into the butter the last time they had all been together in Arbour Square, toasting by the fire. He was brought back to the present as Ann started to speak again.

'Mrs Berringer died of strychnine poisoning. The muscles went into spasms and that would have started within five to fifteen minutes depending on how she took the poison. I suspect she's taken it orally rather than breathing it or having it injected. Someone has put it into something she either ate or drank would be my guess. Doctor Brown told me when we both came that her death would have been due to cardiac arrest in this case. It would have been very painful. We don't have any studies of how toxic it would be in a human being as that would not be ethical. There are cases where it's been unintentional, and, I'm afraid there are also cases where it's been intentional.'

'Do you think someone wanted her to have that sort of death?' Ted asked.

'Yes, otherwise they wouldn't have used it. You know Ted, from cases that arsenic poisoning is common and can be disguised. It can be done over time, bit by bit. But even with arsenic it has a variable success depending on various factors. If someone has a good diet with lots of meat and fish that person can react differently to someone who doesn't have that kind of diet. There are studies being done that the green dye being used in wall paper can kill as a result of the poison in it, but not everyone is affected. The studies I did in Paris even showed that meat is being dipped in arsenic as a fly repellent. While Doctor's don't speak out people will die.' Anne looked out at the scenes of deprivation that they were passing towards the wharfs.

'You did well, Ann. So, definitely not a suicide, despite that note so obviously not in Mrs Berringer's hand-writing. We have a killer and probably someone else who worked over the face and left the note. They wouldn't have known she had signed an agreement for the room, though, so we had something with which to compare the note. Thank-you for helping us,' said Jack. 'Here's to the day when you qualify.'

'If,' said Ann, sadly.

'When,' repeated Jack, smiling at her.

'Here we are,' announced Ted, as they pulled up outside Leman Street. Jack and Ted got down and the cab continued to Arbour Square with Ann.

Inside the station, Sergeant Thick let them know that Hunt and Stan were still not back. There was therefore no news, and no one to give news to. Franks had taken Sam with him and as Sam was effectively off duty at six o'clock Thick assumed it was back to Shadwell, or the Mason's Arms.

'What time are you effectively off duty, Ted?' asked Jack.

'It should have been four o'clock. I think I'll get my head down for a while. We'd better wait for Hunt to come back. What about you?' asked Ted.

Jack nodded about the thought of sleep, but thought of when he could respectably cross the river. 'Franks said we had better disappear, keep moving so we can't be found by that detective.'

'Bit late for you and me, isn't it,' said Ted.

*

Eighteen

By nine o'clock that evening Jack had decided that he was not waiting around any longer. His stomach was erupting with hunger and he felt that he was limited in where he could go to eat as he was still in his uniform. Sandwiches had not satisfied him, Ted having despatched a boy for supplies earlier. He also wanted to get across the river to Camberwell and set himself up for the night on watch so that Harriet could sleep. Without news from Hunt about the arrest of the Policeman that Harriet had identified from the artist's sketch Jack did not want to take any chances in case an arrest had not taken place and the man, or his accomplices, tried again.

Sam had clearly gone home or was still out with Franks. There was no word from either of them.

'Well that was a waste of an evening. I think I'll make tracks to get across the river and call it a day,' said Ted.

'You're right, I'll come with you, and call in and see how Harriet is getting on. Mrs Ardle's expecting me to check things over tonight. Where do you think that Hunt is?' asked Jack.

'Home if he's any sense. If they've made an arrest they've clearly not brought him here or Shadwell. No one is sweating Grace either. We could have a look at him, show willing, then go?' suggested Ted.

Jack nodded and he and Ted went to the cells. Ted slid the opening in the cell door to one side. Grace was asleep, curled up in the foetal position, snoring.

'Looks like an innocent child, not like someone who drove a coach while an American diplomat bled to death. We could try and see if he's prepared to provide us with more information?' suggested Ted.

'Franks thought that we could play Badley and Grace off against each other, see who will cut a deal. I'd be interested to know how he got the booking to drive Mrs Berringer and her gentleman friend in

Windsor. It clearly wasn't done through the Cab Company, so how did he get the work? It hasn't come out of thin air, Ted. That's a long way to drive out of London to collect a lady from the train and drive her around Windsor. He probably did it more than once, so who arranged it?' said Jack.

'I doubt it was Mrs Berringer. I don't think she would have chosen a character like Grace. Perhaps the man she was meeting? That puts him in touch with some dubious types. If he's linked to the Police he's been able to lean on people, so there's a position of power.' Ted indicated to the Constable on duty to open up. The door clanged behind them and Grace came to, momentarily surprised to see two officers in front of him. Then he remembered where he was. He stank, and clearly water had not touched his hands and face that morning.

'You've eaten, I see,' said Ted, glancing at the empty plate.

'Which is more than we have,' said Jack, with a scowl.

'You hit me,' said Grace, pointing at Jack.

'Oh, don't upset him, Mr Grace, he's not very good when he's hungry. Tell you what, I bet you would like a change of scene, wouldn't you? Why not come up to an interview room? The air's not too good down here,' said Ted. 'Constable, organise some tea will you for the three of us and I'll take Mr Grace upstairs.'

Jack blinked a couple of times wondering if Ted had got over-tired by the day. He furrowed his brow to look miserable as that was how Ted had presented him and barked, 'Sugar?'

'Two,' said Grace, confused.

Jack related to how Grace looked as he was confused by the tack that Ted was taking. He banged on the door more aggressively than he actually felt and wondered momentarily if he should accompany it with a snarl. That would probably overdo things, he decided and just left it at the banging. The Constable on the other side unlocked the door and Jack went to make the tea. He carried three mugs into the interview room and set them down on the table so that they slopped. Then he picked up a chair and turned it the wrong way around so that the back would be in front of him, slammed it

down and sat on it, with his elbows resting on the top of it. He stared at Grace and slurped his tea, hungrily.

Ted went into his gentlemanly routine offering Grace the deal.

'We can only give it to one of you. Badley's not going to get it, Detective Sergeant Franks already has aggravated burglary and rape stacked up against him and it's clear he probably finished off the American woman. You weren't there for that, we know. You're just the driver, aren't you? Admittedly you used the cab without your employer's permission and pocketed the fare but all you're doing is driving. Am I right?' asked Ted.

'Exactly. I get a message each time to turn up with a Badley at Windsor. No questions asked, just collect a woman, who's described by what she's wearing, and then wait for the next train and pick up a man. After we'd done it a few times we realised it was always the same two people,' said Grace.

'Who sent you the message?' asked Jack.

'No idea. It came with payment. A guinea. Badley got the same and a uniform. That way it all looked official for the woman, I suppose. She was a diplomat's wife, you know, I made enquiries. After that I said I needed more money so whoever it was sent two guineas. All I had to do was borrow the cab and show up.' Grace took a mouthful of tea.

'What did you think was happening?' asked Ted.

'They were having an affair, it was obvious.' Grace said, 'The woman would go and see her child for about an hour at the school and then it was back in the coach, drive around, no questions asked about what's going on, and then take them back to the station. They'd leave separately again by different trains. It was clear that she was married. She was a loud woman, we could hear some of the things she said from inside the coach, but nothing clear, if you get what I mean. I think she was older than the man that she was meeting as well. He was some big wig as although we never saw his face the cut of his suit was too good for him to be anything else. I was pretty sure he was younger than her. Something about the walk, said that. The only difference in the behaviour was the last time, the woman was upset and we could hear her inside, sobbing. The man kept his voice low all the time but he did a lot of talking.'

Grace looked at Ted, then across at Jack and ran his tongue over his yellow teeth. 'I kept them, the notes, each one, they're at my lodgings.'

'Are they? Handwritten or typed?' asked Ted.

'Who has a typewriter, here?' laughed Grace.

'Americans probably, maybe even "bigwigs." Handwritten then from your response,' said Ted.

'And you're giving us permission to go and get them from your lodgings, aren't you? said Jack, with a scowl.

'Yeah, I could. What's in it for me?' asked Grace.

'Not hanging for the murder of Mrs Berringer,' said Jack, standing up. Grace pushed his own chair back to put some more space between him and Jack. Jack walked to the door, opened it and stuck his head out looking for a Constable. One was coming up the corridor so Jack beckoned him over to the door.

'Paper, a pencil, and an envelope,' said Jack, sharply, with a wink at his colleague. The man grinned and was back in two minutes. Jack pushed the paper and the pencil towards Grace who scribbled a note for his landlady that the police had come to collect some of his things.

'Now, about the American diplomat Berringer, what did you think was going on there?' asked Ted.

'Honest to God, not that he was dead. It was as if he was unconscious and he was all bundled up with these two men pulling him down the path. Kidnap, I thought, maybe a ransom. I was for going then and there but Badley said I was in too deep. The men said I was to go to an address and I thought they said "A" something so I went towards the Whitechapel Road via Aldgate, which is the route I'm used to. It was only when we got over there that one of them started shouting that I'd gone the wrong way and there would be hell to pay. I decided to get out of it and so I crashed the coach. Then the body was on the street, Badley's bending over it, dressed as a policeman of all things, trying to see if the man is coming to and he says to me, he's dead. So, we both did a runner because people were coming over and it wouldn't be long before the real police turned up.' Grace collapsed onto the table with his head in his hands. 'I didn't see murder coming. I swear to God that I had no idea on that morning until the men brought Berringer out of the house that there was anything up. I was for pulling out. Badley and me, we argued most of the way. He kept saying it would go nasty for me as he knew where I lived and would pass it on. I didn't work with him again, and I haven't seen him since.'

'What happened to the two men who were inside with the body?' asked Jack.

'They ran off as soon as we crashed. One of them had a gash on his head and was bleeding.'

'Had you ever seen them before?' asked Jack, forgetting to be curt.

'Never.'

'Thank-you Mr Grace, just a few more questions. Was there any trace of an accent, like an American accent?' asked Ted.

'No, they were London men,' Grace said.

'Did you hear a name mentioned at all when they were putting Berringer in the coach?' asked Jack, still staring at Grace.

'No, I was on the wrong side. Badley might have heard something. All they said to me was what I thought was Aldgate something. And I got that wrong.'

'Right, now we're going to take you back to your cell, so that the other prisoners don't get the wrong idea about you being a police informant. We'll see you in the morning, after we've collected the notes you've kept from your lodgings.' Ted stood up and they took Grace back to the cells.

'What now, Ted?' asked Jack.

'We'll take a cab to his lodgings in Mile End and find those notes he kept. Then home for me in case my missus decides she's had enough of my antics and you can get across and look after Harriet.'

'Sounds good,' said Jack, 'Two cabs in one day!'

'Three, if you play your cards right,' said Ted.

*

The notes giving instructions to Grace were found in a tin on a top shelf in the bedroom that he called home. Jack and Ted left the lodgings and walked to the Mile End Road. Jack flagged down a cab and he and Ted rode towards London Bridge, with St Paul's Cathedral framed against the cloudy sky.

'They're all in the same hand writing. Let's split the notes, Ted, just in case something happens. Then at least we've got some evidence. Is it worth comparing the writing to the suicide note?' suggested Jack.

'Good idea.' Ted put his head out of the carriage and peered up the road. 'Progress is a bit slow around here, isn't it, I thought it would have been quieter at this time of the night.'

'I've almost lost track of time. What time do you think it is?' asked Jack.

'Must be nearly eleven o'clock.'

'Harriet will have given up on me,' said Jack. 'This is the only way to travel, though. Must look odd two police constables in a cab.'

'No choice, now. The ferry will be stopping. Will you step in for a few moments to say hello to the wife? She'd like to wish you a good new year,' asked Ted.

'That's kind, then I must get over to Harriet,' said Jack. He watched a series of cabs roll across the bridge towards them and his brain did a somersault. 'Of course,' he shouted, and Ted jerked with surprise.

'That's why Badley stole the carriage from the coach company and hung onto it. They needed another carriage after the one he and Grace had used to transport the dead Berringer. It doesn't sound as though either Grace or Badley dumped the coach in the Thames. But they must have needed a coach for something. That means Badley is the contact for the man Mrs Berringer was meeting. Franks was right, he is still holding out on us and he knows more. We should go and ......'Ted interrupted Jack.

'No more tonight, Jack. Tomorrow morning, eight o'clock, if you must but not now. Apart from which, you have an appointment with a young lady. Well done, though, and we need to get hold of Franks as Badley is in Shadwell. You and I are on patrol at eight tomorrow and we need to get some sleep. Look, we're here,' said Ted.

'All these are new, aren't they?' asked Jack peering out of the cab as they had pulled into a street lined with semi-detached villas.

'Yes, we didn't want one of the older properties, Margaret thought they were unhealthy. This is nice, newly plastered, and we have a bathroom now with piped water and a toilet in the outhouse. Mains water now, Jack!' said Ted. Jack looked at his animated face and broad smile.

'Good grief, you've got a front garden. You could grow some veg in this,' said Jack, grinning. Ted guffawed.

'Flowers and a bit of a lawn, more like,' said Ted. 'You could have something like this one day.' Ted climbed down from the cab and told the driver to wait. 'Come in and say hello, and then you can get over to Harriet. Wait a minute, that's odd.' Ted paused at the gate.

'What's wrong?' asked Jack as he jumped down from the cab.

'There's a light in the front room. We only use it for high days and holidays. I wonder who's here at this time of the night.' Ted took out keys and opened his front door. The door to the front room was ajar and seated in a comfortable arm chair next to the fire was Tom Hunt.

'Tom,' said Ted, surprised. 'Are you alright?' A door opened further down the hall and a dark-haired woman, in her early thirties with a comfortable build and lively eyes appeared, wiping her hands on a towel. Jack nodded to her and she smiled and came forward to kiss Ted on the cheek.

'Oh, you're home at last. Poor Inspector Hunt has been waiting for you for a couple of hours. Have you eaten both?' she asked.

'Margaret, this is Jack Sargent, who you've heard so much about. Don't offer him food, as he'll eat it,' said Ted with a smile at Jack as he took off his great coat and started to hang it up. Jack hovered, smiling and liking the homely atmosphere.

'Well Tom, what's happened?' asked Ted.

'A lot. I thought you were the one that was likely to come home eventually, Ted, and the safest bet to wait for. Where are you off to Jack?' asked Hunt.

'I'm calling in to make sure Miss Fildew is alright. Mrs Ardle, the cook, said she was upset last night and I thought a police presence might help for a little while, sort of reassure her that she's safe,' explained Jack. 'Have you caught the man, sir?'

Hunt nodded but before he could say anything Margaret Phillips said,

'While you talk, I'll make you something hot. Have you eaten, Ted?' she repeated her question, firmly.

'Yes, but tea would be good, and Jack never refuses food, we should go in and close the door, or we'll have the children down,' said Ted, walking into the front room.

Jack smiled at Margaret and said, 'Nice house,' and then followed Ted into the room while she disappeared down the hall. Jack closed the door and sat on a chair by the window. Ted took the chair opposite Hunt by the fire.

'We've got the man in custody, but in a safe place. He's a detective called Kirby, based at Great Marlborough Street. Morris was there if you remember, Ted, and he knows him. I went over to see Morris about him this afternoon. Morris is making good progress, but it will be a few weeks before he can return and then he'll be in a station for a while. Anyway, Great Marlborough Street is a big division and, of course, Jack, you'll have twigged that its ripe for Golden
Square where the Faceless Woman was found,' Hunt paused as Margaret knocked on the door and then entered with a tray, which she set down on a table next to Jack. She closed the door quietly behind her as she left the room. Jack helped himself to meat and potato pie after a nod from Hunt, and passed the other two men cups of steaming tea.

'He's not talking, Kirby, I mean. Harriet's description will sort him though, and we'll do an identification parade. We can get him for assault, but we can't yet prove anything more. I suspect he's going to benefit by remaining silent,' said Hunt.

'Can we get him to write some lines for us, sir, see if the writing is the same as on these notes?' asked Jack, leaning towards Hunt and pulling two notes from his pocket.

'Good thought, Jack,' said Ted, reaching into his jacket to produce the notes he had kept.

'Where did these come from?' asked Hunt, holding out his hand to take them.

'They're from a cabman, Grace, that we arrested earlier linked with Badley. He was the driver of the cab that had Berringer in it, and also had several jobs meeting Mrs Berringer at Windsor where she sounds as if she had an assignation with a man,' explained Jack. 'He would drive her to the school to visit a child and the man would stay in the cab. Then she'd re-join him and they would drive around and eventually leave separately by different trains. There's four notes we found so that happened at least four times. Grace received payment with the notes. After the first couple of times he twigged it was an opportunity to put the price up. It explains where Badley got the uniform he was wearing from. It was a bit of a charade by the sound of it to make the woman feel safe, being a diplomat's wife. What we do know about the man was he was well-dressed and Grace, the driver, described him as a big-wig, but never managed to see his face.'

'Jack worked it out as we came across here tonight that the cab was disposed of after Berringer's death. We've never found it as you know, which meant that Badley had to get another one, hence the theft of Cunliffe's cab. Badley's the way in for more information, we reckon, Tom,' said Ted.

'That's a job for the morning, then. Probably need to link up with Franks again as Badley's held at Shadwell, isn't he?' asked Hunt.

'Yes. We've not seen Franks, or Sam for hours,' said Jack.

'Well with Kirby, we're unlikely to get him to talk. If he's being protected because of what he knows it may end up with him only being disciplined. It could all get passed off as an awful mistake, that he wasn't following Harriet, and she was hysterical,' said Hunt.

'We need to get Badley to talk then, we can't leave Harriet exposed like this,' said Jack, 'If he gets off he could come after her again.'

'And we could all find that we're in danger anyway. This is higher than Kirby's level. Whoever was involved with Mrs Berringer is in a position of power, has no intention of giving that up and was interested in the soon-to-be widow of a rich man. It doesn't tie up why she was killed. She would still have inherited and after a reasonable time they could have married,' mused Hunt.

'It's the face being destroyed, Tom, Mrs Berringer's face. That action could be separate from the death so that they could try and pass it off as suicide. Tom, we went with Ann Black to the Mortuary today. I pretended to be the doctor standing in for Brown and Ann Black was there with the knowledge. The killer has used poison, strychnine, and it was a nasty death. It's as if someone else has entered the picture, though because the woman was the pathway for riches while she was alive. She was no good to the man that she was involved with dead,' explained Ted. 'Jack's right, we should check the writing against the notes but also against the suicide note.'

'The suicide note wasn't an educated hand like these notes,' said Hunt.

'Badley's denying it but given his track record with violence it could be he was sent to tidy things up, cause a distraction so Mrs Berringer couldn't be linked to the man she had been having an affair with?' suggested Jack.

Hunt sighed, 'Alright, let's get some sleep, and pick it up in the morning. Jack how far do you have to go to get to Harriet's place of work?'

'About five minutes from here and the cab is still outside,' said Jack.

'Good, I'll come with you and drop you and take the cab home,' said Hunt, standing up. 'Look, both of you, don't take any risks and don't go alone into anything. Make sure we know where you are, tomorrow. The man we're dealing with is ruthless, and has a lot to lose. The further we go on this the more dangerous for us and our families it becomes. Goodnight, Ted, thank Margaret for us, will you.'

Jack tapped at the kitchen door and Mrs Ardle, the cook, opened it with a relieved look that he had come. She was in a dressing gown over her cumbersome shape and held the neck together so that nothing showed below her chin.

'Oh, Jack, I thought something had happened to you, as I expected you would be here hours ago. Harriet hasn't gone to bed yet as she wanted to see you. She's up in her room though and is still dressed. Come in the kitchen, I've a plate ready for you. It's a bit dried up as it's been in the warm oven for hours,' Mrs Ardle stood to one side as Jack came in.

'I had to question a man we had arrested earlier today, I am sorry if being so late hasn't helped how Harriet is,' said Jack.

'Have they caught the man?' asked Mrs Ardle.

'Yes, it's as the Inspector thought.' No point in going into detail about how hard the case was going to be to get Kirby convicted, thought Jack.

'You have your dinner, and I'll go and fetch Harriet. I'll have to sit in the snug, I'm afraid so that it's respectable, or the butler will create,' said Mrs Ardle.

Jack nodded as he bent down to lift the covered plate out of the range. The aroma of roast beef started his mouth watering.

'Mrs Ardle, you're an angel, that dinner looks wonderful. Getting a decent dinner has been so much of a problem, today and you wouldn't believe how my stomach has felt for hours.'

Harriet appeared at the door, ten minutes later, with Mrs Ardle behind her. She had put her Sunday dress on that she had worn when she and Jack had first stepped out together. Jack stood, when she walked in, and smiled.

'Just half-an-hour, Harriet and then you must go up to bed. I shall be in there,' said Mrs Ardle, pointing to the butler's snug.

'Alright, Mrs Ardle, thank-you. Hello, Jack, nice you're here again,' said Harriet, holding out her hand. Mrs Ardle was out of sight, and Jack took the hand, and drew her to him.

'The man's being questioned, Harriet. So, he's off the street at the moment. You'll be asked to identify him soon. Look,' Jack said, as he stepped back, but retained hold of her hand, 'Don't go anywhere alone for a while, will you.'

'Have you forgotten that I won't be here after tomorrow?' said Harriet.

Jack hesitated, then said, 'Yes I had. I don't even know where you're going.'

'The house is in Camberwell Grove, but you won't be able to come to the door. You'll get me dismissed if you do. We'll have to arrange to meet on a Sunday somewhere, as that will be my half day. Perhaps at church?' suggested Harriet.

'I'll have to work some Sundays,' said Jack, miserably.

'Well, we can write and work it out. You'll be back over here soon, you said.'

'Yes,' said Jack, uncertainly. 'I'll sit in the kitchen tonight, so you sleep well knowing you're guarded. I'll have to be off at six to get back across the river and I need to call in at my lodgings to get a change of clothes and then to Leman Street parade for eight, or I'll be the one being dismissed.'

'I'll see you in the morning as we'll be up at five o'clock to lay the fires, said Harriet, reaching up and kissing him. At the door she turned and said, 'Thanks for this, Jack, I will sleep better tonight knowing you're here.'

He had been woken by a scullery maid in a mop cap grinning at him as she banged irons against the coal scuttles ready to lay the fires. He had had four hours sleep if he was lucky. Jack's neck had a crick in it due to the uncomfortable position that he had sat in before the dying fire in the grate. He was off at half past five, a packet in his pocket from the cook, and a kiss on the lips from Harriet when Mrs Ardle was not looking. When Jack would see her again he had no idea.

Jack ran to New Road and caught the train to Blackfriars station, hurtling over the bridge in a welter of steam in the early, grey, drizzle of dawn. He succumbed to a cab, looking sadly at the coins as he handed them over to the driver, and rolled into Arbour Square just before seven o'clock, alarming Hannah in the kitchen.

'I'm sorry Hannah,' said Jack, as he came through the kitchen door and dropped his great coat onto the back of the chair by the door. Her face wore its surprised look.

'Oh, it's not you, sir, I can't get an answer from Mr Curzon's room and I know he's in there as he asked me especially, to wake him by 'alf past six this morning. It's now nearly seven o'clock. I've knocked but there's no answer,' said Hannah, flustered.

'I'm going up anyway so I'll look in on him,' said Jack, snaffling a piece of bread and butter as he went through to the back stairs.

Jack knocked on Sam's door and waited. There was no response, so he tried the door knob and the door swung open. Sam was doubled up in his bed with clear traces of vomit on the pillow. Jack's first thought was to open a window as the room smelled rancid but he called from the door, 'Sam, you're unwell,' but there was little coherent response except for delirious rambling. Jack took a deep breath from the air in the hall and went into the room. He bent down and moved the sheet away from Sam's face.

Sam's skin was discoloured and he was rambling and clearly unaware that it was Jack by his bedside.

'I'll get help,' said Jack, and ran for the stairs. It was in his mind to see if Ann was still in the house. He reached the Black's door and rapped on it so that they were in no doubt of the urgency. Ann opened it and he could see that she was on her way out.

'Hello, Jack, good to see you back here. How did yesterday evening go?' Then she stopped as Jack looked in pain.

'Ann, Sam is very ill upstairs. He's vomited and he's a funny colour, and doesn't know me. Could you come and have a look? I think he might be dying.'

'Of course, lead on,' she went to follow him up the stairs, but as an afterthought, turned back and picked up a bag. Jack went ahead two at a time.

'Open the window,' Ann said as they went into Sam's room. Ann pulled back the covers and there was evidence of bloody diarrhoea. 'Oh, goodness,' said Ann. She picked up a hand and looked at the nails, and then gently put the hand down. She checked his eyes and said, 'He's been poisoned, Jack,' said Ann, quietly as if she was commenting on the weather.

'What do we do? You can help him, can't you?' said Jack, coming across from the window and looking searchingly into Ann's eyes.

'Well we have to try. We can see if we can get water into him, and we need to try a blood transfusion.'

'Can you do that?' asked Jack.

'We need a doctor, Jack,' said Ann.

'We've got one, we've got you and you're here now. If you know what to do, Ann, please try. By the time that we get a doctor here he could be dead,' said Jack.

'He may die anyway, Jack, transfusions don't always work,' said Ann.

'Oh, my life,' said Hannah from the doorway. 'I'll get the Inspector,' and they heard her clattering down the stairs shouting at the top of her voice that Sam was dying.

'I can try bleeding him anyway. But we need to inject him with blood, and we need fresh water to pour into him as well. A lot of it. Hannah's coming back and it sounds like Emily and Matthew are with her. Can you stop her coming all the way up and tell her to bring water? Then will you come back and let me take blood from you for Sam?' asked Ann.

'Of course,' said Jack, as he went onto the landing.

Matthew and Emily Doyle were suddenly on the scene as Jack pushed past them and yelled down the stairs to Hannah to bring water and to find a boy who could run to the station in Leman Street with a message for Ted Phillips and Sergeant Thick.

'What's happened?' asked Matthew Doyle.

'He's been poisoned, Matthew. I think it looks like arsenic,' said Ann, without looking at them as she concentrated on finding a syringe in her bag that she was satisfied with. 'Mathew I'm going to try and inject Sam with blood. Jack is willing for me to take his blood, but would you also help Sam by giving your blood as well?'

'Of course,' said Matthew starting to roll up his sleeve.

'I'll go back down to Sarah,' said Emily.

'Yes, of course, we just left her to dash up here,' said Matthew, to Ann.

Emily passed Jack on the stairs and briefly explained that she had left Sarah. He nodded briefly as he climbed back up. Hannah was coming back in through the front door and shouting up that she needed some coins to give a boy to go to the police station. Jack put his hand in his pocket and pulled out shillings and a handful of copper. He lent over the handrail and dropped them down the three flights. Hannah stood back as the coins hit the floor and as she looked up Jack saw she was crying.

'Thanks Hannah, cold water as soon as you can,' he called down to her. She nodded and scrabbled on the floor to pick up the coins. He turned into the bedroom as Ann was drawing the first syringe of blood from Matthew.

*

Thirty minutes had gone by which seemed an age. Still Sam was unconscious but when Ann checked for signs of life they were present. Jack had poured glassfuls of water into him, and he had retched it up. Ann told him to keep going. Now smaller amounts were being given and although he coughed Sam was keeping some of the liquid down. Matthew Doyle had given four lots of blood and now it was Jack's turn.

Then from the hall came a shout, Ted Phillips, Tom Hunt and Stan had come through the kitchen and were looking for everyone.

'Up here,' shouted Matthew.

'How's he doing,' called Ted, from half way up.

'He's still with us,' Matthew said, as they heard the three men start of the third flight of stairs.

'Interesting this,' said Stan, who was now sitting on the top stair. 'I left Franks seeing the police surgeon this morning at Shadwell. He's off colour but nothing like this young lad. I wonder where the pair of them went yesterday? We didn't see Franks back at the station yesterday and he said he went home because he had stomach cramps and a headache and felt so unwell. I only had a brief word with him this morning as I was on my out to come over to Leman Street.'

'Sam has been poisoned,' said Ann, quietly but directly, to Ted. 'If the other policeman that you are mentioning has those symptoms he is showing mild effects, but it still fits. If they were together yesterday then you should look at where they went. You have a poisoner to find. I would hazard a guess that as the woman in the case that you are looking into was poisoned, it could be connected. Right, Jack, that's enough of you or you'll be feeling weak. You and Matthew should both eat something now and rest for a while.'

'Breakfast is on the table, so why don't we go down,' suggested Matthew.

'You look like you could do with something yourself,' Hunt said, taking in Ann's drawn face.

'Not yet,' she said and smiled. 'I'll watch him for a while.'

'I'll keep you company,' said Ted.

The four other men walked slowly down stairs and followed Matthew into the breakfast room. It was still laid and although the hot food had since gone cold there was enough to satisfy.

"Emily must have taken Sarah out. Good thing, the amount of shouting up and down stairs that we were all doing must have been upsetting for the poor little thing,' said Matthew.

Hannah brought fresh tea and gave Jack a meaningful look as she passed him. Wondering what she was trying to communicate Jack put bacon in between two slices of bread and excused himself that he was going to check Hannah was alright. When he walked into the kitchen, Hannah had lined up all the arsenic in the house on the kitchen table, with a book open at the most recent record.

'It wasn't me. They'll say it was me, that I made a mistake, and I'll lose my job, but look, sir, every time we use it we mark it with a date and Mrs Doyle writes her name in the book. See. It all points to being somewhere else they've had poison and not here.' Hannah was crying again.

Jack looked at her bottles to placate her and the register. She blew her nose on a hanky and stuffed it up her sleeve. Once that was done he said, 'Hannah no one will think you're responsible, Sam was out all day and the other detective has symptoms too so it's happened while they've been together somewhere. Someone has got at them to try and stop the investigation that we're on, probably.'

Hannah froze, and then started to cry and speak all at the same time so that her voice came out in a whine. 'No, you don't understand, they were here, in the afternoon. They had tea with Mrs Doyle, I made it, I carried it in and she served it. There were scones and homemade jam as well, the last of the strawberry from the summer. They'll say it was me making a mistake.'

Jack had almost missed what she was saying. He looked at Hannah.

'Did Sam eat dinner here?' asked Jack.

'No, he was up in his room,' said Hannah.

'They must have eaten a meal somewhere together after they'd been to the bank to see Mr Moore, it could have happened there. But why did they come here? Sam, I can understand, but not with Franks? Taking tea with Emily, that's odd,' said Jack, and then he stopped breathing. He walked to the window and looked out onto the oasis that was the garden of a house that he would dream about until his dying day, hoping that one day he too would have a life and home like Inspector Matthew Doyle. Or perhaps not, thought Jack. The oasis was dry and poison had entered its source. Then he spoke, but it was so soft an utterance that Hannah could not catch the word.

'Moore,' he said.

*

Jack had stared out of the window for so long that Hannah thought he was affected by blood fever. He had turned and picked up his great coat which was still on the back of the chair from when he had gone through the kitchen earlier.

'Where does Mrs Doyle usually walk Sarah?' he had asked.

'Up towards the park' Hannah had said.

'Watch the clock, Hannah, and time me for ten minutes. Then go and tell Inspector Hunt that I'm in the park and that he and Stan are to come. Not inspector Doyle, do you understand?'

'Yes, sir,' she had said and the way that she explained it to Inspector Hunt upstairs was that he had the look of a man you wouldn't argue with.

Jack found Emily and Sarah in the park, in the cold, damp air, and they were sitting on wet grass rolling a ball back and forth. Emily saw him and waved.

'I'm glad it's you,' she said. Jack bent down and picked Sarah up, more to get her off the cold ground than anything else. He rolled his great coat up and sat down on it with Sarah on his knee.

'Why Sam?' he asked.

'Because he knew, and I thought there was just a chance,' said Emily.

'I know too,' said Jack, and they looked into each other's eyes.

'But I'm so tired of it now, the pretence, and the trying to keep it all looking normal. It's all over now. It's such a relief.'

'Not yet Emily. I need to know otherwise others will be blamed. How did you do it yesterday?' asked Jack.

'Sugary tea, and in the jam. Sam's greedy for jam, loves it. I thought it would be quick for him, I wanted him to die in his sleep and not wake up. That other man he came with, the one with the beer stains on his waistcoat, hardly ate anything,' Emily laughed, 'but he didn't matter as it was Sam who knew. I could see the doubt in his eyes and then it cleared and he knew.'

'Why did you kill Mrs Berringer?' asked Jack.

'Because she killed the love of my life. She as good as killed him, she knew that man she was involved with was going to have it done. She may not have stabbed him but she knew about it and could have stopped it. She just wanted the money and the position. The marriage was over between them, they were only together so that Arthur kept his work with the consulate. He didn't need to work, you know how rich he was. Did you meet him?' Emily sat back as her mind recalled days that were gone. Jack watched her, suddenly looking animated and young, reliving parties, and dinners, days before her marriage.

'No, I didn't have that pleasure,' he said, and smiled. Emily smiled in return.

'He was charming, and so intellectual, a clever business man, but married. Then father died and I inherited everything, except for the bank directorship, which went to my brother, of course, my adopted brother. You haven't met him, have you either? That's right, it was Sam who met him, that's why Sam knew I'd been in Windsor, because my stupid brother told him yesterday. Clever Sam. What was I saying, Jack?'

'You inherited everything.'

'Yes, and Arthur was so helpful with advice, and we fell in love. And Sarah happened, and Arthur wouldn't divorce his wife because he would lose his position. I was desperate and Matthew Doyle fell in love with me but was so noble and would never pursue me because he was only a Police Inspector. When I found that I was having Sarah, I thought of a way for both of us to carry on without Arthur losing his position. So, I pursued Matthew. Oh, he was hard work, so conscious of everything I had and of not giving me anything. I told him in the end that all I wanted was to be Mrs Matthew Doyle, and that was true,' Emily stopped and looked at Jack's face. 'When did you get the black eye?'

'New Year's Eve,' said Jack. 'Go on, what happened.'

'You know, Jack, like clever Sam. I'll be quick as it won't be long now.'

'Have you taken something, Emily?' asked Jack, as she coughed into her handkerchief.

'It's easier this way, I couldn't bear a trial and the idea of hanging. I married Matthew and we had Sarah, and she is not his. But I thought he has got all my property as we married before the change in the law in 1870, so in a way he was paid for marrying me, and he loves Sarah. He'll look after her, won't he Jack?' Emily paused again, the anxiety in her face.

'He will, and I'll watch out for her too.'

'Yes, she likes you, especially when you sing.'

'I'll do a lot of that with her. What happened with Arthur, Emily?' prompted Jack.

'Oh, Arthur loved her too. He had boys with his wife. Sarah was the one thing that convinced him to finally get a divorce and give up the Consulate. He knew his wife had someone else and anyway it had become a marriage of convenience. He told her, that last time in Windsor. I watched them from the boat we were going on. She didn't know which woman was with him. And then she had him killed in such a horrible way. Matthew actually read the report to me over breakfast. I thought I was going to faint.'

'How did you find her after she disappeared?' asked Jack.

'Oh, a complete chance, we met in Whiteleys. Can you imagine it, the stupid woman tries to disappear and gets bored so she goes to take tea in Whiteleys, and to buy things for her new life, in America. I heard her ordering things to be sent to New York. She gave her address for the bill as a temporary address in Golden Square until the sailing. We actually greeted each other as women who remembered being around the school in Windsor. She didn't realise that I was Arthur's and that Sarah, who she fussed over in the store, was his daughter. Why are you holding her Jack? She likes to play on the grass.'

'It's very wet, Emily, she'll catch a cold. She's quite happy sitting, see, she likes the shiny buttons on the uniform.' Jack smiled at the little girl, and pulled part of the coat over her.

'Leaving her is the hardest thing. You won't tell Matthew she's not his, will you?' begged Emily.

'No, I won't tell Matthew, what would be the point? He loves her and is the father she needs. Go on, Emily, tell me how you saw Mrs Berringer in Golden Square.'

'It was easy to call because I saw the man who had been on the coach in Windsor, coming out of the house. The one who had been pretending to be a policeman. I called and left my card, and then went back the next day. The rest was easy,' Emily's coughing was becoming more pronounced, and she clutched her handkerchief tightly as she felt a spasm.

'What do you mean, what was easy?' asked Jack.

'The strychnine, I wanted her to suffer. It was easy to get hold of, just a little bottle. Then I left. I saw the man from the coach walking towards the house. I suppose he was the person who destroyed the face and left the suicide note. Funny the way circumstances help you. I'm not feeling very well now so I'm going to walk around the park for the last time. Hold Sarah, will you.'

'Why don't you stay with me, Emily, let Ann help you. The others will be coming soon,' said Jack.

'I told you, Jack, I can't stand the idea of hanging. It's better this way. Give Sarah to Matthew will you Jack? She needs someone to love her. Clever Jack, like clever Sam,' said Emily, looking at him for a few seconds. Then, as she walked away through the park, Jack could hear the coughing increasing. She had disappeared into the morning mist as the daylight grew stronger, but he could hear the process of her death. He stood up and held Sarah close, as Inspector Hunt and Stan came running towards him.

'What's happened?' shouted Hunt.

'Emily's confessed to the murder of Mrs Berringer, she poisoned Sam because he worked it out. He and Franks came to the house yesterday, Hannah will tell you. Emily's taken something and she's gone off over to the left.' Stan was starting to run in the direction that Jack pointed to.

'And the child? Has she given anything to the child?' asked Hunt, sharply.

'No, there's no sign of that. I'll take her back to her father,' said Jack.

'And then get Ted and caution Doyle, Jack,' said Hunt,
starting to follow Stan towards the direction of the coughing.

Nineteen

On his way into Leman Street Jack took a diversion to the cab company in order to pay Simon the clerk a guinea for the information about Grace. It was all that was left in the pocket book that had been for his expenses and to pay informers. The days had gone by and he had quietly put his uniform back on that morning to resume his duties on his beat.

Sam had so far survived. So much water had been poured into him that Jack thought he would drown. Jack had said something foolish, joking with Sam that he would soon be back at the station doing the filing with Sergeant Thick and working out other crimes. He had looked at Ann's face for reassurance as he said it and seen the doubt, before she turned away, busying herself with her doctor's bag.

'He has good blood in him, doesn't he, Ann?' Jack had quickly turned it all into a joke but realised that Sam would never fully recover for active duty. He had since been moved to his parent's home as soon as Doctor Brown had said that he could travel. Brown had agreed to front the treatment Sam had been given and they waited and watched for signs of Sam's demise. So far so good, in as much as he was alive.

And all the lodgers had left Arbour Square, now. Hannah was homeless for all he knew and without work, but, thankfully, no one had tried to charge her with poisoning. He wondered if there would ever come a time when homes full of arsenic and docks full of strychnine as rat poison, would stop. The courts were full of poisoning cases.

The eighth of January, 1873. Eight days from his care-free singing in the church on New Year's Eve, and taking tea with Harriet in Westminster on New Year's Day. Harriet, elegant, looking like she belonged in a high-class hotel taking tea, not laying fires wearing a mop cap as she had been the last time he had seen her on that fateful morning.

He turned out of the police dormitory after a night of sleeplessness again. Jack felt the mild south-westerly wind. Love from Devon, he had thought every morning since standing on the bridge at Westminster. That's what Harriet had said. Her mother was sending love to her on the wind. Would this mild, damp weather ever end?

Jack felt that he had aged in the last few days since Emily Doyle's body had been carried by Stan through the park back to Arbour Square. She had been lain on the couch in the room that had held the Christmas Tree until the police van had arrived to take her body to the mortuary.

Hannah had kept Sarah with her in the kitchen, letting the little one cut rounds of pastry using an egg cup to make the shape while Jack had climbed the flights of stairs and then taken Ted from Sam's bedroom and told him what had happened in the park, and that Hunt's orders were for them to charge Doyle with, …. what?

'Not involved in this? Surely Tom doesn't think he was involved in murder? Are you sure that's all he said? Charge him?' asked Ted, incredulously.

'That's all, charge him,' repeated Jack, feeling sick, but noting that he must tell Sam that his fears about Tom Hunt not having the follow through to charge Matthew Doyle had been groundless.

And charge Doyle they had, collusion, party to murder? Jack could not remember what Ted had said. There in the breakfast room Ted had recited the charge, across the white starched linen and luxury, over the boiled eggs and sliced bacon, crisped and cold by then, but before the roaring fire, expertly laid by Hannah that morning. Jack had wondered how Harriet's fires were in Camberwell Green. Doyle had dropped his knife, and that had been the only noise apart from the hiss of the fire. Jack had staggered and the room had swum. Loss of blood, Ann had said, as she wafted smelling salts under his nose when he came around.

'I told you to eat and drink after giving all that blood, Jack, not go wandering in the park,' she handed him tea with sugar with a meaningful tone. Then she had added, 'Even if you did solve the case of the Faceless Woman.'

'Yes, but nothing more laughable than a young constable fainting like a tremulous lady at her first dance,' Stan had said, and had grinned at him. And that had been the only humour in a tragic day.

Jack went to look at the house a week after Emily's self-administered death, finding it closed up, and Matthew Doyle and Sarah nowhere to be seen. Hannah had shut down the house and dropped the keys with Mr Moore, at the County Bank and disappeared. Jack had been to see Mrs Ardle in a kitchen that had once held Harriet Fildew, and asked for a job for Hannah. Mrs Ardle had agreed she could fill the scullery maid's job but he would have to find her quickly. So far, he had not managed to do so.

Jack walked in the park and remembered. The child was safe with Ann, at least, and he shuddered as he thought of what might have happened to Sarah had he, Jack, told the truth about the child's parentage.

Turning back onto the road he walked as usual to check the washing was still on the lines and all secure and did his daily caution to the pretty maids about theft from washing lines, while they giggled at him. Then it was down into the kitchens to accept the home-made biscuits and cups of tea from the cooks. Normality was quite soothing.

*

Franks was in the Mason's Arms as usual by the evening and the two acknowledged each other, Jack now in his labourer's clothes.

'How are you today?' he asked Franks.

'Still no stomach for beer, this is brandy, and the food here is really atrocious. I can't believe I spent so many years eating it. I can only think that I was dazzled by the beautiful Mary, and she was like balm to the system,' said Franks.

'You should go and find her,' said Jack.

'No, really? I'm sure she'll have a dozen men after her, clean young bank clerks and businessmen on holiday.' Franks sipped and stared ahead.

'Well, she may have, but they won't all be a Detective Sergeant who looks good when he takes off a beer sodden waistcoat and smartens himself up. Tell her about your pension,' suggested Jack.

'Oh, that will really do it, talk about a passion killer. I can see her face, hey Mary, I'm an old bloke who has a pension shortly. Please!' laughed Franks.

'You had a narrow escape. Good job you don't like sweet foods or tea,' said Jack, changing the subject.

'Diabolical woman, Emily Doyle. Poor Matthew, his career is finished. And probably Sam's as well. At least they've released Matthew Doyle. The man will disappear, I think, with the child. I spoke to Hunt as we've charged Badley with the murder of Mrs Berringer. Doyle intends to go to Canada and buy a farm. The money is his anyway but he's told Hunt that he will set up a trust for Sarah so that it will all become hers when she comes of age. All that money and such sadness,' said Franks.

'Thank, God, they've let him go. It wasn't the money he wanted. It was Emily. It didn't do them any good, did it because it threw her in the way of Berringer. He must have been a bastard to prey on a young woman in that way. I hope Doyle and the child will be alright in the long run, they'll have each other in a new life and the child need never know about her mother. She's got a father who loves her and it will be a good life out in Canada. Time will go by and hopefully Matthew will find some peace with his little girl, poor man.' Jack waved at the barman to come over.

'I hope the child will never know about her mother, but these things have a way of getting out, in my experience, Jack. You meet someone years later who remembers the name. At least he was spared a hanging with Emily's orchestrated death. It's all over the papers though. Anyway, I have good news for you, young Jack,' said Franks.

'I could do with some,' grinned Jack.

'Badley has confirmed that Kirby was his link, so the man will go down. Apparently threatened to charge Badley with all these heinous crimes if he didn't play ball. We've got Badley on a charge of murder at last, although he's denying it. Ironically for him, Mrs Doyle's account of seeing him return to the house in Golden Square has shown it was too soon for Mrs Berringer to have died of the poison. It's a probability but he'll be charged with causing death through the battering he gave her face. Doctor Brown says that he has consulted an expert toxicologist from the Paris school and it was a matter of minutes after Mrs Doyle left that Badley re-entered the building. She would have died eventually as the breathing would have stopped and she would have suffocated. He could have stopped the death apparently if he'd called for help. Something about Charcoal being used to absorb the poison if you get to the person in time, from what the good doctor said. Instead he's worked her over so although Emily administered the poison, it wasn't that that killed Mrs Berringer in the end. I'm still hoping Badley's going to sing some more and that Kirby will join in. I want that name of the man above Kirby. We'll get him eventually, whoever planned and ordered Berringer's execution. One thing I do not like is a crooked policeman,' said Franks.

'Nor me. I feel like I've aged ten years after the case of the Faceless Woman,' said Jack.

'That would make you about seventeen then, instead of the innocent child you were when we met that first night, before Christmas. Your eye has healed well, by the way. No mark at all. Well, here's Ted. Hello my friend, how are you? Caught up on any sleep yet after the other day?' asked Franks.

'Getting there, Harry. A few more days at home and I'll feel as new. I've got a plan drawn, Jack, for the garden at the end of March. I wondered if you'd like to help?' said Ted.

'Yes, job permitting,' said Jack.

'Where are you staying at the moment, Jack?' asked Ted.

'In the station, back in a dormitory with the snorers of the world. I've asked Sergeant Thick if he'll put me on nights. When am I coming back to New Road, Ted?' Jack looked at his most pleading.

'Ah, well, not just yet. There's still work to be done to get at who was behind the Berringer murder and there's some rotten stuff likely to be linked in Great Marlborough Street Police Station too. Hunt wants you to stay for a bit longer.'

'I'll have to find somewhere to live again, then, or I'll go mad in the dormitory. I'm used to clean shirts and a room to myself now. You've ruined me, Ted,' said Jack with a grin.

'How about a trip down for dinner at Rose's? She's expecting the two of us but I daresay she can stretch to one more, Harry. Come and meet my sister, she's a rare cook and has a place down by the station at Millwall Junction. I've got some good and bad news for you, too, Jack, but I'll save it for after we've eaten.'

The three men walked down towards the Blackwall railway and caught the train down to Millwall Junction. Rose still had a few lights in the windows but was clearly closed to the public, although a few travellers tried the door.

Ted gave a specific knock as a signal that it was him and Rose lifted the curtain, raised her eyebrows to Ted that there was a third man, and unlocked the door.

'Good to see you minus a black eye, Jack,' said Rose. And met Franks' clear gaze with one of her own. 'And Ted, you've brought a new friend with you, I see.'

'I didn't think you'd mind, Rose, the man has been injured with work and hasn't had a decent meal since. Allow me to introduce you to Detective Sergeant Harry Franks from Shadwell. We've been working alongside him on the Berringer cases. You always have so much food, I didn't think that one more would make much difference, just means that Jack doesn't eat as much,' said Ted, with a grin.

'If I'd known that I would have stopped him coming,' said Jack, with a laugh.

'How do you do, Sergeant,' said Rose, holding out her hand to Franks. He took it and held it just a fraction longer than he should have done.

'Much better for being in good company, Miss Rose,' said Franks.

Rose laughed and went into the kitchen and returned with a tureen of stew. She laid a table replete with starched napkins and a tablecloth.

'So, what's the good news, Ted,' asked Jack after his first portion.

'Well, there's good and bad news,' said Ted.

'I heard you the first time but please can you give me the good news first,' said Jack

'The good news is I've found you lodgings with a very good cook, close to a ferry where you can get across and see your girl.'

'You mean?' asked Jack, seeing days stretching ahead of stew.

'My mother and Rose are looking for a lodger, and I'm recommending you,' said Ted, with a wink at Rose, who was smiling in return.

'I'm not sure about this,' interrupted Franks, sitting back in his chair, and sticking his thumbs into his waistcoat pockets. 'I may just have to come and check that he's behaving himself.'

'What about Mary?' asked Jack.

'Who is Mary?' asked Rose.

'No one at all,' said Franks. 'In fact, she's an obsession of Jack's from his time in Brighton, before he joined the force. Keeps trying to take me down there to meet her. I said beauty resides in London and that's where the future Mrs Franks will be found.'

'I see,' said Rose.

'What's the bad news, Ted?' asked Jack.

'Two parts,' said Ted as he swallowed a spoonful of stew, You're in court before Mr Newbury, the magistrate, tomorrow morning.'

'I've just lost my appetite,' said Jack, 'and the second part?'

'There's been a complaint about a young, officious Constable at the Mortuary from a New York detective sporting a diamond in his shirt.'

*

Authors' Note

The novel with Jack Sargent as protagonist is based on the social and criminal history in 1872. Jack Sargent and Arscott Ward were Metropolitan Police Constables in 1872 and Sergeant Thick is better known in the Jack the Ripper investigations later in the century. Both Jack and Arscott married Fildew sisters from Honiton, Devon. Jack Sargent would have coincided in time with Sergeant Thick in the Stepney Division during the 1870's but not in 1872.

Jack and Harriet are ancestors of the authors, but the incidents portrayed, while some are based on actual news reports of the time, are the works of the authors' imaginations.

Books also published by WordHive Ltd.

Chaos Calls to Chaos: The Chris Duncan Series Book One.

Unforced Rhythms: The Chris Duncan Series Book Two

By M.D. Wigg and Jay Heyes

Childrens Books:

Ma and Me: by L. Telfer and J. Ewins

Notes

Chapter One

Edgar Allen Poe, The Murders in the Rue Morgue, first published in 1841. A murder in Paris is solved by a man, C. Auguste Dupin, who finds a hair at the scene of the crime which does not appear human.

Wilkie Collins, The Moonstone, 1868.

Clive Emsley, The Great British Bobby, Quercus, 2010.

Jerome Caminada, "Twenty-Five Years of Detective Life," Manchester: John Heywood 1895. Re-published with an introduction by Peter Riley, Prism Books, Warrington, 1982 and 1985.

Tower Hamlets Independent Newspaper, October to December, 1872.

William Douglas Parish: A Dictionary of the Sussex Dialect and Collection of Provincialisms in Use in the County of Sussex.

Karen Foy, "Life in the Victorian Kitchen," 2014.

Joseph Bullman, Neil Hegarty, and Brian Hill, "The Secret history of our Streets, London, A social history through the houses and streets we live in."

Chapter Two

Camberwellsociety.org.uk

Bradshaw's Handbook 1863. "Bradshaw's Descriptive Railway Hand-Book of Great Britain and Ireland.

British-history.ac.uk

Metropolitan Police Historical Collection, The Life and Police Career of William Edwin Fairbrass, 1806-1876, compiled by Sylvia Fairbrass.

The telegraph, 31 December 2016, Rory Mulholland, Greek ambassador to Brazil murdered by wife's police lover, officials say"

Chapter three

Casebook.org   Sergeant William Thick by Frogg Moody. This sergeant was involved in the investigation of the Jack the Ripper murders. He worked at H division in Leman Street Police Station from 1868, transferring briefly to B division, Chelsea in 1872. He returned to H division Whitechapel in September 1872, and at some point, was promoted to Sergeant. For the purposes of the story we have taken it that his promotion has happened by December 1872.

Disused-stations org.uk

Chapter Four

Illustrated London News, January 4th 1873.

Life in a Victorian Kitchen. Culinary Secrets and Servant's Stories. Karen Foy published 2014.

Chapter Five

Historic Weather at Netweather.tv

Chapter Six

British-history.ac.uk

James Marsh (1836) Account of a method of separating small quantities of arsenic from substances with which it may be mixed. Edinburgh New Philosophical Journal. A. and C. Black. 21: 229-236.

Herschel, William J (1916) The origin of Finger Printing. Oxford University Press. ISBN 978-1-104-66225-7.

Web.bryant.edu Ballistics

Dr Thomas Cream: this case is too late to use but it inspired the idea. A Scottish Canadian: was a poisoner in Chicago in the 1880's, hanged in 1891, London, for strychnine poisoning of several prostitutes. Unsubstantiated claims that he confessed to being Jack the Ripper before his execution. However, he was in prison from 1888.

National Institute for Occupational Safety and Health (NIOSH)

Chapter Seven

Boxing Day: ultimate historyproject.com

Survey of London Vol 43-44: Poplar, Blackwall and the Isle of Dogs. Originally published by London County Council 1994.

Wikipedia: The Great Eastern Main line. Citation: Connor, JE (October 2014) "Bishopsgate (Low Level)". London Railway Record. 81:145.

Elizabeth Garrett Anderson, (1986), "Women in Science: antiquity through the nineteenth century." Cambridge, Mass.: MIT press.

The County Observer and Monmouth Central Advertiser –
Saturday January 6th, 1873: "Boxing Day, and Boxing Night in
London."

Chapter Eight

London Society for the extension of University teaching 1884,
City of London Livery Companies Commission, Report
Volume 1, originally published by Eyre and Spottiswoode,
London, 1884

Chapter Nine

Dio C, Ernest C, Baldwin HF. London: W. Hememamm: 1914.
Dio's Roman History, ncbi.nlm.nih.gov

Campbell JM. Glasgow: Pickering and Inglis, Ltd; 1963.
Dentistry then Now.

Bradshaw's Handbook: continued to be published by his
colleagues and updated after his death. Bradshaw's timetables
continued to be published. After 1923, the railway companies
were combined into the four companies of the Great Western,
London Midland and Scottish, London and North Eastern,
Southern.

Chapter Ten

Stanford's Library Map of London and its Suburbs 1872.

A Century of London Weather, A.L. Marshall, Meteorological
Office, HMSO 1952. Digital.nmla.metoffice.gov.uk

Cab Cultures in Victorian London: Horse-Drawn Cabs, Users
and the City, ca 18340-1914, Fu-Chia Chen, Ph.D, University of
York, Railway Studies. Etheses>whiterose.ac.uk

Chapter Fourteen

———

The Times, December 26th -31st 1872 and January 1st and 22nd 1873: the murder of Harriet Buswell.

Chapter Sixteen

The London Illustrated News January 1873.

Chapter Seventeen

The New York Times 9 December 1857 quoted in Clive Emsley (above).

NIOSH pocket guide to Chemical Hazards 0570.

The Daily Telegraph: 7th October 2016: Lucinda Hawksley. 'Could this Wall Paper Kill You? Victorian Britain's Lethal Obsession with the Perfect Shade of Green.

Chapter Eighteen

Blood groups were not established until the twentieth century. Blood transfusions were attempted for centuries with varying success.

Printed in Great Britain
by Amazon

61429882R00210